Discover the series you can't put down . . .

'A high level of realism . . . the action scenes come thick and fast. Like the father of the modern thriller, Frederick Forsyth, Mariani has a knack for embedding his plots in the fears and preoccupations of their time'

Shots Magazine

'The plot was thrilling . . . but what is all the more thrilling is the fantastic way Mariani moulds historical events into his story'

Guardian

'Scott Mariani is an ebook powerhouse'

The Bookseller

'Hums with energy and pace . . . If you like your conspiracies twisty, your action bone-jarring, and your heroes impossibly dashing, then look no further. The Ben Hope series is exactly what you need'

Mark Dawson

'Slick, serpentine, sharp, and very very entertaining. If you've got a pulse, you'll love Scott Mariani; if you haven't, then maybe you crossed Ben Hope'

Simon Toyne

'Hits thrilling, suspenseful notes . . . a rollickingly good way to spend some time in an easy chair'

USA Today

THE PANDEMIC PLOT

Scott Mariani is the author of the worldwide-acclaimed action-adventure thriller series featuring ex-SAS hero Ben Hope, which has sold millions of copies in Scott's native UK alone. His books have been described as 'James Bond meets Jason Bourne, with a historical twist'. The first Ben Hope book, *The Alchemist's Secret*, spent six straight weeks at #1 on Amazon's Kindle chart, and all the others have been *Sunday Times* bestsellers.

Scott was born in Scotland, studied in Oxford and now lives and writes in a remote setting in rural west Wales. You can find out more about Scott and his work on his official website: www.scottmariani.com

By the same author:

Ben Hope series
The Alchemist's Secret
The Mozart Conspiracy
The Doomsday Prophecy
The Heretic's Treasure
The Shadow Project
The Lost Relic
The Sacred Sword
The Armada Legacy
The Nemesis Program
The Forgotten Holocaust
The Martyr's Curse
The Cassandra Sanction
Star of Africa
The Devil's Kingdom
The Babylon Idol
The Bach Manuscript
The Moscow Cipher
The Rebel's Revenge
Valley of Death
House of War
The Pretender's Gold
The Demon Club

To find out more visit **www.scottmariani.com**

SCOTT MARIANI

THE PANDEMIC PLOT

avon.

Published by AVON
A division of HarperCollins*Publishers*
1 London Bridge Street
London SE1 9GF

www.harpercollins.co.uk

HarperCollins*Publishers*
1st Floor, Watermarque Building, Ringsend Road
Dublin 4, Ireland

A Paperback Original 2021
1

First published in Great Britain by HarperCollins*Publishers* 2021

ISBN: 9780008365530

Typeset in Minion by Palimpsest Book Production Limited, Falkirk, Stirlingshire
Printed and bound in UK by CPI Group (UK) Ltd, Croydon CR0 4YY

MIX
Paper from
responsible sources
FSC™ C007454

This book is produced from independently certified FSC™ paper to ensure responsible forest management.

For more information visit: www.harpercollins.co.uk/green

THE PANDEMIC PLOT

Special thanks to Miriam and Marco, great friends and scientists *extraordinaire*, for figuring out how the bad guys might actually have done it . . .

PROLOGUE

Staffordshire, 1924

Viewed from the road, the splendour of the Bridgnorth Estate seemed to go on for ever. Its thousand or so acres were ringed by a great stone wall that afforded the occasional peep at the rambling country parkland and fine gardens, at whose heart stood the noble old seventeenth-century house.

Wilfred Grey had spent the last six hours travelling here, having departed from his small cottage in rural Northumberland early that summer's morning. As a humble schoolteacher on the meagrest of salaries, his sole means of transportation was the same rattly Francis-Barnett motor-cycle and sidecar combination on which he and his wife Violet had fled London and moved north two years earlier. Violet had done all she could to try to prevent him from coming here today, to no avail. He was weary and stiff after so many hours in the saddle, but as his long journey came to an end, Wilfred's mission was just getting underway and he was determined to see it through to the bitter end.

Wilfred's purpose for coming here meant that he couldn't

just ride in through the gates of the estate. Finding a leafy little lane that skirted along the westernmost perimeter he parked the combination where it wouldn't easily be noticed. He removed his leather goggles and riding gauntlets and left them in the sidecar, but kept on his long waxed cotton coat despite the warmth of the afternoon. The heavy steel weight in his coat pocket slapped against his right hip as he waded through the long grass along the foot of the stone wall. He soon came to the shady spot where a tall, spreading oak tree inside the grounds overhung the top of the wall and made it easy for a young man of his slender build and agility to clamber over.

The nervousness that had been gnawing at Wilfred throughout his journey quickly mounted as he made his way deeper into the grounds. He kept to the shadows and the bushes wherever possible, trying to move as stealthily as he could. He passed an estate worker's cottage where two men were shoeing a horse, but were too preoccupied to notice him as he slipped by. Further on, he could hear the barking of a big dog somewhere nearby, but thankfully there was no sign of it. If not for his beloved Violet anxiously waiting for him at home, Wilfred wouldn't have cared if they let the brute loose on him once his mission was accomplished. Violet was the only reason why he gave a damn for his own skin.

He was sweating as he approached the big house. The Webley service revolver in his coat pocket seemed to become heavier and heavier. He hadn't carried a weapon since coming home from the war six years ago, at the close of that nightmarish period of his life when the real man seemed to have withered away inside him, and all that was left was a frightened ghost called *Lance Corporal* Wilfred Grey. An identity he'd oh-so gratefully left behind him, along with the detested uniform, resuming the gentler occupation he'd followed before that damned conflict began. The gun Wilfred had brought with him here today had been purchased cheap from some ruffian he'd met in a back alley behind a pub the previous evening. Its cylinder was loaded with six cartridges. He prayed he wouldn't need that many to achieve his purpose.

Wilfred hated the gun. It was a bring-back from the war, scuffed and scratched with the marks of combat, and to even look at it was to bring a flood of terrible memories back to his mind. How ironic, he reflected, that after all those experiences that had made him vow never to touch a weapon again, fate should have brought him here, to this place, to kill a man he had never met.

But so be it. Some things were more important than his own personal feelings. Duty must be done. It would be murder, yes. But nobody could have called it cold-blooded, still less unjustified. The taking of this one life paled into insignificance next to the horrors of suffering the man had inflicted on millions of innocent people.

While Wilfred's back yard at home was a modest scrap of ground on which he struggled to grow a few potatoes and cabbages, the Bridgnorth Estate's grand gardens were meticulously tended by full-time staff. Wilfred watched from the cover of a hedge as a gardener tended to a riot of many-coloured roses in a bed beneath an open ground-floor window of the house. The gardener was a stooped old man in hobnail boots, dungarees and a flat cap. He moved like a tortoise and seemed to take for ever to prune a few stems.

At last, the gardener picked up his bucket and tool box and moved on. Shaking badly with nerves and barely daring to breathe, Wilfred remained frozen in his hiding place until the old man had disappeared around the corner of the house.

Now was the time. His heart pounding like a Lewis gun, Wilfred broke away from the hedge and dashed across the lawn to the open window. He waded through the rose bed, trampling the blooms and ignoring the thorns that ripped at his trouser legs. The open window had a thick stone ledge that jutted proud of the wall a couple of feet above his head. He jumped up with both arms raised high, hooked his fingers over the rough stone, dangled for a moment and then scrabbled with his feet to heave and clamber his way over the windowsill. He landed with a soft thud inside the house and instantly sprang to his feet, tearing the revolver from his pocket. He'd had no idea what room of the house he would enter; for all he knew, he'd been about to come face to face with his intended victim.

But the grand music room in which he found himself was unoccupied. Wilfred gazed around him at the elegant furnishings and the magnificent collection of dozens of antique instruments – lutes, violins, harps, highly ornate spinets and harpsichords – that he couldn't have hoped to afford if he taught English twenty-four hours a day for the next hundred years. To be a witness to the living standard obviously enjoyed by such a corrupt and depraved villain when decent and innocent people were left to suffer in conditions of abject poverty only fuelled Wilfred's anger even more, and firmed his resolve.

Wilfred stalked across to the door and peeked out into a

lavish hallway with gleaming marble floor and fine artwork. Over the sonorous tick-tock of a magnificent grandfather clock came the echoing footsteps of a servant whom Wilfred took to be a butler, dressed in a striped waistcoat and carrying a fine china tea set on a silver tray. The butler was an older man, but moved with the ramrod-straight bearing of a British army officer. Many NCOs had retired into service after the war. The butler paused to knock at a door across the hallway, waited a moment and then disappeared inside the room. A minute or two later he re-emerged, the tray now empty, and walked slowly back the way he'd come.

When he was gone, Wilfred gulped a huge breath, eased the door open and tiptoed to the room across the hall. He was dizzy with fear and for a fleeting moment wondered whether he must have lost his sanity, to be doing this. But there was certainly no turning back now.

The room in which he now found himself was a large study filled with bookcases and sunlight that streamed in from tall French windows. The room smelled of aromatic pipe tobacco and burnished leather. The china tea set that the butler had brought in was neatly arrayed on an enormous desk. The man Wilfred had come here to kill was standing with his back to the doorway, reaching up to a bookcase for one of the many leather-bound volumes that crowded the shelves. Hearing the door open, he turned to see his unexpected visitor enter the room. Wilfred recognised him from the single photograph he'd seen. The man was in his early forties, with jet black hair that he wore unfashionably long. His white shirt was open at the neck to reveal a red silk cravat and his patent leather shoes gleamed in the sunlight from the window. He had cold, pale eyes that gazed disinterestedly at Wilfred. Other than a slight pause in his movements he didn't seem especially perturbed by the intrusion. Not even at the sight of the large Webley revolver in Wilfred's hand.

Wilfred closed the door behind him and stepped deeper into the room, desperately trying to hide his near-paralysing terror. By contrast the man remained quite calm. He laid down the book he'd chosen from the bookcase. Stepped casually to the desk, picked up his teacup by the saucer and took a dainty sip. He raised an eyebrow at Wilfred and said, 'I don't believe I was expecting a visitor at this hour.'

'I didn't want you to know I was coming,' Wilfred managed to reply. His voice was so strained with nerves that it sounded like the croak of a dying tuberculosis patient.

The man nodded. 'In that case it would appear that my security arrangements leave something to be desired. How may I be of service to you, sir?'

Wilfred would have preferred that the man didn't speak to him. All he wanted was to get this awful thing done, and leave as quickly as he could. He raised the revolver. His right hand was shaking so badly that he needed to steady it with his left.

'You know why I'm here,' he croaked. 'It's time for you to answer for the terrible things you've done.'

The man smiled. 'I see. Has a jury of my peers found me guilty of some crime that I'm unaware of having committed?'

Wilfred took another step forwards, hoping that his closeness to his target would help his shaky aim to hit its mark. The gun felt heavier than a truck engine. His eyes stung from the sweat that poured down his brow.

'Did you really think you could get away with it?' he rasped.

'Did it never cross your mind that someone would find out?'

'So you've come to murder me, have you?'

'You're the murderer, not me.'

'Really? I must be suffering from somnambulism. Aside from those martial duties I have had the honour of carrying out in the service of King and country, I don't recall having harmed a single soul in my life.'

'You killed my family!'

The man took another sip of tea, gazing at the gun as though it were a feather duster in Wilfred's hand. 'I'm afraid you must be confused, my dear fellow. I don't know you from Adam and I've never met your family. But as you seem so certain that I'm the culprit behind these terrible crimes, I suppose you had better do what's necessary and pull that trigger. That's if you know how.'

'I fought in the war. I know how to shoot.'

'Then get a move on, you bloody fool. The longer you wait, the harder you make it for both of us.'

Wilfred hooked his thumb around the hammer of the revolver and yanked it back until it locked into position. He tried to square the sights on the man's chest, but they wouldn't stay still and his eyesight kept blurring. He took a hand from the gun to wipe the sweat from his eyes. Clenching his teeth, he tightened his finger against the trigger but it seemed rigid, as though something was blocking it. Wilfred knew the blockage was just a figment of his own mind. He tried harder, but the gun only shook worse.

A knowing smile spread across the man's lips. 'Not quite the same when you're not taking pot-shots across no-man's land at some faceless enemy in a trench half a mile away, is it?'

'You filthy bastard.'

The man put down his teacup. 'Look, old chap. There must be another way to settle this. Whatever wrongs you're so convinced I've committed against you and your family, I'm quite happy to compensate you for them.' As he spoke he moved around the corner of the desk, unlocked a drawer and slid it open. 'Regrettably I don't keep a great deal of cash in the house, but I can write you a personal cheque. How does a thousand pounds sound to you? If you don't mind my saying so, you look as though you could use it.'

If Wilfred had been paying attention instead of desperately trying to keep control of his tattered nerves, he might have noticed the way the man was standing with his right hand hovering close to the open drawer. He might have wondered whether it was a chequebook in there, or something else. He might have seen the man's body language as a warning, but he did not.

'I don't want your stinking money,' Wilfred spat back at him.

'Then perhaps you'd care to enlighten a condemned man as to the reason for his impending execution. Because I'm afraid I have no idea what you're talking about, or what grudge you could possibly hold against me. I'm a simple biochemist. Someone who has devoted his entire civilian life to the pursuit of science and the advancement of his fellow man's health and wellbeing.'

Wilfred took one hand away from the gun while he reached inside his coat and tore out the photographic prints he was carrying rolled up in his pocket. A keen amateur photographer, he had taken the images himself on his Pocket Kodak and created the prints in the tiny space he used as a developing room at home. Most of the pictures he took were of nature, or of his beloved Violet and the children. These four were different. They were pictures of documents.

'That's who you are, is it?' Wilfred shouted in fury, barely able to believe the man's brazenness. '*Here's* your pursuit of science. *Here's* your love of your fellow man!' He hurled the prints and they fell to the floor.

The man picked them up. He frowned as he unrolled and examined them.

'There are more,' Wilfred told him. 'These are just a small sample of the evil you've done against the world, you . . . *monster.*' He couldn't think of a stronger word.

The man tossed the photographs on the desk. 'You have no proof. Or else you would have gone to the law, instead of coming here like this.'

'Oh, I think I have all the proof I need. But I know what they would do. Men like you don't face punishment for their crimes. Men like you get away with murder, every time. Just as you think you can buy your way out of this. Well, I'm here to tell you that you can't.'

'Killing me won't bring them back,' the man said.

'No, but at least I'll have the pleasure of knowing you're burning in hell, where you belong.'

And suddenly Wilfred felt the tremors disappear, as though the fear had drained out through his feet. He felt strong. Invincible. He gripped the gun. He would see it through. He would not fail.

But even as Wilfred's finger tightened on the trigger, the man darted a hand into the open desk drawer and came out clutching a small automatic pistol. Two gunshots ripped the air, sharp and piercing in the confines of the room. Wilfred staggered on his feet and looked down in stupefaction at the crimson flowers that were already blossoming over his chest. He opened his mouth to speak, but all that came out was a wheezing gasp. The unfired revolver fell from his hand. His vision quickly began to fade as the darkness rose up and swallowed him.

The very last thing he saw was Violet's face. Then that was gone, too.

The man watched as Wilfred Grey collapsed in a heap on the study floor. Then he calmly walked over to the body and placed a third bullet into Wilfred's head, squarely between the eyes.

The man stepped back to the desk and laid down his Browning .32 automatic next to the empty teacup. He'd have no reason to hide the weapon from the police, when they arrived at the scene. The photographs were another matter. He slipped them inside the drawer, relocked it and pocketed the key. Once the incriminating evidence was out of sight, he rang for his butler.

'Boddington, this blackguard broke into the house, threatened my life and compelled me to defend myself. Kindly get on the telephone to the constabulary, at once.'

In his dream, he is standing barefoot on an empty beach. He is so completely alone that he might be the only living person in the world. The white sand seems to stretch to infinity to his sides and behind him. In front of him, the ocean that had been calm and mirror-smooth just moments earlier is suddenly whipping up into a terrible storm. Black clouds roll in to blot out the sun, driven by a howling wind out of nowhere, lightning rips the sky like jagged knives piercing the darkness and a rumbling cannonade of thunder shakes the ground. Monstrous waves rise impossibly tall from one extreme of the broad ocean horizon to the other, like great towering walls of foaming water, and surge towards the beach gathering power and momentum as they come.

He wants to turn and run back for the safety of the land, but something is wrong because his feet won't move. He looks down and sees that, in the strange way of dreams, they're buried up to the ankles in the wet sand that has set like concrete and holds him in its grip, making him powerless to do anything except stand there and watch.

But now as he remains rooted to the spot and helplessly

staring out to sea, he realises that he's not alone after all. Someone is out there among the giant waves. Above the deafening roar and crash of the storm he can faintly hear their voice crying out to him for help. It's the voice of someone he cares about. He doesn't understand how or why they have come to be stuck out there in the midst of the raging ocean. All he knows is that they're in terrible danger, and he is the only person who can save them.

He struggles to free himself, but the harder he tries to tear his feet out of the rock-hard sand, the more tightly it holds him. He tries to shout, 'Hold on! I'm coming!' But his voice is made tiny by the crash of the waves and the screaming gale that seems to snatch the words from his lips. He can no longer see his loved one or hear their cries for help. All he can do is look on in horror as they slip away from him and fade into nothingness, along with all chance of saving them.

Knowing that nobody else will come.

Facing the black despair of the realisation that he has failed and that they are lost.

12

Chapter 1

The nightmare woke Ben Hope with a start, and he lay awake for the rest of the night listening to the rain drumming on the roof of the former farmhouse in which he lived. At dawn he finally gave up trying to sleep. He threw himself into his morning exercise routine, then pulled on jogging pants and running shoes and headed out to the acres of woods that surrounded his home with his dog, Storm, trotting along at his heels. Running usually helped to clear Ben's mind, but not today. He pushed hard for five miles along the dirt tracks, three full circuits of the Le Val compound, before he stopped to rest among the ivied ruins of the old church that nestled among the trees.

The vividness of his dream was still lingering in his mind as he sat on a crumbling wall and lit a Gauloise. Cigarettes and running didn't go together too well, but the habit had been with him a long time and so he thought *fuck it* and lit one anyway. When the first Gauloise failed to settle his mind, he burned up another. The dog sat close by, watching Ben intently with his great shaggy head cocked to one side and those deep amber eyes filled with a curious expression. He was probably wondering why these silly humans did the things they did. That was a question Ben often asked himself, too.

Ben walked back home, taking his time and deep in thoughts that the beautiful late spring morning and the cheery chorus of the birds in the trees could do little to allay. The Le Val compound was situated in a quiet corner of rural Normandy, set back a long way from the narrow country road that led to it and guarded by tall gates and wire fences. The stone farmhouse at its heart dated back a couple of centuries and had changed little externally in all that time, but nowadays the place served a very different kind of function. Around the cobbled yard stood a variety of other buildings: classrooms, storerooms, an armoury and an accommodation block for the delegates who travelled from far and wide to benefit from the courses taught by Ben and his business associates, who like him were all ex-military. Le Val was a school, of sorts, but it was also a little more than that – as any visitor to the tactical training facility would soon find out when they heard the rattle of gunfire that often shattered the peace of the countryside on a busy range day. One of the more recent innovations to the compound was the killing house, constructed of thick plywood, rubber and car tyres, where Ben and his fellow instructors educated their trainees on the finer points of conducting live-fire CQB hostage rescue and tactical raid operations.

Today wasn't going to be one of those days. No classes were scheduled until later in the week, making for an unusually quiet period in which Ben would have no excuse to keep putting off the mountain of tax and insurance paperwork he'd been successfully avoiding. There was also some maintenance work to be done on the south perimeter fence, the classroom roof had sprung a leak, and they were low on various supplies. Returning to the yard, Ben saw that the Ford Ranger truck belonging to his friend and business partner Jeff Dekker was gone. Which meant that Jeff and their associate Tuesday Fletcher had already set off that morning to pick up materials and provisions, a round trip of seventy-odd miles that would keep them tied up for a few hours.

With the place more or less all to himself for a while, Ben took a shower, brewed up a big pot of strong black coffee and then headed over to the prefabricated office building across from the house to face the unwelcome task of sorting through all his invoices, bills, policies and accounts. Storm met him again at the bottom of the farmhouse steps and acted as though he hadn't seen his favourite human for weeks. Ben loved the big dog. Storm was the undisputed pack leader among the team of guard German shepherds whose job it was to patrol Le Val's forty acres of grounds. But not all the canine residents of the tactical training facility were employed for their security capabilities. Trotting along with Storm was his adoptive little brother and his best friend in the world outside of Ben, a mongrel terrier who went by the appropriate name of Scruffy. Scruffy was really Jude's dog – Jude being Ben's grown-up son who until recently had been living in the States with his girlfriend, Rae. Scruffy had come to join the pack at Le Val during Jude's absence. Pretty much a law unto himself, he spent his days foraging around the barns and buildings in search of rodents, and had formed a strong bond with his much larger companion. Tuesday adored the little guy, but Jeff had started referring to him as 'that ugly mutt' ever since Scruffy had twice sneaked into his quarters and cocked a leg on his boots.

Ben let both dogs into the office, glad of their company as he dug into his administrative chores for the morning. He slumped in his tatty desk chair, turned on the computer, sipped his coffee, fired up another Gauloise, and generally did all he could to procrastinate. As much as he disliked the part of his job that kept him chained to a desk, that wasn't so much the problem. His mind was elsewhere; he was still feeling shaken by the vivid memory of the dream that had kept him awake for most of the night.

He managed to stay focused for all of twenty minutes before the columns of figures and lines of text on his screen began to blur out and his thoughts wandered again. He closed his eyes and saw himself again on the beach with those surreal tsunami waves surging towards the shore. Ben was no kind of a psychologist but it didn't take a genius to figure out that the deadly storm that ravaged the still waters of the sea symbolised the emotional turbulence that had lately turned his life upside down.

The real reason for Ben's downcast mood was a woman called Grace Kirk. Someone who'd become very important to him over the last several months, after a chance meeting brought them together. Grace was a police officer who lived and worked in the Highlands of Scotland. Ben's reasons for visiting the region last winter had been as unexpected as their romance, which had blossomed quickly and led him back north to see her again several times. He had been badly hurt in the past by the ups and downs of his love life and could be reticent about opening up to emotional attachments; but he'd really thought that he and Grace might have a future.

As it turned out, he'd been wrong.

Ben stubbed out his cigarette, and lit another. He knew he was smoking too much, but at least it was better than hitting the whisky this early in the day. *Enough of the damn computer*, he decided. He turned it off, leaned back in his chair with a sigh and tried to empty his mind, but couldn't. For the ten thousandth time, he replayed in his head the phone conversation he'd had with Grace eleven days ago.

Grace had been upset, but she was a strong person and had told him it straight. Her decision to call an end to their relationship had been a tough one to make, and taken her a few weeks to affirm in her own heart before telling him. It wasn't that her feelings for him had cooled, or that she felt he cared any less about her. It wasn't anything he'd said or done to hurt or betray her in any way.

'Then why?' he'd asked her.

'Because it's you, Ben. It's just who you are. Do you understand what I'm trying to say? That's why this will never work.'

And he knew she was right.

Ever since Ben came into her life, Grace had been exposed to danger. She'd been kidnapped once and almost a second time, threatened, witnessed violent deaths and come close to it herself, and all simply because she was involved with a man whose life orbited around trouble and conflict. His was a world of risk. They both knew it wasn't about to change any time soon. And as deeply as she cared for him, she had come to the heartbreaking conclusion that she couldn't be a part of it any longer.

The last escapade had resulted in her having to be evacuated from Scotland to France and placed in the protective care of a former client of Ben's, the billionaire Auguste Kaprisky, whose vast luxury estate was ringed with armed guards. It was a gilded cage, but still a cage, and Grace had deeply resented being whisked away from her life and kept under effective house arrest in a strange country, just because her attachment to Ben made her a target of his enemies. Her sudden and unexplained absence from home had nearly cost her her job, too, something else she wasn't inclined to give up.

'When does it end, Ben?'

'I don't know,' he'd replied after a long pause. He didn't want these things to happen. They just did. Trouble didn't want to leave him alone.

'And what will it be next time?'

'I don't know,' was all he could repeat.

They'd talked for hours on the phone. Grace had cried, and Ben had wanted to cry too.

'I understand why you want it to be this way,' he'd said at the end, when both of them were worn out with emotion. 'It's right for you. I'm okay with that.'

As okay as being mangled in a combine harvester. Or having your innards ripped out by a rusty iron claw.

'I'm going to miss you so much,' she told him.

'Grace—' His voice was a whisper.

'Please don't say it.'

'So long as you know.'

'Me too.'

'Friends?'

'Always,' she said. But he knew he probably wouldn't see her again. Afterwards he'd put the phone down and stood there for a long time staring at it. 'Goodbye,' he'd said to himself, because he couldn't say it to her. The word sounded as crashing and final as a suicide gunshot.

Now, as he reflected back over the symbolism of last night's dream, he thought about the unseen loved one he'd been powerless to save from the raging ocean. It struck him as a terrible irony that the thing he'd feared so desperately when he had to save her from danger in real life had happened anyway, now that she was lost to him.

She's alive, he reminded himself.

That was what mattered most. But it still didn't stop him from feeling as though that iron claw had plunged inside his chest and left him with a big red ragged hole where his heart used to be.

As Ben sat, Storm uncoiled himself from where he and Scruffy had been lying curled up together on the office floor, and came over to him. Ben ran his fingers through the dog's fur as a big sloppy tongue affectionately washed his cheek. Ben said, 'Yeah, I love you too.'

The dog looked at him.

'You think I'm feeling sorry for myself, don't you?' Ben asked him.

The German shepherd panted hot breath in Ben's face but didn't reply. Probably just being diplomatic.

That was when the landline phone on Ben's desk rang. He stared at it for a couple more rings, not really in the mood to talk to anyone. But then he changed his mind and picked up on the fourth ring. Said, 'Le Val.'

'Dad?'

Scruffy looked up with a cocked ear, as if he'd recognised the familiar voice on the other end of the line. Jude sounded breathless and agitated. For him to call Ben 'Dad', something had to be wrong. Ben hadn't heard from him in over a week, and he'd sounded perfectly normal then.

'Dad, I'm in trouble. Terrible trouble. I can't talk long. Tried to call you on your mobile but—'

'Slow down. What are you talking about? What trouble?'

'I've been arrested for murder.'

Chapter 2

It was destined to be a short call, because Jude had the legal right to let someone know where he was but wasn't allowed to speak for long. Ben felt numb and cold as he listened and tried to digest what he was hearing, but Jude was gabbling so fast that he could hardly understand.

'Whoa, Jude. Slow down, you're not making any sense.'

'Tell me something new. *None* of this makes any sense!'

Ben tried to keep his voice steady and calm. He asked, 'When did this happen?'

'Yesterday evening. I've spent the whole night being grilled by the cops. I'm in custody at Abingdon police station.'

Abingdon was one of the bigger towns near the former vicarage that was Jude's family home, situated a few miles south of the city of Oxford that Ben knew very well. A million years ago in a different life, he'd been a student there and attended the same college as Jude's future mother, Michaela Ward.

Ben asked, 'So you're back home again?'

'Yes, and no sooner do I get back here but this guy's murdered and now they're saying I did it!'

'Stay calm. What guy?'

'Duggan! Carter Duggan!'

Ben was blank for a second, then recognised the name, remembering something Jude had told him a few months ago. Carter Duggan had been renting the vicarage through a letting agency while Jude was living in the States. Ben had a dim recollection that Duggan was Canadian, but he knew nothing else about the man. Other than the fact that he was now dead.

'The tenant? You're saying your tenant has been *murdered*?'

'Oh, he's been murdered all right. He was stabbed to death.'

'Where did this happen?'

'In the house,' Jude said. 'Dude was lying right in the middle of the kitchen floor, all kind of crumpled up, with the handle of a bloody great carving knife sticking up out of his chest. If that's not murdered, I don't know what is.'

Ben knew the old vicarage well, had stayed there many times, and had a strong emotional attachment to the place. The idea of something like this happening there was unthinkable, like a violation against something sacred. Jude's description was so graphic that Ben wondered how he could know those details. 'What are you saying, you saw him there?'

'Saw him? It was me who found him! That's why they think I did it. I might . . . I might have touched something. I don't know any more. I've told the story so many times I don't even know what's true and what isn't. I'm losing my mind. You've got to help me, Dad!'

Ben's mind was swimming as he tried to get a handle on

the situation. Storm and Scruffy were looking up at him with anxiety in their eyes. Their acute sense of smell was picking up the stress pheromones he was giving off. He centred himself, controlling his breathing to lower his blood pressure and pulse rate.

Deep in his heart he knew that Jude would never deliberately hurt a soul. Not like his father had. That was part of Ben's DNA that Jude just hadn't inherited, to Ben's great relief. For a time Jude had talked about going into the Navy with a view to trying out for the Special Boat Service, Jeff Dekker's old unit. Ben hadn't been able to imagine his son as a trained killer.

But Ben also knew that things could happen in the heat of the moment. Fights, accidents, crimes of passion, freaks of circumstance. He had to ask. 'Jude. Tell me the honest truth. I only need to hear it from you once, and I swear I won't ask again. You didn't do this, did you?'

Jude exploded on the other end of the line. 'No!' he yelled. 'I'm innocent! How could you doubt me?'

'I don't doubt you, Jude. I just needed to hear you say it.'

'What am I going to do? I've never been arrested for anything before. I don't want to go to jail.'

Ben asked, 'Have they charged you for this?'

'Not yet, but I know they're going to. There's this plain-clothes guy in charge, some prick of a detective who keeps screaming at me like I'd shot the Queen or something. They're going to lock me up and throw away the key. I've got to get out of here! I can't live like that!' Jude's voice was at breaking point.

Ben said, 'Jude.'

'What?'

'Stop. Close your eyes.'

'What for?'

'Just do it.'

A pause. 'Okay, they're closed.'

'Now take a few breaths. Slow and deep, through your nose. Let the tension flow out of your muscles.'

'I'm breathing.'

'Now open your eyes and listen to me like you've never listened to anyone before in your life.'

'I'm listening.'

'You are innocent, Jude. You have nothing to worry about. This whole thing is just some terrible mistake and everything's going to be okay. Do you hear me?'

'I hear you,' Jude replied. But he sounded anything but convinced. Then he said, 'I'm out of time. I've got to go.'

'Jude, I'm coming over there. I'll be with you as soon as I can.'

Then the call was over. Ben sat back in his chair. Picturing his son being marched back to the interview room where the police would continue to grill him until they either let him go or charged him with the crime of murder. Ben wanted to believe it would be the former, but a terrible feeling was building inside him. This wasn't good.

'Jesus.'

He lit a cigarette, reached for the phone and called Jeff's mobile to tell him what had happened and that he had to take off. Jeff was still on the road, in-between stops about twenty miles away. It was like Ben's old friend and business partner to be all serious efficiency in a moment like this. He replied that he and Tuesday were returning to base immediately. 'You need me?'

'No, I'll handle this. I'll be gone by the time you get back.'

'Copy that. Good luck, mate. Give my best to Jude, tell him to keep his chin up, and keep us in the loop.'

'Thanks, Jeff. Talk later.' Ben hung up the phone. He stubbed out his unfinished cigarette, launched himself out of his chair and raced for the door. The dogs leaped to their feet and followed him outside and across to the house. 'You can't come with me, guys. You need to stay and look after things until your uncle Jeff gets back.'

Scruffy looked peeved, but Storm seemed to understand. Ben rushed upstairs and started stuffing essential items into his old green canvas bag. He was no stranger to having to rush off like this, and could be packed and ready to go in three minutes flat. He kept thinking he was dreaming. How the hell could something like this have happened to Jude, of all people?

This was like nothing Ben had had to deal with in the past. If Jude had been kidnapped or was being threatened by dangerous armed assailants, Ben would have known exactly what to do. It had happened before, the time when Jude had found himself a hostage aboard a container ship hijacked by pirates off the coast of Africa. On that occasion, Ben and his comrades had acted decisively and brought him home safely in the end. Their way, playing by their rules. But in this kind of situation Ben knew he was completely outside of his area of expertise. This was a world of courts, judges and lawyers he knew nothing about. He could no more spring his son from a British police cell than he could bust him out of prison, in the worst-case scenario that Jude was remanded in custody.

Maybe it won't happen, he told himself over and over. Maybe by the time he got to Oxfordshire this terrible mistake would have been seen for what it was, Jude would have been released without charge, he'd be back home celebrating his regained freedom and the police would have hauled the real killer into custody.

But the reassuring voice in Ben's head was doing little to alleviate his thumping heart and the tightness in his shoulders as he threw his bag into the back of his car, leapt behind the wheel and took off in a wild spinning of wheels and clouds of dust.

Back on the road again. Heading into the unknown. Ben had no idea what awaited him at the end of his journey. But nothing could have prepared him for the reality.

Chapter 3

Ben's car was a high-performance BMW Alpina, the latest in a succession that had sometimes ended their service at the bottom of rivers, crashed or shot to bits. It was metallic blue, not that he cared since he had never cleaned it anyway. Its one main attribute, as far as he was concerned, was speed. Blistering, scorching, eye-watering power that it delivered in buckets – and he made uncompromising use of that capability as he hurtled away from Le Val and made the journey across northern France to the ferry terminal at Calais. Zipping past traffic as though it were standing still he whittled a four-hour drive into three, broke a ton of speed limits and would probably come home to a stack of fines, but he didn't give a damn.

Before long he was rolling the Alpina onto the car ferry; some ninety minutes later he was roaring off again on British soil. The last time he'd made this crossing, he'd worried about the customs authorities catching him with the firearm that circumstances had forced him to smuggle across the sea. On this occasion he had other concerns on his mind, but there was nothing he could do to update himself on

Jude's predicament until he reached his destination and tried to pry that information out of the police.

He was to be disappointed. After two more hours of manic driving he screeched to a halt in the car park of the Thames Valley police station in Abingdon where Jude was being held. The two-storey modern red-brick building looked to him more like a primary school than a law enforcement command centre, set back from the road on the edge of town amid trees and neat hedges. Trying not to look like a maniac desperado he made himself walk, not run, from the car to the main visitors' reception desk. Some people sat in a waiting area nearby. A desultory-looking female civilian staffer fixed him with a blank gaze from behind a security screen as he explained who he was and why he was here. The staffer spent a long while noting down the details, tapping keys on a computer and made him repeat himself several times while he gritted his teeth and willed himself to keep his patience.

'Your name is Mr Hope?'

'That's correct. Ben Hope.'

'Ben short for Benjamin?'

'Benedict.'

'How do you spell that?'

He spelled it for her.

Tap, tap. She had black fingernails.

'And the person you're enquiring about is Mr Jude Arundale?'

'Arundel.' He spelled that for her as well. 'A-R-U-N-D-E-L. As far as I know, he's still being held here. I just want to know if he's been charged yet.'

She paused the tapping and frowned at him. 'Have either yourself or Mr Arundel had a name change?'

'No, those are our names.'

'But you say he's your son.'

'We have different surnames. Look, it's a long and complicated story that I don't have time to go into right now.' In his rush to get here Ben hadn't foreseen the issue the disparity between their names might flag up, but now he could see where this was going. Welcome to the wonderful land of bureaucracy.

'Are you able to provide any documentary proof of relationship, such as a full birth certificate showing your identity as parent?'

Ben sighed. 'No, I don't have anything like that.'

'Do you and your son live together?'

He was about to reply truthfully, 'No, we never have, not for any great length of time,' then realised that answer would just make things worse. 'He's his own person. He owns a home here. I live in France.' He took out his driving licence to show her. She gave it only a cursory glance.

'If you could have provided something like a utility bill to show you're both resident at the same address, that might have been something. Is there nothing you can show me to prove that you're related?'

'Not really,' he admitted. That sense of being out of place and helpless was coming back strong. This just wasn't his world.

'Then I'm sorry, Mr . . . uh . . .'

'Hope.'

'I'm sorry, Mr Hope, but without proof of relationship

I'm not allowed to give you the information you're asking for.'

'I just want to know if he's been charged, that's all. A simple yes or no. It's not much to ask.'

'I'm sorry, but I just can't. Look at it from my position. You could be anybody.'

'Please. You could tell me by nodding or shaking your head. Nobody would even know.'

'It's my job.'

'He's my son.'

Her lips tightened into a firm line and her eyes hardened with a look of finality. This conversation was over.

Ben stared at her. The people in the waiting area were all craning their necks to watch the minor drama playing out at the reception desk. He felt his shoulders sag and knew he had to give it up. 'Fine,' he said, and turned away from the desk and walked out of the reception area feeling stupid and frustrated.

Back outside, he lit a Gauloise and turned to gaze at the police station, wondering where Jude might be inside. He imagined that the custody suite would be somewhere in the bowels of the building, comprising interview rooms and cells, some of them probably painted pink to make for a less threatening environment for vulnerable detainees or folks of a special snowflake disposition. Which did nothing to soften the harsh predicament of a person condemned to spend the next indeterminate period of their life behind bars. If charged with the murder of Carter Duggan, Jude would find himself being transported to a real prison that didn't look like a primary school surrounded by pretty gardens, and didn't coddle its inmates with the fake comfort of pink cells. For all Ben knew, Jude was already there.

One thing was for sure: unless he was prepared to break in through the police station roof, abseil through a window or camp outside the building on the off-chance of getting a glimpse of Jude, he wasn't going to find out anything more here. The afternoon sun was beginning to sink in the sky. He finished the cigarette and flicked the stub into the bushes, then thought *fuck it* and stalked irritably back to his car.

With nowhere else to go he drove west and north across Oxfordshire, a dogleg route of twenty-two miles that took him from Abingdon to the village of Little Denton. It was a familiar road that always filled him with bittersweet memories. The village was one of the few in the area that had remained unspoilt by developers. The houses were mostly Cotswold stone and many older cottages retained their thatched roofs. The little church where the Reverend Simeon Arundel had once delivered his sermons still rang its bells on a Sunday morning as it had been doing for centuries. Ben turned off by the village pub, wound his way along a twisty lane running parallel to the Thames, and arrived at the ivy-covered vicarage that stood surrounded by trees behind a high stone wall. He sighed as he reached the place. Before it had become Jude's, this had been the home of two very dear friends whom he still missed badly.

When Ben told people that the family background to his relationship with Jude was a long and complicated story, he wasn't just giving them the brush-off. It was also a story fraught with pain and sadness.

Jude's mother Michaela and her husband, Simeon, had

raised the boy with a secret that was revealed to nobody until after their tragic deaths in a car smash. For most of his life, Jude had been under the natural impression that his dad was Simeon Arundel, the much-loved vicar of Little Denton, whom his mother had married before he was born. The truth was that Jude's biological father was the wild young theology student and future soldier with whom she'd had a short, turbulent and passionate fling when they were all at university together: Ben Hope. They'd been something of a gang, the three of them, but the unhappy breakup of Ben and Michaela's whirlwind relationship had ended all that. He'd been just too much of a handful, back in those days. Soon afterwards, when Ben's unpredictable life path had led him to veer away from his studies and join the army, Michaela had confessed to Simeon something Ben had no clue about: that she was pregnant.

One of the kindest and most principled men Ben had ever known, Simeon Arundel had been there for Michaela all those years, and been honoured to bring up Jude as his own son. Had he and Michaela not met such an untimely end, they might have told him the truth one day; but the secret had gone with them to their graves and only a posthumous letter from Michaela had revealed the secret to Ben and, accidentally, to Jude.

At the time, it had been hard to tell which of the two of them was more shocked by the bombshell discovery. For Ben, it had been the crushing guilt of learning that he'd inadvertently left Michaela in the lurch all those years earlier, combined with the stunning strangeness of becoming a parent for the first time in his life. As for Jude, the poor kid's whole world had been turned upside down and inside out, and he'd had a hard time dealing with the fact that this person he barely knew, and then only as a distant friend of the family, was actually his father. The relationship between Ben and Jude had started out pretty rocky and gone through a lot of ups and downs before they'd gradually been able to come to terms with the impact it had made on both their lives. More than a son, Ben felt that he'd gained a friend.

And now this.

It felt very strange not to drive up the crunchy driveway to the house. Ben's reason for parking the Alpina outside the gates instead was that the vicarage grounds were already full of vehicles. Thames Valley Police had invaded. The Arundel family home was now the scene of the crime, festooned with blue and white POLICE LINE DO NOT CROSS cordon tape. A forensic investigation van was parked close to the front door with a squad car on each side. Ben noticed that one of the squad cars was crushing part of a rose bed that Michaela had planted long ago, and which Jude had lovingly tended in his mother's memory. Ben didn't like that very much.

As he stepped out of the Alpina and walked through the gates towards the house, he noticed something else. Not all four vehicles parked outside the house were painted in blue, white and lurid yellow livery with the shield emblem of Thames Valley Police on their bonnet. The odd one out was unusual. Very unusual. An ordinary unmarked cop car would have caught his eye but this one stood out like an elephant in a sheep enclosure. It was a massive black 1970 Plymouth Barracuda, as long and wide as a canal barge. The American muscle car made the police fleet vehicles look like Dinky toys. But what really drew Ben's attention was that he'd seen it before.

He paused beside the huge car, peered in the window and was greeted by a furious barking and a flurry of black and tan fur and snapping teeth from inside. The big German shepherd was better than any anti-theft alarm, that was for sure. Ben smiled at the dog. 'Hello, Radar.'

Continuing towards the house, Ben ducked under a tape cordon and spotted a uniformed cop emerge from the front door and head for the squad car that was parked on Michaela's roses. The officer saw him, stopped and fixed Ben with an icy stare. 'Hey, you. Can't you see this is a crime scene? No access to members of the public.'

Ben kept walking. He said, 'Where's McAllister?'

Which completely threw the cop off his rhythm. He blinked at Ben and stammered, 'H-how . . . w-what . . . w-why . . .'

Ben had come to Little Denton wanting to see inside the house, but now he'd changed his mind. Partly because he knew the police wouldn't let him in, partly because the forensic people would already have found anything worth finding, and partly because the presence of the big black Barracuda told him who was presiding over the crime scene investigation. He said to the uniform, 'Tell him that Ben Hope is here and wants to talk to him.'

The officer stared at Ben for a beat longer, then nodded without another word and disappeared back inside the house.

Ben lit up a Gauloise as he waited outside. A few moments

later, the owner of the muscle car, Detective Inspector Tom McAllister, stepped out to meet him.

McAllister was a big guy, broad-shouldered and ugly, but possessed of a rugged kind of charm. His Ulster accent was only a little softened by all the years he'd spent on the Thames Valley force.

'Ben Hope. I thought it must be some kind of frigging joke. How come you're not dead by now?'

'Nice to see you again too, Tom.'

Chapter 4

Ben had first crossed paths with DI McAllister a while back, when a trip to Oxford for a reunion event at his old college had brought with it the inevitable trouble that seemed to dog him everywhere he went. It had been the start of, if not a beautiful friendship, then at least a particular sort of unusual relationship.

Ben's past experiences as a freelance kidnap and hostage rescue specialist had ingrained in him a certain mistrust of law enforcement officers in general, and he often didn't get along too well with them. Grace Kirk had been one notable exception to that rule. Thames Valley Police Detective Inspector Tom McAllister had been another. Ben had found the Northern Irish cop to be a rough diamond and a straight shooter. He was also a dyed-in-the-wool maverick who thought outside the box, tended to bend the rules now and then, and had had his own run-ins with his superiors who regarded him as a loose cannon. Ben could resonate with that.

'I'm still alive,' he replied. 'And I see you're still in the game. Not quit the force to open your own restaurant yet?'

McAllister scowled and shook his head. 'So, if I may ask,

what the frig are you doing here? You may have noticed that you're walking into a restricted area.'

'So have the wizards at Thames Valley worked out who killed him?'

'Killed who?'

'Come on, McAllister. No need to play those games with me. Carter Duggan. The guy who was stabbed to death here last night.'

McAllister's face crumpled up into an expression of curious puzzlement. 'Certainly seem to have the inside track, Hope. In which case you ought to know that they already have someone in custody.'

Ben noticed the 'they', instead of a 'we'. Ever the outsider, that McAllister. He replied, 'I was aware of that. The problem is that they've got the wrong person.'

'And so you've come to confess that you did it, is that right?' McAllister said with a nasty grin.

'Actually, I was more hoping that I could prevail upon the forces of law and order to see the error of their ways and nail the real killer. Or else I might have to give them a helping hand.'

Cops generally didn't like it when civilians threatened to get mixed up in their investigations, especially ex-Special Forces soldiers with a known talent for mayhem and bedlam. McAllister didn't seem especially perturbed but said, 'I'm a little fuzzy on your involvement in this case.'

It was time for Ben to come clean. 'The suspect in custody for killing Duggan is my son. That's why I'm here.'

McAllister frowned. This was news. 'Hold on a minute. Jude Arundel is your *son*?'

'That's what I said.'

'Bullshit. Arundel's parents were Simeon and Michaela Arundel and they're dead.'

Ben held his eye. 'Tom. Look at me. Am I the kind of person who would bullshit you about something like this?'

McAllister returned Ben's look for a long moment, then nodded. He glanced back at the house, peering through the open doorway at all the activity that was taking place inside. He turned back to Ben and said, 'Walk with me a minute. I don't want those eedjits inside to overhear.'

McAllister descended the steps from the front door and the two of them strolled away from the house. 'You're serious, aren't you?'

'I've never been more serious in my life,' Ben said.

'*Your* son?'

'It's a long story. You just have to believe me.'

McAllister heaved a sigh. 'You might be a lot of things, Hope, but you're no liar. I believe you. Okay, so how much do you know?'

'When I talked to Jude earlier he hadn't been charged with it yet. I've just come from the Abingdon station. Tried to find out what's happening but they wouldn't talk to me.'

'I hate to be the bearer of bad news,' McAllister said. 'They charged your boy with murder late this morning.'

Ben felt a great weight pull at his heart. He took a deep breath. 'How bad does it look for him?'

'Not good. His prints are all over the handle of the knife, for a start. Results came through this morning. That's what clinched it.'

'There has to be some other reason for that.'

McAllister shrugged. 'No sign of forced entry, suggests the killer had a key to the house. And it wasn't a robbery, either. Duggan had two hundred quid cash in his pocket and was wearing a fancy Tag Heuer watch that your average opportunistic crook would've whipped off his wrist faster than you can say Jack Robinson. Plus, there are two witness statements that he was seen having a hell of an argument with the victim earlier in the day. About what, I can't tell you. In fact I shouldn't be saying any of this to you.'

Ben remembered what Jude had told him about the grilling he'd received in the police cells. 'Were you one of the interviewing officers?'

McAllister shook his head and replied, 'No, I'm a latecomer to this party. Just come off the case of the Rose Hill polka-dot underwear rapist, who I'm happy to say is now behind bars. The chiefs didn't put me on this assignment until this morning, after Jude was charged. Lucky me, eh?'

Ben wished that he knew more, and that Jude had had time to tell him about it. 'He's headstrong. And he can be a handful to deal with.'

'Just like his old man?'

'But he's not a murderer. He did not do this.'

'Tell that to the judge.'

'Who was Carter Duggan?' Ben asked.

'I only know what I know,' McAllister replied. 'Canadian citizen, native of Ottawa, here in the UK on a temporary visitor's stamp. Fifty years old, six-one, sixteen stone. He's an ex-cop who spent seventeen years with the Ontario Provincial Police, retired in 2012 with the rank of detective staff sergeant.'

'What was he doing here in Little Denton?'

'I'm looking into it.'

They had walked as far as McAllister's car. McAllister opened the door and cranked down the window to give the dog some more air. Radar stuck his head out and painted his master's face with a huge pink tongue, the same way that Storm did with Ben. McAllister patted him lovingly, in a way that made Ben suddenly yearn to be home again.

Ben curled his fingers and offered his hand for the dog to sniff. He asked, 'So what happens next?'

McAllister replied, 'His bail hearing is set for tomorrow morning at Oxford Magistrates' Court in front of District Judge Crapper. That's moving along pretty fast. He might've had to sit waiting a lot longer. Means he gets to enjoy the hospitality of the Abingdon station custody suite for another night. Nothing anyone can do until the hearing.'

Ben dreaded asking. 'How likely is he to be granted bail?'

McAllister shrugged. 'Letter of the law? According to Section one-one-four, paragraph two, of the Coroners and Justice Act, bail may not be granted unless the court's satisfied that there's no significant risk of the suspect trying to make a break for it or hurt anyone else. So technically, the kid could be freed tomorrow as long as someone's willing to enter into a recognisance.'

'Speak English, McAllister.'

'In layman's terms, it means to act as his guarantor and cough up a large amount of cash if the suspect breaks the conditions of his bail.'

'He won't break them,' Ben said.

'That's up to you to persuade the court,' McAllister replied.

'Though I wouldn't get my hopes up, pal. In real life it all hangs on what the Crown Prosecution Service push for. This was a nasty killing and I don't see the CPS taking a light touch here. They'll already be leaning on Judge Crapper to side with their decision.'

'But Crapper still gets the final say, doesn't he?'

McAllister made a noncommittal yes-and-no kind of gesture. 'Aye, he does in theory, but he's got a reputation for being a weak auld bugger. He knows if he grants bail against the Public Prosecutor's recommendation, then it'll get automatically appealed to the High Court and that could drag on for ever and make him look bad if the appeal's upheld. I'd expect him to take the path of least resistance, cave in to the Crown like he generally does and order your boy to be remanded in Bullingdon Prison until his trial date. Which could be months away.'

Another heavy weight tugged harder inside Ben's chest. He felt a numbness spreading through him. 'Where's Bullingdon?'

'Arncott, near Bicester.'

Ben knew the old market town because of MoD Bicester, the Ministry of Defence's biggest ordnance depot. He'd been there once when part of the regular army, prior to his SAS days. It was about twenty miles away from Little Denton. But once Jude was banged up inside, he'd be so far out of Ben's protective reach that it might as well be on the moon.

'You said this was a nasty killing,' he said. 'Just how nasty are we talking about?'

'Murder weapon was a large cookery knife. Belongs to a matching set from the block on the kitchen counter. Nice ones, too. Misono.' McAllister was a keen chef in his home life. Ben had once seen him take time out at a murder scene to admire the victim's collection of copper saucepans. He knew a thing or two about cookery knives, as well. 'Sharp's not the word. You could chiffonade basil with it and the leaves'd feel like they were coming off in perfect ribbons in your hand. So you can imagine what a bit of determined hack and stab work did to this poor bastard.'

Ben didn't have to imagine, because he'd seen similar or worse done to people in the past. For Jude to do something so brutal and violent to another human being, he'd have to have lost his mind and been on hallucinogenic drugs. It was simply unthinkable.

Ben was about to reply when the patter of tyres on gravel made them both turn and glance towards the gates, to see another unmarked police car turning in off the road and rolling up the vicarage drive. McAllister looked at the approaching car with a dismal expression. 'Oh, shite.'

Chapter 5

'It's Forbsie,' McAllister said. 'What the hell is that wee skitter doing here?'

Forbsie was Detective Superintendent Alan Forbes, McAllister's superior and nemesis. Ben had met him once before, too. And another time long before that, back when Ben was a student and Forbsie was still in uniform, an occasion that had resulted in Forbsie getting covered in human excrement. That, too, was a long story, and not one that had done anything to endear Ben to the man.

'You'd best get out of here,' McAllister warned him. 'There'll be hell to pay if he spots you hanging around.'

A row of conifer trees stood next to McAllister's Plymouth, planted there by Michaela a long time ago. Ben stepped behind them so that Forbes wouldn't see him. 'Thanks for the advice, anyway, for what it's worth.'

Forbes's car reached the top of the driveway and rolled to a halt. The Detective Super was the only person inside. He looked just the way Ben remembered him, a reedy-looking individual with a dyed black comb-over and a moustache that bristled like the hairs on the back of an angry cat.

McAllister seemed about to go over to meet his superior, but then paused and instead moved behind the trees closer to Ben, so that Forbes couldn't see him either. With a thoughtful twinkle in his eye he asked, 'Where are you staying?'

With all the rushing around, Ben hadn't given it an instant's thought. 'I don't know. A hotel, I suppose.'

'You can come and doss on my couch, if you like. Then we can talk more.'

'Isn't that a little unconventional, for the cop leading the investigation to offer to discuss the case?'

'I'm an unconventional kind of guy,' McAllister said with an alligator grin. 'This way I get to keep an eye on you. Last time you poked your nose into a police investigation on my turf we ended up with a bloody war kicking off and an estate block that looked like something from Beirut, 1982.'

'I wouldn't know anything about that,' Ben said. He remembered the occasion well. He'd disappeared long before the police armed response vehicles had come screaming to the scene.

'Anyhow, the dog likes you.'

'Then how can I refuse?'

'Meet me at the Trout at Tadpole Bridge tonight at eight o'clock. My place isn't far from there.' McAllister pressed a business card into Ben's hand. 'Here's my number in case you change your mind.'

Ben slipped further behind the conifers as Forbes stepped out of his unmarked police car and began strutting towards the house. McAllister went over to greet him. They shared a couple of brief words and then went inside. Ben waited until McAllister shut the front door behind them, then emerged from the cover of the trees and walked quickly back to his car.

It was after five in the afternoon and Ben now had almost three hours to kill before meeting McAllister. He got into the Alpina and took off out of the village with no clue where he was going. There was no way for him to contact Jude or do anything more to help him until the bail hearing in Oxford tomorrow. He felt sick with worry and his mind was buzzing with so many thoughts that he could barely think straight. He was soon lost in the deep countryside that lay all around Little Denton. Fields and farms and signposts and the occasional house flashed by, but he scarcely even noticed them.

After a few minutes on the road he began to worry about losing concentration at the wheel, and pulled over in a grassy field gate entrance across the road from a patch of woodland. He sat there for almost an hour, staring into space and thinking about what Jude must be doing and feeling at this moment.

Restlessness getting the better of him, he climbed out of the car and crossed the road to go wandering a while in the forest, hoping that it would help to clear his mind. It felt good to move. He found a track through the trees that reminded him of his woodland paths at Le Val, and his walking pace stepped up to a jog, then to a run as the energy coursing through him found its release. His feet pounded the dirt. Twigs lashed his face. He sprinted faster, and faster, pushing himself to maximum speed and holding it there for as long as he could, until the burn in his legs made him stop. He had run almost a mile through the woods.

Ben spent some time resting on a fallen tree and giving in once more to the temptation of his Gauloises. The run had helped to flush some of the turmoil from his head, but he could still feel it all hovering over him like a black storm cloud. As early evening came he made a quick call to Jeff at Le Val to update him.

Jeff sounded shocked that Jude had been charged with the murder. Ben wished he'd had better news to give. He promised to phone Jeff again when he knew more. When the call was finished, he used his phone to locate the rendez-vous point for his meeting with Tom McAllister at eight. He made his way back to the Alpina and set off, giving himself plenty of time to get there.

The Trout at Tadpole Bridge lay a few miles away in rural west Oxfordshire, by the Thames close to a place called Buckland Marsh. Ben drove over the old stone humpback bridge and turned into the car park of the historic inn. It was two minutes to eight and McAllister's car wasn't there yet. Ben wandered inside. The decor was the usual old-world, rustic-chic style of these Oxfordshire country establishments. Aged oak beams as thick as tree trunks, uneven flagstone floor and a fireplace flanked by stacks of logs. Something about the place struck him as vaguely familiar, and after a moment he realised with sadness that he might have come here on one of his legendary pub crawls with Simeon Arundel, all those years ago. Back then, even among the wealthy elite of Oxford, it had been a rare privilege for a student to possess their very own set of wheels – and Simeon's bright red classic Lotus Elan had earned him both the envy of the young gentlemen and the admiration of the ladies, in equal measure. Ben had fond memories of those summer nights zapping about the county in their Quixotic quest to sample every variety of real ale known to mankind.

It had been in the same red Lotus that Simeon and Michaela would later meet their deaths. They were still so young. Ben missed them both badly.

He ordered a double scotch, no ice, no water. Most of the pub tables were occupied and he didn't much feel like company anyway, so carried his drink out to the beer garden and sat alone where he could see the road. He'd been waiting just seven minutes when he heard the unmistakable V8 rumble of McAllister's car approaching; then the Barracuda appeared on the bridge and came rolling up next to Ben's Alpina in the car park. Ben quickly downed the last of his drink and walked over to meet him. McAllister rolled down his window and said, 'Follow me.'

Chapter 6

McAllister led Ben deeper into the countryside, through a web of single-track lanes that in places were little wider than the huge Plymouth. After passing through a hamlet called Chimney McAllister's car turned off the road and Ben followed him along a rutted private track overhung by thick tree cover, which wound and snaked down towards the river. The lane petered out near an ancient, semi-derelict watermill which still had its wheel and most of its stone walls intact, but not much else. McAllister pulled up and clambered out of his car, and Ben stepped out to join him.

'Here it is,' McAllister announced, spreading his arms out wide. 'Home sweet home.'

For a moment Ben wondered if McAllister was having him on, or whether the detective was really crazy enough to live in a crumbling ruin – but then, glancing around him, he noticed the little path through the trees that led up to a small cottage half-hidden among the foliage. He said, 'You certainly found yourself a remote spot to live in, McAllister.'

'Aye, well, it suits us.' McAllister tipped his driver's seat forwards to let the dog out. Radar jumped from the car and bounded over to investigate their guest.

'Come on up to the house and have a drink while I get dinner on. Hungry?'

'I haven't eaten a thing all day.'

'Then you've come to the right place.'

McAllister led the way up to the cottage. A small conservatory at the front doubled as a greenhouse and was filled with culinary herbs. The combined aromas of rosemary, thyme, sage and dozens of others that Ben couldn't identify were a harbinger of the gastronomic treats in store. The inside of the house was as rustic as the exterior, and as lived-in as a comfortable old shoe. Ben liked the place immediately. Warning him to mind his head on the low beams, McAllister hustled into a bedroom and reappeared a minute later, having changed out of his dark work suit into a pair of worn jeans and a baggy shirt. He headed straight for the kitchen. 'Beer?'

'Beer is fine,' Ben replied.

McAllister's kitchen was a hard-worked space, cluttered but well organised, with gleaming wood surfaces and copper pots hanging over a range. He yanked open a fridge that was as big as his car, pulled out a couple of bottles and tossed one to Ben, along with an opener.

'Langtree Hundred?' Ben said, looking at the label.

'Local ale. I order it by the crateload. Couldn't be without it.'

'I take it there's no Mrs McAllister.'

'Just me and the dog. If there's a woman out there who'd put up with a crusty old fart like me, she hasn't turned up yet.'

'You're not that old.'

'But definitely crusty.' McAllister seemed to relish the idea, and so Ben wasn't about to disabuse him of that notion. The cop was poised to dive back inside the cavernous fridge when his expression suddenly froze to a look of horror. 'Jesus Christ, I just had a terrible thought. You're not a vegetarian, are you?'

'If it walks, crawls, swims or flies I'll eat it.'

'Thank God for that.' McAllister reached into the fridge and came out with a covered pan. Inside it, two enormous steaks had been marinating in wine with some kind of herb seasoning that smelled so aromatic, Ben could have eaten them raw. 'Not that I have a problem with it, mind,' McAllister added. 'There are oodles of wonderful dishes you can make without meat. It's not like them Vulcans.'

'Vegans.'

'Whatever. You can't cook a thing for them. Imagine braised carrots and celery or sautéed potatoes without butter. Or worse, with frigging soya margarine.'

'Unthinkable,' Ben said.

'Heresy is what it is. You don't have a soul if you don't eat proper food. Just my opinion. Not that I give a damn about offending people. I've been doing that all my life.'

Ben smiled. 'You want some help getting dinner going?'

'Think I'll manage. Help yourself to another beer. It's a warm evening. Thought we could eat outside. Okay?'

Ben hung around in the background and watched as the cop got to work, filled with dynamism. It was clear from the expression of pure contentment that spread over his craggy face that McAllister loved cooking much more than he did his chosen profession. After he'd removed a few more items from the fridge he bustled back outside and over to an adjoining outbuilding, from which he dragged a Texas-style barbecue smoker that was roughly the size and shape of a small steam locomotive, with a tall stove pipe at one end. Next he grabbed a sack of charcoal, which he proudly showed Ben. 'Make it myself out of oak and hickory. Can't abide these newfangled gas-fired things.'

McAllister set about lighting the fire, filling the air with smoke. While he was waiting for the coals to come up to temperature he returned to the kitchen to prepare a salad made up of different varieties of organic lettuce from his vegetable garden. Then, once the barbecue was glowing red, he took the two steaks from their marinade pan and laid them with a flourish on the grill.

'Rib eye cuts,' he declared, as they began to sizzle and give off a wonderful smell. 'Best steak in the world for grilling. The marinade's the secret to making them even more tender. They'll be ready in no time.'

When the steaks were done, it was time to get out the wine. McAllister, of course, had a great bottle of red set by, opened well in advance so that the wine could breathe, and at the perfect temperature. They sat down to eat at a trestle table in the cottage garden overlooking the riverside with a view of the old mill. The dog lay happily on the grass nearby. Butterflies fluttered around the wild buddleia and the lazy Thames burbled by in the background. Ben hadn't thought he would have much of an appetite under the circumstances, but the steaks were unbelievably tender and tasted even better than they looked and smelled. The wine was equally delicious and Ben attacked it with gusto. He needed this. If he was to do battle to help Jude's predicament, in whatever way he could, then he would need all the energy and strength he could get.

'You eat like this every night?'

McAllister shrugged. 'Oh, this is nothing fancy. Sometimes I'll blag a few hours off in the afternoon and spend some time doing something special. Not that I'm that good, you know?'

'This is good enough.'

They talked for a while about the old watermill, which McAllister was slowly restoring with the long-term goal of creating his own restaurant, the Three Bay Leaves. 'Three leaves together like an Irish shamrock, see?'

'I get it. Very artful.'

'It won't be the biggest or swankiest restaurant in the county. Just the best. We'll do eighteen to twenty covers a night, tops. When word gets around, you'll have to book a month in advance.'

'So you mean to quit the force eventually.'

'That's my dream. But to make it come true is no mean feat, on my salary.' McAllister was doing all the work himself. An old odd-bod called Sparrowhawk, who lived on a river boat, cruised up now and then to lend a helping hand, but it was slow progress. McAllister didn't envisage handing in his resignation any time soon. 'Besides,' he said through a mouthful of steak, 'what would they do without me?'

By the time they'd finished eating and a second bottle of wine was flowing, the conversation drifted back to Jude. 'I never knew you had kids,' McAllister said.

'Neither did I, for twenty years.'

'Oh, I see. Like that.'

'No,' Ben said. 'Not like that.'

'Let me guess. It's a long story.'

Ben said, 'Tell me more about the witnesses.'

Chapter 7

McAllister said, 'They're the Heneghan sisters. A couple of old biddies who've been living together in the same wee house in Little Denton since about 1947, with a couple dozen moggies. Elsie's ninety and Maureen's eighty-four. From what I can gather talking to the locals, they spend their days going around shaking a collection can for animal charities, and woe betide you if you don't bung them some change when they come a-calling. Seems they were doing their usual rounds of the village early yesterday afternoon when they happened to turn up at the vicarage and heard a load of shouting going on inside. When they peered in the front door, there was your boy Jude having a pretty strong argument with the tenant, Carter Duggan. According to their police statements, which are identical, it was Jude who was doing most of the shouting. They described him as being a lot more aggressive and threatening than Duggan.'

'Threatening in what way?'

McAllister reached for the wine and topped their glasses up. 'How about "Shut your mouth or I'll kill you"? Sounds pretty threatening.'

Ben was stunned. 'Jude said that?'

'Each of the Heneghan sisters made an independent state-ment, and they both reported what he said more or less word for word.'

'Jude's never threatened anyone in his life before.'

'Well, he has now.'

'Was he drunk?'

'Clean as a whistle. Tested negative for alcohol or drugs on admission to the station.'

'Which has to mean that Duggan provoked him somehow. The guy must have said something really terrible to wind Jude up that much. Shut your mouth about what?'

'We don't know,' McAllister replied. 'Whatever Duggan might have said, the Heneghan sisters got there too late to hear it. And your boy refused to tell the questioning officers anything more. All we know is, he made the threat.'

Ben swallowed some more wine, along with his frustra-tion, and said grimly, 'Okay. But the sisters didn't witness Jude assaulting Duggan in any way.'

'No, their turning up interrupted the argument. At that point Jude pushed past them, went storming out of the vicarage and over to the garage, and took off like a bat out of hell in a silver Toyota. DVLA records show that it's his own car.'

Ben asked, 'How did he get to the vicarage?'

'Local taxi firm picked him up from Faringdon railway station.'

'So that explains why he was at the vicarage,' Ben said. 'He went there to pick up his car. Perfectly innocent thing to do.'

'Fair enough. So why were they arguing?'

Ben couldn't answer that. 'What happened next?'

McAllister said, 'We know that he went from there to a hotel in Marcham, and booked a room for the night. CCTV footage shows him leaving the hotel on foot to visit a nearby fish and chip shop early that evening. Didn't go into any pubs or have anything to drink, as we already know from his test result. Later that evening he drove back to Little Denton, and returned to the vicarage.'

'You don't have CCTV video of that. There isn't a camera anywhere in the whole village.'

'No, which makes the timing a little hazy because we don't know exactly when he got there,' McAllister said. 'Here's what we do know. At eight-twenty that evening the old guy next door was in his garden when he heard what he described as a short, sharp, blood-curdling scream from the vicarage. I love that word, "blood-curdling". You'd be amazed how often it comes up in police statements.'

'Go on.'

'It was a man's voice screaming. After that, silence. The neighbour was wondering what the hell was up, but he didn't want to intrude, or maybe he was a bit freaked out by it. So he tried phoning the vicarage's landline number to ask if everything was okay. No reply. After a few more minutes the old guy goes round there in person to check things out. He notices the silver Toyota in the driveway, which hadn't been there earlier. Duggan's car was a black Ford Mondeo, a rental. Anyhow, the old guy knocks on the door. Still no reply, but at this point he notices that the door's ajar, and he gets a feeling that something's definitely wrong. He's a little nervous but does what most folks would do, and goes inside calling "Hello? Hello? Is everything all right?" And that's when he found the body.'

'In the kitchen,' Ben said, recalling what Jude had told him.

McAllister nodded. 'Lake of blood all over the floor, and there's Carter Duggan lying in the middle of it, hacked to bits and dead as disco with the knife stuck up to its hilt in his chest.'

'Jude told me he was the one who found Duggan.'

McAllister made a sceptical snorting noise. 'Well, I'm not going to say he was the one who *found* him first. But he was definitely there in the room before the neighbour walked in. The old guy's police statement describes him standing right over the body, kind of staring at it in fascination. When he noticed the old guy in the doorway, he turned slowly to look at him and just said, "He's dead." It was the neighbour who called 999. Your boy was apprehended twenty-two minutes later, when the officers got to the scene.'

'So Jude didn't try to leave the scene?'

'No, he sat and waited quietly for the police to arrive.'

'And you don't find that strange, for a guilty man not to run?'

McAllister made that noncommittal gesture of his. 'It's not actually that unusual for killers to let themselves get arrested like that. It's as if they've resigned themselves, knowing that it'll only make it worse for them if they try to evade capture. If the armed response boys get called in, you're liable to end up riddled with bullets.'

'That makes sense,' Ben said. 'Except Jude isn't a killer.'

'His fingerprints all over the knife say otherwise.'

'Were Jude's the only prints on it?'

'No, there were two sets. Duggan had been handling the knife, too. Which is pretty unremarkable, seeing as he was living there. Unless you're going to claim that he stabbed himself?'

Ben lit a cigarette. The sun was sinking behind the trees, casting a golden light over the river. He said, 'I still can't understand why Jude's prints could have been on the knife.'

'Um, well, there is one fairly obvious explanation,' McAllister said. 'Chances are that when you pick up a knife to murder someone, unless you wear gloves, you'll leave a neat little trail for the forensic guys.'

'Excluding that possibility,' Ben said, shaking his head. 'Which I am. Because it's not possible that it happened that way.'

McAllister gave him a heavy stare. 'You really want to believe that, don't you? Okay, so how else do you explain it?'

'He's only just come back from the USA and this guy was living in his house. Is it possible that the prints were on the knife the whole time he was away?'

McAllister considered it briefly. 'Technically, if they're not smudged or wiped away, prints can remain on a clean, smooth surface for years. They're basically oil, so they don't evaporate. But you're talking about a key item of kitchen equipment that's in daily use and washed and dried each time afterwards. How many thousands of times have I cleaned my knives?'

'Not everyone's a chef like you. Maybe Duggan ate out

every night, or lived mostly on takeaways. He might have handled the knife once or twice but never needed to clean it.'

'Possible,' McAllister said. 'But answer me this. Suppose there's a third person involved, this hypothetical mystery killer who managed to sneak into the house, do the dirty and disappear again like a ghost. Why did they just happen to pick up a knife that was already there? If they'd turned up at the house intending to murder Duggan for whatever reason, wouldn't they have brought their own weapon? What kind of murderer comes unprepared?'

Ben had already thought about that. 'Just because the killer used the knife from Jude's kitchen, it doesn't mean he came unprepared. He could have been carrying his own knife or any other kind of weapon, but he just didn't happen to use it.'

'How does that work?'

'Easy. Duggan's in the kitchen when he hears a noise that alerts him to the presence of an intruder. Feeling threatened, he grabs the knife from the block. Next thing, he's attacked, tries to defend himself. There's a struggle, but the intruder gets the better of him and uses the knife against him. The intruder's wearing gloves, so he leaves no prints on the handle.'

McAllister looked doubtful. 'Duggan was an ex-cop and a fairly big, tough guy. He'd know how to take care of himself.'

'He'd been out of the police a long time,' Ben said. 'Besides, if we're honest, how many active police officers do you know who can withstand a serious lethal attack from an expert?'

'So now your hypothetical intruder is some kind of Ninja assassin.'

Ben said, 'He got in and out without anyone noticing, and left a dead man in his wake. That takes skill.'

'I see. And all this just happens to take place moments before Jude arrives on the scene. Sorry, I'm not buying it.'

Ben thought for a moment. 'Okay. Backtrack. You said that the neighbour tried to phone Duggan after hearing the scream, but then some time went by before they went over to knock on the door. How much of a time interval are we looking at?'

McAllister said, 'He was a little vague in his statement. We know the exact time he called next door, and when he dialled 999. It leaves a realistic window of maybe eight to ten minutes.'

'Long enough for the real killer to have disappeared, and for Jude to turn up and find Duggan lying there dead. Next thing, the neighbour walks in and sees him standing over the body.'

'Just by chance. Very convenient.'

'Or very inconvenient for him, if he didn't do it,' Ben said. 'It's his house. He grew up there. Nothing too amazing about his wanting to hang around the place.'

'Hmm. Technically it was Duggan's house at the time, being as he had a proper tenancy lease through a rental agency.'

'All the same, there could be a hundred reasons why Jude could have gone back there.'

'The most obvious one being to carry out the murder threat that he'd made earlier the same day, in front of eyewitnesses. That's how everyone's going to see it.'

'Then they'd be wrong,' Ben said. 'Did Jude have the victim's blood on him?'

'On his shoes, plenty of it.'

'That doesn't prove anything. Sounds like you couldn't walk into that kitchen without standing in a puddle of blood. What about his hands, his clothes?'

McAllister hesitated, and said nothing.

'Come on, McAllister. You don't stab and hack a man to death, up close and personal, without getting covered in blood. Especially if he's not inclined to just stand there and let you do it. You get it up to your elbows, on your face, in your hair.'

'Speaking from experience, are you?'

'You know what I used to do for a living,' Ben said. 'I was trained to neutralise the enemy by whatever means are most appropriate. Knives are silent and effective. It's an ugly business but that's how it is.'

'Jeez. The biggest thing I ever carved up was a side of pork. I don't know, maybe he could have wiped himself clean before the cops arrived.'

'Blood is tacky and sticky. You need a long, hot shower to get it off.'

'Or maybe he just didn't get any on him.'

'No chance,' Ben said. 'There has to be another explanation as to what he was doing there at that moment.'

'But what if there isn't?' McAllister countered.

'He didn't do it.'

'He's the only one with any motive. He threatened the guy.'

'Duggan was a cop. You make enemies, in that line of work. Someone he put in jail, or a relative.'

'Tell me about it. But I'm presuming his enemies are in

Canada. Why would they jump on a plane and come all the way out to a quiet little Oxfordshire village to do the dirty?'

Ben made no reply.

'I don't blame you,' McAllister said. 'Of course you don't want to believe it. You're a decent guy. But you're also sounding like a guy who's desperately clutching at straws to exonerate his son. Problem is, whichever way you cut it, he looks guilty as hell.'

Chapter 8

Ben sat up long after McAllister had gone to bed that night. The old battered couch in the cottage's living room was comfortable enough, and God knew Ben had slept in a lot of worse places in his life. But there was nothing he could do to still his mind except drink himself unconscious – and he wanted to appear reasonably fresh for Jude's bail hearing in the morning, not smelling like a brewery. Around four a.m. his fatigue finally got the better of him and he drifted off into a troubled sleep.

He was awake again just two hours later, and took a fretful walk along the riverbank with Radar as he thought about the long day ahead. McAllister was up soon afterwards, and brewed a pot of excellent coffee. He explained to Ben that he wouldn't be at the hearing because he had a fresh missing persons case to investigate, and a few doors to knock on that day. Ben wished him good luck with it.

By eight, Ben was driving into Oxford. He left the Alpina in a park and ride and took an overcrowded bus into the city centre. He might have enjoyed being back in his favourite English city, under different conditions. The Magistrates' Court in Speedwell Street, just a short walk from his old college, was a grime-streaked modern building that had to be a contender for one of the ugliest in Oxford. Ben got there at nine o'clock sharp with thirty minutes to spare before the hearing began. In a downstairs lobby he met Jude's court-appointed lawyer, a pimply youth by the name of Dorian Simms who, judging by the brief conversation Ben had with him, didn't appear any more confident in Jude's innocence than Tom McAllister. So much for the defence advocate having faith in his client.

Ben had a request for Simms. 'As Jude's only relative, I'd like to address the court on his behalf. Can you arrange that with the judge for me?'

Simms frowned and glanced at his watch, not pleased at the extra workload this quick errand would place on him. 'I'd have to hurry. We've only got a few minutes.'

'Then you'd best hurry,' Ben said, looking him in the eye. 'Now, here's what I need you to tell him.'

Simms scurried off to catch Judge Crapper in his chambers and convey Ben's message before the hearing began. Ben paced in the lobby, waiting. With two minutes to go, Simms returned to say that the request had been granted.

The courtroom wasn't one of those grand wood-panelled rooms in which Ben had always imagined great legal dramas playing out. The walls were institutional beige and the seating was like office furniture. A clerk ushered Ben to a seat near the front. Simms sat at a table nearby and opened a briefcase, shuffling papers about with a serious air, like a real lawyer. More people came in and took their places towards the rear. Ben had no idea who anyone was. As he was painfully aware, he was a total stranger to this alien world.

Ben hadn't laid eyes Jude in months, not since before he'd gone off to America, and his heart was thumping at the surreal prospect of seeing his son as a prisoner accused of murder. When Jude was brought into the courtroom by two guards and made to stand in the dock, Ben's stomach tightened into knots. As a remand prisoner, Jude was allowed to wear his own clothes. His unruly mop of blond hair had grown a little longer, and he was a little leaner than before. Ben had never seen him looking so grim and strained. As Jude caught sight of his father sitting there, he lit up momentarily and seemed about to call over to him. Ben signalled to him to keep quiet and stay cool.

District Judge Crapper appeared from another side door and wedged himself into position behind his bench. He was grey and old and quite fat, wore half-moon spectacles and a look of world-weariness, and seemed to have difficulty walking. After a few preliminaries, the bail hearing got underway. The court was presented with the facts of the case, which sounded even more worryingly cut-and-dried than McAllister's account of them. The witness statements claiming to have seen and heard Jude threatening the victim were damning enough; the grisly details of the crime, Jude's presence at the scene and his fingerprints on the murder weapon made his guilt look obvious. Ben found it all hard to listen to, and sat with his hands jammed between his knees. Jude stood in the dock completely stone-faced, his eyes fixed on some spot on the wall opposite.

When the matters of the case had been heard in excruciating detail, the district judge turned to peer at Jude and said, 'Mr Arundel, you understand the charges against you?'

'Of course I bloody do,' Jude replied loudly, holding his chin up in defiance. 'I'm not an idiot. But I didn't do it!'

Simms shot to his feet, anxious to intervene before Jude did himself any more damage. 'Sir, my client is fully aware of the gravity of these charges, and wishes to plead not guilty.'

'Thank you, Mr Simms,' said Crapper, casting a steely eye across the courtroom and apparently unfazed by Jude's minor outburst. 'As the court is aware, the purpose of this preliminary hearing is not to determine the accused's innocence or guilt, but to decide whether bail should be granted in this case. Under Section Four of the Bail Act of 1976 all accused persons have a right to bail, subject to conditions determined by this court. However, the potential grounds for refusing bail are set out in Schedule 1 of the Act, whereby remand in custody pending trial may be ruled applicable. Now, I understand we have someone here who wishes to speak for the accused?'

Ben took that as his cue. He stood and gave his name for the court, stating for the record that he was the nearest living relative of the defendant. Speaking in the same clear, careful tones as he'd used back in the day for addressing military briefings, he explained that in his opinion Jude Arundel posed not the slightest flight risk in the event of his being released on bail. Nor was he likely to start interfering with or threatening witnesses, to commit any further offences or pose a threat to public order in any way. This was the first time in his life that he'd ever found himself on the wrong side of the law, and he was a totally responsible citizen, etc., etc. By the time Ben had finished with him, the defendant sounded as though he should be canonised Saint Jude.

The judge studied some notes in front of him. 'I understand, Major Hope, that you are the father of the accused?'

Ben disliked the use of his former military rank, but in situations like this it served a useful purpose. He wouldn't have instructed Simms to let it be known to the judge, otherwise. 'That's correct.'

'And this father-son relationship is despite the disparity between your surnames, Hope and Arundel.'

Ben gave an inward sigh. Not this again. It hung over him like a curse, and the only response he could give was his old standby. 'Long story, your Honour.'

The judge nodded sagely. 'Very well. We can get into that later. For the moment, Major Hope, are you willing to enter into a recognisance, as a guarantee to the court that conditions of bail would be met?'

Crapper was studying Ben with sharp eyes over the rims of his half-moon glasses. Ben felt the pressure on him to make the best use of this moment. He was depending on Crapper not being quite as much of a weakling as McAllister had made him out.

Ben cleared his throat. 'Yes, your Honour, I am. I'd also like to reiterate for the court that my son has never broken a law or hurt a soul in his life. His past record is completely clean and there's no reason for anyone to suppose that he would ever break the conditions of his bail, if granted. He will comply with any travel restriction or curfew conditions imposed by the court during that time. As a former officer of HM Armed Forces I will assume responsibility for seeing that he behaves himself.' He added, 'Trust me, there's nothing this court can do to him that I won't, if he doesn't.'

This brought a few quiet chuckles from the back of the room. The judge offered a small smile, and nodded again. Ben sensed that the old man was on his side. His heart began to race with anticipation that the judge would rule in favour of granting bail.

But before the judge could speak, Jude suddenly gripped the railing of the dock and yelled at the top of his voice, 'This whole thing is totally insane! I'm innocent!'

For a bewildered moment, all the air seemed to have been sucked out of the room. Ben glared hard at Jude, but to no avail. Jude shouted, 'I didn't kill the guy! You hear me? Anyone who thinks I did needs his fucking head read!'

District Judge Crapper banged his gavel and said sternly, 'Mr Simms, please get your client under control at once.'

But at this point the only way to shut Jude up would have been to shoot him. In a tone of fury that filled the entire courtroom and could not have been missed by anyone standing outside within fifteen yards of its doors he screamed, 'And I swear, you lock me up in jail for this, and I'll escape! I'll disappear and you'll never see me again! You hear me, you bastards?'

The court dissolved into chaos. The judge banged angrily and demanded that Jude be removed. His guards stepped up, grabbed him by both arms and whisked him hurriedly out of the door through which they'd come. For which Ben was immensely grateful, because otherwise he might have been seriously tempted to leap across the courtroom and personally strangle him. Simms was sitting with his head in his hands. The judge's face was purple as he went on banging and calling for silence.

When at last the buzz died away, Judge Crapper rasped, 'Well, I think that settles that. Bail in this case is hereby denied. I order the suspect to be remanded in custody pending trial, the date of which shall be determined in due course.'

Chapter 9

It was 9.53 a.m. The hearing had come to a crashing end after just twenty-three minutes, and it had taken Jude a matter of seconds to torpedo any possibility of being released that day – or any day, until he was formally tried for murder months from now.

As the courthouse emptied around him Ben remained in his seat, staring at the vacant dock where Jude had been just a moment ago and struggling with the mixed emotions that washed through him. For all his anger towards Jude for having just obliterated his own chances of getting bail, it was hard not to feel a sense of pride at the way he'd stood up to proclaim his innocence. And as Ben sat there searching his own conscience, he couldn't help but privately admit to himself that, back in the wild days of his youth, he might very well have done exactly the same thing, let the chips fall where they may and damn the consequences.

Maybe being crazy was just incurably embedded in the Hope family DNA.

When Ben finally exited the empty courtroom, he found Simms hanging around outside in the corridor. The lawyer looked pale and anxious, and kept shaking his head in disbelief. 'I've never seen anything like it. What was he thinking? I'm certain that the judge was about to rule in his favour.'

Ben wished that he knew more about the workings of the law and wasn't so dependent on Simms for advice. 'Is there any way out of it?'

Simms heaved an exasperated sigh. 'Oh sure, he can always reapply for bail. Though he doesn't have a snowball's chance in hell of its being granted, after that performance. He couldn't possibly have done a better job of persuading the court that he was a major flight risk if they were stupid enough to let him walk free.'

'But it can't hurt to try, can it?'

Simms shrugged. 'Frankly, it'd be a waste of time and I have better things to do. Not all of my clients are hell-bent on landing themselves in jail.'

'Still, I'd like you to apply on his behalf. If they agree to another hearing I'll make sure he doesn't misbehave again.'

'He'd have to grovel on his knees and beg for mercy. Tell them he had a momentary lapse of sanity or something. Blame it on the stress of being in jail.'

Ben didn't see Jude doing that, but promised, 'I'll speak to him. When can I see him?'

'Not for a while. It'll take a few hours before he's transferred from the holding facility to Bullingdon Prison. I might be able to arrange a visit later in the day.'

'I'd appreciate that, Mr Simms. Thanks.'

Ben gave Simms his mobile number and asked him to keep in touch. Simms didn't look too happy about it, but agreed to call him later. With that, clasping his briefcase, he scuttled off down the hallway and disappeared through a door. Ben wasn't sure whether Simms would even bother to call him. But he was wrong. Four hours later, at three minutes to two in the afternoon, Ben's phone buzzed.

At that moment, he was walking through Christ Church Meadow, a blessed haven of serenity right in the middle of Oxford that lay insulated from all the bustle and noise, dirt and traffic of the city. He'd left the splendid ivied rear facade of Meadow Buildings behind him and cut down the broad tree-lined footpath to the river, to wander awhile along its banks and watch the rowers come swishing by in their long racing boats and single sculls. It was a beautiful day to be walking free under the wide blue sky. Not so great for an innocent man slammed behind bars. Earlier, from a pub beer garden where Ben had allowed himself to consume just enough single malt scotch to smooth the edge off his nerves while staying sufficiently sober to jump in his car at a moment's notice, he'd called Jeff Dekker to give him the promised update on Jude's situation. Jeff had sounded every bit as depressed as Ben was feeling himself.

Simms said, 'Visiting time at Bullingdon ends at quarter to four and I managed to get you a slot for the last hour. Technically you needed to have booked a day in advance, but I called in a favour. Which means you owe me.'

Simms sounded sullen and pissed off, but at that moment he'd just become Ben's best buddy. He added, 'Don't forget to bring ID or they won't let you in. And be sure to arrive early, because there'll be a wait. You know how to get there?'

Ben was already running. 'I'm on my way.'

After a rumbling, jerking, grindingly slow bus ride from

St Aldates through the city centre and up Woodstock Road to the park and ride, Ben clambered into the Alpina and burned rubber north-eastwards in the direction of Bicester. It was a twenty-five-minute drive, if you abided by the speed limits. He followed the signs saying HM PRISON BULLINGDON that led off the main road to Jude's new abode, home to about eleven hundred residents. The cluster of red-roofed prison buildings stood within an irregular octagon of high walls surrounded by open fields. Checkpoints and cameras, guards and wire fences were everywhere, and despite the green areas, playing fields and gardens the place was every bit as forbidding and gloomy as Ben had imagined. He'd been inside prisons before and they weren't his favourite environments to spend time in. From the visitors' car park he walked up to the reception building.

The strict procedure of the ID security check was like an assembly line as visitors were made to go through different rooms. Before a new door could open, the one behind it had to be closed. Step by step, you left the free world behind you. The pat-down search included a sniffing from a security dog that didn't look as friendly as Storm or Radar. Ben was asked to remove his jacket and surrender his phone as well as his cash-filled wallet, as visitors were forbidden from carrying more than £10 into the prison, and then only in coins for use in the vending machines. He received a lecture from a dead-eyed officer on the strict rules of his visit, and after a long wait was then ushered through several more layers of security before finally being admitted into the visiting block.

A low mutter of conversation and the cries of restless,

distressed children filled the room as a dozen or so prisoners and their loved ones used their allotted hour of visiting time. The room was equipped with rows of low tables flanked by plastic chairs, everything bolted rigidly down. Some artificial plants had been placed here and there in an attempt to provide some semblance of a comforting environment for the sake of the families, but it wasn't working. Though one or two inmates seemed to be sharing a more joyful moment with their loved ones the atmosphere was mostly tense and overhung with fear, anxiety, sadness, embarrassment, humiliation and frustration. Private conversation was impossible in the presence of the team of watchful, unsmiling security personnel who hovered on standby in the background, listening to every word as though all dialogue were potentially suspicious and ready to step in to prevent old Ma Barker from slipping her beloved nephew a home-baked fruitcake with a file inside.

Jude was already sitting there waiting for Ben, hunched over his table and looking weary, gaunt and thoroughly depressed after having spent only a matter of hours in his new home. Though permitted to wear his own clothing he was dressed in grey jogging bottoms and a light blue T-shirt. He didn't stand up as Ben approached, as the rules of the visit dictated that he wasn't to leave his seat. Ben took his place opposite him at the low table. Physical contact wasn't allowed. The two of them sat there in silence for a few moments, neither wanting to be the first to speak.

It was Ben who finally broke the silence. 'Well, that was a smart play.'

'They weren't going to give me bail anyway,' Jude replied.

'We'll never know now, will we?'

'So I suppose you've come to give me a pep talk.'

'I'm surprised you haven't escaped yet. I thought no prison could hold you.'

'I'll get out of here. I swear it.'

'You're an idiot.'

'I'm innocent.'

'I know you are,' Ben said. 'Now tell me the whole thing again, from the start.'

Chapter 10

'There's not much to tell,' Jude said. 'I've lived in Little Denton most of my life. So when I got back home from America, that's where I headed. My car was there, and I'd nowhere else to stay.'

'Except you couldn't,' Ben said. 'Not with the house let to a tenant.'

'I wasn't going to ask him to leave or anything,' Jude protested. 'I thought maybe, if I asked nicely, Duggan might be cool about letting me stay in the annexe.'

Jude was referring to the self-contained extension that Simeon and Michaela had added to the vicarage years earlier, to create an extra space for visitors. He went on, 'It's got its own little bathroom and kitchen. He was just one guy, with the whole rest of the house to himself. I wouldn't have been in his way. I was even happy to knock something off the rent, in return for letting me stay there. It seemed to me like a reasonable enough idea. How was I to know that Duggan wasn't a reasonable kind of person?'

Ben asked, 'You hadn't met him before?'

'Never laid eyes on the guy. Spencer and Grady, the letting

agency, took care of all that stuff, vetting clients and so on. As a matter of fact, the house was let to a Ms E something, can't remember her surname, on Duggan's behalf. I think he might have been working for her, but I don't know much about it.'

'Okay,' Ben said, eager to recap the details. 'So what happened, you came home, knocked on the door, introduced yourself as the homeowner and put this proposal to him?'

'Not quite,' Jude said. 'What happened is that when I turned up at the house, nobody was around. I knocked a few times, called a few times, and there was no answer. Then I walked around the back and saw that the French window to the garden was open. So I went inside.'

'Just like that, uninvited?'

Jude shrugged. 'Look, I'd just come from the airport. I suppose I wasn't thinking straight. I was knackered and jetlagged and feeling kind of low. It felt so good to be home, after all the shitty things that've happened in the last while, what with me and Rae splitting up. I still really miss her.'

Ben didn't share that sentiment, but said nothing.

'Duggan was obviously somewhere around,' Jude went on. 'I could smell fresh coffee and the radio was on. I was expecting him to appear at any minute, had it all worked out what I was going to say to him. After a couple of minutes of hanging around waiting for the guy to show up, I suddenly realised I was starving. You can't eat that slop they serve on aeroplanes and I'd not had a bite all day. So I did what anyone would do. I went into the kitchen to make myself a sandwich.'

'I'm not sure that anyone would have done that,' Ben said. 'It wasn't your house.'

'Hey, hang me. What's a bit of bread and cheese? I found a chunk of cheddar, a jar of pickled gherkins in the fridge and a sliced white loaf in the bread bin. Laid everything out, grabbed a knife from the block and was just about to start dicing up the pickles when this angry-looking dude appears in the doorway.'

'Hold on,' Ben said. 'The knife. Are we talking about the same one—?'

Jude nodded. 'Yeah. The one he was killed with.'

Ben understood now how Jude's fingerprints could have got on the knife, by perfectly innocent means. In which case, his worst crime was simply being a silly damn fool who'd wandered into someone else's home to make a sandwich.

'That was the first time I saw Duggan,' Jude said. 'Right nasty-looking piece of work the guy was, too. And not too pleased to see me, either. Like the three bears coming home to find Goldilocks eating their porridge.'

'Under the circumstances—' Ben began.

'Yeah, well, wasn't like I was robbing the place,' Jude protested. 'The stupid sod started on at me before I could get a word in: "Who the eff are you? What the effing hell are you doing in my effing house?" Like that. Really stroppy. So, you know me, always trying to be Mr Nice Guy. I'm doing my best to smile and look pleasant, and I apologised and told him who I was, how I'd just returned from abroad and needed a place to stay. As sweetly as possible, I asked him if he wouldn't mind letting me have the annexe, in return for knocking a hundred quid a month off the rent for the remainder of his lease. If he'd agreed, I'd have called the agency right away.'

'But I'd imagine he wasn't in agreement.'

'Not exactly, no. Started going on at me about the terms of the contract, and how it still had a couple of months to run, and how until then this was his place and I was an effing intruder and he'd call the effing police if I didn't clear off right away.'

'Maybe you should have,' Ben said.

'I thought I could make the guy see sense. "Come on," I said to him. "Be reasonable." He stared at me like I'm a moron, replied "Even if you are who you say you are, why the hell should I let you stay here?" To which I answered, "Because I've got nowhere else to go". And that was when he came out with the thing that pissed me off. I'd been pretty cool until then.'

'What did he say?'

'He said, "That's not my effing problem, is it? Haven't you got any friends you can stay with? What about your parents? Can't they give you a bed? Or maybe they find you as annoying as I do."'

Ben thought, *Ouch*.

'I just lost my rag,' Jude said, shaking his head ruefully. 'He shouldn't have brought Mum and Da— I mean, Simeon – into it like that.'

'And so you threatened him,' Ben said. 'You told him if he didn't keep his mouth shut, you were going to kill him.'

'Yeah, I admit I did kind of shoot off a bit. I didn't mean it, of course. I was wound up, that's all. It's still a raw nerve.'

'At which point, the Heneghan sisters turned up, collecting for their cat charity, just in time to hear you making the threat against Duggan.'

'Those two old harpies,' Jude replied with a grunt of sour disapproval. 'They've never liked me, since I was a little kid. Used to whinge to Mum whenever I cycled along the pavement past their house. One time they even accused me of trying to run over some mangy cat of theirs. Total lie. I never came near the horrible thing.'

'But it would appear that their witness statement was accurate, all the same.'

'They heard what they heard, but they didn't understand what was going on,' Jude replied irritably. 'That's what matters, isn't it?'

Ben's neck and shoulders felt as tense as steel cables and he wished he could light up a Gauloise. There were so many things he wanted to say, but held back because there seemed little point in rubbing salt in Jude's wounds. What was done, was done. At the same time, he was furious at his son's pig-headedness. Duggan might have been an unpleasant character but it was hard not to agree with some of what he'd said. Why couldn't Jude have gone to stay with a friend instead? Or rented a place of his own? Or come to stay at Le Val, where he was always welcome? He wasn't entirely penniless and could do as he pleased. If he'd needed money, Ben would gladly have sent him some. And why, why had he allowed Duggan to get under his skin like that?

'Next, you ran to get your car from the garage, and you took off. Correct?' Ben already knew the bare facts, but he wanted to hear the rest from Jude's own lips.

Jude nodded. 'I didn't really know where I was going. Ended up at this shithole hotel in Marcham. I hung around there for a few hours, went to get some fish and chips, but they tasted like shit, too. Or maybe it was just me. I was feeling really bad about the whole thing, thinking I'd acted like a real prick and shouldn't have reacted to Duggan the way I did. It wasn't his fault. So I got in the car and drove back to Little Denton, to apologise to the guy for my stupid behaviour.' He gave a shudder. 'Too late. There he was, the poor bastard, lying in a pool of blood. I can still see it, every time I close my eyes. Can't sleep. Can't think about anything else. How could anyone believe I'd do a thing like that?'

'Why didn't you tell the police the reason you went back there?'

'Because it's private and personal. They'd start asking all kinds of questions about our family and I didn't want to have to answer them. And also because I was in shock. I wasn't thinking straight. I could hardly speak. It was like some horrible dream that I couldn't wake up from. It still feels that way.'

'Did you tell them the reason why your prints were on the knife?'

'No, because who would believe it anyway? Especially not that officious bastard who muscled into the interview room while they were questioning me, and started yelling his head off at me. You could tell all he wanted was to get me to confess to it, so he could lock me away and claim all the glory.'

'Who was he?'

'A senior officer. I don't remember his name. Short, reedy. Black comb-over. Hitler moustache.'

'Forbes?'

Jude nodded. 'That's him. Nasty pompous little shit. Even

if I'd wanted to tell them the whole truth, I wasn't going to talk to him. Nothing would make him change his mind that I'm guilty.'

'Sooner or later you're going to have to start helping yourself,' Ben told him. 'You're an innocent man. They'll come around to understanding that, but not if you go on acting the way you did today in court.'

'Pretty daft,' Jude admitted. 'Seem to be making a habit of that, don't I?'

'You're not on your own, Jude. I'm not going away until this thing is sorted out.'

They talked a while longer. Jude was growing tired and emotional, and Ben tried to cheer him up by changing the subject to fill him in on life at Le Val. 'When this is over, you should come and spend time there with us.' He smiled. 'Scruffy misses you.'

But Jude couldn't be consoled. 'When this is over,' he muttered glumly, 'I'll either be a fugitive on the run, or I'll be dead. I can't survive in prison, Dad.'

Ben was about to reply when a guard came up to say their time was over. They managed a brief goodbye, and then Jude was led away with his head hanging low. Ben was escorted from the visitors' centre, retrieved his things and returned to the car. As he drove away, Jude's last words to him were still ringing in his ears.

'No,' he promised himself. 'That's not how this will end.'

Chapter 11

The more Ben mulled over the facts, the crazier the situation appeared and the more questions stacked up in his mind. Whoever had killed Carter Duggan was a slick and brutal operator who'd managed to commit the murder completely unseen. And must have had a reason for doing it, which was a question nobody seemed to be interested in answering because, as far as they were concerned, they had their man.

Who actually *was* Carter Duggan? Why was he living in Jude's house? Who was the woman, this 'Ms E something', who had apparently rented the property on his behalf, and for whom Jude thought Duggan worked? Worked in what capacity?

As he drove aimlessly around the Oxfordshire countryside Ben briefly considered calling the letting agency, to try to find out the woman's name. But he knew the attempt would be futile, as they inevitably wouldn't divulge the information. Short of breaking into their offices and ransacking their files, he was locked out of the loop. But he knew someone who might be prevailed upon to fill in the missing details for him.

Ben pulled over, found Tom McAllister's business card and punched the number into his mobile. When the cop picked up the call, sounding harassed and irritable, Ben said, 'What's for dinner tonight?'

'What the frig do you think I'm running, Cairns's Lodging House?'

'Cairns's what?'

'Just something my mother used to say. Roll up anytime after seven. I'm doing a new recipe. Be nice to try it out on someone.'

'Sounds ominous. Should I bring anything to drink, seeing as I invited myself?'

'Just bring yourself. I've got enough booze here to knock out half the British Army.'

By the time Ben arrived at McAllister's place just after seven, the brightness of the day had turned to a sultry and overcast evening and the darkening clouds offered a hint of thunder. He was greeted enthusiastically by Radar and wandered inside the cottage where he found McAllister burning up the kitchen like a one-man catering corps. The cop was in the process of laying out two fat, juicy-looking chicken supremes on a thick chopping board, while something was sizzling in a heavy copper skillet on the range.

Ben said, 'Let me know if I need to call the fire brigade.'

'Piss off,' McAllister snapped back at him without turning around. 'Everything's under control.' He waved an arm in the direction of the fridge. 'Grab yourself a beer, and one for me, will you?'

Ben cracked two bottles open and leaned against the kitchen counter, out of McAllister's way. The beer was cold and crisp, and almost instantly he felt some of the tension oozing out of his muscles. 'Good day at the office?'

'No, I had a shit day at the office. Like I always do. Drawer on the left. Make yourself useful there and chuck me the rolling pin.'

The rolling pin was more like a police truncheon. With a gusto that bordered on violence McAllister set about battering the chicken breasts as though they were about to escape. Ben watched as the cop flattened them out thinly, then laid slices of mozzarella cheese, Parma ham and a stem of fresh asparagus on each. Delicately and expertly, he rolled them up and tied them with thin string into parcels. Meanwhile a pan of olive oil and melted butter was heating to smoking hot temperature. McAllister flung the chicken parcels into the pan, and soon the aroma was filling the kitchen. With a lot of rattling and scraping he fried the chicken until the outside was browning nicely, then turned it down to simmer with garlic and white wine while putting the finishing touches to the sautéed potatoes that were in the copper skillet: a generous knob of butter, fresh-chopped rosemary and more garlic, crushed and diced to a pulp.

As McAllister worked his magic, Ben gazed around the kitchen and his eye settled on a cork notice board that hung on a wall between two cupboards. A collection of wine labels and old photos were pinned to it, and out of curiosity he stepped over to examine them. There were several pictures of Radar growing up, from a cute six-week-old black and tan ball of fur to a gangly-legged adolescent. Beside them were some prints of the watermill in various earlier stages of renovation, one of them showing McAllister posing with a long-haired, white-bearded fellow whom Ben took to be his helper, Sparrowhawk. Half-hidden behind a snowy scene of the cottage in winter was an expired Thames Valley Police warrant card showing a somewhat more youthful McAllister, with the rank of Detective Sergeant.

'Nice mugshot,' Ben commented.

'Hmm? Oh, that,' McAllister replied absently as he tasted his sauce with a wooden spoon, smacked his lips and grabbed a salt grinder to add some more seasoning. 'You're really supposed to dispose of them when they're expired. But someone told me I looked like Liam Neeson in that photo, so I sort of hung onto it as a keepsake.'

'Liam Neeson? You reckon?' Ben had to squint to see the resemblance.

'We're ready,' McAllister declared with a flourish. 'While I plate this up, would you grab the bottle of Sauvignon Blanc from the freezer?'

'Gladly.'

They ate indoors, at a small round table by a window. McAllister fixed Ben with an expectant look as he took his first bite of the chicken parcels. 'Well, what do you think?'

'I think you need to get that restaurant opened soon.'

'Bung me half a million and I'll be in business a month from now.'

They ate in silence for a few minutes, because the food was almost too tasty to talk over. The white wine, chilled to perfection and incredibly smooth, started disappearing too quickly. Ben hadn't forgotten his reason for wanting to come here this evening, but he was careful not to come straight out asking for the name of the mysterious 'Ms E something'. Planning to work around to it, he said, 'I saw Jude today.'

'Hm. How was he?'

'Not good.'

'As you'd expect.'

'He told me something he hasn't told the police.'

'I'm all ears.'

Ben told McAllister about the real reason for Jude's fingerprints being on the knife. McAllister chewed pensively as he listened. 'Well, I know what Forbsie would say about that. He'd say Jude could easily have thought that one up in retrospect and has no proof to back it up.'

'Forbes has made his mind up, then,' Ben said.

'Oh, they've got their man, no question about it. And Forbsie doesn't much like asking questions, once he's got the answer he wants.'

'But you do,' Ben said. He sensed a certain scepticism in McAllister's manner that hadn't been in evidence yesterday. Maybe the cop had been doing his own mulling over of the situation.

McAllister gave a dry smile. 'Aye, well, maybe that's why Forbsie and I don't get along so well. I usually just stay away from the guy. But I can't always. Today was one of those days.'

Ben got the feeling McAllister was leading to something. 'Why, what happened today?'

McAllister sloshed more of the white wine into their glasses. The first bottle was nearly gone. 'Did you know that Duggan wasn't the official tenant of the vicarage?'

A bulb lit up in Ben's brain. It seemed as though McAllister was about to fill in the missing information he was interested in, without even being asked. Maybe the cop had the gift of clairvoyance. Or maybe there was a trail here, and they were both sniffing their way along it. He put down his fork, looking intently across the table at the cop. 'I know that the person paying the rent was a Ms E something. Jude told me he couldn't remember her surname.'

'Ms Emily Bowman. Fifty-eight years old, divorced, parents deceased, no kids, lives alone in one of those great big fancy houses up in Boars Hill. And she can well afford it. She's the founder and CEO of a successful company called "The Culture Collection". Started out as a cottage industry making Victorian-style curtain designs twenty years ago and now has a string of stores across the country and a thriving home decor mail order business that does a million pounds of orders a month.'

'Jude said that he thought Duggan was working for her in some capacity. Was he a company employee?'

McAllister shook his head. 'No, she hired him privately.'

'To do what?'

'I told you yesterday that I was looking into Duggan's background. Turns out that when he quit the Ontario Provincial Police in 2012, he went solo as a private investigator. Actually made quite a name for himself, and his services were in demand both in Canada and elsewhere. He flew over here six weeks ago to take up residence in Little Denton.'

'So Duggan was investigating something for Emily Bowman. But what?'

'I asked her that myself,' McAllister said. 'As part of my

job to put together a profile of the victim. She told me that he was hired to look into historical records and gather research information on past members of her family. Mainly to do with her grandmother, but she wasn't any more specific than that and I couldn't press her for details.'

'Why Duggan? Was he a genealogist as well as a detective?'

'He seems to have had some expertise in that field. Four years ago he cracked a cold murder case dating back to the late eighties in Victoria, Canada. Frig, I can't talk with an empty wine glass in front of me. Hold on while I fetch another bottle.'

McAllister was back a moment later, ripping the cap off the second ice-cold Sauvignon and sploshing it into their empty glasses. 'Where was I? Oh, aye. It's something called genetic genealogy. Had to look it up. The idea is that if you go back far enough, everyone's related to everyone else. If the average family has two to three kids, then a typical individual could potentially have nearly two hundred third cousins, almost a thousand fourth cousins and nearly five thousand fifth cousins. What Duggan did was use family trees to ID a previously unknown suspect, who then turned out to have DNA matching samples on the victim. It was a brilliant bit of work and got some media attention at the time. That's how she must've found him. And being rich, it was no big deal to fly him over to England and put him up in posh digs for a few weeks while he did the job.'

'But you don't know the specifics?'

McAllister shrugged. 'It was a private matter between her and Duggan. Unless I have reason to suspect they were up to something fishy, it's none of my business.'

'Fair enough. But you still haven't told me what happened today.'

'Ms Bowman called the police late yesterday evening to report that a strange black Mercedes was hanging around outside her house. Didn't manage to get the registration but she claimed she'd seen the same car following her earlier in the day, too. Coming so soon after Duggan's murder, it freaked her out and she was scared someone was watching her.'

Ben felt a tingle of excitement. This could be important. 'And?'

'A patrol unit was sent out to take a look around. No black Mercedes. No sign of anything suspicious. Official conclusion is that Ms Bowman just got an attack of the jitters and fell prey to her own imagination. Which could be right. But all the same, I suggested to Forbsie this morning that maybe we should post a surveillance car at her home for a couple of days, just to make sure.'

'I take it he didn't agree to that.'

'Apparently our resources are stretched paper-thin as it is, what with police budgets getting slashed every year, and we can't be expending precious manpower every time a member of the public gets it in their head that there's a bogeyman lurking in the garden. I said fine, but what if she's not just imagining it? He demanded to know if I was implying there was a connection to the Duggan case. I told him that until the suspect in custody is properly convicted, that's all he is, a suspect, and that we can't afford to jump to conclusions or rest on our laurels. That didn't go down too well with old Forbsie. Stirring up trouble as usual,

McAllister. Not a team player. A maverick who likes being perverse just for the hell of it. Undermining the integrity of the force. Wasting police time and taxpayers' money. Yadda, yadda. I walked out of his office.'

'Are you going to pursue it with Emily Bowman? What if there's something going on that we don't know about?'

'Forget it. Until the black Mercedes comes back, if it ever does, I'm officially warned off. I might not love my job sometimes, but I'd prefer to keep it.'

Now Ben was getting a clear picture of what McAllister was thinking. The cop wasn't saying so openly, but he was privately doubtful that Jude had killed Duggan, and was pissed off that his superiors, Forbsie in particular, had been so quick to accept the mantra of Jude's guilt. That was the real reason why he was so willing to feed information to Ben. McAllister needed a capable ally to get to the bottom of Jude's case. Partly for the sake of proper justice, but also partly to get the upper hand over a superior officer he'd been at loggerheads with for years.

Ben said, 'You might have Forbes hanging over you watching every move, but I don't.'

McAllister smiled. 'As long as you behave yourself, then I can't stop you. More wine?'

Much later, after McAllister had finally retired to bed, Ben went outside and walked back down to the river's edge to drink in the sounds of the night. He loved the darkness, always had. The air was thick and sultry and tingling with the subtle electrical charge of a coming storm. Sporadic dull flashes illuminated the clouds many miles off to the north and a softly menacing rumble rolled across the horizon, like the light and sound of a tank battle in the distance. It felt to Ben as though something far greater was stirring up there in the starless sky. Elemental forces gathering their power, slowly building in intensity as they waited for the moment to unleash their fury, when the strobing violence of the lightning would shrink your pupils to pinpricks and the thunder felt as though it could split the earth in two.

Ben wondered if Jude could sense it too, and if he could see the faraway flashes from his cell window.

Something was coming. Something deadly and terrible. It wasn't here yet, but it would be soon.

Ben gazed at the dark river, and wondered if that something lay within himself.

Chapter 12

From the moment he'd arrived, Jude had been discovering that life in prison was all about strict routine. HMP Bullingdon operated a twelve-hour day, with prisoners unlocked from their cells between 7 a.m. and 7 p.m., and kept closed up for the remaining twelve. Meals were served in the large mess hall, and with a daily catering budget allowance of around £2 per prisoner, the food was as revolting as he'd expected it to be.

He was by no means the first newbie finding his feet in this stark, bewildering and sometimes terrifying new environment. About a quarter of Bullingdon's residents were, like him, remand prisoners still awaiting trial for a whole variety of crimes, alleged or actual. For the first week of their stay, inmates were put through an induction process where they were able to share problems and concerns, were schooled in the rules and ways of prison life and required to sit basic tests to decide what kind of educational courses they might pursue while inside. Shortly after his arrival Jude was interviewed by a prison counsellor who asked him how he was feeling. He replied, 'Oh, wonderful. Never been so happy,' and afterwards wondered whether his sarcasm had got him listed as a potential troublemaker. To hell with them.

A facility originally designed to contain just seven hundred inmates was now crammed with over eleven hundred, with the result that fewer and fewer cells offered the luxury and privacy of single-person accommodation. Before getting here Jude had been fervently hoping that he'd be allocated a cell to himself, and had been dismayed to be told he'd be sharing. As it turned out, though, Jude's worries were quickly relieved when he was introduced to his new cellmate. Big Dave Flynn was a soft-spoken man in his early forties, and the kind of person Jude might have described as a 'gentle giant' if not for the fact that Dave readily admitted that he was here because he'd badly mangled and almost killed, with his bare hands, a drug dealer who'd been selling crack to his fifteen-year-old daughter, Charmaine. The dealer, once he'd eventually limped out of hospital, got off virtually scot-free (in terms of legal justice, at any rate), while Dave was sentenced to six years for grievous bodily harm with intent. He'd settled peacefully into prison life, kept himself largely to himself and read the Bible a lot. His wife and his daughter, now nineteen and happily drug-free, came to visit him every week.

Dave listened calmly and patiently to Jude's story. He was fascinated to know that Jude had grown up as the son of a vicar, and appeared to sympathise deeply with his plight though he offered no comment on Jude's protestations of innocence.

In truth, Dave told him, life here wasn't really all bad. Everyone was kept busy, with a variety of jobs and activities on offer. The most popular job was working for the DHL mail service, for the whopping pay of £30 a week. Others worked in the prison garden, in the kitchen or helping to maintain the buildings while learning trades like carpentry and plastering. 'There's a decent enough library, too,' he said, 'and if you're into that kind of thing you might get a job there.'

As to the darker side of life here, Dave was able to fill Jude in on the finer points you'd never be told by the officers. Drug smuggling was far more of a problem than the authorities would admit, even though the prison was full of signs and posters discouraging their use. The place was awash with them, and prisoners used whatever they could get hold of. Dave hated drugs, after what had happened to his daughter, and he was quite an authority on the subject. He explained that some of the most popular, cheap and easily obtainable illicit substances in circulation among the inmates were synthetic lab-made concoctions such as 'black mamba', and especially 'spice', Bullingdon's number one favourite, which users smoked, ate or made tea with.

'I'm not into that stuff,' Jude assured him.

'Keep it that way,' Dave replied, in a voice that suggested that, if Jude *had* been into that stuff, his cellmate's gentle demeanour might be liable to do a sudden polarity-flip. Dave explained that spice was highly addictive and harder to come off than heroin. Such 'zombie drugs' were also known to have an unpredictable effect on the user, including triggering psychotic episodes and terrifying hallucinations. As a result the prison had a growing problem with violent outbursts, self-injury and attempted suicide. 'What makes it even worse,'

Dave told him, 'is that the prison's badly understaffed because of all the bloody budget cuts. More and more of the senior officers who knew their jobs and kept a lid on things are leaving, and they're being replaced by inexperienced staff who aren't up to the job.'

Which was bad news, as Dave went on to warn Jude, considering the fact that, on top of the drug problem, bullying and intimidation were part of the darker reality of prison life. 'It means you've got to look out for yourself, 'coz if something kicks off, half the time there ain't gonna be a guard around to break it up. You need eyes in the back of your head.'

Jude had come to Bullingdon knowing that he'd be mixing with a lot of nasty characters, and he counted himself highly lucky to have found a friend and mentor on his first day. His next close encounter wasn't such a positive experience. It happened that same afternoon, as he was heading over to the prison mess hall for dinner after an exploratory tour of the prison library. Half his mind was engaged with making his way through the confusing maze of corridors and metal stairways; the other half was reflecting sadly on his meeting with Ben earlier. He had sensed Ben's contained anger, hidden behind a veneer of tenderness and patience and love, but simmering like a pressure cooker. Jude had not only let himself down badly; he'd let Ben down too.

Those were all the thoughts tumbling around in his head when, caught unawares, he was suddenly cornered against a wall by an inmate he instantly sensed didn't have friendly intentions. The man was a good ten years older than Jude and a few inches shorter, but lean and whippy and dangerous-looking, like a ferret. There was a nasty gleam in his eyes and he had a missing ear, as though it had been slashed off with a razor. The scar extended all the way across his cheek to the corner of his mouth, giving his lip a ferocious curl.

The ferret planted an accusing finger in the middle of Jude's chest and snarled, 'Hoi, new boy. I seen you comin' in and I don't like your fuckin' face.'

Jude might have replied, 'Look who's talking.' Instead he wisely remained silent. He didn't much like the guy's finger poking at his chest, either, but sensed that to grab it and twist it away from him would quickly lead to violent consequences.

'What are you gonna do about that?' the ferret rasped. The scar made him spit when he talked.

'Look, I don't want trouble,' Jude said. 'I'll stay out of your way, if that's what you want. Please, let me pass.'

But the ferret wasn't ready to let him go. 'How'd you like to have your fuckin' teeth smashed down your throat?'

'I wouldn't.'

'Just remember, new boy. I'm watchin' you. You see me comin' you better get out of my fuckin' way. Get it?'

'No problem,' Jude muttered. 'I get it.'

The ferret held the finger there a moment longer to make his point, then dropped it and allowed Jude to slip away from him. He laughed loudly as Jude hurried off, feeling humiliated and shaken.

In the crowded, noisy mess hall a few minutes later, Jude spotted an empty seat next to his new friend Big Dave and carried his tray over to join him. The pile of grey slop on his plate was meant to be scrambled eggs, but it looked more like wet mortar. He wasn't feeling remotely hungry, and not because of the terrible food. 'What's the matter?' Dave asked, seeing his expression, and Jude related the encounter with the ferret.

'That's Mickey Lowman,' Dave replied, recognising Jude's description of the scar and the slashed-off ear. 'Real nutjob. Guy's high on spice most of the time. He was three years into an eight-year sentence for armed robbery when they caught him with a knife he'd engraved with the name of a guard he wanted to kill. When the judge was slapping a couple extra years onto his sentence, he threatened to kill him, too.'

'I've never seen the guy in my life before,' Jude protested. 'What the hell did I ever do to him?'

'You didn't need to. He's just a psychotic moron. You're not the first remand newbie he's collared that way.'

'Has he ever hurt anyone?'

Dave shovelled a massive forkful of curry into his mouth. It looked and smelled like dog food. He nodded. 'One or two.'

'Great start,' Jude groaned. 'Just my luck to fall foul of the most dangerous man in Bullingdon.'

'Oh, no,' Big Dave replied with a chuckle. 'Forget Mickey Lowman. You want dangerous? *There's* dangerous.'

Dave discreetly pointed out a middle-aged man who was sitting quietly hunched over his plate at another table on the far side of the room. The man was almost as large as Dave, with shoulders like an ox and a shaven head that gleamed in the harsh neon lights of the mess. He was surrounded by a gang of companions who seemed to defer to him while huddled protectively around. The group exuded an aura of menace and Jude noticed the way that other prisoners seemed to give them a wide berth.

'Who is he?' Jude asked.

'You're looking at Luan Copja,' Dave told him. 'The man, the legend. An Albanian crime boss who used to be the head of a sixty-million-pound organised crime empire, until they banged him up. He's serving twenty-three years without parole for human trafficking and involvement in various grisly murders, extortion and torture. They say he once tied a rival drug lord into a chair and pushed red-hot skewers through his eyeballs. On another occasion he apparently disapproved of his daughter's choice of fiancé, because Prince Charming had a habit of showing his arse to people. Old Luan had his men teach him the error of his ways, by beating the poor bugger so badly with steel pipes that he'll be spending the rest of his life sucking baby food out of a tube.'

'Jesus.'

'Not that Luan's allowed being inside to slow him down too much. Rumour has it that he's proved quite capable of running his business from behind bars. His gang of body-guards are all killers who'll slice your head off in a heartbeat if you even look at him sideways.'

'I won't look at him at all.'

'Hey, it's only prison gossip,' Dave said, shovelling down more of the unspeakable food. 'Could all be bullshit, for all you know. But all the same, that is someone you definitely need to stay well away from.'

Chapter 13

Just four miles from Oxford city centre, set against a sweeping panorama of hills and woodland under a perfectly unbroken pale blue sky: this was Boars Hill, one of Oxfordshire's most exclusive residential areas, whose stately mansions and rambling historic cottages were surrounded by scenic views people gave millions for. Ben had set out early from McAllister's place half an hour ago. Last night's promise of a storm had passed over to make way for a clear and beautiful morning and the climbing sun peeked brightly through the trees as he neared his destination, but the residue of its sullen menace was still hanging over his mind, like the aftermath of a bad dream.

Ben had decided to pay Emily Bowman an unannounced visit, in the hope of catching her off her guard and more amenable to talking to him. The grand house had once been part of the Berkeley Castle Estate and now stood within its own well-tended acres, which included a tennis court, indoor pool, stable block and an emerald green, white-fenced meadow with some horses peacefully grazing. Being the founder and CEO of the Culture Collection obviously paid well. Ben rolled through the gates into a courtyard flanked by a triple garage on one side and a range of converted cottage buildings on the other. A Volvo estate and a smaller hatchback were parked in front of the house. Ben slotted in next to them and walked towards the entrance, rehearsing in his mind what he needed to say. Getting Emily Bowman to talk to him might not be easy.

The doorbell was a heavy brass affair nestling among the ivy that surrounded the carved oak front door. Ben pressed it with a knuckle and stepped back. A minute later the door swung open, somewhat tentatively it seemed to him, and he recognised the face of Ms Emily Bowman from her company website. She was tall and thin in a sporty kind of way, and could easily have passed for the ladies' captain at a swanky golf club – which, Ben thought, she possibly was. Her hair was nicely swept back in a silver wave and she wore a tweedy kilt skirt and a buttercup-yellow silk blouse with a string of pearls. Her expression was more severe than in her website photo and Ben thought she looked nervous and agitated, but that could just have been the combined effect of her state of anxiety and finding a slightly tousled, rumpled blond stranger in sunglasses and a leather jacket standing on her doorstep. He suddenly wished that he'd shaved and paid more attention to his hair that morning.

Ben removed his shades and said, 'Ms Bowman?'

She opened the door a little wider and stood framed in the doorway, looking at him uncertainly. Behind her was a long airy-looking hallway, at the far end of which Ben could see a short-haired portly woman with red cheeks scurrying back and forth stowing things into boxes. The housekeeper, he guessed. A collection of expensive leather travel bags were lined up in the hallway, packed and bulging. It looked as if someone was planning a trip away, and for longer than just a few days.

'I'm Emily Bowman. Who are you?'

'My name is Ben Hope. I apologise for turning up unexpectedly like this, but it's an important matter and I'd really like to speak with you, if I may.'

Ben's well-honed spider sense suddenly told him he was being watched from behind, and he glanced quickly around to see that a white-haired man in his late sixties or early seventies had emerged from behind the cottage buildings by the house. He looked like a seasoned old countryman, a groundskeeper or an estate manager, wearing a tatty Barbour shooting jacket and a flat cap and cradling an old hammer shotgun in his arms. He moved a few steps and stopped, eyeing Ben from a distance. The message wasn't particularly subtle. Ben wondered whether all unexpected visitors to the house were met with a loaded twelve-bore.

Emily Bowman looked cagily at Ben and asked, 'Concerning what?'

He replied, 'Concerning the tragic demise of your former employee, Mr Carter Duggan.'

Her eyes narrowed. 'Are you with the police?'

Better hope I'm not, he thought, thinking about the shotgun. 'No, and I'm not a private investigator like Mr Duggan, either. I'm just a private citizen, Ms Bowman, same as you.' Ben slipped a Le Val business card from his pocket and held it out to her.

She hesitated, plucked the card from his fingers but barely

even glanced at it and folded her arms. He'd been right: getting her to talk to him wasn't going to be a pushover.

'How did you know Mr Duggan worked for me?' she asked suspiciously. 'I don't believe that information has been made public knowledge.'

Ben didn't want to reveal his real source, so someone else had to take the fall. He said, 'I spoke to someone at the Spencer and Grady letting agency yesterday. I'm afraid they let it slip that you rented the vicarage on Mr Duggan's behalf. Which is the reason why I came here this morning.'

Emily Bowman didn't look pleased. 'Oh, they did, did they? Then I shall have to have a word with them.'

'Ms Bowman, I promise you that I'm legit, and I really need your help. May I come inside? I won't take up too much of your time.'

'If you're not with the police, then I don't see why—'

'The person accused of the murder, Jude Arundel, is my son,' Ben cut in. All the heartfelt emotion trapped inside him came out in the tone of his voice. He was surprised at how raw it sounded. Emily Bowman blinked a couple of times and cocked her head as though trying to decide whether he was telling the truth. Her severe expression seemed to soften a little. Confusion clouded her eyes. 'Your son? But—'

'Different surnames, I know. Long story.'

The old man with the shotgun was still standing there like a loyal watchdog. Ben said, 'Ms Bowman, I need to speak to you because I don't believe that Jude killed your employee, and until someone finds out who did there's an innocent man rotting in prison.'

'Isn't it the police's job to be dealing with this?'

'The police have already got their man, as far as their top brass are concerned. The detective who was in charge of the investigation isn't so convinced, but his hands are tied. Please, Ms Bowman. Maybe I'm clutching at straws here, but you're the only person involved who knew Carter Duggan alive.'

She heaved a sigh, flustered. 'Well, all right, then. You'd better come inside. But you can't stay long. I'm terribly busy at the moment.'

Ben thanked her and stepped into the house. It was cool and spacious and very tastefully decorated inside, but he sensed an apprehensive atmosphere hanging in the air. The portly housekeeper was still bustling about packing things. As they passed by her she looked tentatively up from her duties and said in a small voice, 'I'm all done with the kitchenware, Ms Bowman. Did you want me to pack the things from the second wardrobe, too?'

'Thank you, Margo. Yes, please,' Emily Bowman replied, glancing at her watch. It was hard to tell which one of them looked more edgy.

It was clear to Ben what was going on. Emily Bowman was afraid of something; so were her housekeeper and the old guy outside, and he was certain this had to do with the mysterious black Mercedes and her call to the police two nights ago. He would have loved to ask her about it, but he'd already said too much about Tom McAllister and to probe so deep would be opening the cop up to all kinds of trouble. Ben asked casually, 'Looks like you're going somewhere?'

'Just a short holiday,' Emily Bowman replied, a little stiffly. 'You were lucky to catch me, actually. I'll be leaving within

the next hour or two. This way, please. We can talk in here.'
She led him to a door and showed him through to a huge
living room with tall windows and a view over miles of
countryside. She left the door open. 'Now, Mr, uh' – glancing
at his business card – 'Mr Hope. What exactly is it you think
I can help you with?'

'I'm just fishing for all the information I can get,' Ben
said. 'Any blanks you can fill in for me.'

She shook her head. 'I don't know what to tell you. Yes,
it's true, Mr Duggan was working for me. I contacted him
a couple of months ago, and asked him to come over to
Britain to carry out a private investigation. It's a personal
matter, concerning my family history. I chose to employ
him because of his expertise in that kind of research. He
came highly recommended and he was doing a very good
job until . . . well, we needn't go into what happened, need
we? But I don't see of what concern the details of his investigation would be to anyone except myself. I'm certainly not
willing to discuss them with anyone on the outside. That's
what I told the police, too.'

'I understand. I don't mean to pry.'

'Beyond that, I really don't know anything. I barely knew
the gentleman, outside of our brief business acquaintance.'

'What kind of man was he?'

'Straightforward, direct, matter-of-fact. I liked his no-
nonsense approach. He was the old-school type. No fancy
gadgets and technology. Just good old-fashioned detective
work.'

Ben asked, 'The work he was doing for you, was it in the
local area?'

She hesitated before replying. 'I don't mind telling you that much. No, my family were originally from London and then relocated to the north of England before I was born. Mr Duggan's research required him to do a bit of travelling here and there, expenses I was only too happy to cover. I chose to rent accommodation for him locally so that he and I could meet regularly in person and discuss his ongoing findings. There are also some family papers that are precious to me and I keep here at the house, to which he needed access. We had a few discussions, but sadly that was the end of it.'

Ben asked, 'During these discussions, did Mr Duggan ever say anything to you that might have struck you as odd?'

'Not that I can think of. Odd how?'

Something flashed in Emily Bowman's eyes as she said it. Ben was an expert at reading faces and he could see conflict in her expression, like a ripple disturbing calm waters. Something being held back. He pressed on, picking his words very carefully. 'I mean, did you have any reason to suppose he was concerned, or that he might have been in some kind of danger?'

'No. I understood he was killed because of some argument. With . . .' She flushed, uncomfortable. 'With your son. I have no children, but I'm sure that if I did, I wouldn't want to believe them capable of something so dreadful. I understand your wanting to protect him. But at the same time, from what I gather, the evidence all points to his guilt. Didn't he make a threat against Mr Duggan's life?'

'The argument was over something Mr Duggan said about Jude's past,' Ben said. 'Something very painful that made him lose his rag for just a moment. Jude said what he said, in the heat of the moment. I imagine we've all said things like that. Doesn't make us murderers.'

'Then . . . if you don't think . . . who—?'

'It wasn't a robbery. And it's pretty unlikely that it was someone settling an old score from back home in Canada. And random attacks by psychopathic killers don't tend to happen much in quiet country villages. Which means there has to be another reason why someone with the appropriate skillset slipped into the house, stabbed a man to death and then disappeared without leaving a trace or a witness. There isn't a lot to go on. That's why I came here hoping to find out more. Because there are pieces of this puzzle that are missing, and I need to find out what they are. Anything you can tell me about Duggan, anything at all, might offer a clue.'

Emily Bowman looked perplexed. 'I've already told you all I can. There really isn't any more.'

'And it couldn't have anything to do with what Mr Duggan was investigating for you, about your family?'

'Not in the least,' she replied curtly. 'Why would it?'

There'd been a moment earlier when Ben had thought she might tell him something, but that moment was gone and now she was closing up again. With nothing to lose, he decided to take the plunge. 'What about you, Ms Bowman? Have you noticed anything strange or suspicious, anything that made you feel worried or threatened?'

Her face went two shades paler, the muscles around her eyes clenched like iron and she replied very quickly, 'No. Nothing like that. Why would I?'

Liar, he thought. It couldn't have been any clearer if she'd had it printed across her forehead.

'Only, I wondered if maybe that was why you were taking a sudden holiday. Seems like your helper is in quite a rush to get things packed up. And your friend with the shotgun looks like he's on the lookout for trouble.'

Her lips clamped into a tight, bloodless line. She looked at her watch and shook her head. 'Mr Hope, I'm afraid I don't think there's any way I can help you. I'm very sorry for what's happened to your family, but I really am very busy and I think it's time for you to leave.'

And with that, the conversation was officially terminated. Ben could do nothing more. Except to leave her with something to think about after he was gone.

Looking Emily Bowman in the eye he said, 'You know what, Ms Bowman? I believe that you're holding something back. And if you are, then you need to understand that an innocent young man will spend the next several years in prison and his life will be destroyed, just because you didn't have the guts to speak up. Remember that.'

She stared back at him and said nothing. A muscle in her cheek twitched.

'I've written my mobile number on the back of the card I gave you,' he told her. 'Please, give me a call if you change your mind.'

'I doubt that.'

'Thanks for your time, Ms Bowman. Enjoy your holiday. I can see myself out.'

The old guy with the twelve-bore was still watching the house, as though he was ready to start blasting at the first wrong move. Ben could so easily have walked over there and wrapped the barrels around his neck before he even knew what was happening, but that wouldn't have been fair. Or else Ben might have grabbed him, dragged him back behind the row of cottages and made him spill whatever it was that Emily Bowman was so afraid of. But Ben doubted that she'd have told the old guy much, other than to be on the lookout for strange visitors to the house.

Deciding to ignore him, he walked back to the Alpina. Emily Bowman's watchdog didn't take his beady gaze off Ben until he was speeding out of the gate.

Ben drove away with a fierce surge of conviction that there was much more to Ms Bowman and her dealings with the late private investigator than met the eye. There was little point in trying to persuade her to reveal more. But if the secret she was obviously holding onto was the cause of her sudden and unexpected holiday, then the empty house would offer Ben the perfect opportunity to return that night and have a look for those precious family papers. If they were so important to Duggan's research, Ben wanted to see them too.

Enough dabbling around. The time had come to find out what the hell was going on.

Chapter 14

Ben now had the remainder of the daylight hours to kill before he returned to Emily Bowman's home, and he intended to make full use of that time. He drove back to Little Denton, but instead of entering the village he rounded its outskirts and left the car tucked among a stand of beech trees off the quiet country road, some eighth of a mile from the vicarage as the crow flew. There were too many prying eyes in that village, and what he was about to do required a little discretion.

Hopping over a ramshackle fence he scrambled down a slope knee-high in rough grass and cow parsley, and made his way into a small patch of woodland. Beyond the trees was a path, now mostly grown over, which led to an old wooden gate. It was an emotional walk for Ben, because the last time he'd been here was with Jude's mother, Michaela Arundel, years ago on a crisp and sunny winter day when the two of them had gone for a wander through the countryside with Scruffy, the family's adopted mongrel, running rings around them. That walk had been the last time Ben had ever been alone with his old love. Just a few hours later, she and Simeon were dead.

The gate, secured by a rusty padlock but all too easy to hop over, was the rear entrance to the Arundels' long, sloping and now sadly overgrown back garden. It was flanked on both sides by a screen of unclipped conifers that shielded him from view of the neighbouring houses as he walked up towards the vicarage. If Ben had been an intruder planning on sneaking into the property undetected, this was the way he'd have come. And in fact he *was* an intruder planning on doing exactly that.

The house was still festooned with police tape, but nobody was around. Ben carefully approached the back door and examined the frame and the Yale lock. According to McAllister, the police had found no signs of forced entry, and so far Ben could find none either. Carter Duggan's killer had either come in another way, or maybe he'd been equipped with a handy universal bump key like the one that Ben now used to defeat the lock. Seconds later, he was inside.

The vicarage was a rambling old house, built on here and there over the course of many years to create a labyrinth of rooms and passageways. The back hallway led to a utility room and scullery, from which one exit led up a backstair and the other through a recessed secondary doorway into the kitchen.

The kitchen, scene of the murder, was Ben's first port of call. Though nobody could have guessed that just a couple of days earlier, a man had lain here stabbed to death in a pool of blood. The room had been left spotless in the wake of the forensic team and Ben could only visualise the scene and try to imagine how the whole thing had gone down. If the killer had entered the house from the rear garden, he could very easily have come into the kitchen by the same route Ben just had. Ben knew from past memory that the rear doorway into the room was very little used. While the rest of the room was brightly lit from the window, the recess in which it lay was a shady little passage eight feet deep. Ben could easily picture how the victim could have been oblivious of the intruder's presence lurking there in the moments before the attack: Duggan standing at the counter, pottering about or brewing a pot of coffee or whatever his last actions had been, his back to the door, totally unawares until the killer struck.

But it was all guesswork, and there was little more to be learned from the kitchen. Ben slipped out of the room the way he'd come in, and used the creaky backstair to climb up to the first floor. The stairway emerged in a narrow passage with a bathroom at one end and several doors off it to the left and right: main bedroom, second and third bedrooms, study. Ben checked the study first, because if Duggan had been using it for his work he might have left behind some useful clue to explain just how the hell his research might have led to his own untimely death.

Once upon a time, the place had been a clutter of Simeon's vast collection of theology books and the desk had been all but hidden under the heaps of paperwork that came with running a busy parish. But as Ben stepped into the room he saw that the desk was clear. Checking the contents of its drawers, he found two paperclips, some dust balls and a dead moth. So much for useful clues.

Ben went from the study into the main bedroom, on the assumption that it was the one the tenant would have used.

He was right. Duggan's belongings were still in the bedroom and ensuite bathroom, presumably waiting to be shipped back to Canada by his next of kin, if he had any, but it hadn't happened yet. Ben went through them but found nothing of any interest – the usual male toiletry items, a tube of haemorrhoid cream, a couple of issues of a Canadian outdoors and hunting magazine, a dog-eared paperback detective novel, a local newspaper from a week ago – until he opened up the double wardrobe and checked the clothes inside.

Duggan had brought a minimum of things from Canada. Some underwear and folded shirts and spare socks were arranged on a shelf, along with a spare pair of tan leather brogues. Three wooden hangers hung from a brass rail. The one on the left held a single-breasted grey suit wrapped in a plastic cover. A couple of pairs of well-creased khaki chino trousers hung from the one in the middle, their pockets empty except for a paper tissue. On the right hanger was a tweed sports jacket. The suit looked immaculate but the tweed was much used and slightly frayed, as though it was Duggan's daily wear. Ben went through it. In the inside breast pocket was a takeaway Indian restaurant menu; the left side pocket contained two spare buttons in a plastic wrapper; and in the right side pocket Ben found a beer mat.

He examined it. A small, circular piece of card, a bespoke item printed for a pub Ben guessed Duggan had visited during his stay in the UK. The mat smelled faintly of stale beer. On the front was the name of the pub, the Man O'War, with a picture of an old sailing ship. On the back, Ben read, '*The Man O'War has been the local public house in Hunstanton since the late 18th century, and was originally built from the timbers of a warship wrecked against the nearby cliffs in 1776. Many changes have been made over the years but we continue to honour our traditional role at the heart of the community! Jack and Sally welcome you aboard.'*

Which was all good promotional material for the Man O'War, but what was it doing in Duggan's pocket? Ben didn't know Hunstanton, though it was a safe bet that it was a long way from landlocked Oxfordshire. A quick check on his phone revealed that Hunstanton was a seaside town in Norfolk, about 135 miles and a three-hour drive away.

That set him thinking. Emily Bowman had told him that Duggan's work for her involved travelling about the country. She'd also said her family had relocated from London to the north of England at some point. Norfolk, stuck out on the easternmost bulge of England's coastline, was only on about the same midland latitude as Birmingham, not particularly far north at all. What family leads could Duggan have been following up there?

For a discouraging moment Ben was thinking that this was all going nowhere, and that he was just chasing shadows. But then he noticed the faint handwriting that had been messily scribbled by someone, presumably Duggan, in biro along the top edge of the mat.

ACHILLES-14 / Galliard

Ben had no idea what it could mean, but instinct told him to hang onto the mat, in case it was important somehow. He slipped it into his own pocket and went on searching through the rest of Duggan's things until he was certain he'd find nothing more, and left the bedroom.

The other two bedrooms were empty and hadn't been used in a while, beds made up tight and undisturbed dust on the surfaces. Still wondering where the killer could have got in, Ben went into the bathroom near the backstair – and that was where he found what the police had missed. The upstairs bathroom belonged to the older part of the vicarage, and still had the original windows and fittings. The windows were set low, just above floor level with a broad wooden sill. The catches were of the old-fashioned zero-security variety, just a couple of curly cast-iron handles with a thin locking tab that wouldn't require much pressure from outside to pop open. Replacing them with something more modern had been one of those jobs that Ben had urged Jude to take care of when he'd inherited the place, but Jude wasn't any more of a DIY handyman than Simeon had been.

Sure enough, one window was open a narrow crack, with just a few flakes of paint and a couple of small splinters on the sill to show that it had been recently pried open. Maybe if McAllister's nemesis Forbsie hadn't shut down the investigation in the belief that they'd solved the case, the cops would have found the forced window. Ben knelt by it and looked out. There was a mature sycamore tree growing too close to the house, which had spread out considerably since the last time Ben had been here. Even in Simeon and Michaela's day they'd fretted about falling branches damaging the roof. Like with the windows, Ben's advice to Jude had been to lop the damn thing, but Jude had refused on sentimental grounds.

Ben considered the distance from the nearest branches to the window. One particular limb looked thick enough to support the weight of a man, and the gap wasn't far. A nimble climber, not too heavy, could easily have leaned across to the outside ledge while prying open the window. Not easy, but it could be done. On their way out, the intruder would just pull the window shut behind them before escaping back down the tree.

Ben thought about the lack of any bloodstains on the bathroom floor, or the passage and the backstair. As he'd pointed out to McAllister, the killer was likely to have been covered with it. But a clever operator – a pro – could have worn disposable overalls and overshoes that they quickly stripped off after the deed was done, and stuffed in a bag. That way they'd leave little or nothing of a trail to follow.

Ben returned down the backstair, headed outside into the garden and went over to examine the tree. It didn't take him long to find the fresh scrape on the bark about six feet off the ground, and the recently snapped limb a few feet higher up.

Ben thought, *No signs of forced entry, my arse.*

He'd learned something, but he still had too little to go on. Tonight, he would learn more.

Ben slipped back out of the property the way he'd come in. He was walking through the patch of woodland in the direction of his car when his phone went.

To his surprise, the call was from Emily Bowman. She sounded upset and worried, and suddenly wanting to talk to him after all.

'Mr Hope?'

'I didn't expect to hear back from you.'

Her next words stole the breath from his mouth and halted him in mid-stride.

'I know your son is innocent.'

Chapter 15

'Are you hearing me?' Emily Bowman said. 'Your son didn't kill Carter Duggan. There's no way he could possibly have been involved.'

Ben was almost too stunned to reply. He leaned against a tree and clasped the phone tight against his ear. 'How do you know this?'

'Please. I need to talk to you. Can we meet again?'

Ben didn't want to wait that long. 'We can, but I need you to tell me now. What do you know? And why the change of heart?'

She replied, 'What you said to me before, about destroying the life of an innocent young man . . . it really stayed with me. I can't live with that thought. I'm not a selfish person. I'm a person who's afraid. Terribly afraid. And I'm someone who needs your help, Mr Hope. After you left, I looked you up by the web address on your card, and I saw what you do.'

Ben was confused. 'I don't understand. Why does it matter who I am, and what I do?'

'Because you protect people,' she replied. 'That's what I need.'

'You're asking me to protect you?'

'Or else I thought perhaps you could recommend someone in that line of work. I have to have the best, and I need them to start immediately. I don't care how much I have to pay. I have to get away from here as quickly as I can, and I have a place to hide, but I don't want to be alone. What if those people find me?' Her voice sounded hollow with fear and she was talking so fast she was tripping over her words.

'Slow down. Explain why you need protection. Who's going to find you? What does this have to do with Duggan, and Jude?'

'I . . . I'm in terrible trouble. I should never have involved Mr Duggan in this. It's all my fault.'

'This is about your family history?'

She gulped a deep breath and tried to speak. 'Our family has a secret, Mr Hope. A horrible secret that people have died for, and I'm terrified that more people will die because of it. My mother, Glencora Bowman, knew it. It was only after she passed away, when I was going through her things, that I came across Violet's journal. Well, it was really more like a memoir. You might say a confession, even.'

'Violet?'

'My grandmother. Years after the event, she wrote it all down in a book. It wasn't meant to be read by anyone else but her. When she died, my mother read it and then kept it hidden away.'

Ben asked, 'Years after what event?'

'It's too long a story to go into now. I promise I'll tell you everything when you get here.'

Ben had to bite back his frustration. 'And this secret book is the reason you hired Carter Duggan?'

'Yes. The things my grandmother wrote . . . I was so disturbed by them that I had to find out more. I didn't know where to start. I needed help, if I was ever going to get to the truth.'

'And did he?'

'Yes, and I believe that what he discovered cost him his life and now I'm so afraid the same is going to happen to me.'

Now Ben understood more clearly why she'd seemed in such a hurry to get away from home earlier. There seemed little point in asking her what Duggan had discovered. Instead he asked, 'Are you still at the house?'

'Yes, but I'm frightened to stay much longer in case they return.'

'Who, the people in the black Mercedes?'

Emily Bowman was too panic-stricken to be taken aback that he knew about that. 'There isn't time to talk about this by phone. How fast can you get over here? I can explain everything to you when you arrive. Then you'll see why it's just not possible that your son killed Mr Duggan. Please, Mr Hope. Will you help me?'

'I'll help you,' he agreed. 'But on one condition. That whatever information you've got to tell me that gets Jude off the hook, you'll repeat in a formal police statement to Detective Inspector Tom McAllister.'

'Anything,' she said desperately. 'Just hurry. Please!'

'I'm on my way,' he said, and ended the call.

Ben ran for the car. The Alpina's twin-turbo engine fired up with a roar and the fat tyres spun hard into the dirt. As he surged away towards Boars Hill the excitement was running hot through his veins that he'd found a witness who could exonerate Jude. Things were moving quickly now. He thought about calling McAllister to fill him in on this unexpected development – but then decided to leave it until after he'd spoken with her.

If Ben had acted on that initial impulse to tell the cop where he was going, he'd soon have come to regret it.

It was only a twenty-minute drive from Little Denton to Boars Hill, even without shredding every speed limit in sight as Ben often tended to do when he was in a hurry. But a few miles out from the village, he cursed as he saw the tail of slow-moving traffic ahead. A queue of a dozen or more cars was stuck behind a lumbering farm machine, with unbroken streams of cars zipping the other way at seventy. Overtaking would have been suicidal.

Ben joined the line and for the next several minutes impatiently settled down to a thirty-mile-an-hour pace, lighting up a Gauloise to soften his frustration. Peering past the line of traffic he could see a layby coming up on the left, but the farm machine made no attempt to pull in to let people pass.

The people you meet when you don't have a gun. Ben swore a little more loudly and drummed his fingers on the wheel. 'Come on. Come on.'

Finally spotting a break in the oncoming traffic he saw his chance and stamped his foot to the floor. The eight-speed auto transmission kicked down a few gears and the revs soared to a fruity howl as he swerved out into the right-hand lane to overtake the dawdling queue as though it was standing still. It wasn't often on Oxfordshire's overcrowded main roads that he got the chance to demonstrate the fact that the Alpina D3 bi-turbo was the world's fastest production diesel car, with a skilled and fearless driver at the wheel.

But for all that, by the time Ben reached his destination a few minutes later, it was already too late.

He knew from the moment he raced into the courtyard of the big house that something was wrong. The old guy with the shotgun was still pretty much in the same spot that Ben had seen him last. But he'd been on his feet before, and now he was lying sprawled out and immobile on the gravel, flat on his back with his arms and legs outspread. He didn't look as if he'd died of a heart attack.

Ben skidded the Alpina to a halt on the loose gravel and burst out of his driver's door, keeping low as he ran over to the body on the ground. The old guy's eyes stared emptily up at him. The chequered shirt he was wearing under his Barbour jacket was soaked almost black with blood, all down the front. Ben tore the shirt open from the neck and saw the two large-calibre bullet holes that had punched his chest three inches apart. Heart shot and lung shot. There was little point in feeling for a pulse. But the dead man's skin was still warm to the touch.

Which meant he'd been alive until very recently.

Which meant that whatever was happening inside the house was just minutes old, or still ongoing.

Ben didn't have time to think about it. He simply had to act.

The man's shotgun was still clenched in one lifeless hand. Ben peeled away the fingers and wrenched it free. Twin hammers, twin triggers; it was a seriously old-fashioned tool probably dating back to the time of the last King Edward. One barrel of the gun had been fired, and not long ago judging by the sweetish tang of freshly burnt powder Ben could smell as he cracked open the action and ejected the spent case. The second barrel was still loaded, its hammer cocked. The old guy had managed to get off just a single shot before the opposing gunfire had cut him down.

Ben knelt over the corpse and quickly searched through the pockets of the Barbour jacket, found a handful of loose cartridges and grabbed them. He swung away from the body and ran back to the car, crouching for cover behind its front wing as he reloaded the spent shell. He looked over at the house, listened hard; could see nothing, could hear nothing. No sounds of violent disturbance from within. No gunfire came from the windows. The place seemed empty, but he sensed it wasn't.

He cocked the second hammer, thought *fuck it*, surged to his feet and sprinted towards the house. The front door was lying ajar. To go crashing through like a stormtrooper was a sure way of getting yourself shot by anyone who might be lurking in the hallway. He eased the door silently open the rest of the way and peered inside.

The hallway was empty. That was, apart from the corpse of Margo, Emily Bowman's housekeeper. She was sitting slumped in a chair with her head lolling against her left shoulder and her tongue hanging out. Her face was laced with blood from a large bullet hole in the dead centre of her forehead. Another – the killer's first shot, Ben guessed – had drilled her through the chest. A pool of red at her feet reflected the light from the open doorway.

Something shiny and golden twinkled from the edge of the blood pool. Ben didn't need to pick it up to know what it was: a spent cartridge case from a .45 automatic. One shooter could have entered the house, or a two-man team. Both armed with high-capacity pistols. Ben was under-gunned, but even an antiquated twelve-gauge was a supremely deadly weapon, in the right hands.

The packed boxes and bags were still in the same place. It looked as though Emily Bowman had delayed her escape just a little too long. But where was she?

Ben hunted quickly through the downstairs rooms. The house seemed even bigger than it looked from outside, and it took him a whole two minutes to clear the ground floor. There was no sign of her. Racing back past Margo's sitting body he headed up the stairs.

And that was where he found Emily Bowman.

Chapter 16

At the top of the stairs, an elegant U-shaped galleried mezzanine landing with an ornate white wood balustrade partly overlooked the ground floor to Ben's right. To his left ran a series of closed white wood doors, separated by gilt-framed paintings and ornamental statuettes. Diaphanous light filtered down from a stained-glass dome set into the ceiling far above. A wrought-iron spiral staircase at the far end of the landing led up to the second floor.

Ben stalked cautiously along the landing, slow but urgent, clutching the shotgun and ready to react at the tiniest noise or movement. The carpeting was thick and silent underfoot. He checked the first door to his left and found an airy, graceful bathroom with a Victorian tub and satin drapes veiling a tall window. The second and third doors were both empty bedrooms. He quietly closed each door and moved on.

Halfway along the landing something on the richly-carpeted floor caught his eye. It was a bright, fresh spatter of blood that hadn't yet soaked into the fibres. It was followed by a trail of spots. There was a red smear on the handrail of the balustrade.

Ben stopped breathing. A couple of steps ahead of him was the fourth door. The first three had been closed but this one was open a few inches. There was another blood spatter across the middle of the door at chest height, garish and livid against the glossy white paintwork. Ben nudged the door the rest of the way open with his toe. He already had a bad feeling what he was going to see inside.

Emily Bowman was lying face-down half across the bed with one leg hanging off the edge. The tweedy kilt skirt was riding up to her waist. Part of her right shoulder had been blown away, the buttercup-yellow silk blouse stained crimson. There were two more bullet holes in her, one in her back and one at the base of her skull.

Ben stepped into the bedroom and stood over her. He could easily piece together the evidence to picture the whole scene: Emily Bowman had been upstairs when she'd heard the first exchange of gunfire coming from outside, followed quickly afterwards by the shots in the hallway below. Gripped by panic, she'd started running for the stairs when she must have been confronted by the killer or killers coming up from the ground floor. Turning back in horror to run the other way; then the shot blasting out; the bullet slamming into her right shoulder, the blood spraying. Emily had wobbled but she hadn't fallen. Using the handrail to steady herself she'd managed to get as far as the fourth door and burst through it at the same moment that the second bullet caught her in the back. The white flash. Already dying on her feet as she staggered into the bedroom and then collapsed face-down onto the bed.

Then the killer, or killers, had calmly walked into the

bedroom after her, and executed her with a last cold-blooded shot to the back of the head.

Ben gently rolled her over. The brutal damage to her face was what he would have expected from a large-calibre point-blank gunshot exit wound. He'd seen worse, but right now he couldn't remember when.

He was sickened, angered and saddened at the sight of her lying there. If he had got here a few minutes sooner, she might still have been alive. And whatever secret she'd been about to reveal to him might still have been Jude's best chance of exoneration. Now that, too had been snuffed out with a bullet to the head.

Ben had seen enough. He was turning away from the dead woman when he heard a noise from another part of the house. He froze. Listening hard. There it was again. The soft but unmistakable sound of someone moving around upstairs. A moment later, the muffled thump of a door slamming, followed a few seconds after by footsteps. Ben closed his eyes to focus on their rhythm and decided they were those of two people. In the next instant he heard a voice mutter something he didn't catch, and another in reply.

He stepped out of the bedroom with the shotgun clenched against his hip and finger on the trigger, in time to see two men reaching the bottom of the spiral staircase at the far end of the mezzanine landing. Both wearing dark trousers and black lightweight bomber jackets zipped up to the neck. Both armed with chunky black pistols. One was carrying a backpack over his shoulder. The two of them were smiling like a pair of buddies enjoying a joke. They had just murdered three people, and they were smiling.

Ben wanted them alive. But he knew well enough that things often didn't work out that way.

The jokey smiles dropped as both men simultaneously saw Ben emerge from the bedroom door. They were professionals. Well drilled. And their response was instant. The pistols came up in unison and they both opened fire at once, fast and furious, in a rattling *blamblamblamblam* that sounded like a blast from a machine pistol. But Ben's own responses were honed smoother and even more second-nature instinctive. Even as their weapons were swinging up to take aim at him and he read the hard looks of intent in their eyes he gave up on the idea of taking them alive.

He let off the right barrel of the shotgun. The shattering blast filled the air like a bombshell going off and the gun kicked ferociously in his hands. As the incoming swarm of gunfire smacked into the plaster and punched through the bloodstained wood of the open door next to him he ducked back inside the bedroom without seeing where his shot had gone, and dived over Emily Bowman's body to take cover behind the bed. A bed wasn't ideal protection from large-calibre gunfire but it was better than a flimsy partition wall. Ben cracked open the shotgun and flicked the empty, smoking hull from the right-hand barrel. He quickly slid in another shell in its place, thumbed back the hammer and ducked his head down lower as another staccato burst of shots rattled from the landing, sounding closer. They were firing randomly through the wall in the hope that at least one bullet would find its mark. One of them smacked into Emily Bowman's body with a meaty thud. Another smashed an antique glass Tiffany lamp by the bedside and toppled it over.

In a lull between shots Ben heard the soft *thud* and oiled-metal *clack* of a pistol having its empty magazine being ejected and dumped to the floor, and a fresh one being quickly, expertly rammed in. He levelled the shotgun over the top of the bed towards the area of bedroom wall behind which the sound had come, wrapped his index and middle fingers around both triggers and let off both barrels at once.

Not something you could do with a modern shotgun. Twice the noise, twice the recoil. And twice the downrange destruction. The blast blew a ragged round hole in the wall, the size of a marine porthole. Chunks of plaster and splintered bits of stud battening flew in all directions.

Ben's ears sang from the deafening explosion, but he could hear well enough to tell that the gunfire from the landing had stuttered to a halt. Peering through the hole in the wall, he could see no movement outside. He quickly reloaded his empty gun with his last two cartridges.

Just then, he saw a dark shape scurry past the bullet-riddled bedroom doorway. He leaped to his feet, vaulted over Emily Bowman and the bed and ran out onto the landing in pursuit. Glancing left, he saw one man down, lying inert near the foot of the spiral staircase, the front of his bomber jacket ripped up. To Ben's right, the second guy was escaping towards the stairs, still carrying the backpack over his shoulder and moving with a pronounced lurch in his step. He was hit and leaking blood in his wake, but still in the game. He was also Ben's best remaining chance of finding out who these killers were, and who they worked for.

Ben pointed the shotgun at him and could have cut him

down in his tracks. Instead he held his fire and yelled, 'Stop! Toss the weapon!'

The lurching, limping figure wasn't ready to give up the fight just yet. At the sound of Ben's voice he wheeled around with his own and his dead associate's pistols in both hands and delivered a wild volley of shots. An alabaster statuette on a plinth blew apart three inches from Ben's elbow. Ben thought *You asked for it*, stood his ground with bullets burning past him and fired off one barrel as the guy crashed through the last door before the stairs. The door frame disintegrated into spinning splinters and dust, but thanks to Ben's hesitation the guy was marginally ahead of the curve and made it through into the room. Ben raced for the doorway, bracing for more shots punching back at him through the wall.

The other side of it was the airy, graceful bathroom that Ben had checked minutes earlier. He rounded the edge of the shattered door frame just in time to see the injured man lurching past the Victorian bathtub and shoving hard through the drapes against the tall window. Before Ben could do anything to stop him, there was a tinkle of smashing glass as the window crashed violently open; then the man was through and leaping into space.

Ben hurried across to the broken window just in time to see him slithering and tumbling down the slope of the roof, dislodging tiles as he went. As he reached the overhanging edge the man tried to grapple for the guttering to break his fall, missed, and dropped out of sight. Then he was gone.

Chapter 17

For all Ben could tell, the guy had gone plummeting to his death. Ben had no intention of following him there. He swore and backed away from the window, ran out of the bathroom, pounded down the stairs, sprinted past the body of the housekeeper still sitting in the chair, and burst outside.

At a sprint he rounded the side of the house towards where the man had fallen. He looked up at the roof: it had to have been a twenty-five-foot drop, high enough to break bones or possibly kill you if you landed badly on the kind of hard paving that skirted the house walls. Ben was half expecting to see a broken-necked corpse, but what he found instead left him with mixed emotions. Partly positive, because dead men don't talk and he wanted this one alive – and he was, because all there was of him on the paving was some blood. And partly negative, because now Ben had no idea where he'd gone.

He scouted for a blood trail, but it was scanty and then vanished altogether. The guy was hurt but he wasn't bleeding to death, and he was probably putting pressure on the wound to cover his tracks. Ben found one small red spatter on the gravel, the size of a penny, and decided that the man must have gone down the avenue that separated the house from the indoor pool building next to it.

Ben ran the length of the gap and emerged from the other end. There was no sign of the man anywhere to be seen. The pool house was all windows, and peering through them Ben could see he wasn't in there either. Ben now found himself standing at a T-junction where the path forked right and left: to his left, Emily Bowman's tennis court and an area of lovely garden with a small apple orchard; to his right, the large horse paddock Ben had seen on his approach to the house. One way or the other, he had to choose. If he picked the wrong one, there was every chance that his man would get away.

If in doubt, turn left had been Ben's watchword for years. If it came down to a coin toss, that was the way he'd go.

That was when he noticed the horses.

There were five of them, two bays, a big, handsome chestnut and a pair of greys, one of them just a foal. That morning Emily Bowman's little herd had all been lazily grazing at the lush summer grass. Now they had moved off to the far side of the paddock and were milling nervously over by the fence, snorting and neighing loudly. The sounds of gunfire from inside the house might have spooked them, but Ben's instinct told him the animals had taken fright at something that had happened more recently than that. Something from just moments ago. Horses were extremely sensitive and could read human body language even better than a dog. When people behaved erratically or angrily around them, their natural prey animal's self-preservation instinct kicked in. If a hurt and desperate man had come running past their paddock just now, the horses would have picked up on the furious vibes he was giving off, and they'd want nothing to do with him.

Ben was suddenly certain that his quarry had gone that way.

Trusting his instinct, he turned right and sprinted past the paddock fence. The big chestnut saw him and wheeled around, whinnying. Ben ran on, one eye to the ground, searching for more blood spots but seeing nothing. Past the edge of the paddock was a stable block, and beyond that again was a long, large wooden barn. It had tall double doors to allow large machinery in and out, but those doors were padlocked. Whereas the smaller person-sized door inset in one of them was cracked open a few inches. Ben saw the small blood splash a few feet from the entrance and a red smudge on the door handle, and suddenly knew that his instinct had been right.

He approached the door with the shotgun levelled and ready. In a strong, clear voice he called out, 'Okay, I know you're in there. Come on out with your hands on your head, and I won't shoot. You've got five seconds. Four . . . three . . .'

But Ben never reached two. The roar of a loud-revving engine suddenly erupted into life from within the barn. In the next instant the tall double doors burst open and flew apart in a storm of ripping planks and flying splinters as a big utility tractor rammed through and came charging straight towards him.

Ben flung himself out of its path, dropping the shotgun. The tractor surged past and narrowly missed him. He rolled on the ground, sprang back to his feet and went to retrieve his fallen weapon, but saw that its barrels had been crushed flat under the tractor's knobbly wheels. The man inside the cab grappled at the wheel as he brought the machine back round in a tight circle to try to run Ben down again. Its front end was crumpled from the impact, one headlight dangling. The tarpaulin it must have been covered with was trailing along behind, along with all kinds of tangled-up junk that had been piled up next to it – rolls of fencing wire, a reel of high-tensile steel cable that had got itself enmeshed around the front axle, an old horse blanket.

The tractor came roaring back at him. He waited until the last instant and then leaped out of its path a second time, and it smashed into the edge of the barn, ripping off the remnants of one shattered door and carrying away a corner joist with a force that almost collapsed the entire building. The tractor forced its way through the wreckage like a Panzer tank and kept going, coughing out a black cloud of diesel smoke as it accelerated hard away. Now it looked as if the man at the wheel had given up on the idea of squashing Ben to death, and was intent on making his escape. Somewhere close nearby, he and his accomplice must have had a getaway car hidden. If the man could get to it before Ben stopped him, he'd be gone.

Ben ran after the tractor, thinking that he could jump onto the dragging tarpaulin and grab a solid handhold so he could scramble up onto the rear of the vehicle. He managed to get one foot on the tarp, then the other. But the big rear wheels and bendy plastic mudguards gave him nothing to latch onto, and it was impossible to stay upright.

He fell, and was instantly in danger of getting tangled up in the folds of the thick plastic and either mangled under a wheel or eviscerated by a trailing length of barbed wire. The tractor was gaining speed now as it headed away from the outbuildings. Thirty miles an hour felt uncomfortably fast when you were being dragged over the rough ground. Ben fought to disentangle himself from the tarpaulin and was suddenly free, rolling in the dirt. Then he was back on his feet, scraped and battered but mindless of the pain as he resumed the chase. As fast a runner as he was, the tractor was steadily drawing away from him. A heavy roll of fencing wire unsnagged itself from its undercarriage and Ben swerved out of its way as it came bouncing towards him. The cable reel being dragged along in its wake began to unravel. The high-tensile steel swished along the ground behind it like a silver snake.

Ahead, a closed metal gateway blocked off a compacted-earth path that ran parallel with a grassy bank. At the bottom of the slope was a large pond with lilies and ducks and an ornamental fountain at its centre. The path cut across Emily Bowman's property to another gate in the distance, which Ben saw marked the perimeter. That was where the man and his accomplice had left their car. That was where he was desperately trying to get back to now.

The tractor veered towards the gate. Engine revving to the max, wheels churning up the dirt, oily black smoke pumping from its exhaust stack, the slinky silver cable tailing along in its wake. It smashed into the gate with a juddering crash. The gate was strong galvanised steel, hinged to a metal post embedded in concrete. It was bent and buckled by the impact, but still held. The tractor crunched into reverse, lumbered back a few feet and then came at it again. This time, the gate ripped off its hinges and the big wheels crushed it flat.

That was the moment Ben saw his chance. The tension had momentarily gone out of the steel cable as the tractor negotiated the gate. Fifteen yards behind, Ben snatched the end of the cable off the ground at the same instant that the tractor took off again. In another second it would be ripped from his hands. He raced for the ruined gateway. The gate was toast but the thick galvanised post was deeply enough embedded in the concrete to have remained intact. Ben very quickly looped the end of the cable around it, made it fast and stepped back as the slack was taken up and the braided steel rope snapped as taut as a piano string.

With a rending *crunch* the strain wrenched the post to a forty-five-degree angle. But it held. So did the cable. You could have dangled a battleship from that cable. And the other end of it was solidly attached to the tractor's front axle.

Something had to give.

And it did.

Chapter 18

The tractor's rear wheels lifted off the ground and the vehicle flipped tail over nose and sideways at the same time, coming down with a rending crunch that flattened the roof and sent bits of debris flying in all directions. The front axle, together with suspension parts and steering linkages, was ripped clean away. One wheel went bouncing off down the grassy slope and hit the pond water with a huge splash, scattering the ducks that were dabbling there among the lilies. The dismembered vehicle rolled a couple more times, and its destructive momentum began to carry it down the embankment towards the water.

Ben's heart was thumping as he sprinted after it. Invoking the forces of mayhem and devastation was an easily overdone thing, especially when you needed to keep your enemy at least alive enough to press information out of him. The man at the wheel might have been crushed to death by the flattened roof, or he might now be trapped inside the wreck as it splashed down into the pond and sank to the bottom. Either was a bad outcome; but then Ben saw the guy spilling out of the wreck as it rolled down the embankment, battered and bloody but still perfectly alive. He was still clutching his backpack as he staggered to his feet, fell and then struggled upright again, just as the tractor hit the pond with an explosion of spray like a depth charge.

The man broke into a limping, lumbering run and tried to escape towards the perimeter fence. He threw a wild-eyed look back over his shoulder, saw Ben rapidly gaining on him, jerked a pistol from his belt and pointed it. His aim was wild and the bullet missed his target by several feet. Ben flinched at the flat report of the gunshot but kept running.

The pistol was empty now, slide locked back. A surge of triumph burned through Ben's veins. The man had just spent his last chance of getting away. And he knew it. With a shout of rage and frustration he hurled the dead weapon at Ben's head. Ben ducked it and the missile sailed over his shoulder. The man kept running, but it was a hopeless effort. Ben was on him in the next three strides, and tackled him with a force that made him drop his backpack and go tumbling on his face.

The man fought him like an animal, with the desperation that comes with having nothing left to lose. Ben pinned his thrashing, kicking body to the grass and hit him hard in the face, twice, three times, but still he kept on fighting. His mouth was streaming blood, red teeth bared in a grimace of hate. His clawed fingers raked at Ben's face and tried to gouge his eyes and get a grip around his throat. Ben hit him again, but the man barely seemed to feel it. He bent up his right leg as though he was about to try to kick Ben off him – his right hand let go of Ben's throat for an instant and shot down to his ankle – and suddenly there was a small boot knife in his fist, a leaf-bladed dagger that flashed towards Ben's ribs with lethal force.

Ben writhed his body away from the blade and rolled over onto his back, and the man rolled with him, now riding on top and trying to plunge the dagger into Ben's chest. The needle-sharp, double-edged blade was within three inches of his heart when he blocked the man's wrist and twisted it hard and felt the crackle of ripping cartilage. The guy didn't seem to care. He managed to get a hold of the knife with his other hand and kept on battling. No pain. No fear. Kill or be killed. Ben knew there was only one way he was going to disable this enemy. This was a fight to the death now.

Locked together, they tumbled down the embankment towards the pond, where the grass was all flattened and ripped up by the rolling tractor. Its rear end still jutted up from the muddied, rippling surface of the water. Over and over. Ben swallowed a gasp of air before the shock of the icy-cold water jolted him, and next thing the roar of the murky water was in his ears and his vision was clouded by weeds and lichen and bubbles, so that he could no longer see his enemy as the two of them sank deeper towards the mud at the bottom of the pond. If one of them didn't win this fight in the next minute, they were both going to end up drowned.

On the edge of panic now. Fighting as hard as he'd ever fought in his life. Driving the guy against the submerged tractor chassis, striking with everything he had: knees, feet, fists, head. Suddenly realising that the enemy wasn't fighting back any longer. His body going limp.

Ben grasped him by the collar of his jacket and used the

last of his energy reserve to kick and struggle back up to the surface. He gasped for air as his head burst from the water and swam for the edge, dragging the limp form behind him. The guy barely seemed to be breathing.

Both of them were covered in green-black pond weeds and lilies. As Ben hauled the unresponsive body up onto the bank, he suddenly saw why he'd stopped fighting. In their frenzied rolling tumble down the slope the knife intended for Ben had ended up stuck deep in the killer's own chest. Which seemed like a suitable end for him, if he was the man who'd murdered Carter Duggan. He was fading fast. But Ben didn't want him to die, not just yet. He grabbed the man by the collar and shook him. 'Who are you? Who are you working for?'

No reply. The guy spat up a load of pink foamy pond water. He muttered something unintelligible; then his eyes rolled over white and the last remnant of life in him slipped away, along with anything Ben might have got out of him.

Ben frisked the body for any kind of identification, but wasn't surprised to find nothing. Professional assassins don't show up for work with their wallet and driving licence in their pocket. This man wasn't even carrying a phone. Ben took out his own phone and used it to take a mugshot of the dead man's pallid, battered features. Leaving the body lying there on the sodden, muddied grass, he wiped the worst of the pond vegetation from his clothes and walked squelching over to where the dead man's backpack had fallen. Its contents were Ben's only possible clue why the killers had attacked Emily Bowman's house. He picked it up, unzipped it open and found what was inside.

140

It was a book. An old, slim journal bound in tatty, faded red leather. There was no inscription on the cover but its yellowed and dusty pages were filled with cursive handwriting of a style that instantly dated it back a good number of decades, maybe to the 1940s or older. The things Emily Bowman had told him came flooding back into his mind.

'Our family has a secret. A horrible secret that people have died for. And I'm terrified that more will die because of it.'

The journal in his hands had belonged to Emily's grandmother, found hidden among her daughter Glencora's possessions after her death. He recalled the things Emily had said about the disturbing revelations that had impelled her to hire Carter Duggan to help her discover more about her family history.

Ben wanted to know more, too, because his gut told him that here was the key to the whole thing. He now had two pieces of evidence: the book and the Man O'War beer mat he'd lifted from Duggan's jacket back at the vicarage.

Ben took the beer mat from his pocket and gazed at it and the memoir in turn. Somehow, these two items were connected, and he was determined to find out how and why. But this was neither the time nor the place to start trying to figure out the mystery. He slipped the beer mat into the pages of the book and replaced it inside the backpack, zipped it and slung it over his shoulder.

Nearby lay the empty pistol that the dead guy had tried to brain him with. A SIG forty-calibre auto, well oiled and nearly brand new. Not a piece of equipment that the average common thug could get hold of too easily in free Britain. Ben slipped it into his pocket. Next on his checklist was the crushed shotgun, still lying among the wreckage of the half-ruined wooden barn. He wiped it down for prints. He had no desire to be traced to the events here today, when the police eventually arrived on the scene. Which could be a long time away. Worried about the horses, he jogged over to the paddock to check there was enough water in their drinking trough to last them.

There was nothing he could do for the bodies of the killers' three victims. Returning upstairs he examined the corpse near the foot of the spiral staircase. Like his associate's, the man's pockets were devoid of ID, but Ben did find a spare loaded magazine for his identical SIG pistol, which suddenly made the captured weapon much more useful. Ben used his phone to take another mugshot.

The two men had been coming down the spiral staircase when Ben had encountered them. He climbed the iron steps to the second floor and emerged onto an upper galleried landing with more rooms radiating off it. Emily Bowman had made her office up here, from which she had run her considerable and growing business empire. The office had been recently searched. Desk drawers ripped out, files dumped on the floor, papers everywhere. In the midst of the mess, Ben found the card he'd given her earlier that day lying on a desk next to a computer that was whirring softly in dormant mode. He nudged the mouse and the screen flashed into life.

As she'd admitted to him on the phone earlier, Emily Bowman had been checking out his profile on the Le Val website. It gave scant information about his military back-ground, but enough to convey an impression of his experience to a prospective client in need of help. And more than enough to raise plenty of unwanted questions about his possible connection to a murdered woman, when the police searched the house.

Ben used a knuckle to tap keys, closing the webpage and then deleting the record of her visit there from the computer's search history. He pocketed the business card, then left the study. Next door was a comfortable library with three walls covered in floor-to-ceiling bookshelves and some tastefully-worn leather armchairs with reading lamps. It was immediately clear that this was where the killers had focused their search, telling Ben that they must have known in advance they were hunting for a book – a very particular sort of book, the one that he now had in his possession. The shelves had been roughly ransacked, dozens of books, files and periodicals dumped all over the floor. But they hadn't needed to take the whole room apart: wherever Emily had been hiding her grandmother's memoir, she obviously hadn't done a great job of concealing it.

Touching nothing else, Ben headed back downstairs, passed by the dead bodies of the housekeeper and the old guy, and returned to his car. Thirty seconds later, he was gone without a trace of his ever having been there. From Boars Hill he cut eastwards along Foxcombe Road and Hinksey Hill until he hit the A34 bypass northbound and put his foot down, creating as much distance between himself and the crime scene as he could before the incident was reported.

It takes a while for the mind and body to climb down from a combat situation. Ben was on edge and couldn't concentrate simultaneously on driving and the thousand thoughts whirling through his mind. He needed somewhere to sit alone in peace and take stock of the new situation, so turning off the dual carriageway at Botley he headed a few miles further along the Eynsham road to a spot near the river that he knew well, near Pinkhill Lock.

Leaving the car he wandered down to the water's edge carrying the backpack he'd taken from Emily Bowman's place, and drank in the stillness: just the soft lapping of the river at its banks, the cawing of crows circling above the trees and a muted rumble of traffic in the distance. Ben sat by the slow-moving river and lit a cigarette. The landscape of sun-parched fields was yellow and flat; behind the trees to the east was Farmoor Reservoir, with the sailing club on its far shore. A small bevy of swans sailed past downstream like a convoy of galleons. He used to come out here with Michaela, once upon a time. Michaela loved the swans.

Closing his eyes, he drew in the acrid but somehow soothing cigarette smoke and let the dust settle on his turbulent thoughts. Things were happening at a pace now. For reasons still unclear, the death count had just multiplied and this time there was no way the police could pin the blame on Jude. Maybe being kept out of mischief in a prison cell was the best place he could be at this moment. But would the fresh killings be enough to exonerate him from Carter Duggan's murder? The evidence against him wasn't any the weaker for it, and the cops didn't generally go around dropping charges for no good reason. No, Ben sensed that Jude wasn't out of the woods yet.

He opened the backpack and took out the slim leather-bound book. On the inside cover, in faded handwriting, was the name Violet Bowman and beneath it the date April, 1946. Emily Bowman had called the book her grandmother's confession. It was a strange word to use. A confession of what?

Ben was about to find out. He began to read, and an incredible story slowly unfolded before his eyes.

Chapter 19

Violet Bowman's memoir was composed in the plain, simple hand and straightforward prose of someone who was perfectly literate but lacked the benefits of a formal education. It opened with a line that sounded exactly like the confession that Emily Bowman had described it as.

My name is Violet Bowman, but it wasn't always. It sometimes seems to me as though I've lived several different lives, and parts of my past seem to me like a dream now, like some story that I once read. Perhaps that's why I put pen to paper now, all these years later, as a reminder to myself that it was real, and that I can never be forgiven for my part in the pain and suffering of those I loved so dearly.

Ben read on.

I was born Violet Littleton in 1905, the only child of a poor but respectable Christian family in Cornwall. My father had been a miner, but he fell sickly when I was very young and I can barely remember a time when he was not bedridden for much of the day, seldom appearing at mealtimes and almost never venturing outdoors. My poor mother worked as a seamstress and did the best she could to raise me more or less alone. Times were often hard and I knew hunger from an early age. I cannot say I ever really attended school, or at any rate not so as to have anything much to show for it. I was a simple girl, attended to my duties and tried to be good and love God, as I was taught.

In the early spring of 1922, at the age of seventeen, with great sadness and reluctance I left my parents' home for the very first time and travelled to London in search of work. The Great War had caused terrible economic harm to our community in Cornwall and we were struggling like never before. I was a resourceful girl, not afraid of working hard. It was time for me to be brave and grown-up and support my family, though I had never seen London before and was very afraid and lonely in such a strange, bewildering new environment. With the small amount of money my mother had given me I took a room in a boarding house, a very austere place.

Within just a few days I found a job at the Osram Hammersmith Lamp and Valve Works, on a production line making tungsten lamps, or what we would call light bulbs now. It was a huge building dating back to the last century, with a great dome that had been added in 1920, and a big golden sign that said 'Osram Lamps' that you could see for miles. Over two thousand people worked at the plant, a lot of them women.

The war had brought big changes for us, creating jobs that had once been seen as men's work. Women made munitions, worked in coal mines, drove lorries. Some people called it a social revolution, but when the soldiers came back from the war a lot of those women were sacked from their jobs or had to go on working for less pay than the men. There was always talk that we were exploited, but what else was a poor girl to do in those times? I felt lucky to have a job at all.

I was one of a large crowd of women of all ages who sat at benches all day, operating machines. Sometimes I would be clamping the lamp filament tails, or working the lamp capping machine, but most of the time I was at the final inspection and testing station, sorting out the bulbs that worked from those that didn't. The testing machines were temperamental and sometimes you'd get an electric shock. The bulbs that passed inspection were hung on a rack, and the rest were put in a bin. Men would come and collect the bulbs into crates and take them away. Hundreds and thousands of them all day long, clink clink clink. It was soulless work. The noise inside that great big building would make your ears bleed, the hours were terrible long and the pay was small, but I stuck at it and sent as much money home as I could, to support my parents. I lived in cold-water lodgings near the railway, a damp attic room that was little better than a slum. I had been taught to read and write by a kind old lady named Beatrice Powell back in Cornwall, for whom I used to sew, and in what little spare time I had I tried to educate myself by reading books. But I was often too exhausted by the long hours of hard work.

The one thing that made life at the factory more bearable was my friendship with a co-worker there, a red-haired Irish girl a year older than me. Her name was Kitty Kelly and her family was from Limerick, though she was an orphan. Kitty and I got on like sisters. On a Sunday we would sometimes take a tram to Hyde Park, or visit a cheap tea room that was the only place where we could afford to treat ourselves, apart from our occasional outing to the pictures to see one of our favourites like Charlie Chaplin or Douglas Fairbanks. She lived in even worse lodgings than mine, above a butcher's shop in North End Road, and we sometimes talked about getting a place together.

One day Kitty didn't appear at work, and nobody seemed to know where she was. I was worried, and that evening I went over to her lodgings, only to be told by her landlady that she had left without giving any forwarding address. I was terribly sad and upset, and I felt abandoned and hurt that my best friend had gone off without telling me. It didn't seem like her.

For the next six months I continued to labour hard at the factory, but it was an unhappy time with no real friends to soften the hardship and few people to talk to. A new foreman had started there, a coarse brute of a man by the name of Herbert Slacker who paid me too much attention and was always staring at me. I was quite afraid of him, and did my best to avoid his company.

Then one day, as the factory whistle blew and all the workers were swarming out of the gates, I heard a familiar voice calling my name, and I looked around to see a well dressed young woman standing in the street and smiling at me. To begin with I didn't recognise her, and all I could do was stare in confusion.

'Sure, don't you know me, Violet?'

It was Kitty!

'Aye, it's me all right,' she laughed. 'Stop looking at me as if you'd seen a ghost. Come on, I'll treat you to a high tea.'

I was already so amazed that I could hardly manage to say a word. But then, to my even greater astonishment, Kitty called a cab and the two of us rode across London to an expensive tea room in Regent's Street. I had never been anywhere like it, all those people in their fancy clothes, and there was me, a factory girl in my old coat and worn-out shoes. I could still hardly believe that the fine lady sitting beside me was my old friend from the Lamp and Valve Works. She no longer looked like a malnourished working-class girl. Her curly red hair had a shine to it, and her green eyes were bright, her skin clear. She was beautiful! I couldn't help but notice the way all the men in the tea room were looking at her and how the waiters fawned over her.

At last I was able to ask all the questions that had been tying up my tongue until now. 'Kitty, what happened to you? Where did you go?'

And that was when, leaning across the table and speaking in a hushed voice, Kitty told me the most incredible thing I'd ever heard in my life. Kitty had found a new job, as a member of a group whose existence was new to me. They were called the Forty Elephants.

'Who are they?' I asked, filled with excitement. It was a very peculiar name, and in my mind I was imagining all kinds of strange and wonderful things. Was it a theatre? A circus?

'Bless you, no,' Kitty said, laughing. Then she lowered her voice again and looked around to make sure nobody was listening. 'We're crooks.'

I was so shocked I couldn't speak as Kitty told me all about it. The Forty Elephants were one of London's biggest crime gangs, all made up of young women, who would go into expensive shops and steal everything from perfumes to jewellery to luxury clothes. Nobody knew quite how they had got their name, but Kitty said it might be because their headquarters was the Elephant and Castle pub in Lambeth, where they were mixed up with the all-male mob of the same name. Other people said that it was because they were so huge with their loot when leaving the stores they robbed that they looked like elephants. In those days, women wore bustles and heavy clothing, useful for hiding stolen goods.

'We work for a girl called Annie Diamond, though most people call her Diamond Annie,' Kitty explained. 'She grew up in the same workhouse as Charlie Chaplin! And has been leader of the gang since the age of only nineteen. They call her "Queen of the Forty Thieves". She's still barely twenty-six, but look out if you cross her.'

The gang was so big and well-organised, Kitty said, that it had spread out of London and operated in cities as far away as Liverpool. Their method was tried and tested and very effective. A group of young girls would go into a fancy store, all dressed up, often wearing fur coats and muffs even when the weather was warm. Diamond Annie liked to recruit prettier girls, because they were less likely to be questioned or challenged by male shop staff, and one or two of them could use their charms to distract the sales assistants while the rest of them were filling up their muffs and stuffing their pockets with anything they could snatch – wrist watches, gold necklaces, whatever could bring a good price on the black market. A great deal of practice had made them excellent thieves. Then they would hurry out of the store, jump into a waiting cab and vanish.

Other Elephants got work as maids working in the homes of wealthy families. They would spend a week or two making an inventory of all the valuables in the house, then wait until the family were out before they would call in their accomplices and the place would be stripped bare.

'But Kitty,' I said, so aghast that I could barely keep my voice down, 'this is stealing! It's wrong!'

Kitty just shrugged her shoulders, with a smile. 'Aye, to be sure, there's no other word for it. But we're stealing from folks who can afford it. They've already got more money than they can spend.' She glanced around the tea room and pointed out a group of wealthy-looking ladies at a nearby table. 'Look at them, Violet. Covered in gold and pearls and fox-fur stoles. How many of them would even miss a trinket or two? And here's another thing,' she added quite vehemently, losing her smile. 'If the shoe was on the other foot and you was the one with the money and the jewels, you think there's one of these fine upstanding people who wouldn't rob you four ways to Sunday, give them half a chance?'

'It's still wrong,' I insisted.

'I'll tell you what's wrong,' Kitty replied. 'That's for a good, sweet, kind-hearted girl like you to waste her life away working in a factory for a parcel of greedy pigs who would leave you to die in the gutter. Look at the state of you – sure your eyes are like two burnt holes in a blanket. They're wearing you out.'

'It's not that bad,' I tried to protest.

'You're no better than a slave to them, Violet. They don't give a — about you.'

I was speechless. I had never heard a girl say — before.

'Anyhow,' Kitty went on. 'I don't intend to spend the rest of me life doing this. I've got a plan. I'm not going to spend all I earn. I'm already putting some money by and in ten years or so, I'll have made enough to buy a little tea room of me own. Maybe not as posh as this one. Something simple. I'll bake Irish bread and scones and folks who've left the old country to live in England will come from miles around. Got it all worked out, see? I'm going to call the place Kitty Ryan's. After me Gran. That was her maiden name and she was good to me when I was a little girl.'

'I don't know what to say, Kitty.'

'Say you'll join us,' Kitty replied, her green eyes sparkling as bright as the emerald ring I had noticed on her finger. 'They're always looking for new girls and you're pretty enough to suit them – or at least you could be, with a bit of sprucing up, your hair done and some new clothes. I can put in a good word for you, so I can. You'll be well looked after. Look at me, sure – would you ever have believed it? I've got me own rooms in a respectable house, me own money to spend on nice things. I really am putting on the posh. Look at this dazzler,' she added, holding it up to show me more closely. 'I've never had it so good.'

'I'm so happy to see you again,' I said to Kitty after a long moment's silence. 'And I'm glad that you're doing well. I just wish that there could be some other way.'

'Life is hard, ducky. Do yourself a favour.'

'I can't, Kitty. I couldn't. I just wasn't raised that way and I couldn't live with myself. I would rather be poor, even a slave as you say, than to be a criminal.'

We talked a little while longer, but my heart was heavy. Finding an excuse to leave, I thanked Kitty for the tea, and took her new address. We made plans to stay in touch and go out together as we used to. Little did I know it as I left the tea room, but I would be seeing Kitty again sooner than I thought.

Three days later at the factory, Slacker finally acted on the vile, salacious urge that I had been seeing building up in him for weeks. I was at my inspection station when he interrupted my work and directed me to go to fetch something from a storeroom. I suspected something, but couldn't refuse an order from a supervisor. But the moment I entered the empty storeroom he suddenly appeared, and locked the door shut behind him.

I tried to cry for help, but before I knew what was happening he pushed me to the ground and stood over me, unbuckling his belt and saying the most disgusting things. I was just a simple girl and knew virtually nothing of the world, but I understood very well what his intentions were. To this day I'm sure that the filthy animal would certainly have forced himself on me, if another foreman had not happened to visit the storeroom just in time and, finding the door strangely locked from inside, started thumping on it. Startled, Slacker pulled up his trousers and beat a hasty retreat.

An older, wiser and more confident girl living in a more modern time might have reported him, but I was young and frightened and this was 1922, when a woman's word counted for far less in society. Instead, I said nothing to anyone about the incident, left my job that very same day and immediately began looking for other employment, to no avail. Within a short time I realised that for an uneducated girl like me, the factory offered the best chance of half-decent work I could hope for. That hope was gone now, and every door seemed closed to me. Every door but one.

The next morning, after a long and sleepless night of struggling with my conscience, I spent all my remaining money on a cab ride to Kitty's house. She was happy to see me, and even happier when I confessed that I was reconsidering her offer of recruiting me to the Forty Elephants.

And that is how I, Violet Bowman, still a month short of my eighteenth birthday, became a professional criminal.

Chapter 20

Ben found himself drawn in by the simple directness of Violet's narrative. He'd never heard of the Forty Elephants before and had no idea of what to expect next, but a strange sense of foreboding told him that Violet's account was leading to dark places. He read on.

Soon afterwards, I was introduced to the leader of the gang, a right hard case if ever there was one. She was tall, over five feet and eight inches in height, and had been a criminal since 1912, aged sixteen. Her father, Thomas Diamond, was said to have once put the Lord Mayor of London's head through a glass door – and the daughter seemed to me no less of a tough, intimidating character. I soon saw how she had earned the nickname 'Diamond Annie', from the diamond rings she wore on every finger.

With Kitty vouching for me, I was soon inducted into the gang and introduced to other members, like Maggie Hill, who had a terrible reputation for violence, Louisa Diamond, Annie's younger sister, and Lilian Goldstein, who also worked for a smash-and-grab gang led by a woman called Ruby Sparks. The rules were simple: learn the ropes, do as you're told and keep your mouth shut; don't get caught, and if you do, never rat on your fellow Elephants. Lastly, Diamond Annie instructed me, was I to take up with any young fellow, I must get her approval first. Annie herself was unmarried and most of the girls were single. Any men in their lives had to be completely trustworthy and any hint of betrayal would be severely punished. How severely, I could only guess – but afterwards another member of the gang warned me: 'See them rings she wears? Ain't just to look pretty, dear. She took a bloke's eye out with a single punch once, and she'll do the same to anyone who looks at her wrong. 'Ard as bleedin' nails she is.'

I was in now; there was no backing out. But as rough and vicious as she might have been, Diamond Annie was a skilled leader who drilled and organised her gang with military precision. On my first mission as a fledgling member, just two days afterwards, I was posted as a lookout in the street outside while half a dozen Elephants, Kitty among them, swiftly and expertly plundered fur coats and bolts of silk worth hundreds of pounds from one of London's most prestigious department stores, one of several raids that were taking place simultaneously across the city. I was terrified, but excited and elated all at once, as though my blood had turned to champagne (which I had never yet tasted, but would come to enjoy a good deal).

That evening the Forty Elephants celebrated their successful mission with a wild party and I must confess to having drunk rather too much, being completely unused to wine. I had never laughed so much in all my life. Diamond Annie herself came up to me and, with a smile, pressed into my hand the biggest sum of money I had ever seen, let alone dreamed of possessing.

'You earned it, my girl,' she said. 'And there's plenty more where that came from. Here, have another drink!'

After having me act as lookout on a few more occasions, Annie decided to give me my first 'proper' assignment and I discovered to my amazement that I had something of a talent for the job. I came out of that first robbery wearing so many layers of fashionable underwear and other expensive garments under my coat that, just as Kitty had described, a slip of an eighteen-year-old suddenly resembled one of the great lumbering creatures from which our gang had got its name.

At that point, I am ashamed to say that I was quite seduced by the lifestyle into which I had been plunged. I had fine clothes, trinkets and baubles, a better place to live and a pocketful of money. My social life revolved almost entirely around the Forty Elephants, whose parties were a regular feature. Many of the girls drove fast cars and were often employed as getaway drivers, or to transport groups of gang members further afield whenever Annie decided that London was too 'hot'. There was always the risk of getting caught, but somehow that just excited me more. The whole thing was like a game, every new job an elating challenge.

And yet, as time went and the novelty of no longer being poor began to wear off, my conscience began to suffer. I hadn't been raised this way, and deep down in my heart I knew that what we were doing was terribly wrong. A few times I tried to share my feelings with Kitty, but she just laughed and said, 'Look around you, girl. Times are good. Maybe you'd rather be back in the factory, making light bulbs ten hours a day with that Herbert Slacker's hand up your skirt?'

A turning point for me was when, with permission from

*Diamond Annie, I took a train back home to Cornwall to visit
my parents for the first time in the nearly eighteen months
since I had left for London. My father was still as unwell as
ever, and I thought my mother had aged a lot during my
absence. My mother, of course, knew from the larger sums of
money I had been sending home lately that my circumstances
had changed, though I hadn't breathed a word of the truth to
her. But when she saw me in my newfound splendour (though
I had made a conscious effort to dress down for the visit) she
was immediately suspicious and refused to believe my story
that I had been promoted to the top floor of the factory, as an
administrator. How was it possible for an unschooled girl to
have enjoyed such career advancement after just a few short
months? What was I getting up to? Where did all this money
come from? What kinds of sordid liaisons had I become entan-
gled in? Was I the mistress of some wealthy cad? God help us,
had I fallen into prostitution?*

*My mother's hostility took me completely by surprise, and
her questioning went on so that I broke down under its pressure
and confessed all to her, in floods of tears. Hearing my story
my mother became pale with anger, called me a villain and a
disgrace and ordered me out of her house, banishing me from
ever returning and declaring that any money I sent from then
on would be thrown straight on the fire. I wept, I begged; to
no avail. I returned to London a scandalous woman, disowned,
disinherited and broken-hearted.*

*For the next period of my life, while remaining with the
Forty Elephants, I vowed to work towards creating a better,
more honest future for myself. Kitty had her dreams of setting
up her own tea room; for my part I decided to further my*

education. I started crying off the gang's parties and instead attending evening classes to improve my reading and writing skills, my aim being to gain some qualifications in typing and shorthand and perhaps become a clerk or a secretary. These classes were taught at a charity school run by Mrs Evelyn Clifford, an aristocratic lady and a Fabian.

Feigning some lingering, debilitating illness, I turned down several jobs for the Elephants in the hope that Diamond Annie wouldn't smell a lie. The hardest part was to fool my old friend Kitty Kelly, who I sensed was disappointed in her recruit and had cooled somewhat towards me, which saddened me greatly. But the more determined I became to pursue my new future, the more I found myself living in fear that the gang would find me out. When I went to my night classes I took a variety of more and more convoluted routes, constantly glancing over my shoulder in terror of seeing our fearsome leader chasing after me with her ringed fists clenched and ready to gouge my eyes out.

Still, I remained set on my course. It was at the night school that I met a handsome young schoolmaster called Wilfred Grey, who had volunteered to teach English there two evenings a week. Over the following months, he and I grew closer. Sometimes, we met outside of class, and he would read to me and encourage me to read to him, gently correcting me where I went wrong. Wilfred's favourite books were the novels of Anthony Trollope. I had never heard of him, of course, but I was too embarrassed to say.

Gradually, oh so slowly but with a wonderful feeling that it could not have been any other way, we began to fall in love. Looking back, I think it crept up on both of us, and each was just as surprised as the other. Wilfred believed my tale that I was a lady's maid. I felt so bad lying to him, but what else could I do?

His own story was terribly sad. He had served as an infantryman in the war, and returned from the unspeakable horrors of the battlefield renouncing all violence against his fellow Man only to discover that his entire family – his parents, a brother and a sister – had died in the devastating Spanish influenza epidemic that had begun to sweep Europe during the last months of the conflict and claimed untold numbers of lives. He was still much affected by the grief of their loss. I had never seen a man cry before, as he did when he shared his sorrow with me, and I was deeply moved. This was a sweet, tender, soft-spoken and so, so gentle soul with whom I could imagine spending the rest of my life. When he proposed to me in April 1923, I said yes without a second's hesitation.

Now I really was in a mess. Because of course I knew that Diamond Annie would never approve of Wilfred as a match for one of her girls. He was an outsider to our community of crooks and mobsters, a decent and respectable gent even if he had little money, and because of that he was a threat to them. Not long before, I had heard something that sent shivers down my spine. It was the story of a past gang member called Eliza, who had become engaged to a young man called Harry, of whom Annie did not approve. Eliza disobeyed and broke away from the Elephants to marry him, with terrible consequences. The very morning of their union the newlyweds were viciously attacked in the street right in front of the church. The constabulary were called to the disturbance and a violent gun battle erupted in which people were killed – including poor Harry, shot in the heart on his wedding day. I would not, could not allow something like that to happen to Wilfred. If I was to break, it had to be a clean break.

I no longer had any choice but to confess the truth to him, praying to God that he wouldn't react the way my mother had. 'I need you to know, my love,' I said to him through my tears. 'I need you to know, even if you hate me for it. Even if you leave me.'

But I had found the most loving and understanding man in the world, who listened to my confession without a word of judgement. 'You did what you felt you had to do, Violet. That took great courage. Now you need to find the courage to do what's right. Then you and I will leave this city, get married, set up home and begin a whole new life together.'

It sounded so wonderful. But how could we hope to make such a dream come true? My ill-gotten gains had fallen off lately as my commitment to the Elephants slackened. As for Wilfred, he earned so little that he had nothing saved at all. The escape he talked about would cost money, lots of money.

'I have a plan,' I said. 'One more job. One more, and I'm done, I swear.'

'Is there no other way?' he asked, pained.

'Please trust me,' I replied earnestly. 'I can put some cash in our pockets. Not a fortune that we can live off for ever, but enough to make our break and see us through until we find our feet.'

He agreed.

In truth, the job had already been lined up. Feeling that I had the potential for it, Annie had been pressuring me for some time to undertake the most daring robbery of my career to date. Now I accepted it. My appointment having been set up using false references, I was to take up a housekeeper's post at a large, luxurious apartment in Park Lane, the London home of a wealthy gentleman who spent most of his time at his country mansion. I would remain there for two weeks, during which time I would 'case the joint' as Annie described it, and arrange for a convenient time for my fellow Elephants to invade the apartment and pick it clean of anything of value.

It was painful to me not to see Wilfred for those long two weeks. I soldiered through it, however, trying to close my mind to the immorality of what I was about to do. In the event everything went beautifully. When at the perfect moment I called in my fellow gang members to do their worst, I took the opportunity to supplement my share of the robbery by filling a large cloth bag with valuables. The gentleman had a great collection of silverware, some very fine collectables, a pair of gold cufflinks and a jewelled pocket watch I found in a drawer, its reverse engraved with the owner's name; in another I found a thick bundle of cash that I guessed the gentleman must use for expenses during his visits to London. All of it I grabbed quickly, before the rest of the Elephants arrived.

Lastly, running my eye along a bookcase filled with magnificent tomes, I spied a breathtakingly beautiful edition of an Anthony Trollope novel I had heard Wilfred talking about with great enthusiasm. I had never seen a finer looking book. The cover was inlaid with mother of pearl and gold, as much a piece of art as a book. Its title was 'Can You Forgive Her', which I suppose I must have unconsciously considered an apt choice, though this thought process was furthest from my mind as I snatched the book to offer Wilfred as a gift. I fleetingly noticed that it seemed unusually heavy, but there was no time to dwell on the notion as, the very next moment, the Elephants came thumping on the door and I had to rush to let them in, first making sure that my bag of valuables was out of sight.

Within thirty minutes, they had finished their work and they escaped to a stolen van, laden with goods. Alone again in the now-bare apartment, I retrieved my personal spoils, locked up and left on foot.

The robbery had been a roaring success for the Forty Elephants, netting several thousand pounds' worth of loot, not to mention the few hundred more that I had managed to rob from the robbers. If Diamond Annie had known what I was really up to, she would have taken more than an eye for my disloyalty. In fact I wasn't alone in this solo enterprise, because during my time with the gang I had managed to make contact with a 'fence' who now took from me the gold watch (passing it on to a crooked jeweller who could erase the true owner's engraved name), the cufflinks and various other items in exchange for a pretty sum. Added to my percentage of the takings, the reward for having played an instrumental part, this amounted to enough cash to fund Wilfred's and my escape from London and keep us going for a while in our new home. The handsome edition of 'Can You Forgive Her', I kept for myself as planned, waiting for the right moment to present it to my beloved.

Two days later, as rich as we ever would be again, Wilfred and I fled from London never to return. We thought it was the start of a bright new future for us.

How horribly wrong we were! We couldn't have known it then, but we had just sealed our doom.

Chapter 21

And so, we were on our way. The very last thing I did in London was to use some of my ill-gotten gains from the robbery to purchase a secondhand motorcycle combination, the cheapest form of transport we could avail ourselves of. With Wilfred in the saddle, myself wrapped up cosy and warm in the sidecar and our scant belongings strapped to the baggage rack we waved a final farewell to the city and set off on the long, long, rattly, shaky journey northwards.

Our new home was a simple but cosy little stone cottage we had found for rent in Northumberland, far away from the troubles we were leaving behind. It had a small garden, which seemed like a vast estate to us, plenty of room to start a vegetable plot. We were alone at the end of a tiny, lonely road that wound through a moor a mile or so from the village. The countryside reminded me a little of where I had grown up, but somewhat wilder and much colder.

On our first evening there, I cooked us a dinner of chicken and potatoes, and we opened a bottle of wine we had brought from London as a special luxury. As we finished our meal I said to him, 'Wilf, I have a present for you. I wanted to keep it until we got here, as a surprise.'

With that, I proudly presented Wilfred with the beautiful Anthony Trollope novel I had taken from the Park Lane apartment, thinking that he would be pleased. But to my dismay his reaction was anything but favourable, becoming very cross with me and refusing to accept the gift.

'I won't have it, Violet! Do you hear me, I won't have it. How could you have thought otherwise?'

'But you agreed that I should do that last job,' I protested, deeply hurt and stung. 'You knew what it involved. You knew I would be taking things that didn't belong to me. One little book – what difference does it make?'

'I agreed for you to do one last job, yes. But I didn't consent to become your accomplice, and I want no part in it. This is stealing!'

'Yes! Stealing!' I shouted back at him. 'Stealing, for us, for our future. You benefit from my crime as much as I do. It could not be helped, Wilfred. Please tell me, where else were we going to get this money from? How else were we going to get this place, you a poor schoolteacher with barely two farthings to rub together? Or the motorcycle? You had no objections there, as I recall.'

But for all my attempts to reason with my beloved, he staunchly refused to accept the book. Close to tears and quite resenting his rejection of my loving gift, I thrust it in a bag and set off across the moonlit moor with the intention of tossing it in the nearest river, from the humped stone bridge quarter of a mile from the cottage. Deep down I think I knew I had done wrong in taking the book, however I might try to justify it to myself – had not seen it as theft at the time, or at least not in the same order of theft as the rest of the things I had taken – and it was dawning on me how foolish I had been for thinking he would be happy with it. Into the river with it, then, and good riddance!

But then as I strode over the moor my pace slackened and I stopped, and took the book from my bag and looked at it again in the moonlight – and I thought how very beautiful it was, and what an awful shame it would be to destroy it. So, calming my emotions, I decided to keep the book hidden in some secret corner of our home, in the hope that one day Wilfred would change his mind.

How, how, I wish I had acted on my first impulse and rid us of that damned book forever. That book was the ruination of everything.

The next morning, our brief quarrel all but forgotten and its immediate cause now safely stowed away out of sight in the cottage's dusty attic, we began our new life in earnest. Wilfred had already found a schoolmaster's position at the village school, having written a letter of application while still in London. He embarked on his new job determined to impress and succeed, while I set about making our humble little cottage into a perfect home.

We had been passing ourselves off as husband and wife during this time, for the sake of appearances, and using the name 'Mrs Grey' allowed me to erase the identity of Violet Littleton, my shadow-self, now a fugitive from much more dangerous people than the law. But after only two weeks we ended the pretence by getting married for real: the quietest and most private ceremony there ever was, a few miles away in

Rothbury, nothing like the splendid white wedding all girls dream of, but for all that it was the happiest day of my life! At that point, it seemed impossible to believe that all our past troubles could ever return to haunt us.

Ben skimmed over the next dozen or so pages of Violet's memoir, which were an account of the basic but generally happy existence the newlywed Mr and Mrs Grey enjoyed together in rural Northumberland, a million miles from the world they'd known. Planting cabbages and potatoes; fetching eggs and milk from the local farm; pumping water from their own well; gathering firewood; helping Joe the shepherd rescue lambs from the snow; whitewashing the walls of the little cottage in springtime: all the trappings of simple country living a century ago. Within a year of their escape from the city, a child was born – a boy whom they named Charlie; then in late 1923, a second, this time a girl, called Glencora after a favourite Anthony Trollope character of Wilfred's. Absorbed in motherhood, totally devoted to her little son and baby daughter, Violet was able to put her former life almost completely behind her, as though it had never happened. The nightmares in which Diamond Annie would appear at the foot of the bed, ringed fists clenched and grinning maniacally, faded and disappeared. Over time, too, the memory of the stolen book wrapped in a blanket up in the attic slipped from her mind. The one aspect of her time in London that continued to linger in her thoughts was her lost friendship with Kitty. Violet often reflected sadly on the happy days they'd spent together, as close as sisters. She'd have loved to write, perhaps start a correspondence, find out how Kitty was doing, learn if she'd ever progressed with her dream of opening up her own tea room and a thousand other questions she yearned to ask her old friend; but it was too dangerous, and possibly for Kitty, too.

Meanwhile, Wilfred flourished in his teaching job and was as loved by his pupils as he was praised by his superiors. He was soon offered a better employment contract, with slightly more pay that enabled him to pursue his passion for photography. The bad old days were surely now far behind them.

The way Violet wrote about that period of her life, lingering over the details with a sense of nostalgia so heavy you could almost taste her tears, Ben knew the next chapter of the story would be the darkest. His head was spinning with anticipation. Did Diamond Annie and the Forty Elephants have a wider role to play in this mystery? Was that what this was all about: some kind of gangland vendetta dating back nearly a hundred years? Had Emily Bowman hired Carter Duggan to unravel her dead grandmother's connections to modern-day organised crime? And what was the significance of the book she'd taken from the apartment in Park Lane? The way it kept resurfacing in Violet's narrative hinted it was somehow more important than it seemed. But how?

Whatever he was about to learn, the core truth of the Bowman family secret now seemed tantalisingly close.

And as Ben went on reading, he soon discovered that he'd been right. But at the same time, he'd been very, very wrong.

I will never forget the day that everything suddenly changed, and the blissful life Wilfred and I had been leading came to an end as though the walls had come crashing down around us. The day was June fifteenth, 1924.

It started innocently enough. Wilfred was at school that morning when the kitchen basin sprang a leak: the cause being a disconnected drain-pipe, threatening to flood the entire floor, and I with a great mound of dirty linen to wash. Living in the countryside had taught me some rudimentary home maintenance skills, and I resolved to fix the problem myself. Wilfred kept his tools in the sidecar and so had taken them to work, but I recalled having seen a box of old spanners in the attic. Glencora was asleep in her cot. Little Charlie was quietly playing with the wooden train his father had made him. Leaving the children in peace, up I went to the attic to retrieve the box.

How much more dusty and cobwebbed the place had become since I had last been up there. It was while I was searching around among the old crates, broken chairs and assorted junk that I came across the hidden book. So much time had passed, so many events had filled my life that I had managed to completely forget about it until now. Unwrapping the heavy package from its towel and looking at it once more in the dusty light of the attic window was like revisiting the past. Its beauty, its weightiness, the quality of its manufacture, struck me all over again.

Only then did I realise that I had never even opened the book beyond its first couple of gold-edged pages. Doing so now, I began to find myself drawn into the prose of its esteemed author – my reading skills and appreciation of literature had continued to improve greatly over the years. But then as I leafed over from page nine to page ten, I discovered to my utter amazement that the book owed its substantial heft to more than just the magnificence of its binding. Instead of a printed page I found myself frowning in confusion at a grey metal plate with a recessed keyhole. It wasn't a book, it was a safe!

Speechless, I carried it back down from the attic to examine more closely in the light. The thin-walled but strong metal box had been fitted with great expertise inside the body of the book, which had clearly been selected for the purpose on the basis of its size and thickness. Every leaf from the tenth page to the last had had its centre cut away and been laboriously glued to its neighbour, to form a rectangular hollow several inches long and wide into which the secret compartment had been solidly mounted. As to what was inside, with the lid securely locked and no key I could have no idea. Nothing rattled within, when shaken; it could have been empty.

By the time Wilfred returned home from school later that day, I was still so bewildered by my discovery that I could not bring myself to keep it from him. At first he seemed perplexed and irritated at me for having brought back up the subject of our old, forgotten argument – why would I do such a thing? But then, as I thrust the book into his unwilling hands and made him see for himself the surprise it contained, he was no less stunned than I had been.

'What do you suppose is inside?' I asked him.

'I don't know,' he replied. 'It may be nothing at all. Or it may be something of particular value that we should attempt to return anonymously to its true owner, which we can safely do now so much time has passed. And then, Violet, we will put this behind us and never, ever speak of it again. Do we agree?'

Meekly, hanging my head, I consented. Whereupon, Wilfred tucked the book under his arm, grabbed his roll of tools from the sidecar and disappeared into the tiny room that doubled as his study and his darkroom, bolting the door after him. Soon afterwards I could hear the taps and scrapes as he set to work opening the lock. He was a mechanically-minded man and tenacious, despite his gentle nature. Once started on a challenge he found it difficult to let go of, even for the promise of a nice bowl of stew for dinner. He was in there for hours. It was his private domain, which I respected, but every so often I would come and knock at the door and ask how things were coming along. By now the sounds from inside had stopped, and I was sure he must have either succeeded in opening the safe or given up trying. But when he barely responded to me I went off to attend to the children, then some time later retired to bed.

When I woke just after dawn, Wilf's side of the bed was unslept in. He was no longer in his darkroom, where on his workbench I found the book safe prised open and empty; but he himself was nowhere to be seen. Long after he should have set out for work, his motorcycle combination was still parked outside. When he eventually appeared he was sullen, moody and virtually silent. I asked, 'Darling, are you unwell? Tell me what I can do for you.' But he ignored me and locked himself away.

I knew beyond a doubt that something he had discovered inside the book's hidden compartment had affected him deeply. What that something might be, was impossible for me to guess at. Later that morning I tried again. 'Please, Wilf, why can't you talk to me? I'm worried about you. Please come out.'

Leaning close to the door I could detect the pungent chemical smell of his developing chemicals. 'Are you printing photographs? Can I see?' He always loved to show me his latest pictures. But now all he said was 'I'm busy.'

At dinner that night, finally rejoining his family, he still would barely talk to me. I had never seen him look so grim. 'Is it something I have done wrong?' I asked, desperate for some kind of explanation for the sudden change that had come over him.

'No. It has nothing to do with you.'

'Then won't you tell me what's upsetting you so much? Something you found inside the book, I know. And what pictures were you developing earlier? What's the secret? I'm begging you. If something is hurting you, can't you share it with me?'

'Papers,' he muttered, closing his eyes. Then he looked angry with himself, as though he had said too much.

'Papers? What papers? Is that what you were photographing? Why?'

Wilfred sighed and ran his fingers through his hair. 'Please don't ask, Violet. It's better that you don't know.'

It went on like that for three days, Wilfred acting in the same way, withdrawn, silent and plainly terribly unhappy. Something seemed to be eating him from inside, and nothing I could say or do would get him to open up to me. He would disappear for long periods, sometimes on his motorcycle, sometimes on foot. I didn't know if he had taken time off work; I later would discover that he had resigned from his job.

Late on the evening of the third day, as a violent thunderstorm shook the cottage, Wilfred sat me down at the kitchen table and told me there was something he must do. 'My plans are made. Don't try to change my mind. I'll be leaving in the morning.'

'Leaving?' I cried. 'Where are you going?'

'I daresay you'll find out soon enough,' he replied darkly.

'Take me with you!'

'No, Violet.' Reaching out to grip my hand tightly, he looked into my eyes with the utmost intensity of emotion, as though he was bursting with pain. 'And you will have to leave this place, too,' he said. 'After what must happen now, you and the children will no longer be safe here. Lie low. Take care of our babies.'

'I don't understand,' I sobbed, melting into tears. 'What must happen? Why must you go? What are you talking about?'

But he just shook his head. 'All the necessary arrangements are made. When I'm gone you will find an envelope. In it are some documents, along with some money. God knows I wish it were more. Make the best use of it that you can, my darling. And whatever happens, never, ever forget that I loved you with all my heart.'

The next morning, Wilfred rode off and I never saw him again.

Chapter 22

This was a stunning twist in the tale, and it took Ben by surprise as he sat there glued to the narrative. Just as he'd been starting to think this was all about the Forty Elephants, now that idea was blown away. Suddenly, Violet's story had shifted to centre on the Anthony Trollope novel she'd stolen from the London apartment – or, more correctly, what was inside it. Whatever Wilfred had found in there, these obscure 'papers' that he'd refused to tell her anything about had spelled disaster for them.

Just how much of a disaster, Ben was about to find out.

Streaming tears of sadness and confusion, a crying baby in my arms and a badly distraught little boy clutching at my skirt, I watched forlornly as Wilfred disappeared over the horizon. When he was gone I ran to his room where I found the promised envelope. Inside was a thin bundle of cash, a rental lease on a house in Whitby, a hundred miles away, a rail ticket and a letter, sealed in its own envelope. It was addressed to 'My Darling Wife Violet'.

I felt so sick with bewilderment that I could barely read, or hold the letter still in my trembling hands. My eyes took in the words but my mind couldn't comprehend them.

'I must do what I must do,' he wrote. 'And if my plan succeeds, I will become notorious. You will hear things about me, Violet. They will say I was a common burglar, a murderer and monster, the lowest kind of human being, that I cruelly took the life not just of an innocent soul but of a great and worthy patriot and a gentleman who supported our nation in the late war. Please don't listen to their lies, Violet. And no matter what happens to me – whether I am killed in my attempt or whether I am taken, tried and hanged for my crime, as I surely must be according to our laws – you must try to believe that I acted with the noblest and least selfish of intentions.

'It breaks my heart to leave you and our beautiful children, but in all conscience I have no choice. A murderer I may become, but my sins in comparison to that man's will be like a candle glow next to a thousand suns. No more evil person ever walked this earth, nor is likely to again until the day the Devil rises from Hell to claim our world for his own.

'I cannot tell you more, my dearest. Trust that my secrecy on this matter is purely for your protection, for this is a secret too dangerous to be shared with those whom I love. I know this is a great deal to ask of you, but I pray you will understand. And now, Violet, I must ask two more things of you: firstly that you destroy this letter the moment you have read it, lest its possession should implicate you in this affair.

'Secondly, though I know you will find it hard to accept, I ask that you leave home as fast as you can. Whatever happens, I have no doubt that the police will come to interrogate you, and it would be in your interests to avoid them. Even if I succeed in my quest, there will be more evil men seeking revenge for my actions, and they are likely to trace me to my address. Furthermore, news of my crime will travel fast and the press will be in an uproar over the affair. It makes no odds for my name and face to be displayed in every newspaper in the land, but the efforts of some over-zealous reporter could all too easily compromise your anonymity and place you at risk from the villainous characters you left behind in London, who may also come looking for you.

'I would sooner have gouged out my own eyes than put you in danger, my darling, if I had had any choice in the matter. I did not; and for that reason it is urgently important that you waste no time in following my instructions. Abandon the cottage (the lease is soon up for renewal in any case) and take the train to Whitby. You will find the address of the house enclosed herein, along with a note of introduction to the landlord, Mr Cruickshank, a fine gentleman who comes highly recommended and I believe will treat you well. He will know you as Mrs Halsted, and that is the name you must use to protect your identity. The money I have provided will last a while, at least, and I know that you will soon be back on your feet again. The bright, resourceful girl I first met has grown into the most remarkable woman I have ever known. You will have a great life without me, Violet. I wish, wish, wish that I could have been a more worthy husband to you. I hope you will forgive me.

'Go, Violet, I implore you. Kiss the children for me and remember I will always be with you in my heart.'

I could not believe it. I would not believe it. And I could not bring myself to abandon our home so lightly. When I had wept out every last tear that my body had to give I resolved to wait for Wilfred's return. But he did not return either that day nor the next, nor the next after that. Still I waited, and waited. I waited too long.

My first visitors arrived on the afternoon of the second day. I was outside with the children gathering wild strawberries for our pudding when I heard the sound of an approaching vehicle in the distance. At first I thought it was Wilfred and my heart leapt into my mouth. But before I was foolish enough to go running to meet him I realised the sound was of a Tin Lizzie motor truck, and my excitement turned to dread – all the more so when, watching from the bushes, I saw that the truck was carrying two constables in their black coats and tall helmets. Were they coming to tell me that something terrible had happened to my husband? I was terrified that was so, but I still refused to believe it. Or perhaps they were coming to arrest me for my part in whatever he had done! Remembering his advice to avoid them, I kept the children quiet and we remained in hiding. The constables walked up to the cottage, knocked and waited, knocked and waited, then shrugged their shoulders and climbed back into their truck and left.

I should have taken the police's visit as my cue to leave the cottage that same day, but I was paralysed by indecision. It was the worst mistake I have ever made in my life. Because that evening, my second visitors appeared.

I was in the kitchen when I saw the headlights of a pair of motor cars approaching on the moor road, still in the distance. The police returning, or worse? Gripped by a rising panic I rushed upstairs to grab Glencora from her cot and rouse little Charlie from his bed. With my infant daughter in my arms *and holding my son's hand, urging him to keep quiet and praying the baby would do the same, I hurried from the cottage before the motor cars could arrive, and the three of us hid in a rocky dip some distance away. The night was still and cool. Charlie was sobbing and I clasped him tight to comfort him as we watched the cars pull up outside the cottage garden wall. My heart was beating so hard that I could hear it thumping like a drum.*

It was very clear that they were not the police. Six plainly-dressed men armed with revolvers emerged from the motor cars and broke into two groups of three. One group disappeared around the rear of the cottage while the other briskly entered the front door without knocking. They looked very severe and set in their purpose.

'Mummy, I'm frightened,' Charlie whispered in my ear.

He could not have been any more frightened than I was, but I had to act strong for him. 'Shush, my darling. We're perfectly safe here.'

'Where's Minnow?' Minnow was his pet kitten, a present from Joe the shepherd. Charlie was much devoted to the little creature.

'Minnow's fine,' I assured him in a tense whisper. 'Quiet, now.'

All six men had now entered the cottage. I could see lights and movement inside. I heard the crash of something breaking; then a moment later my heart began to beat even faster and I gasped at the sight of flickering flames in the kitchen window. Lord help us, they were setting fire to the place!

The blaze spread very fast, as if the men had set it going with petrol. Its roar filled the air and flames were soon gushing from every window. The men had left as quickly as they arrived, returning to their cars and driving away. But I was terrified they would come back and find us.

That was when I ran, tears flooding down my face, clutching the bouncing, howling weight of baby Glencora to my shoulder and still clasping Charlie's hand. Wilfred's envelope was in my pocket. It was everything I had in the world except for my children.

'Minnow!' Charlie's shout burst from his lips at the same moment that he tore his hand from mine and began running back towards the burning cottage. 'Minnow!'

'Charlie! Stop!' I cried out, but he kept on running. I had Glencora; I couldn't catch him.

And as I watched in unutterable horror, my child ran inside the burning cottage in search of his pet kitten. I screamed his name, over and over, until I thought I would scream my throat out. The heat of the flames was intense and the smoke stung my eyes. Then, with a terrible cracking sound followed by a rending crash, the cottage roof collapsed inside the shell of the walls.

'Charlie!'

But my little boy was gone.

It was hard to read Violet's account of the days that followed. Though she stuck mainly to the facts as they had occurred, the pervasive sense of tragedy seeped through her writing like blood through a bandage. How long she sat staring at the burnt-out cottage before her neighbours from the farm found her, she didn't say. Wanting to avoid any police involvement she made no mention of the arsonists, and told her neighbours that little Charlie was with his father. Exactly what she said to them wasn't clear, but she persuaded them to take her to Rothbury, the nearby town where she and Wilfred had been married, with some story of meeting him there. Ben could only wonder at the incredible self-control she must have had, while inside she was crumbling into an emotional wreck.

Television was still in the future, and in 1924 public radio broadcasting was in its infancy. Few residents of rural Northumberland would have had their own set, Violet's farming neighbours included, and so it wasn't until she reached the town that she saw the newspaper headline screaming from every paper stand: Wilfred Grey, a local schoolmaster and war veteran, had been killed while attempting to murder a respectable citizen in his home in Staffordshire.

To Ben's frustration, Violet seemed to gloss over the facts of the incident, as though she'd been afraid to give too much away even in a private memoir. All she revealed in her account was that Wilfred's would-be victim had got the better of him, shot him dead on the spot and called the police. Back in those distant days when the British government still trusted its citizens to defend their life and property with armed force, private handgun ownership had been common-place. Wilfred must have known the risk, going in. Even if he'd succeeded, he'd have faced the death penalty for cold-blooded murder.

But what was Wilfred doing there in the first place? What could have possessed a mild-mannered schoolteacher, an ordinary man with a stable career and a young family, still less a man who had witnessed at first hand the horrors of war and renounced violence, to travel hundreds of miles southwards to break into a person's home and try to kill them? If Violet had any answers to those questions, she was keeping them to herself, leaving Ben with only one logical conclusion to draw: that it had to do with the enigmatic papers or documents he'd found inside the hollow book.

Whatever the case, in the space of two days Violet had now lost nearly everything in her world, first her little boy, now her beloved husband. Waving goodbye to her life in Northumberland she rode the train to Whitby on the Yorkshire coast and took up residence in the house that Wilfred had rented. Following his instructions she used the name Halsted, and for the next month tried to pick up what little pieces of her life she could, while focusing her energy on taking care of her infant daughter Glencora.

Violet's story of that time seemed to be told as if through a veil, strangely detached. It was clear that she'd fallen into a state of depression, even suffered a mental breakdown. How she'd managed to hold it together, Ben had no idea. The pressure on her must have been tremendous, combined with the racking sense of guilt she felt, believing that she'd brought this whole thing down on her family. If she hadn't got involved in criminal activities, if she hadn't taken the book, her husband and child would still have been alive.

Violet hadn't settled for long in Whitby, and spent the next two and a half years moving aimlessly from town to town, county to county, working through a succession of short-term jobs. Eventually, in January 1927, she'd landed employment as a typist at a solicitor's practice in York. That was where she'd met Eric Bowman, a young clerk working in the same office. Her description of him portrayed a kind, decent man, plodding and unexciting but steady and dependable. In April 1929, they were married. Violet changed Glencora's surname to Bowman, partly for the sake of propriety but mainly to place another layer over her real identity.

Years went by. Violet and Eric's marriage produced no children, but Glencora's stepfather doted on her and happily regarded her as his own daughter. The family lived comfortably until the outbreak of a new war in 1939, when Eric joined the RAF. On 17 October 1942, the Lancaster bomber in which he was serving as a crewman was shot down during a raid on the Schneider Kreuznach industrial works at Le Creusot in eastern France.

It wasn't until nearly four years after Eric's death that Violet, now a widow twice over, finally put pen to paper and set down her long and sad story, with no intention of ever allowing anyone else to read it.

Chapter 23

Ben closed the book and looked around him, realising he must have lost track of time as he'd sat there absorbed in Violet Bowman's story. The day had worn on; the sunlight on the river was softer, and the swans were long gone. He stood and stretched his muscles, aching now from the fight earlier, and it occurred to him that he hadn't eaten a bite since leaving McAllister's early that morning.

Ben slipped the book into his pocket and paced the riverbank, lighting up another Gauloise to help him think. What had he gained? The events of Violet Littleton-Grey-Bowman's life were stunning, but the secret at their core remained mostly intact, like the gold bars inside a bank vault that resisted the most determined efforts to blast it open. Nothing in the memoir explained what Wilfred Grey had found inside the hollow book, or what had made him take that fateful decision knowing it would destroy him and his family.

Had the London townhouse where Violet had carried out her last job for the Forty Elephants belonged to the same man Wilfred would later attempt to kill? Who was he? What had he done to make Wilfred believe he was so evil? Who were the arsonists who had come to burn down the cottage, and caused the death of the little boy? Did they work for Wilfred's would-be victim and was this the act of reprisal that Wilfred had predicted? What secret could have been so terrible that Violet was too afraid ever to breathe a word of it to anyone, even after it claimed the lives of her husband and child?

And on, and on. The more questions filled Ben's head, the fewer answers he could find. This was why Emily Bowman had also needed to take the steps she had, to help her understand the fate of the grandfather and uncle she'd never known.

Ben's first piece of evidence had taken him so far, but not far enough. Now he needed to turn to the second.

Carter Duggan's beer mat was still clasped between the pages of the memoir, like a bookmark. Ben examined it again, trying to make sense of the clues that Duggan had scribbled on it. More than ever, he was certain that these two items fitted together somehow, and that if he could decipher the code he could unlock the missing details from the memoir. That was what Duggan had been trying to do, and what he'd learned had been enough to get him killed.

ACHILLES-14 / Galliard. What could it mean? Was it some kind of weird riddle? Or a code? Ben hated codes and wasn't so keen on riddles, either. Or maybe it was neither of those things.

'Think, Hope, think,' he muttered to himself. The name Achilles was a no-brainer, in and of itself. You didn't have to have studied history to have heard of the greatest and most ferocious warrior of ancient Greek legend, the hero of

Homer's *Iliad*, blessed with almost immortal power after being dipped by the heel in the river Styx as a baby. Son of a king and a water nymph goddess, slayer of the Trojan prince Hector and the driving force behind the fall of the city of Troy.

Okay, fine, but it was perfectly meaningless to Ben in this context. As for the number fourteen suffix, it made the name look like a code or a formula, or even a military designation. But signifying what? Without further information, he couldn't even guess.

Moving on to the word 'Galliard', that one had even less meaning to Ben. Taking out his phone to look it up online, he found that Galliard was a musical term for a kind of dance that had been popular in the Renaissance. A couple of companies had appropriated the name as a brand, one a large property development firm and the other a big pharmaceutical company. Another blank.

If you couldn't think your way through a problem, sometimes it paid to try to think your way around it. Ben reflected on Duggan scribbling those words on a pub beer mat, and what circumstances might have led him to do that. In a world of flashy digital tech it seemed like an old-school thing to do, but then the investigator had been an old-school, low-technology kind of guy, according to his employer. This was a traditional street cop who belonged to the era when detectives and their informants met in smoky bars like spies of old, hunched secretively over strong drinks and passed information scribbled on cigarette packets and matchboxes. Gone were those days – or maybe not quite.

The location of the Man O'War pub in Norfolk was

another potential clue. Had Duggan travelled to the east coast to meet someone there – someone with information critical to his investigation? The scribbles could have been his way of making notes during the conversation if, say, his informant had refused to be recorded. It might be a long shot. But if it wasn't, then the identity of the person Duggan had gone there to meet was of particular interest to Ben.

And short of raising Carter Duggan from the dead to ask him, there seemed only one way of finding that out.

Now, in the late afternoon, Ben hacked further westwards from the city and headed back towards Tom McAllister's place. He felt bad about what he was about to do, but a plan was forming in his head. Arriving at the cottage sometime before six, he saw that the Plymouth wasn't there. That suited him just fine. As he stepped out of the Alpina there was a furious barking, and Radar came tearing out from behind the outbuildings, tail high, hackles bristling and ready to repel intruders in German shepherd style. McAllister hadn't taken the dog to work with him that day, which could have been a problem – but when Radar recognised Ben his threatening behaviour instantly softened and he trotted over to lick his hand and let himself be petted, as docile as a puppy.

'Tell him I'm sorry about this,' Ben said. His regret was genuine, but he had no choice. The lock on the cottage door took him seconds to defeat with his bump key, and he was in. Radar trotted at his heel and followed him into the kitchen. Ben opened a cupboard and found a box of dog biscuits.

'Hungry?' He tossed one and Radar snatched it out of the air. Ben was hungry too, and felt a pang of temptation to check out whatever goodies might be in McAllister's fridge. But he hadn't come here to raid the guy's food supplies. There was something else he wanted to steal instead.

The expired police warrant card was still pinned to the cork notice board on the wall where Ben had seen it last. He plucked out the drawing pin and took it down, examining the ID photo of the younger Detective Sergeant McAllister more closely. Liam Neeson it was not; it didn't look too much like Ben either, but it had the Thames Valley force logo nicely emblazoned on it and the words POLICE OFFICER in bold red, and would do just fine for what he had in mind.

Ben delicately repositioned the photo on the notice board that had been half-hiding the card, so that McAllister was less likely to spot the empty space right away. Then he slipped the card into his wallet and left, the dog still trotting along after him wagging his tail. 'See you around, buddy,' Ben told Radar as he climbed back in the car.

He'd been inside the cottage less than four minutes, and now the time was just gone six p.m. His plan was coming together.

Ben fired up the Alpina. Next stop: the Norfolk coast.

Chapter 24

Jude had figured that if he could just manage to avoid Mickey Lowman, the ferrety-featured, one-eared bundle of charm he'd encountered on his first day in HMP Bullingdon, then he could at least reckon on a reasonably quiet life here behind bars. That was, for the short time he'd be detained in this place. He still had no idea how he'd do it, but his desire to escape burned more strongly with every passing hour.

Yeah, you and the other thousand guys in this shithole, he thought dejectedly as he made his way back to his cell from the prison library that afternoon. You didn't have to be a genius to work out that escape was the top-rated fantasy on the mind of every man in here.

But I'm innocent, Jude reminded himself. How many of his fellow inmates could genuinely vow and declare that they'd been purely a victim of circumstance, just happening to be in the wrong place at the wrong time? He seemed to make a habit of that, he reflected bitterly. Like the time he'd *just happened* to get a crewman job on an African container ship that *just happened* to get itself hijacked by pirates.

And as he walked around the next corner, Jude suddenly discovered that he'd blundered into the same situation yet again: because he'd just happened to turn into a passageway in which he found himself alone with none other than the hulking figure of Luan Copja, the Albanian crime boss.

For once, the most dangerous man in Bullingdon seemed to be without his gang of cutthroat bodyguards. Jude swallowed nervously and paused in his step, trying not to think of eyeballs and red-hot skewers. He'd been in the presence of some pretty nasty characters before now – the Congolese warlord General Jean-Pierre Khosa might just about rival the likes of Luan Copja for nastiness – and in general they weren't his favourite company. Was the correct prison etiquette to walk on by without acknowledging the man, or to offer some gesture of deference? Copja was lumbering along in the other direction, moving slowly like a great ponderous bear and paying Jude as much attention as if he'd been a flea crawling on the ground, so Jude decided to do the same. They passed by one another without a word.

And then the brief encounter would have been over, and Jude and the crime boss would have gone their separate ways. But that wasn't how it played out.

Wrong place, wrong time.

In the next instant, a third man appeared in the corridor, emerging from the head of a metal stairway. He was lean and bald and sunken-cheeked, with tattoos lacing both sides of his neck. He wasn't looking at Jude, but Jude saw the way the bald man was staring at Copja. The Albanian didn't seem to notice him, and kept on slowly up the passageway. The bald man stalked after him, face tense, his body language full of intent, pace quickening step on step. Something appeared in his right fist. Something long, dull and pointed.

It was a shank.

As the scene unfolded as though in slow motion right before his eyes, Jude could see what was about to take place. He'd thought prison hit jobs only happened in movies, but this was real and a man was about to die.

He was under no illusion that the intended victim was any kind of angel. Copja more than certainly had it coming, many times over. But something in Jude's nature just couldn't allow him to stand by and let this happen in front of him. He ran after the bald man and yelled, 'Hey! You! Stop!'

The Albanian jumped like a bull jolted by a cattle prod, and whirled around. The bald man hesitated in his step and glanced back at Jude with his teeth bared in rage. Nobody else was about. For a second Jude, Luan Copja and his attacker just froze, locked in a three-way standoff. Copja could have made a break for it, but there was little chance he could outrun his leaner, faster assailant. He seemed calm. Watching the knifeman. Watching Jude. A thread of a smile on his lips, a wily, knowing expression in his eyes.

'Turn around and walk away, my friend, and you get to live through this day. Or else you will see what will happen to you, hey?' Copja's voice was deep and his accent was thick.

The knifeman's eyes were darting as he quickly worked out his best move. He looked to Jude like a serious and highly motivated thug who wasn't about to be deterred from carrying out his business. Jude thought he was probably getting well paid for it, and faced harsh consequences if he failed. Which meant that by intervening in this private murder attempt and becoming the only thing standing between the hunter and his bounty, Jude had just put himself on the line.

Still, Jude couldn't back down. It just wasn't in him. Call it genetics. Call it what you like. Pure foolhardy stupidity, perhaps. Jude said, 'You heard the man. Come on, you don't want to hurt anybody.'

'Back off, arsehole,' the bald guy snarled. 'Unless you want some of this too, do you?'

'Seriously. You need to drop that thing and walk away right now,' Jude warned him.

'Or what? You gonna take it from me?'

Jude could see the hard hate and desperation flashing in the guy's eyes, and knew he was going to make a lunge at him.

When Jude had gone through his phase of wanting to enlist in the Navy and train to join up with the Special Boat Service, he'd spent some time learning some principles of combat from Jeff Dekker at Le Val. Jeff had showed him some pretty neat tricks. One of those that Jude had mastered quite well during those sessions was a way of disarming someone coming at you with a bladed weapon. He'd practised it quite a bit, although he and Jeff had only ever done it with a plastic training knife. If this maniac made a slash at him, it would be the first time Jude had faced a confrontation with the real thing, and his knees suddenly turned to water at the thought.

'Expect to get cut,' Jeff had warned him. 'Even the best of

the best will avoid getting into a tangle with a live blade, if there's any way out.'

But right now, Jude didn't have any way out.

And then his worst fear came true, because the guy did come at him.

The knifeman wanted Jude out of the way as fast and efficiently as possible, so that he could turn his attentions to his main target and get the hell away before guards turned up. He clutched the shank in an underhand grip, held it high and rushed at Jude trying to punch the blade downwards into his upper chest or throat. There was a lot of inherent power in that movement, using the full tension of the back and triceps muscles to drive the weapon down hard and fast. But Jude had tactics and leverage on his side. Jeff's training flashing through his mind, he deflected the arm clutching the knife and twisted it sideways while pushing the guy's elbow in the opposite direction as it came driving down under its own momentum. The move put breaking strain on the knifeman's shoulder joint and he contorted his body in a bid to reduce the pressure. But Jude followed it through smoothly until the guy was being cranked over sideways in screaming agony, losing his balance and totally unable to prevent it from happening.

As Jeff Dekker had taught him, 'If you can get it to that point, it's game over for the bugger.' And it was. As the pain shredded his nerve endings his fingers involuntarily lost their grip on the handle of the shank. The weapon tumbled to the floor, followed shortly thereafter by its owner. To Jude's amazement and no small relief, the disarming move had worked perfectly.

The bald guy was struggling and thrashing on the floor. Jude still had a grip on his arm. What to do now? Stamp on his head or something? Jude was unwilling to hurt him too much, but it was like having a tiger by the tail. Before Jude had time to decide either way, he heard rushing steps and voices coming up behind, and spun around fully expecting to be rushed by a squad of prison guards.

He was wrong. Three of Luan Copja's henchmen, the same ones he'd seen clustered around their boss in the mess hall, now arrived on the scene to take charge. One of them motioned to Jude to let go of the bald guy's arm. They swarmed around the body on the floor, piling in a furious barrage of kicks and stamps. The bald guy was curled up in a foetal position, trying to protect his face, but in seconds the blood was streaming. Then two of them backed off to attend to their boss while the third threw himself on top of their victim, something in his hand, his arm pumping rapidly. *Shtick-shtick-shtick-shtick*; a high-pitched scream; more blood appearing.

Jude was numb, but before he could react someone yelled 'Guard!' The two henchmen with Copja hustled him quickly towards the head of the stairwell. The third one jumped up from the now inert body of the bald guy, grabbed Jude's arm in a pincer grip and said in his heavy accent, 'We must run.' There was blood on his face.

Luan Copja growled 'Wait!' His henchmen hesitated, darting anxious glances up the passageway where racing footsteps and raised voices were getting closer every second. Copja stepped over to Jude and placed a hand like a crushing hydraulic press on his shoulder. 'Little man, you have saved my life. Thank you,' Copja rumbled, looking Jude earnestly in the eyes.

'We must go!'

The guards were coming. The pair of men hustled Copja down the stairs. The third led Jude the other way along the passage. 'Hurry! Hurry!' A siren had begun to blare. Legs pounding. Heart racing. Tingling with adrenalin and shock. Jude's escort dragged him around a corner and pressed him up against a wall. 'You are a good boy. You say nothing to no one about this. Okay?'

'O-okay,' was all Jude could say. Then Copja's henchman was gone, vanished like smoke.

Jude hurried back to his cell, where Big Dave was reading a magazine on his bunk. 'You okay?'

'I'm fine,' Jude said, somehow collecting himself.

'What's going on out there?'

'I don't know. Think there was a fight. I didn't see anything.'

Big Dave peered at him over the top of the magazine. 'Sure you're okay?'

'Why shouldn't I be? Nothing to do with me.'

'Never said it was, did I?'

Jude clambered up to the relative privacy of the top bunk to close his eyes and let his heart rate settle. He felt sick to his stomach. And something told him this business wasn't over yet.

Chapter 25

It was a UPS delivery driver who found the gunshot body of Emily Bowman's grounds manager in the yard of the big house in Boars Hill just after four o'clock that afternoon and called the police. When the officers arrived on the scene, they made the grisly discoveries of three more corpses inside the house and a fifth elsewhere in the grounds. In response to the bloodbath, Thames Valley rolled out an armed response SWAT team, and soon the property was cordoned off and resembling a war zone swarming with troops, while a helicopter thudded back and forth overhead. The usual show of force that the cowboys liked to put on when the actual threat was long since gone.

In the midst of the mayhem, Tom McAllister's black Barracuda was waved through the cordon and rumbled into the yard to join the fleet of marked patrol cars and armed response vehicles, ambulances and coroner's vans already there. A forensic tent had been set up around the body out front. They were still in the process of bagging up the house-keeper's corpse in the front hallway as McAllister walked in. 'Thins' Waller, head of Forensics, was taking a momentary break from the slaughterhouse and had just got off the phone to his wife to say he was going to be working late.

'Jesus wept, I've seen some godawful bloody messes, but never anything quite like this,' Waller muttered, shaking his head.

'What've we got?'

'Two unidentified shooters and about a million spent rounds of forty-calibre ammunition. Mrs Bowman copped one in the shoulder, one in the back and one in the back of the head. Execution style. This was a professional hit, make no mistake.'

'Until someone hit the hitters,' McAllister said.

Waller nodded. 'Looks that way. Or a couple of them, at any rate. One's got his guts blown out with a shotgun, the other's been stabbed, drowned and beaten half to death. Looks like a bloody battlefield out back.'

'So there's another shooter still at large,' McAllister said. 'A third player, with a different agenda. Except he turned up here too late to stop them.'

'These people have been dead since this morning. Long enough for your mystery shooter to be a thousand miles away by now. I don't envy you, McAllister.'

'Thanks. I was hoping you might have some brilliant ideas to share with me.'

'That's your department,' Waller said sourly. 'My job's to gather evidence, not to have brilliant ideas. And I've got enough work on here to keep me busy for weeks. I'm getting too damn old for this crap.'

'Aye, you're not the only one. Yowch.' McAllister winced and pressed his hand against his right cheek.

'Toothache?' Waller said, knowingly.

'Just a twinge. Started last night.'

'Now I envy you even less, Detective Inspector.'

As McAllister threaded his way through the house, a coroner's team passed him on the stairs, carrying Emily Bowman's body on a covered gurney. Anger rose inside him, thinking about her 999 distress call after seeing the black Mercedes. If that fool Forbes had allowed him to post a patrol car outside the house, none of this might have happened.

There were a lot of loose jigsaw pieces floating around in McAllister's mind right now, but only two questions stood out. Who had reason to kill Emily Bowman? And who turned up to take down the killers?

He was pondering the first question, absently tonguing his tender tooth and hoping it wouldn't get any worse, when his phone buzzed.

'Hi, Sweetie.' There was only one person in the world who would ever call him Sweetie with anything approaching sincerity, and that was Detective Sergeant Billie Flowers. Billie sang bluesy, soulful jazz in clubs when she wasn't working nights, and had a voice to match. Right now she was still at HQ and McAllister had set her to work going through Emily Bowman's recent phone records.

'Anything?'

'Not a lot,' she admitted. 'Except that the last call she made was to a prepaid mobile account. No way we can trace the owner's identity.'

'Got the number?'

Billie read it off. McAllister grabbed a biro and wrote it on the back of his hand. The number looked vaguely familiar to him.

'That's all for now,' she said brightly. 'I'll call you back when I've cracked the case.'

He was putting the phone away when it rang again. 'Christ, can a man get no frigging . . . This is McAllister.'

'I expect to be kept updated, Detective Inspector.' The unlovely tones of Superintendent Forbes rattling his eardrum.

'I just got here. Sir.'

'Have you put a trace out on all black Mercedes in the area?' Forbsie demanded. Can you believe this frigging eedjit, McAllister thought. He felt like replying, 'I thought that was all in her imagination.' Instead he answered truthfully, 'Yes, we have, and nothing unusual or suspicious has come back.'

'Then I suggest you widen the net, McAllister. Obviously I have to do your job for you, seeing as you clearly have no ideas of your own.'

Stay calm. Stay calm. 'I do have one, sir,' McAllister said. 'I think we need to consider the implications for the Arundel case, don't you?'

'Implications?'

'You don't think this puts a different light on things? The fact that Carter Duggan's employer has now been murdered too, while the original suspect was locked up in Bullingdon?'

Forbsie huffed. 'That's for the court to decide. I don't see the connection myself. There could be all kinds of reasons. Arundel could have had an accomplice, for example. Makes sense to me,' he added, already warming to his own on-the-spot unsubstantiated hypothesis.

'Hold on, I'm losing the signal,' McAllister lied, cupping the handset with his hand to muffle himself. 'Go . . . f— . . . y—' He ended the call in disgust, thinking that next time he saw Forbsie he should wring his scrawny neck and be done with it. Or maybe not.

He spent another while touring the crime scene, taking the details in for himself while pondering the second question that had been in his mind. The first was still impossible to answer for the moment, but solving the burning issue of who had caught up with Emily Bowman's killers might not be such a hard one. He looked at the prepaid, untraceable mobile phone number he'd written on the back of his hand, the last call she had made, and realised where he'd seen the number before. It was Ben Hope's.

'*You might have Forbes hanging over you watching every move, but I don't,*' Hope had said to him last night.

To which McAllister had replied, '*As long as you behave yourself, then I can't stop you.*'

But now McAllister was getting worried that he might not be able to stop Hope, whether he behaved himself or not.

Chapter 26

It was approaching nine o'clock that evening by the time Ben arrived in the seaside resort of Hunstanton. Though it was situated on England's east coast, the town itself faced west across the broad estuary of the Wash, and the sun had just finished setting over the sea as Ben parked the car. The Man O'War pub was a traditional low-slung inn not far from Hunstanton's famous striped sedimentary cliffs.

A cool westerly breeze was blowing inshore. He zipped up his leather jacket and walked inside the pub. The nautical theme – ship's bells and wheels and naval art all over the walls – added to the old-world ambience of low ancient beams made from ship's timbers, rough-clad walls and tiny windows. The place was fairly busy and filled with laughter, music and the smell of fried food wafting over from the little restaurant section in one corner. Ben's mouth watered, because he'd still eaten nothing since breakfast. He had a strong hankering for some liquid refreshment, too, but as he was here on duty – albeit fraudulently – it might not be appropriate to walk up to the bar and order a big plate of food and a double scotch.

A portly, cheerful middle-aged barman and a younger woman with red hair in a ponytail were enjoying a break in between serving drinks and laughing over a joke as Ben approached. The barman smiled at him and said, 'What'll it be, mate?'

Ben swallowed back the last bit of temptation, took out his wallet and flashed Tom McAllister's warrant card, holding it out in such a way that his thumb masked most of the ID photograph and letting the guy see it just long enough for him to register the big red POLICE OFFICER lettering. 'I'm Detective Inspector Tom McAllister, Thames Valley Police,' he declared, as though he'd been saying it for half his life. In fact this wasn't by any means the first time that he'd impersonated a police officer, so he was used to adopting the role. It certainly made the job of getting people's coop- eration far easier, without having to point a gun at them. Much more civilised. The bar staff's reaction to the warrant card was the predictable mix of surprise, unease and defer- ence to authority. If either of them thought that this slightly tousled, unshaven blond-haired stranger in leather jacket and jeans was an unlikely sort of Detective Chief Inspector, they didn't show it.

'What can I do for you, officer?' the barman asked.

Ben put away the warrant card, took out his phone and brought up the mugshot image that he'd lifted from Carter Duggan's website earlier that day. Jude had said the man looked like a nasty piece of work, and he hadn't been entirely wrong: the cold eyes, the high patrician brow, the hooked nose and thin lips all hinted at a tough and arrogant kind of customer.

'I'm making inquiries about whether this man visited the area within the last month or so,' Ben explained. 'We have reason to believe that he visited this pub, possibly to meet someone. I'm wondering if you or any of your staff might remember having seen him?'

The barman scrutinised Duggan's picture and his female colleague stepped closer to look, cocking her head. 'I'm pretty good at faces but I don't recognise him,' she said. 'Then again I'm only here three days a week so I could've not been working that day. What about you, Harry?'

Harry seemed keen to help and he was staring holes in Ben's phone screen, but after a long pause he shook his head. 'I can't say for sure. I might have seen him, but . . . You don't have any idea when we're talking about?'

'I don't have a specific date,' Ben said, feeling his heart beginning to sink. Maybe this had been too much of a long shot, after all.

'Trixie might know,' the woman suggested brightly. 'She's here almost every hour God sends. Hang on.' She disappeared through a door behind the bar, calling, 'Hey, Trixie, got a moment?'

Trixie emerged soon afterwards, a kitchen apron strapped around her ample middle. She had short, spiky black hair, heavy eye makeup and a ring through her nose. She gave Ben a lingering look that turned to one of surprise when told that he was a police detective. 'It wasn't me, I swear,' she joked, putting up her hands. 'I had nothing to do with it.'

'I'll let you off that one, Trixie,' Ben said. 'All I want to know is whether anyone here at the Man O'War might have seen this man during the last few weeks.'

'What's he done?' Trixie asked, frowning at Duggan's picture.

'Not much,' Ben replied. 'He's dead. This is a murder inquiry, so anything you can tell me would be much appreciated.'

'No shit,' Trixie breathed. 'Ugly sort of dude, wasn't he? We get a lot of ugly dudes in here. I serve the tables six days a week, so I should know.' Her eyes narrowed to thin white slits within the pools of black makeup. 'Wait a minute. I know what's throwing me off. Did he have a beard?'

'Everybody's got a sodding beard these days,' the red-haired barmaid muttered. 'Disgusting.'

'Takes me back to the seventies,' Harry said, pulling a pint for a customer who'd come up to the bar. 'We were a hairy bunch back then. When I still had hair.' Ben was thrown by Trixie's question, because he had no idea whether Duggan had had a beard at the time of his death or not. 'He might have had,' was all he could reply. The master detective at work.

Trixie tapped at the phone screen with a fingertip. 'Yeah, yeah, he had a big old straggly face fungus like a pirate captain or something. Fit right in with the decor in this place. American guy, yeah?'

With that, Ben felt a tingle of excitement and knew that Trixie was on the right track. 'Canadian.'

'Whatever. They all sound the same to me. He was here Wednesday before last. May fifth. About twenty past eight in the evening, until around nine-thirty.'

Which seemed to Ben like an incredibly pinpointed answer to arrive at, from zero information just moments earlier. He asked, 'Are you sure?'

Trixie nodded. 'Uh-huh. The night we had the big birthday party going on. Table three. Jack Curran's fiftieth.'

'Oh, yeah,' Harry remembered, now finished with his customer and putting the money in the register. 'I wasn't here,' their red-haired colleague commented, helpfully.

'Lucky you,' Trixie said. 'We were run off our bloody feet. Right rowdy lot, they were. That's how I remember it, because the Yank pirate captain and his buddy made a big deal about all the noise the party were making, and moved to the window table over there' – pointing – 'so's they could hear themselves talk. Jack Curran called them a couple of anti-social such-and-suches. Kept yelling for them to come and join the fun. And what a lot of fun they had, too. They smashed about fifty glasses that night.'

'Right, right,' Harry said. 'It's all coming back to me now. I remember the guy.'

'What can you tell me about the person he was with?' Ben asked, hoping that might be coming back, too. Apparently not, because Harry looked blank. Trixie shrugged and said, 'Just a guy. Oldish, nothing I could really tell you. He might've been in here before, or he might not.'

Ben pointed up at the CCTV security camera that was watching them from above the bar. He'd noticed more of them on his way in, positioned around the interior and exterior of the building. Aside from the fact that he was currently being filmed in the criminal act of impersonating a police officer, which wasn't an ideal arrangement, the damn things might be of some use now that Trixie had helped him to narrow down their time window. He asked, 'How long do you keep your CCTV security footage?'

'Law says we have to keep it stored for thirty days,' Harry said.

Trixie giggled. 'Even the cops don't know the law.'

Busted. 'I'm not that kind of cop,' Ben said.

'I'll say,' she replied suggestively.

'I'd like to view it, if I may.'

Harry shrugged. 'Sure, no problem. Come into the office. Molly, can you cover for me for a few minutes?' he asked the red-haired barmaid.

'Do you need me?' Trixie asked, hopeful.

'You've been a great help, Trixie,' Ben told her. 'I wouldn't want to keep you from your job.'

'Do I get, like, a medal or something?'

'Can't do that, but I promise never to arrest you for any crime, no matter how heinous.'

'Cool.'

Ben went through behind the bar and followed Harry into a little backroom with a cluttered desk, a row of filing cabinets and a computer terminal on a table. He was glad that he didn't have to be alone in the office with Trixie. A split-screen video monitor showed the live recorded images from the cameras, in real time. 'The recordings are all kept on that hard drive,' Harry explained, pointing at a black box plugged into the back of the computer. 'Pull up a chair, Inspector. Shouldn't take me long to find the footage you're looking for.'

Harry clicked here and there, opened up a program and hovered over the keyboard as an empty search box popped up. 'What day was it again?'

'May fifth, sometime after eight p.m.,' Ben reminded him.

'Got it.' Harry rattled more keys, clicked and tapped again, and said, 'Okay, here we are.' He hit a play button and the computer lit up with a similar version of the split-screen image on the other monitor, showing various views of the pub's interior and exterior. One covered the car park and beer garden, another monitored the front entrance. The inside of the pub and the corridor leading to the toilets were visible from different angles. If there were blind spots, they were minimal. A little time and date counter in the bottom corner read May 5, 8 p.m. Harry asked, 'You want me to zoom in on any particular screen?'

Ben pulled his chair closer. 'No, keep them all open for the moment.'

At that time of the evening, it seemed that neither Carter Duggan nor his unknown friend had yet arrived. The car park outside was still relatively empty. Inside, Ben could see Trixie and another waitress scurrying about serving food to some diners and preparing a large table that he guessed was for the birthday party.

He asked Harry if he could fast-forward the footage. At a click of a mouse the time counter started to run at quadruple speed. Trixie and the other waitress became super-animated figures, zipping about like ants. At 8.07, cars began to hurtle into the car park and the first of the birthday party arrivals came pouring through the door, crowded the bar and gathered around their table. At nine minutes past, a lone male figure, tall, bearded, broad-shouldered, wearing a tweed sports jacket, appeared on the front door monitor, walking up towards the pub. As he pushed inside he vanished momentarily and then reappeared on the monitors covering the lounge bar area. Ben said to Harry, 'Bring it back to normal speed.'

No question about it, the solitary new arrival was a hairier version of the same Carter Duggan whose image Ben had on his phone. Moving normally now, Duggan paused inside the door, checked his watch and glanced around him as though looking for someone; then went to the bar, ordered a pint of beer and made his way back across to an empty table away from the growing crowd of partyers. Ben pointed to the section of the monitor with the best view of Duggan's table and asked Harry if he could zoom in on that screen.

Duggan settled in place and quietly sipped his beer, glancing now and again at his watch and keeping an eye on the door. More people were turning up now, mostly in twos and threes, and the place was filling. At 8.12, the door swung open once more and this time another man entered on his own. As Duggan had done, he paused near the doorway, looked around, and his gaze landed on Duggan, who had seen him come in and half-rose to his feet, waving. The man walked over to the table and they shook hands, a little stiffly and formally, not like friends but rather two people who had never met in person before.

Duggan's contact was an older man, slightly built with receding grey hair. He wore a neat grey suit and looked fairly affluent. After a brief detour via the bar, the pair settled at their table. The older man pointed at Duggan's pocket and seemed to say something that Duggan was unhappy about. The Canadian paused a beat, then took out his phone and laid it on the table. The older man picked it up as though checking it, then left it lying between them as they fell into deep conversation.

Behind them, the party was getting into full swing, centred around its boisterous birthday boy, a red-faced loudmouth who was waving his beer around and looked like he was having a great time. Duggan shot the party table a few disgruntled looks as the volume rose, and after a few more minutes he broke off his conversation and motioned towards the window seat as though suggesting to his contact that they should move there. It was just as Trixie had described. Once reseated further from the partyers, their quiet, private conversation resumed. The older man seemed to be doing much of the talking. Who was he, and what were he and Duggan talking about?

Ben asked Harry to fast-forward again. The time counter wound onwards at high speed. Nine o'clock came and went. The levels in the men's glasses were dropping, Duggan's more slowly than his companion's. At 9.03 p.m. the older man stood up and returned to the bar for a refill. While he was gone, Duggan reached across the table, slid a beer mat off its edge and into his lap, whipped a pen from the breast pocket of his tweed jacket and was seen to scribble something on the mat.

Bingo.

Ben asked Harry to replay that moment at normal speed. As the older man returned from the bar with his second drink, Duggan quickly slipped the beer mat into his pocket.

'Do you know him?' Ben asked, pointing at the older man.

'I can't say that I do,' Harry said, looking doubtful. 'He's not exactly what you'd call distinctive looking, is he?'

Just then the office door opened and Molly, the red-haired barmaid, said, 'Harry, the Theakston keg needs changing. I can't get the gas valve thing open.'

'I'll be there in a moment.' Harry looked nervously at Ben. 'I need to take care of this.'

'Don't worry about it,' Ben replied. 'You've been very helpful.' Which was true enough, though what had been gained from it was virtually nil. He still had no idea why Carter Duggan had come here to meet the older man, the purpose of their conversation and the meaning of what Duggan had written on the beer mat. Apart from that, it had been a highly successful mission.

'Sorry we couldn't do more for you, Inspector.' Harry must have been able to see the disappointment on his face. Ben stood up from his chair and was about to reply when Molly happened to glance across at the computer monitor; something caught her eye and she pointed and said, 'Hey, that's Joe.'

A superbright magnesium flare erupted in pyrotechnic splendour in Ben's mind. He said, 'Joe?'

She nodded casually. 'Uh-huh. Joe Brewster.' She was completely sure of it, not a shred of doubt in her eyes. 'I've not seen him in the pub before, but I know him. My mum used to work in his shop.'

Ben asked, 'What shop is that?'

'The little antique book place in town. It's right on the High Street. You can't miss it.' Then Molly frowned, suddenly remembering who Ben was, or at any rate who he was pretending to be. 'Is Joe in trouble?'

Ben smiled and shook his head. 'Not at all. I was just

210

eliminating a lead in my inquiry. Routine stuff, happens all the time. Mr Brewster's got nothing at all to worry about, as far as I'm concerned.'

'I'm pleased to hear it,' Molly replied, the frown melting.

'I'd better go and get this keg sorted out,' Harry said. 'Is there anything else we can do for you, officer?'

'As a matter of fact there is,' Ben said. 'Can you grill me a steak, medium rare, with chips, a couple of beers and a double shot of your best single malt scotch?'

Chapter 27

Within hours of the fatal stabbing of the inmate whose name had now emerged as Jimmy Leggitt, HMP Bullingdon Prison was in an uproar. The governor and her staff flew aggressively into action, making all the expected sabre-rattling media statements in which they vowed to weed out the perpetrators and tighten up security, threatening a total lockdown of the facility pending a major investigation. There were cell searches for weapons, grillings and interrogations of the usual suspects, and the rumour mill went into overdrive.

Jude was aware of the curious way Big Dave kept looking at him, as though secretly wondering whether he knew more than he was letting on. 'You're kind of quiet,' he commented during dinner that evening.

'I'm just feeling a bit tired,' Jude said. 'This place gets me down.' As if that even needed mentioning.

'Yeah, well, better get used to it, pal, 'cause you're gonna be here for a good while yet,' Dave told him, shovelling food. Jude said no more. He'd noticed that Luan Copja and his men were absent from the mess hall.

After dinner they had fifteen minutes before the 7 p.m.

twelve-hour lock-up. Dave declared that he was going for a walk and had to see someone about something. Jude wandered back to the cell alone, hopped up onto his bunk and was getting immersed in the much-thumbed Clive Cussler thriller he'd borrowed from the prison library when the door opened. 'Enjoy your evening stroll?' he asked, without looking up from his book.

'Hey, my friend,' said a deep, rumbling, heavily accented voice that didn't belong to big Dave. Jude laid down his book and glanced around, startled, but somehow he wasn't too surprised to see Luan Copja standing in the cell doorway, flanked by two of his henchmen: the one who'd done the dirty on Jimmy Leggitt and the one who'd whisked Jude away from the scene. Jude wondered if the third one was somewhere outside, keeping Big Dave at bay – because something told him that Copja was here for a private conversation. The Albanian was smiling and looked relaxed, but there was a hard gleam in his eye.

'Been talking to people about you,' Copja said.

'I hardly know anyone here,' Jude replied.

'But they know you. I heard you had a problem with some asshole.'

Jude shrugged. 'Not really.'

'The guy with the one ear,' one of Copja's henchmen said, pointing to the side of his own head. 'Name is Lowman. Mickey Lowman. He talks too much. Been going around telling folks he made you piss your pants and cry like a baby.'

'He's full of shit,' Jude said defensively. 'I can look after myself.'

Copja grinned. 'Sure you can. Sure. But we can all look

after each other too, right? That's what friends are for, no? And you and me are friends now. You do something for me, I do something for you.'

'I'm not asking for anything from you,' Jude said.

'You are proud,' Copja said. 'I like that.'

Jude sensed they were building up to something. Then out it came. The other henchman, the knife killer, looked penetratingly at him and said, 'You don't like it here, right?'

Which seemed like the strangest question for one prison inmate to ask another. Jude quipped back, 'Are you kidding? I'm having the time of my life. After the court sets me free, I was thinking maybe I'll ask to stay on.'

The crime boss thought that was hilarious. He reached out a fist the size of a pineapple and thumped Jude's shoulder so hard it would leave a bruise. 'You're a funny guy.' But his knife killer henchman went on looking at him, unsmiling. 'You could always leave. Would you like that?'

'Sure,' Jude replied. 'I'm working on getting out of here just as soon as I can.'

'Is that right?' Copja said, suddenly serious again. 'How do you think you will do that?'

'Oh, I have a master plan,' Jude told him.

'You hear that, boys? He has a plan.' Copja tapped the side of his nose. 'Plan is good, my friend. But you got to plan it right.' Then he winked at Jude. 'See you around.'

With that, the three of them turned and walked off. Jude let out a long breath, leaned back down on his bunk and thought, 'What the hell was *that* all about?'

Chapter 28

Feeling invigorated with half a pound of grilled steak inside him and the pleasant burn of the whisky on his lips, Ben left the Man O'War shortly after ten-thirty and drove around Hunstanton. Passing down High Street he spotted the tiny little shop, sandwiched between a jewellery store and a coffee bar, with a retro painted sign saying BREWSTER'S ANTI-QUARIAN BOOKS. The windows were shuttered for the night and there was nothing Ben could do until morning. He drove on until he found a hotel, a grand old house that was just a two-minute walk from the beach and had vacancies.

The four-poster bed and balcony with a panoramic view of the moonlit seascape were much more luxury than a man like him needed, but sometimes you had to go with the flow. He dumped his bag on an armchair, locked his captured SIG pistol in the combination safe next to the bed, raided the mini-bar for another whisky and took a walk down to the beach to breathe the night air and listen to the crash and roar of the surf.

'I'm getting closer, Jude,' he murmured to himself, barely audible over the waves.

But was he really, or was that just what he needed to believe?

He took his time the following morning, filled with impatience to be there waiting when Brewster opened up the shop but opting instead to let the guy settle into his daily routine and catch him at his most unawares. It was a bright morning and the sunlight dappled the sea with a billion twinkling diamonds. He went for a run on the beach, took a long shower, drank two large black coffees in the hotel bar and smoked a Gauloise on his balcony before heading back into the town.

It was 9.25 when Ben parked the car down the busy, bustling High Street from Brewster's Antiquarian Books and walked up to the shop, brushed and shaved and looking a little more like the respectable plainclothes police officer he'd be masquerading as one more time. A bell tinkled as he entered. The shop was a quaint old place, not especially well maintained, peeling paint and saggy floorboards. It seemed even tinier on the inside than it appeared from outside, crammed from floor to ceiling with aisles of dusty, faintly mildewed-smelling tomes that Ben found hard to imagine anybody wanting. Judging by the emptiness of the shop, it seemed that the citizens of Hunstanton generally felt the same way.

The only other living soul in the place was a young woman standing behind the counter, by the window with a view of the street behind her. She smiled sweetly at Ben and wished him good morning. 'Please feel free to browse all you like.'

'Actually, I was hoping to speak to the proprietor, Mr Brewster. Is he around?'

The young woman's smile melted quickly and there was a dart of nervousness in her eyes. Ben wondered whether Brewster had told her to be wary of anyone looking for him. If that was so, it was interesting. The news of Carter Duggan's death would have reached his ears as well as anyone else's, but maybe Mr Brewster understood a little more about the reasons behind it. If Brewster was worried because he knew why Duggan died, that meant he was potentially in on the secret. The young woman replied hesitantly, 'Uh, ah, may I ask what it's . . .'

Ben took out the warrant card. This time he kept his thumb over the Thames Valley police logo and crest as well as McAllister's picture, because he needed her to think he was a local cop. 'Police. Is Mr Brewster here?'

Mixed emotions showed on her face, a combination of relief and worry. 'Is there some problem?'

Ben gave her a reassuring smile. 'We've received reports of a gang of specialist book thieves operating in the area,' he told her, improvising wildly. 'I'm speaking to owners of shops like this one, to advise them to be on the lookout. It really would be better for me to talk to Mr Brewster in person.'

The young woman looked blank. Swallowed. 'Oh. I see. That's awful. Uh, you just missed him, I'm afraid. He only came in for a few minutes this morning to collect some paperwork.'

Ben regretted that he hadn't got here sooner. 'He's gone home?'

She glanced out of the window and pointed across the street at a silver Volvo estate parked a little way down on the opposite side. 'His car's still there. He said he was popping over to the chemist's. You might still be able to catch him.'

Ben thanked her and left the shop. Glancing down the street he saw the pharmacy sign forty yards away on the opposite side, near where the silver Volvo was parked. He was crossing the road when he saw the slightly built, grey-haired man from the Man O'War's CCTV footage emerge from the chemist's shop clutching a paper bag. Picking up a prescription, Ben thought. He hoped Brewster's health wasn't too fragile. He needed the guy to be in reasonable condition when he started getting some answers out of him.

Brewster reached the silver Volvo before Ben could flag him down, and got in. A puff of exhaust, his indicator flashed, and Brewster pulled out into the traffic and set off. Ben hurried to the Alpina, jumped behind the wheel and followed him.

Brewster drove southwards out of Hunstanton and along a fast A road that cut diagonally inland, past suburban housing and a heritage centre and a leisure resort and a golf club. Traffic was thin and Ben hung cautiously back, keeping the Volvo just in sight for a couple more miles, until he saw it turn off the main road, following a sign for Sedgeford. Not wanting to lose him Ben sped for the turning, accelerated hard to close the gap and then slowed again as the Volvo came back into sight. Sedgeford was a medium-sized village with a lot of red-brick and stone houses. The other side of it, Brewster's indicator flashed again and he turned into the driveway of a large, impressive country home that stood a good distance from its nearest neighbour, with stripy lawns and stone barns, elegant arched windows and tall chimneys.

Ben rolled to a halt a little way from the driveway entrance and walked up to the property. From what he'd seen of the area, he would have guessed that housing prices around here were sky-high. Brewster's home looked like a lot of house for someone who owned such a humble, slightly decaying little secondhand bookshop that was unlikely to generate a hell of a lot of revenue. Maybe he was just a rich eccentric.

One thing Brewster wasn't was a keen gardener. As Ben approached the house he noticed the overgrown lawn and the unclipped shrubs that were encroaching on the bay window in front. The Volvo was parked around the back, ticking gently as it cooled. Ben knocked at the door and waited a minute before it opened.

Brewster had been home long enough to take off his coat and put on a comfortable cardigan and slippers. His expression was anxious as he peered from the doorway. Up close, his complexion looked sickly and yellowish. Not a well man, by the look of him. Ben held up the warrant card. 'May I have a word, Mr Brewster?'

'I . . . Is this about the book thieves?' Brewster's young helper must have phoned him on his mobile while he was en route back home.

'We should talk inside, if that's all right with you,' Ben replied.

Brewster seemed reluctant, but led Ben into the house. The interior, like the outside, spoke of an income level far above anything the shop could earn him, unless he had some racket going on the side. Brewster led him down a flagstone passage to a living room full of classic leather and oak. The bay window overlooking the front lawn was the one Ben had seen on his approach, the view half blocked by over-grown shrubs and bushes.

'Is Mrs Brewster at home?' Ben asked.

'There is no Mrs Brewster,' Brewster replied. 'I live alone.'

Exactly what Ben had expected to hear, judging from the state of the garden. Most married men wheeled out the lawnmower at least now and then, for the sake of harmony. 'My mistake.'

'Can I offer you a cup of tea, Inspector . . . I'm sorry, I didn't catch your name.'

'No, thanks. Have a seat, Mr Brewster.'

Brewster perched nervously on the edge of a large wing chair. Ben positioned himself on a sofa between Brewster and the door. He said, 'I'm afraid I misled you regarding the nature of my visit today, Mr Brewster. The fact is, I haven't come here to talk about gangs of book thieves. I'm here to talk about a man, recently deceased, called Carter Duggan.'

Brewster turned pale and flinched as though Ben had slapped him. 'Carter who?'

'Come on, Mr Brewster. Let's not play games. I have evidence to show that Duggan travelled to Hunstanton on May fifth, and that you had a meeting at the Man O'War pub. You're a known associate of a murder victim, and I believe you have important information to share.'

Brewster chewed his lip anxiously and glanced towards the door as though he wanted to bolt through it. 'I . . . yes, uh, I knew that he had been murdered. Was I supposed to come forward to the police? Am I in trouble?'

'Not necessarily,' Ben said, laying on the ambiguity like a weapon and playing Good Cop and Bad Cop rolled into one. 'But I'd like you to tell me what your meeting was about. Did you know Mr Duggan personally?'

'Not at all. Never met him before in my life.'

Which Ben had already suspected. But his question was just a bridge to lead on to his next: 'Then why would he have travelled across half the country to meet up with a total stranger?'

A long pause. 'I was asked to talk to him,' Brewster confessed.

That was strange. Ben said, 'Asked by whom?'

Brewster was sweating. 'I'm not in any trouble?' he repeated.

'Not unless you've done something wrong.'

'I haven't. I swear.'

'Then you have nothing to fear,' Ben told him.

Brewster pulled at his fingers as he spoke. 'I can explain, but it's complicated. You see, Mr Duggan was interested in some information that an associate of mine has. It was my associate he first reached out to.'

The joys of phony authority. Doors that normally had to be smashed down just flew wide open when people thought you were a copper. Ben asked, 'And your associate is who, exactly?'

'Someone who, for particular reasons, is very, very careful about whom he meets,' Brewster replied mysteriously. 'And so, he asked me to contact Duggan, arrange a face-to-face with him and get a sense of whether he was genuine. I set up the meeting, careful to arrange it in a public place where I'd be safe.'

'Had you any reason to believe you wouldn't be safe

otherwise?' Ben asked. 'Meaning, did you or your associate regard Duggan as a threat?'

'Not especially,' Brewster said. 'We were aware of his background, of course, though that in itself wasn't a concern. But those were the rules I was set. If I had thought Duggan was kosher, my associate would have agreed to meet him in person. After speaking with Mr Duggan, however, I decided it was better to err on the side of caution. He seemed too interested in money.'

'I think you'd better explain,' Ben said.

Brewster shifted nervously around on the edge of his seat, knowing he'd already committed himself. 'Do I have to?'

'If it has a bearing on my investigation,' Ben said, 'then I'm afraid you do.'

'There's, well, you see, there's quite a bit of background to it. It's a long story.'

'I love long stories,' Ben said. 'And I'm all ears.'

Brewster sat there knitting his fingers and frowning deeply. He heaved a deep sigh, then went on: 'In my career I worked as a senior chemist within the R&D department, then later in sales and marketing, for a well-known pharmaceutical company. One that I prefer to remain anonymous.'

'For the moment,' Ben agreed, wondering where the hell this unexpected twist was leading. 'Go on.'

'Three years ago, I began to form suspicions that the company I worked for was involved in illegal activities. These have never been proven, which is the reason I'm careful not to name names.'

A recent memory flashed into Ben's mind, of the big pharmaceutical company that Duggan's beer mat scribbles had prompted him to look up. It had seemed like a blind alley at the time. He asked, 'Is the company called Galliard?'

Brewster's face turned a shade paler at the mention of the name. 'The Galliard Group. Then you know already.'

'I have my sources. What kind of illegal activities?'

Sweating profusely, Brewster hesitated a few moments. 'Why are the police asking me this? Are my former employers under criminal investigation? Am I going to be asked to testify?'

'Answer the question,' Ben said. 'Or you will be in trouble.'

Brewster sighed. 'Oh, God. Very well. Do you know what botox is?'

The question threw Ben a little off track. He replied, 'It's a beauty treatment. Some kind of gunk that a lot of women with more money than sense get injected into their face to help with wrinkles.' Not that any of the women in his life had ever subjected themselves to such bizarre tortures, as far as he was aware. Then again, so much of what the opposite sex did was, and would remain, a perfect enigma to him.

Brewster nodded. 'Correct. How it works is by paralysing the nerve signals to the muscles, so they can't contract, and the lines around the eyes, mouth and forehead become softer and less noticeable. It's actually the most popular non-surgical cosmetic treatment in Britain and several other countries, hugely in demand. The product is widely manufactured under many different trade names, and generates a fortune in income for companies like the one I worked for.'

'The Galliard Group,' Ben said.

'Correct. Like all their competitors, they can't produce

223

enough of it. As well as the beauty industry it's also used in mainstream medicine to treat a variety of conditions, such as muscle spasms and migraine. But if its millions of happy users knew what it really is, they might think twice about having the stuff pumped into them.'

Chapter 29

Brewster explained. 'Botox is short for botulinum toxin, a neurotoxic protein that is in fact the most deadly poisonous chemical substance known to man. In doses only slightly higher than those routinely used in cosmetic medicine, it causes paralysis and rapid death by respiratory failure. Extremely small doses can be, and are, fatal. To give you an idea of just how lethal it is, one gram of hydrogen cyanide, as used in Nazi death camps during the Holocaust, has the power to kill six people. By comparison that same single gram of botulinum toxin, ingested, would be easily sufficient to kill over five million people. If aerosolised, that number potentially rises to one and a half billion people.'

Those seemed like crazy numbers to Ben. 'One *gram*?'

'Correct.'

'So your former employers manufactured this stuff.'

Brewster nodded. 'Oh, by the truckload. They still do. And as I said, they're by no means the only company producing it. '

'You said you suspected them of illegal activities. I gather they're not breaking any laws simply by making botulinum for the beauty industry.'

'No, none at all,' Brewster replied. 'It's all perfectly legit, on the face of it. Some people, myself included, find it somewhat ironic, not to mention dangerously insane, that a substance of such eminent lethality managed to become the first biological toxin to be licensed for human treatment, back in 2002, and is now a multi-billion-dollar industry in its own right. But whether or not you think it should be banned, it's very much legal. My suspicions arose only by chance.'

'This is what you talked about with Carter Duggan?' Ben asked, trying to see where it was going.

'It's all connected,' Brewster replied. 'I did say it was a complex story.'

'Then keep talking.'

'As I told you, most of my career was spent in the laboratory, and then in sales and marketing,' Brewster went on reluctantly. 'Six years ago, a few months before my retirement, I was asked to stand in for a sick colleague in another department, part of whose job involved warehouse inspections. It was a responsible position and I was a trusted long-time staff member, and I was happy to fill in. Now, the company manufactures many different product lines and has thousands of clients around the world. I was responsible for checking details of shipments to their respective destinations overseas. Everything was carefully coded and organised. In theory, the system should have almost run itself and errors and oversights should have been virtually impossible.

'But one day, not long after I took over my new duties, I came across a packing slip attached to an unusually large botox shipment with the destination put down as Sirte, Libya, with a code that didn't seem to match my paperwork. When I cross-checked it against the computer records, I discovered that no such shipment was due, and the code didn't seem to exist. By the time I had finished double-checking, the shipment was sent on its way even though I hadn't signed off on it. When I mentioned this irregularity to my superiors, I was pretty much given the brush-off and told that some clients used a different coding system or other. It was all a bit odd and vague, but at the time I let it go. Then a few weeks later, the same thing happened again. This time, the destination was Baghdad, Iraq. When I went back into the system to check the shipment codes, the records had strangely disappeared. As though someone had been purposely trying to hide the tracks of those botox shipments. Now I was beginning to think something fishy was going on.'

'You were concerned that shipments of the toxin could find their way into the wrong hands?' Ben said.

Brewster nodded. 'Who wouldn't be? Botulinum toxin has been used as a bioweapon many times in the past. The US Government produced it under the codename "Agent X" during World War Two. It's thought the Japanese conducted experiments with it on Chinese, Korean and American POWs. Later on, in the 1980s, the German Red Army Faction terror group were caught manufacturing the rubbish, thankfully before they had the chance to use it. So here I was, looking at these mysterious shipments that appeared to have been sent without a trace to some of the world's more politically unstable regions, both of which had, or have had, strong ties to terrorism. And we're talking about seriously large amounts of product, hundreds of pounds. If someone with evil intentions could release even just a tiny pinch of it in the air outdoors, at least ten per cent of all the people downwind for a third of a mile would die a horrible death, or at the very least be severely incapacitated. Imagine the effect of a concerted attack within a confined space like a city subway system at rush hour. It's unthinkable.'

'Did you report your suspicions to anyone?'

'I never got the chance,' Brewster said. 'It appeared that my computer checks hadn't gone unnoticed. Soon afterwards, I was invited up to the top floor of the company building and brought in to meet a pair of chief executives I'd never seen before. I was informed that for economic reasons Galliard were thinning out their senior personnel who'd been there for twenty-five years or more, and that my name was on the list. They were offering an extremely generous golden handshake. So generous, that you'd have to be an idiot not to see it for what it was, kiss-off money.'

'How many other Galliard staffers were offered the same deal?'

'As far as I was ever able to ascertain, I was the only one. Their layoffs story was a lie. It was a transparent attempt to silence me, because they knew about my suspicions.'

'How much of a payoff are we talking about?' Ben asked.

'Just a shade over a million pounds. Part of the deal was that I had to sign a non-disclosure agreement that prohibits me from discussing any aspect of my work for the Galliard Group, to anyone, for as long as I live. So you understand my reticence in telling you all this. Not that anyone would ever be able to prove that the company was illegally peddling lethal biotoxins to dodgy clients. They're far too clever, and extremely rich and powerful.'

'And you took the money.'

'You'd have to be a bloody fool to turn down an offer like that. I retired here to the coast, bought this house, opened the shop as a hobby business – I've always had a passion for old books – and I've been very comfortable for the last five years. Financially speaking, anyway. My health's falling apart and I'm plagued by my conscience. That's why I stayed in touch with Miles. Especially after what happened to Suzie.'

Ben blinked. He was missing something. 'Hold on. Miles and Suzie? Who are they?'

Brewster looked annoyed with himself for having let the names slip, but it was too late to take it back now. He shrugged and said, 'You see, I wasn't the only one who suspected that Galliard were up to no good. Other people had doubts, too. But not everyone got off as lightly as I did.'

'Did Miles and Suzie work for the company too?'

'That's where the two of them met. He was a lab technician and she worked in the accounts department. Poor girl,' Brewster added, shaking his head sadly. 'Those filthy bastards.'

'What happened to her?'

'She was killed in a terrible car smash, about a year after I retired from the company. In fact "killed" doesn't quite do it justice. She was decapitated. It was horrible.'

'By "filthy bastards" I'm assuming you don't believe it was an accident,' Ben said.

'No, I don't,' Brewster replied. 'These people are as ruthless as they're rich and powerful. Makes me think about what might have happened to me, if I hadn't taken the deal.'

'And Miles?'

'He quit his job after that. He was destroyed by what happened, and for a long time I was certain he was going to do something crazy to get his revenge on them, but he didn't. Now he keeps a low profile, uses a different name. I'm not quite sure what he does for money.'

Ben was thinking hard. 'Is this Miles your associate? The person Carter Duggan first contacted, before you were asked to meet with him?'

'That's right,' Brewster admitted.

'If he keeps such a low profile, then how was Duggan able to find him?'

'Miles is much more involved in these things than I am. He posts articles on the dark web about the illegal activities of pharmaceutical companies. I can only assume that Duggan was a skilled enough investigator to come across his name and decide to get in touch.'

Ben was slowly piecing the fragments together. 'Let me get this clear. Are you saying that Duggan approached your associate to learn more about Galliard's shipments of botulinum to suspect countries? Is that what this is all about?'

Brewster fell silent for a long moment. Sweat was rolling down his brow. He puffed out his cheeks and sighed. Then he said, 'No, that's not the reason. I told you there was a lot of background. Everything I've told you is leading up to the real story. Because Galliard have been involved in terrible things for many, many years. Long before my time. I can only tell you so much. Miles is the real expert on the matter.'

Ben looked at him and could see he was telling the truth. Brewster was scared to death, and wouldn't have been willing

to reveal a fraction of what he had, if he hadn't been intimidated into it by Ben's fake police persona. Or unless he'd
had a gun pointed at his head. The SIG pistol was in Ben's
pocket for that reason, just in case it proved necessary.

Ben asked Brewster, 'What's Achilles Fourteen?'

Brewster looked confused for a second, then the look of
fear in his eyes became even more acute. 'I . . . I . . . how
did you . . ?'

Ben said, 'You made Duggan hand over his phone before
you started talking, so that he couldn't record the conversation. Who carries a tape recorder any more? I'm guessing
that was part of Miles's rules of engagement. But the moment
you turned your back and went to the bar for another drink,
Duggan grabbed a beer mat from the table and used it to
scribble down a couple of notes. Now I know what one of
them means. But I think the other is even more important,
and now you're going to tell me. I repeat, what is Achilles
Fourteen?'

Brewster stared at him, his pallid face suddenly flushing
purple. He jerked unsteadily to his feet, as though the sudden
movement made him dizzy. 'Wait a minute. There's no way
the police know any of this. Because if you did, you wouldn't
have come to me, you'd have gone after Galliard. You're no
police officer. Let me see that warrant card again.'

Ben said patiently, 'Sit down, Mr Brewster.'

'You're working for Galliard, aren't you? You're fishing to
find out how much I know and then you're going to murder
me like you murdered Duggan. Admit it! Think I didn't
know you people have been following me, watching every
move I've made ever since our meeting?' Brewster let out a

wild laugh. 'Go on and kill me, then. Put a bullet in my brain. You'll be doing me a favour. My doctor says I'll be dead in six months anyway. You want to know what it feels like, swallowing fifty pills a day?'

Ben stood up, pulled the SIG from his pocket and pointed it at him. 'I don't work for Galliard, but you can rest assured that I'll do whatever it takes to make you talk to me. Make this easy on yourself, Brewster. Tell me what Achilles Fourteen is, and I'm gone.'

There was a moment's silence as they stood facing off.

And that was when the attack came.

Chapter 30

At the top of a high-rise corporate headquarters building, alone in a palatial office suite with a panoramic view of the city, were two men. One of them, seated in a plush leather chair behind his enormous desk and gazing deep in thought out of the window, was the CEO and president of the multi-billion-pound company that had been founded by his illustrious grandfather all the way back in 1908. The senior executive with him, pacing up and down the length of the huge Qashgai rug in front of the desk with a phone clamped to his ear, was his immediate subordinate and VP of the corporation, a man named Jasper Hogan.

The Chief found Hogan's pacing profoundly irritating, but he sat quietly gritting his teeth and waiting for the feedback from the phone conversation he was having with one of their associates in another part of the country. Their man on the ground was doing most of the talking, while Hogan prompted him with terse questions like 'Are you sure?' and 'What are they doing in there?' and 'Are your people in position?'

Hogan's boss closed his eyes and reflected on the situation.

A lesser man might have been deeply unsettled, even panicked, by the events of the last few days. But like his father and his grandfather before him, he was a robust and determined individual who refused to accept that any crisis, however threatening, couldn't be handled. He'd faced serious challenges before, and not only survived them but seen his company thrive and grow from strength to strength regardless.

Still, he was perplexed, even worried.

Young Arundel's chance appearance at the crime scene and subsequent arrest for the murder of Carter Duggan had seemed like a stroke of luck at first. But then Ben Hope had come along and changed everything.

It had been one of their trusted agents, present at Oxford Magistrates' Court the morning of the bail hearing, who had reported back to them the surprise development that Arundel's biological father had entered the equation. Until that moment, they'd all been under the impression that Arundel's parents were both deceased. Which wouldn't in its own right have presented a problem, except for the fact that a swift and extensive background check of this Major Hope's military record (or the parts of it that they'd been able to access) had revealed the slightly shocking truth that the only living relative of the man who was conveniently taking the fall for the elimination of Carter Duggan was an experienced and battle-hardened professional warrior, leader and strategist with a list of credentials they'd have longed to be able to make use of for themselves, under different circumstances. Few of the men they now and then had had occasion to employ to take care of certain unpleasant matters were half as qualified. Some were military veterans themselves, specialised in the uglier kind of contract work that men with their particular skillsets were able to carry out: it was one of those that the Chief's second-in-command was talking to on the phone at this moment. Needless to say, the troops on the ground had no idea who their real employers were, or what purpose they were serving by following their orders.

For the first couple of days after Arundel was carted off to jail, all had been quiet. During that brief lull, the Chief and Hogan had dared to hope that their concerns were unfounded. Maybe Arundel's father would simply return to his home in France and hold back from getting involved. Maybe everything would be okay. But yesterday that optimism had been blown to pieces when their clean-up operation against Emily Bowman had turned into their worst nightmare. The meticulously planned disappearance of the bodies, the burning of the house to erase all evidence, couldn't have been more disastrously aborted. Fine, Bowman was dead, but the operation had failed in its main objective. The lid was off the box now. The police were involved. Questions would be asked. And you didn't need to possess the gift of clairvoyance to work out who was responsible for wiping out their operatives.

Ben Hope was back in the picture. And he was an even more serious liability than they'd feared. Because now the Chief and his co-conspirator Hogan suspected that Hope might have made off with the important piece of evidence their operatives had been sent there to obtain, the memoir of Emily Bowman's grandmother Violet that had sparked

Carter Duggan's potentially damaging investigation into their company's activities in the first place. If the memoir had now fallen into Hope's hands, it meant he was on their trail, too. A man like him could hurt them far, far more than some greedy washed-up ex-cop from Ottawa. What did Hope know? How close was he to working out the whole truth?

And now, as though yesterday's developments weren't troubling enough, had come this morning's news from the leader of the operatives who'd been deployed to the east coast to eliminate Joe Brewster.

This time, the Chief and his second-in-command weren't taking any chances. In the wake of the messed-up Bowman operation the clean-up team was bigger and better equipped than the first. No more unmitigated bloodbaths. Their orders were to move in hard, fast, silently and unseen, snatch Brewster from his home and discreetly remove him to a prearranged location where he would be injected with a carefully selected and blended cocktail of chemicals that would be swiftly lethal and untraceable. Brewster's medical reports, which they had no problem hacking into, showed that his health prognosis was poor, at best, giving them a nice opportunity to take advantage of. Once he was dead, the body would be returned to his home, changed into pyjamas and tucked up in bed; and as far as the rest of the world was concerned, poor old Joe Brewster had tragically succumbed to the illness that had been slowly eating him away. They'd send flowers to his funeral.

But that plan, too, was now sunk. When the snatch team had turned up at Brewster's house that morning with the intention of either taking him right away or waiting until he got home from the shop, they'd discovered not only that their target was at home but that he had a visitor. The blue BMW Alpina D3 with French plates and left-hand-drive was parked near the gate, and it was registered to their new nemesis, Ben Hope.

When the team leader got straight on the phone to alert his bosses, it sparked a red alert. There was no longer any question that Hope knew far more than he should – enough to have led him to Brewster, which meant he was tagging Duggan's footsteps quite closely. Which also meant he knew what they themselves had only recently discovered, ironically thanks to Duggan: that Brewster had key information concerning their organisation and its illegal activities. Information that must not be allowed to spread any further.

The Chief had had enough of listening to Hogan prattling on the phone. He swivelled around from the window and silenced the conversation with an impatient gesture. 'For God's sake, we need to put an end to this right now.'

Hogan pulled the phone from his ear and cupped the handset. 'What do I tell him?'

The Chief didn't need long to consider the remaining options.

He replied, 'Change of plan. Tell him to move in and shoot them both.'

Chapter 31

If Ben's full attention hadn't been fixed on Joe Brewster at that moment, he might have sooner noticed the stirring in the overgrown bushes outside the window. It was his sixth sense that saved him, that almost preternatural instinct honed through half a lifetime of danger and warfare to alert him when an enemy was close.

A fraction of a second before the shotgun blasts destroyed the centre panes of the bay window, Ben was already wheeling away and swivelling his drawn weapon. At the same instant the figures of two men were rearing up out of the bushes, both dressed in black, both clutching short-barrelled auto twelve-gauges that they levelled to their shoulders and fired. Glass and buckshot sprayed into the room to the sound of twin bombshells. Brewster screamed, staggered and fell, pulling the wing chair down with him.

Ben didn't know if Brewster was hit. There was no time to find out. Just like there was no time to take careful aim at the enemy before they emptied their weapons into the room and killed everything living inside. Ben was a fast pistol shot. Sweeping multiple targets right to left he was super-fast; sweeping left to right he was exceptional. He set his front sight on the guy on the left, centre of mass, pure instinct, gun and hand and eyes and brain all melding into one, and double-tapped his target before the muzzle blurred ten degrees right to engage the other even as the first one crumpled at the knees and began to fall.

Then, silence. Smoke oozed from the muzzle of Ben's gun. Four rounds gone. Fourteen remaining. No reloads. Once they were gone, they were gone. And there was no telling how many assailants he was up against. One thing he knew for sure, they would attack harder and in greater numbers than they had at Emily Bowman's house – and he knew the reason why. It was because this time, they knew he was here.

One body was twitching in the bushes outside the shattered window; the other was inert. The air in the room was sweet with the tang of burnt powder. Ben raced over to Brewster. He had blood on his face where he'd been hit by flying glass, but after a quick pat-down Ben decided he hadn't taken any buckshot. Ben grabbed an arm and gathered him up. 'On your feet, Mr Brewster. We don't have a lot of time.'

He'd got to Emily Bowman's house too late to save her. This time, he was ahead of the curve, if only by a hair. And he was damned if he was going to let them have Brewster so easily.

Ben could hear more men swarming inside the house. While the first two had stalked up to the front window, others had invaded from the rear. He contemplated the risks of trying to escape through the shattered window and decided they were too high. No telling how many more could be lurking in the garden, ready to appear from nowhere and blast them at the vulnerable moment when Ben was helping Brewster out. No, their best chance was to run the gauntlet through the house.

'Wh-what's going on?' Brewster muttered. His eyes were darting and he was pale. The effects of shock kicking in.

'Come on. Move.' Ben wrapped an arm around him and held him close, holding the pistol one-handed as they made their way towards the door. They were three steps from it when a percussive blast sounded from the other side. Wood splinters and plaster exploded from the frame. They were trying to pin him in here, which meant more were racing towards the front window, ready to pour in overwhelming firepower. Ben wasn't content to wait for them. He punched three rounds through the door as fast as he could pull the trigger, and heard a short, sharp cry from the other side. Eleven rounds left. The door hinged outwards. He crashed it open with a savage kick and saw the man down in the passage nearby, lying spread out in a red pool, still clutching his weapon in one dead hand. Another man was making a hurried retreat down the passage, firing behind him as he went: a wild shot that gouged a trench out of the wall a foot from Ben's shoulder. Ben chased him with two more rounds, but the running man managed to reach cover around the corner and the pistol bullets slammed harmlessly into the plaster.

Nine rounds left. Ben jumped over the body, dragging Brewster along with him by the wrist. Brewster made no attempt to resist him, dazed and muttering 'Oh my God, oh my God'. Ben had no time to stoop down and gather up the dead man's fallen weapon, and with Brewster in tow he couldn't handle a heavy shotgun one-handed as well as a pistol. No point in checking the body for ID because there wouldn't be any. Ben pressed on, every nerve in his body jangling as he sensed the presence of the enemy all around. Brewster was like a dead weight trailing along behind him, severely compromising his ability to fight. But there was no way he was letting Brewster go.

Ahead, the man around the corner ducked back out with his shotgun pointing from the hip and squeezed off a shot, missing Ben and Brewster but blowing a wall lamp into pieces. Ben popped two more fast shots back at him, so fast that the snapping reports sounded like one, and this time the man didn't duck back around the corner fast enough. Blood flew up the wall. He stumbled and slipped and went down.

Four men dead, seven rounds left. It was a dangerous balance. *Keep moving.* Ben kept an iron grip on Brewster's wrist and jerked him along behind him. The guy on the floor wasn't quite dead yet, sliding around in his own blood and trying to get to his feet. He wouldn't last long. Not worth wasting another bullet over. Ben trampled him brutally, dashed his head against the floor and moved on. Around the corner, the way ahead was clear. The front entrance hallway was in sight. But several more rooms lay to their left and right, before they could reach the door.

There was no going back now. Ben strode fast up the passage. A door to the left flew open; a figure stepping out to block his path; the big fat O of the shotgun muzzle ready to rip loose a deadly blast. Ben could no longer afford the luxury of double- and triple-taps. When the pressure was on, you just had to be faster and more accurate. His sights locked on target and he fired once and the forty-calibre bullet smacked the man in the dead centre of the forehead and he tumbled back, crashing into a wall and leaving a red streak down the flowery wallpaper as he slid to the floor.

Five men down for thirteen rounds gone, only six remaining. Getting close to the entrance hall now. Then they were at the door and bursting through to the outside. Ben was ready to confront more attackers appearing from any direction, but there were none. Had he got them all? It was too risky an assumption to make, but despite himself he felt a stab of relief and triumph penetrate the adrenalin-charged battle mist like a shard of sunlight.

'Where are we going?' Brewster mumbled. 'This is my home! I'm not leaving!'

'Shut up and keep moving,' Ben told him. They hurried past Brewster's Volvo, and around the side of the house towards the gate. Just the other side of it, a black van was parked. The attackers must have rolled up to the house in neutral with the engine off, or Ben would have heard them coming. These were professionals. But professionals paid by whom?

The keys were still in the van's ignition. Ben reached in the open window and plucked them out and hurled them over a hedge into the neighbouring field.

'Where are we going?' Brewster gasped. He was clutching at his chest and having trouble breathing.

'To my car.'

'Please, stop, I can't run any more.'

Ben bent at the waist, pushed his shoulder into Brewster's

middle and wrapped an arm around the man's thighs and hoisted him up into a fireman's lift. He'd carried plenty of men like this before, when they were injured in battle or training. Those were big, burly comrades in peak physical condition and full kit; Joe Brewster was a spindly little guy with barely a scrap of muscle on him. Ben ran for the Alpina. Still no sign of anyone coming after them. Maybe there really was nobody left to come after them. Still, Ben didn't want to put it to the test. He reached the car, blipped the locks and tore open the back door and bundled Brewster inside.

'Where are you taking me?'

'Somewhere safe.'

Ben ran around to the driver's door and jumped in behind the wheel. Instants later the engine's throaty howl rasped loud, the tyres bit down hard into the dirt and sprayed mud and grass into the air as the Alpina took off like a missile.

They were away clean.

And then, suddenly, they weren't.

As Ben accelerated away from the house, three men burst from the roadside bushes just ahead of them and sprinted into the road. They'd skirted around the side of the house in an attempt to head him off. Planting themselves in his path like a human roadblock. Bringing their weapons to bear on the speeding car.

Ben yelled at Brewster to get his head down and did the same, ducking down behind the dash and driving blind as he rammed his foot down and hurtled straight towards the men in the road. A ragged series of blasts hit the front of the car like hammers and the windscreen above Ben's head dissolved into an opaque web of cracks. Then the nose of the Alpina ploughed into the legs of one of the men with a grisly thump before he was able to get out of the way, and his body rolled and cartwheeled up over the bonnet and the roof. The white windscreen was painted red. Then he was tumbling lifelessly to the ground in their wake. His two companions had managed to sidestep the impact of the car and delivered their point-blank blasts into its left flank as it surged by them, blowing out the side window and what was left of the windscreen.

Ben straightened up behind the wheel, glass fragments cascading off him, yelling, 'Brewster? You okay?' No reply from the back. Brewster was still hunkered down low in the space between the seats.

Ben yelled, 'Hold on tight!' as he stamped on the brake and threw the car into a sideways skid so that it howled to a halt broadside across the road, tyres smoking, rocking violently on its suspension. The two shooters were coming on with their weapons raised, pumping shot after shot into the Alpina's flank.

If there had been just one man left standing, Ben would have dearly wanted to turn the car around and go after him, run him down and take him alive to find out who the hell he was working for. But not two; and now it was too late because it was just a matter of time before one of the shotgun blasts ended him. Ben extended his pistol and rattled off all six of his remaining bullets, rapid-fire. One man went down, then the other. And then there were no rounds left in Ben's pistol, and nobody left to shoot at.

Now Ben saw a car coming down the road, from the direction of beyond Brewster's house. It was still several hundred yards away, but it was approaching fast and in less than thirty seconds it would reach the slaughterhouse scene with dead bodies strewn about the middle of the road. Ben had no intention of being around when that happened. He stamped on the gas and took off again, leaving black ribbons behind him. Fifty miles an hour; the needle climbing to seventy; to ninety. The wind blast from the glassless screen filled the car like a hurricane, making tears stream from his eyes. He drove like a wild man for two miles along the empty country roads, then pulled over and twisted around in his seat to look into the back.

'Brewster?'

That was when Ben saw the gaping gunshot wound in Brewster's neck.

Chapter 32

They say that dead men don't talk. But Joe Brewster had one last piece of information to offer from beyond the grave. When Ben checked the mobile phone he found in Brewster's trouser pocket he discovered among his contacts list a number for someone called Miles Redfield.

Miles, the former Galliard Group employee whose girlfriend Suzie had been killed in a possibly suspicious car smash. Miles, the person Brewster had described as 'the real expert' on the dubious practices of the company, whatever those might be. Were Galliard behind this whole thing, rubbing out anyone who threatened to get too close to their secrets? Was that the trail Carter Duggan had been on? What had Brewster meant when he'd said that Duggan was too interested in money? And how did any of this connect with the memoir of Violet Bowman and the unexplained death of her husband Wilfred almost a century ago? Trying to figure out the puzzle felt like walking into a mind maze that could trap you forever and drive you crazy for lack of answers.

Ben was banking on Miles Redfield having those answers. But it wasn't something that could be done over the phone.

Before he could go any further, he needed to find alternative transport. The Alpina looked exactly like a car that had been in the middle of a furious gun battle, and with a dead body in the back Ben preferred to avoid drawing too much attention to himself.

Ben wasn't sentimental about motor vehicles. Nobody who'd destroyed as many of them as he had, by various means, could afford to get too attached. But the prospect of getting rid of the car presented a challenge. You could burn it; you could bury it; you could dump it in the sea. Or you could simply abandon it and hope nobody would ever find it. All of which alternatives were either wishful thinking, practically unfeasible or completely useless. He was going to have to improvise.

The opportunity came five miles further down the road when Ben skirted by a village and saw a sign that said RICK'S SCRAPYARD. The place was just beyond the edge of the village, surrounded by ragged wire mesh fencing and filled with heaps of rusted-out bodyshells and axles and tyres and old gearboxes. Ben liked scrapyards. They were great places to make things disappear. At the centre of this one, visible from the gates, was a crane with a magnet the size of a tractor wheel dangling from four chains. Next to the crane, some kind of giant machine was rumbling and gnashing and grinding. A car crusher.

Ben drove in through the gates. There was a hut that doubled as a reception office, but it appeared empty. The only person in sight was a kid who was perched up in the cab of the crane, yanking levers and preparing to demolish an ancient Toyota pickup. Ben stepped out of the Alpina and walked over, waving with a friendly smile. The kid waved back, grinning a goofy grin. He couldn't have been more than seventeen, and looked inoffensive but perhaps not quite the full ticket. In a different setting he might have been sitting on a rundown porch wearing a backward baseball cap and plucking a banjo. Ben guessed that the machine couldn't be that hard to operate.

'Are you Rick?' Ben yelled over the noise, knowing he wasn't. The kid stopped what he was doing, paused the crane and shook his head. 'He's my dad. He's not here.'

Which was what Ben had wanted to hear. He reached for his wallet and shelled out five twenties that he held up towards the crane cab. The kid gawped at the money and said, 'What's that for?'

'It's yours, if you buzz off for ten minutes and don't tell your dad I was here.'

The kid considered this, poking out his tongue in concentration, then nodded. 'Okay.'

When he had disappeared inside the hut, Ben ran back to the Alpina and parked it next to the Toyota pickup, emptied all his things from inside, then clambered up into the crane cab. He ran his eye across the controls, quickly figuring it out. The crane grumbled and rumbled and rotated on its base until the giant magnet dangled from its chinking, rusty chains directly above the Alpina's roof. A tug of a lever, and the magnet descended and clamped into place with a loud *clang*. Another tug, and the chains snapped taut and up came the car with its buckshot-riddled panels, its blown-out windows and its hidden back seat passenger.

Ben swivelled the crane around until the car was suspended

over the crusher, gently swaying. The jaws of the great hydraulic press waited below. Ben felt a slight pang, more for Brewster's sake than for the car's. It was a hell of a way to be buried. He wondered if he should say a prayer, but nothing appropriate came to mind. So he thought *fuck it*, bade a quick goodbye to the vehicle and its occupant, and pulled the lever that lowered the car into the maw of the crusher. At the press of a button the monster machine went to work with a terrible crumpling and crunching.

By the time the kid returned from the hut, the D3 Alpina had been transformed into a cubic metre of compacted metal and plastic with a human body encased somewhere inside.

'That your car?' the kid asked.

'Used to be.' Ben jumped down from the crane cab, took his wallet back out and offered the kid another sheaf of notes.

'What's that for?' the kid repeated, eyes bugging at the cash.

Ben pointed at a line-up of old bangers that were awaiting scrapping. He said, 'That's for the keys to any of those that still runs.'

Fifteen minutes later he drove off in his new acquisition, a twenty-year-old wreck of a brown Land Rover Defender with one red door, a rotted chassis, mouldy seats and a holed exhaust held on with a wire coat hanger. If the thing had a couple hundred miles left in it before it crumbled into a pile of rust, that was good enough for him.

He called Miles Redfield from the road.

'Joe?' said the nervous voice on the line.

'Joe Brewster is dead. Unless you want to wind up dead, too, you need to talk to me.'

Chapter 33

Miles Redfield sounded like a man living in fear. At first, he was unwilling even to talk, and Ben twice had to persuade him not to hang up the call.

'Why should I trust you? I don't know who the hell you are.'

Ben spoke calmly and patiently. He repeated, 'Someone with a personal interest in knowing what's behind the murder of a man called Carter Duggan. I believe it's connected to a company called Galliard.' He added, 'And the death of your girlfriend Suzie.'

There was a long, heavy silence on the line, then a sigh. 'She wasn't my girlfriend. She was my fiancée. We were about to get married when they killed her.'

'Then meet me,' Ben said. 'I need to know what you know.'

'Why?'

'Because if what you're saying is right, these people are going down.'

Miles Redfield asked, 'And you're going to take them down?'

'Who else is going to do it? You?'

'You've no idea what you're talking about. Not the remotest clue who these people are, what they're capable of.'

Ben replied, 'I think I have a reasonable idea. But I need your help, Miles. What's it to be?'

Another long pause, another sigh. 'All right. I'll meet with you.'

They arranged it for late that night. Miles Redfield lived in Tower Hamlets in London, and gave Ben directions to a supermarket car park. 'If I think this is a setup, you'll never see me,' he warned. 'And you should know that I'm armed.'

It would have been a two-and-a-half-hour drive in an average car and under two in the Alpina, but the struggling Land Rover only just managed to make the distance in three. It was raining heavily as Ben reached his destination, using his phone GPS to navigate through the slick, wet night streets. He parked in the furthest corner of the supermarket car park, giving him a wide-angle field of view as he waited, smoking in the darkness and watching through the rainwater ripples that ran down his screen.

The rendezvous was set for eleven-thirty. Twenty minutes before the appointed hour, Ben saw a Volkswagen Beetle that was in almost as terrible condition as his Land Rover pull into the near-empty car park and cruise slowly under the lights. Ben slid down in his seat and watched as the Beetle circled the whole car park as though searching for something, then retreated to the shadows of the opposite corner. Three minutes later, Ben saw a raincoated figure slip furtively out of the Beetle and skulk away to hide behind a row of recycling banks.

Miles Redfield might have thought he was being cautious by turning up early and getting into a concealed position to spy from a distance, but he wasn't very good at it. Not good enough to notice Ben's ghostlike exit from the back of the Land Rover, if indeed he'd noticed the vehicle at all. And certainly not good enough to have any idea of what was coming as Ben spent a full fifteen minutes skirting the edge of the car park, methodically slipping from cover to cover, moving as only a person trained in urban covert operations knew how to move.

The first Miles Redfield knew that he wasn't alone was when Ben was standing right behind him, and reached out of the shadows to touch him on the shoulder. The guy jumped as though he'd been shot, crashed into the nearest of the recycling banks and almost fell over, grappling to wrench something from his jacket pocket and getting all tied up. He'd been right about being armed, for what it was worth. Ben snatched the plastic BB gun from his hands as it appeared. 'Don't be silly, Miles. I'm not going to hurt you. Now let's go somewhere we can talk.'

Ben followed the Beetle through the night streets as Miles Redfield reluctantly led him back to his place. He lived in a poky second-floor flat in a downbeat-looking estate that was all grubby concrete stairways and rusty iron railings and graffiti-sprayed walls. The rain was falling more heavily now. They were both dripping as Miles showed Ben inside the flat and offered him a cup of tea. For once in his life, Ben accepted, just because it was warm and wet.

They carried their steaming mugs from the minuscule kitchen into a tiny, dismal living room and Ben settled on a threadbare sofa opposite his nervous host. They sat in silence for a few moments, if the drumming of the rain on the windows, the aggressive thump of rap music, the howl of a baby coming through the paper-thin walls either side and the shriek of a police siren a few blocks away could be called silence.

Ben glanced around him at the room. There was hardly a corner that wasn't piled high with stacks of books and bulging files, periodicals and boxes of old newspapers. Papers and notebooks covered the floor and more sheets were stuck all over the walls. It looked like the room of a demented student swotting for impossibly difficult final exams or feverishly working on some abstruse PhD thesis. Miles Redfield obviously spent a great deal of time in here. But for what purpose? Ben was about to find out.

Slowly, Miles Redfield began to talk. He apologised for the state of his home, which sadly reflected the level of poverty he was forced to endure. Because he lived under a false name he was reduced to doing whatever menial cash-paid day jobs he could find here and there. By night he blogged on the dark web, immersed himself in his studies and research, and had devoted himself to preaching the evils of the Galliard Group and its ilk. When he mentioned Galliard a blaze of hatred burned through the sadness in his eyes. At the root of it all was his bitterness over what he believed they'd done to his fiancée. He laid down his mug for a moment to fetch a framed photo from a side table. He clasped it lovingly in his hands, then held it out for Ben to see. 'That was her.' The picture showed a happy, smiling young woman with golden hair and vivid blue eyes.

'I'm sorry about Suzie,' Ben said. 'And about your friend Joe Brewster. I did everything I could. I won't fail again.'

'I don't understand why you're involved in this,' Miles said, and Ben gave him a quick summary of events since Jude's arrest for the murder of Carter Duggan.

'What's Galliard to you?'

'Nothing,' Ben replied. 'I'm interested in one thing only. Nailing the guilty man so that the innocent man can go free.'

'How much do you know?'

'Only what Brewster was able to tell me. If this whole thing is about botulinum toxin, then there's a lot that I don't understand. Such as what the hell the connection can be between a dodgy pharmaceutical company and a dead woman's handwritten life story from the 1920s.'

Miles gave a bitter laugh. 'I can't tell you about that. But one thing I can assure you of is that Galliard's crimes go well beyond what Joe might have told you. He didn't know the half of it.'

'Then I think you'd better fill me in on the rest,' Ben said. 'From the beginning.'

And so Miles did.

The first part of his story overlapped with what Brewster had already told Ben. He had been working as a laboratory chemist for the Galliard Group for a couple of years when he'd met Suzie Morton, a recent hire in the accounts department. After not too many weeks, they'd fallen deeply in love. Miles choked up every time he mentioned her name.

As well as being the best thing that had ever come into his life, Suzie had been a genius at accounts. She'd been the first to notice certain carefully concealed anomalies in the books, all of them mysteriously pertaining to shipments of Galliard's own brand of botox to customers in particular parts of the Middle East and North Africa. When she shared her findings with Miles, he was at first hard-pressed to believe it, then intrigued, then horrified and angry.

'I knew she was right. Before I knew it, I was fully on board. The deeper we dug, the more the anomalies didn't add up.' The pair had soon come to the conclusion that Galliard were selling highly suspiciously large quantities of botulinum toxin, under its own beauty skincare brand, to countries that didn't normally have a great demand for beauty products. Payments were being deliberately obfuscated, straw man accounts created, shipping codes doctored.

'We got even more suspicious when the leader of the opposition party of a certain African country that happened to have received a Galliard shipment a month earlier, along with his entire family and retinue, reportedly died of an unknown cause with symptoms that resembled botulism poisoning. We couldn't find any solid connection, but what if Galliard was secretly supplying dictators and terrorists with deadly poisons under the guise of beauty products? We became fixated on the idea.'

Even more so, when Miles and Suzie found out through the grapevine that a senior supervisor called Joe Brewster had been let go after going around asking questions about similar concerns.

'We met with Joe a couple of times outside work, but at that time he didn't want to know. He'd had his big money payoff and was scared to get involved. Soon afterwards he bought a new house and moved away from the area. We were alone again, and determined to find concrete evidence that Galliard were committing crimes. Suspicions weren't enough. Once we'd got some irrefutable proof under our belts, we'd be able to go to the authorities.'

'So I'm guessing you never did,' Ben said, 'or you would have.'

'I'm coming to that. Deep under the Galliard HQ building is a network of cellars where old archive documents are stored. We had a crazy idea that we might find something incriminating down there, and crazy ideas lead to crazy actions. One day we stayed behind after work, hiding until everyone had gone home. When it was night, dodging security patrols we sneaked down to the basement and broke into some safes.'

Miles went to slurp his tea, but it had gone cold. 'We didn't find what we were looking for. What we found instead was something far, far worse. Something that makes peddling botulinum toxin to terrorists look like petty crime.'

Ben guessed what was coming. 'Achilles Fourteen?'

Miles peered at him curiously with narrowed eyes. 'Achilles?'

'That's the name Joe Brewster gave to Duggan. I thought it looked like a code of some kind. Or a military designation. I sense that you know the real answer.'

'I do,' Miles replied. 'But before I tell you, are you sure you want to go down this road? Because if you do, there's no coming back. You should be careful what you wish for.'

'You're damn right I'm sure,' Ben said.

So Miles told him. 'What we found in a safe down in that

basement were old photographs of documents dating back to the time of the First World War, over a hundred years ago.'

Chapter 34

The revelation made Ben's mind start to whir. The historical connection linked back to the time period of Violet's memoir and the subject of Carter Duggan's research for Emily Bowman. 'Keep talking. I want it all.'

Miles Redfield asked, 'What do you know about mustard gas?'

Ben's heart was thumping. 'Only that it was a pretty damned nasty chemical weapon, back in the day, and it had nothing to do with mustard.'

Miles nodded. 'Its chemical name is bis(2-chloroethyl) sulfide. It's colourless in pure liquid form but in the First World War a more impure form was used that had a mustard colour and an odour similar to horseradish or garlic, hence the name – like you say, it had nothing to do with mustard. It was a powerful irritant that caused chemical burns and severe blistering on contact. Initial exposure was symptomless but by the time the skin infection showed itself, it was too late to take preventative measures. The mortality rate was only around two to three per cent, but those who suffered burns from it faced a long hospitalisation, plus a greatly increased chance of developing cancer in later life.'

Ben said nothing. He was remembering that Wilfred Grey had served in World War One. Had he been one of those long-term victims of the gas? Maybe; but it didn't address the question of what he'd found inside the hollow book Violet had stolen from the London apartment.

Miles went on, 'In other words it was nasty, but it wasn't a great battlefield weapon because its effects were too limited and slow. What do you care if the enemy soldier who's trying to blow your brains out gets cancer twenty years later? You want him dead now, so he can't pull a trigger. Right?'

Ben couldn't argue with that logic. 'Go on.'

Miles said, 'Officially, the Brits didn't deploy mustard gas until as late as 1917, but the Germans had been using it fairly extensively. His Majesty's Government was under pressure to fight fire with fire. The idea of spraying chemical agents on the enemy was appealing but they wanted something better, more effective, that could not only take out enemy troops but bring a rapid end to a conflict that everyone had thought would be over in a matter of months but seemed to be dragging on with no end in sight. So the British War Office set up a secret department within MI1, Military Intelligence, with the remit to develop more effective chemical weapons that could help to win the war quickly and decisively. In early 1915 a lucrative government contract was handed to a private British company called Clarkson Chemicals, which had been founded in 1908 by its owner Elliot Clarkson. Their top secret objective, officially classified to this day, was to create a more potent, faster-acting form of mustard gas. It wasn't until

259

decades later, in the Second World War, that they'd realise you could boost the gas's lethal properties by distilling it in its liquid form. At that stage, they were still searching.

'Clarkson put together a small team of chemists, named Ivor Holloway, Alf Liddell and Cecil Watson, and set them to work in a closed lab environment with orders not to come out until they'd cracked it. All were young, single men who'd been spared from the draft in order to serve their country in a different way. The team spent several fruitless months working around the clock on a whole series of dead ends. But then they made a chance discovery that yielded results far beyond what they could have imagined.

'The first tests were carried out on rats at the Clarkson laboratory. The enhanced mustard gas they were developing produced the same relatively low instant death rate among the rats, until it was observed that some of the rats succumbed much more quickly. This was potentially exciting news, but the scientists discovered to their disappointment that the higher death rate among these rats wasn't due to the gas, but to an influenza-like viral illness that had spread among some of the lab rat population. In itself, the virus wasn't especially harmful to them, only affecting the older and weaker ones, and nor was it communicable to humans. Healthy rats were largely unaffected by it, even if infected. So, no great shakes. Back to the drawing board they went.'

'Hold on,' Ben cut in. 'Just how do you know all this?' The more he listened, the more he wondered how a semi-employed former lab chemist and blogger could get their hands on classified Military Intelligence files from a hundred years ago.

'From the lab reports of the time, which were among the papers that Suzie and I found buried in the basement,' Miles replied. 'Now listen, because this is where it gets interesting. Then the miracle happened, at least as far as the Clarkson team were concerned. Within days of the sick rats dying from the mustard gas exposure, Ivor Holloway came into the lab early one morning during Christmas 1915 to find every single rat dead. Not just dead, but showing all kinds of horrible symptoms: blistering, blackened flesh that looked burnt, destroyed organs. Their cages were filled with blood from where they'd been haemorrhaging from the nose, mouth, ears and even eyes. Their skin was covered in dark blotches that almost resembled the classic buboes of the Black Death. It was wildly more severe than anything the scientists had seen in their previous testing. Holloway summoned his team members Cecil Watson and Alf Liddell, and showed them what had happened. Clarkson, enjoying Christmas with relatives in Scotland, was notified by phone. At first, none of the scientists could understand what the hell had happened, though they knew they were definitely onto something. What nobody had reckoned on at the time, now much better understood, was that mustard gas has strong mutagenic effects.'

'Explain "mutagenic",' Ben said.

'It means that the exposure to the gas can induce mutations to the DNA of the host,' Miles replied. 'You see, unlike cells, viruses can't replicate by themselves. They need to take over the protein synthesis factory in a living cell and reprogram it to make copies of the virus. At the same time, different types of virus work in different ways. An RNA virus like the flu has an extremely high rate of genetic mutation, thousands of times higher than a DNA virus like, say smallpox or herpes, changing so fast that the immune system can't build up a resistance to it.'

'Which is why you can't vaccinate against it so easily,' Ben said, working hard to keep up with the science.

'Correct, because it's always changing. It's called hyper-mutability. Now, combine that effect with the mutagenic properties of mustard gas, and you have an explosive mixture. It turned out that exposure to the mustard gas agent had caused a completely unpredicted mutation to the footprint of the comparatively innocuous RNA virus that had affected the initial batch of sick rats, with lethal results. Autopsies on the dead rats showed extensive damage to the lungs, similar to the effects of mustard gas, but much more devas-tating, and also to the heart and the brain. The scientists clearly had managed, by chance, to stumble on a very deadly pathogen.'

Miles continued, 'But the effect went further than that. In addition to its supercharged virulence, at the same time the mutated virus had now acquired the ability to affect individuals of a different species. It had gone zoonotic, able to infect not just rats but humans too, with just as high a fatality rate. The team found this out for themselves the hard way. Very soon after the discovery of the dead rats, Ivor Holloway fell severely ill. He was twenty-four years old and had been a college boxing champion and a competitive runner. Immune system like a tank, you'd imagine, but he was dead in two days, and was soon followed by his two colleagues. Liddell was the last to go. Before his death he was able to note the details of the others' symptoms, and some of his own, in the lab reports. The effects of the disease agent were horrific, producing all the same symptoms as the infected rats. Holloway died in excruciating pain all over his body. After his death his skin was so discoloured that the corpse could have been taken for that of a black man. Watson bled to death from the ears, eyes and nose, and his lungs had turned to mush.'

Ben said nothing. He was getting a bad feeling about this.

'Rushing back from Scotland on hearing of the disaster, Clarkson had the lab decontaminated by scientists in the 1915 equivalent of hazmat suits. The bodies of the rodent and human victims were put in isolation. As Clarkson discovered more about what had happened, he began to realise that he had stumbled on something incredible. He'd been hired to deliver a military biotechnology that could stamp out the enemy hard and fast and bring the war to an end. And that was exactly what he now had. They called the weapon Achlys-14.'

Chapter 35

'Achlys,' Ben said. 'Not Achilles?'

Miles Redfield shook his head. 'No, not Achilles. I'm guessing that Duggan misheard the name while he was talking to Joe. I suppose it was an easy mistake to make. They kind of sound alike.'

Which suddenly changed everything. It made sense that Duggan might have made that simple error, trying to glean information from his contact inside a noisy pub with a party going on. And it also explained Joe Brewster's initial look of confusion when asked about 'Achilles-14'. Now Ben's memory kicked in sharply and he remembered what he'd long ago read about the name Achlys, back in the dim and distant days when he'd studied theology. They hadn't just been taught about the monotheistic gods of the mainstream religions.

He said, 'Achlys was the Greek goddess who symbolised the mist of death.'

Miles nodded. 'Yeah, I looked her up too. She was also the goddess of deadly poisons, who distilled toxic drugs made from flowers and used them to turn humans into beasts. Quite appropriate, don't you think? I imagine that some classical-minded ex-public-school boffin in the War Department probably came up with the name. The number fourteen represents the fourteen attempts it took to refine the mustard gas agent into something altogether more lethal.'

How the War Department had first gone about deploying Clarkson's weapon was unknown, Miles explained. But just weeks afterwards, German troops in France had begun to come down with a mysterious and unprecedented illness that quickly ravaged their ranks. Within a terrifyingly short space of time, the strange disease had become the scourge of the Imperial German army and its allies on the front. The intelligence reports that filtered back home delighted the British government and especially Military Intelligence, who were privy to secrets that were probably withheld from the vast majority of elected politicians, including the Prime Minister Herbert Asquith. Their plan to devastate the enemy forces was working beautifully.

'And then it all started to go terribly wrong,' Miles said. 'In retrospect, the most horrible thing about it was that Clarkson and his Intelligence cronies could have been so naive they didn't see it coming. Or that they could have been so utterly cynical that they could let something so awful happen. Either way, their wonder weapon was soon totally out of control.'

World War One, 'the war to end all wars', had mushroomed from a relatively minor diplomatic flap to becoming almost the most horrendous and murderous military conflict in history, at that time second only to the Mongol conquests of the thirteenth century and eclipsing even the bloodbath of the Napoleonic Wars. It had torn Europe completely apart both physically and geopolitically, affected virtually every corner of the planet and involved some sixty million combatants. But something even deadlier and more powerful was brewing in the background.

'It was no wonder,' Miles reflected, 'how easily the disease spread from the enemy forces it had been meant for, and ripped through our own troops. As horrific as the death tolls from the sausage grinder of the battlefields might have been, the numbers of fatalities from the infection were often five or six times higher. In September, October and November of 1918 alone, allied troop hospitals in Europe recorded over 300,000 casualties of the disease, many of whom died. It affected so many soldiers on all sides so quickly and aggressively that things got to the point where nurses in field hospitals were wrapping up still-living men in bodybags and putting death tags on them, to save time. There's no telling how many more thousands of bodies left rotting in the trenches, presumed to have been casualties of war, were actually victims of the disease.

'But the battlefields were just the beginning. The transport of troops from so many countries to and from the battlefields was the biggest movement of people that the world had ever seen. Soldiers brought it home to their respective countries when they went on leave or were invalided out of the army, and at the end of the war when they all flooded home. The virus spread on ocean liners, it spread by rail. Across all of Europe, into America, Russia, China, India and South East Asia. It was a true global pandemic.'

'You're talking about the Spanish flu,' Ben said. 'I'd heard about it. I had no idea it was this bad.'

'You and most folks,' Miles replied. 'One of the most incredible things about it is that it's been largely forgotten today. But as for the name "Spanish flu", forget it. It was only given that label because the world press didn't start taking it seriously until around the time it was hitting Spain. There could also have been a bit of media disinformation going on, to hide the real origin of the disease. It certainly wasn't Spanish. And I don't think it was flu, either. It was something else. Something nobody had ever seen before, and for good reason.'

'Are you seriously trying to say it was man-made?'

Miles shrugged. 'Who's to say it wasn't? Even to this day, we've never really got to the bottom of what could have caused it. There were lots of vague theories at the time, like the one that the disease might have originated in a large field hospital in Étaples in north-west France, which was a rural area rich in goose, duck and pig farms that could have harboured the virus. Truth is, they literally didn't know what had hit them. But if you look at the evidence, you can't avoid the fact that the symptoms of this so-called influenza were uncannily similar to the effects of Achlys-14. It didn't behave like any kind of flu anyone had ever seen. Patients' fevers ran so high some doctors believed it was some terrible form of malaria. The excruciating bone and joint pain it caused made other medical experts think they were dealing with dengue fever, which you'd normally find in the tropics.

'But it was far, far worse than that. Victims often bled heavily from the nose, ears, mouth and eyes, just like the lab rats and chemists at the Clarkson laboratory. Lung damage in the infected was so severe that surgeons compared it to the ravages of mustard gas. *Mustard gas.* Ringing any bells? Pockets of gas would bubble up from under the skin as it leaked out of their ruptured lungs. The collapse of the lungs stopped the supply of oxygen to the blood, which caused the condition called cyanosis where the skin turns dark blue. Many of the dead were so badly discoloured that you couldn't tell the body of a white man from a black man.'

'Just like Holloway, the lab chemist,' Ben said.

'Exactly like Holloway, and his colleagues too. Now that it was out among the general population, the blackening of the bodies of the dead caused panic among troops and civilians who started to believe it was a return of the dreaded bubonic plague. Meanwhile the list of strange symptoms goes on. Autopsies of the dead showed that the disease caused damage not just to the lungs, but to the brain. Which was further evidence it was very unlikely to have been any kind of influenza, because flu doesn't cause neurological problems like that. Yet the rare survivors of this disease were often left with permanent brain damage and altered behaviour, like psychosis. After the epidemic spread to the USA, President Woodrow Wilson fell gravely ill from it and recovered, but was left with strange neurological symptoms and a changed personality. Some historians think that could even have been a contributing factor to the rise of World War Two.'

Ben wanted to say something, but there was nothing he could do but listen grimly as the rain kept pattering on the windows and Miles Redfield kept talking.

'There were other big differences between influenza and this disease. Your normal influenza epidemic tends to infect the very young or the very old, creating a U-shaped curve that leaves the middle age groups largely unaffected. Most fatalities are among older people, especially those with serious pre-existing health conditions. But this epidemic attacked indiscriminately. Young, old, healthy, sick, it didn't matter. People in the prime of life were struck down along with everybody else. It's estimated that five to ten per cent of the world's healthy young adults were wiped out by it. The world's best medical experts were flummoxed. By 1919, they began to agree that the epidemic was viral. But where had it come from? In Britain and the USA, ironically but not surprisingly, theories ran rife that it was something artificially cooked up in an evil German plot to destroy them. And how could it be cured? Nobody knew that either. Medical treatments for the disease were almost completely ineffective. They ranged from bleeding to enemas, to saline and glucose injections, alcohol, heroin, morphine, and some weird cocktails of lard mixed with chloroform or turpentine. Some of those treatments probably caused more deaths on top of those produced by the disease itself. Folk cures included stuffing salt up children's noses, hanging magic charms around your neck, and gargling with disinfectant. In every affected country – which was most of the developed world – trains and buses were fumigated. The public were made to wear masks and told to stay apart. Social contact was shut down tight. Families broken up. Couples becoming afraid to kiss one another. Men, women and children dropping dead in the streets of major cities everywhere, their bodies turning black where they lay and nobody daring to touch them. An aura of fear hanging over everyone's life, and with good reason. Whole areas evacuated, public spaces turning into ghost towns. Economies devastated.'

'How many people died?' Ben asked.

'A lot would be an understatement. From when it appeared out of nowhere to when it suddenly seemed to peter out without a trace, the pandemic killed an estimated fifty to a hundred million people, out of a global population of less than two billion. Proportionately, that would be the equivalent of a casualty rate of up to 430 million people, if a pandemic of that lethality were to strike the world today.'

Ben shook his head. 'Jesus.'

'To put it another way, the so-called Spanish flu claimed more lives in its first twenty-five weeks than the AIDS virus did in its first twenty-five years. In America alone, it killed more people in a single year than the combined combat casualties of both world wars, Korea and Vietnam. Nothing else in history, no war or famine or natural disaster, not the scourges of bubonic plague or smallpox, has ever caused as much devastation as the mysterious "Spanish flu" that never was.'

'But what if you were wrong about this?' Ben said. 'What if it really were just a very, very bad flu outbreak?'

'Then it would have to be an impossible freak of nature. Listen, the influenza virus has been around for a long, long time. The first global flu pandemic was in 1580, and at least sixteen other major epidemics happened in the next three centuries, some of them deadly enough to wipe out entire cities. In the modern age, the Asian flu of 1957–8 killed up to four million people, out of a world population that was well below half of what it is today. Which, I'll grant you, is pretty bad. Ten years later, the Hong Kong flu claimed a few more million and was the last really serious epidemic of its kind. But anyone who tries to compare any of them with the devastation of the Spanish flu is badly in need of a history lesson. It was the single most savage killing force of human beings that ever existed. And I'm certain beyond a doubt that the man who started it all was Sir Elliot Clarkson.'

Chapter 36

Clarkson, Clarkson, Clarkson. The name kept coming back like a bad smell. He was a player in this for sure, but Ben needed to know how and why. 'Tell me more about this Sir Elliot.'

'I've read all I could find about the man. He was born in 1883, the son of a wealthy merchant. Public-school education, showed an amazing flair for chemistry at a young age, graduated from Cambridge and founded his chemical company in 1908, when he was just twenty-five. Clarkson Chemicals made money in fertilisers, printing ink and other ventures, before he got into the munitions business and patented a new formula for smokeless gunpowder that was claimed to produce more velocity with less pressure.'

'That was how he came to the attention of the War Office?'

'And how he was awarded the contract to produce their secret weapon after just seven years in business, aged thirty-two. That was his big break. And needless to say, he did very well out of it. I don't imagine that the top brass were too pleased after the Achlys-14 experiment went so badly wrong. But luckily for him, the government were so satisfied with his initial results that they gave him a knighthood and showered him with money. He'd already been a rich man before the war, with a big estate in Staffordshire, a posh home in London, and all of that. By the end of it, his wealth had more than tripled. He used his fortune to build Clarkson Chemicals into a much larger company called Galliard Pharmaceuticals, now the Galliard Group.'

And there was the Galliard connection Ben had been expecting. But something else Miles had just said struck a chord in his ear. 'An estate in Staffordshire?'

'It had come to him by inheritance,' Miles said. 'The Bridgnorth Estate, a thousand-odd acres and a great big seventeenth-century manor house.'

'And you say he had a place in London, too?'

'Seems he wasn't much of an urbanite and just kept an apartment here for when he was in town on business. Park Lane, I think it was. Slumming it, as one does.'

With an almost audible click, Ben felt another chunk of the puzzle sliding into place in his mind. The 'respectable citizen' Wilfred Grey had gone to kill on that fateful day in 1924, and died trying, lived in Staffordshire. The city property from which Violet had stolen the Anthony Trollope novel the year before had been described in her memoir as '*a large, luxurious apartment in Park Lane, the London home of a wealthy gentleman who spent most of his time at his country mansion*'.

Ben was now able to link up the events, like fragments of a mosaic that were slowly drawing together into a coherent picture. He thought back to Violet's memoir and wondered at the twist of fate that had just happened to lead her, in her last ever robbery for the Forty Elephants, to the luxury London pad of none other than Sir Elliot Clarkson. And to have been drawn to the ornate, beautiful book that just happened to contain a secret stash of notes – secretly and somewhat carelessly stored at his apartment, saying a lot about the man's casual, cynical attitude towards what he'd done – revealing the true origin of the devastating outbreak. The hidden evidence of his complicity in what had to be, if any of this was true, the biggest mass murder in history.

Elsewhere in her memoir Violet had described Wilfred's grief over the loss of his parents, his brother and his sister in the Spanish flu pandemic. The discovery of the papers hidden inside the book had given Wilfred all the reason in the world to want to take revenge on the man he had discovered, by chance, was its orchestrator. His crime had been one of passion; his only mistake had been to let his enemy get the better of him.

'What happened to Sir Elliot in the end?' Ben asked.

'Apart from becoming richer and richer and dying very peacefully in 1978 at the ripe old age of ninety-five, nothing. He never had to account for what he'd done, and enjoyed a much better life than he deserved. Galliard Pharmaceuticals went from strength to strength, prospered through World War Two, swallowed up a bunch of smaller rivals and became the Galliard Group in 1963. His only disappointment in life was his son Robert, who was born in 1929. Clarkson had always intended him to take over the firm one day, but Robert went his own way and ended up in Paris after the war, doing the bohemian artist thing in Montmartre and hanging out with boozy poets and actors. By the time Robert's son was born in 1966, the old man had pretty much written him off. But Sir Elliot doted on his grandson, Gregory. He was a precocious little boy who showed a real talent for science at a young age, unlike his father, who'd never had a talent for anything except spending the family money.

'In the meantime, Robert Clarkson's career as an artist had gone south, predictably enough, and he'd degenerated into a full-blown alcoholic and drug addict. He died soon after Gregory's eighth birthday. The mother was some French actress and had been out of the picture for a while. Probably relieved to be shot of his worthless son, old Elliot took the boy under his wing, moved him into the Bridgnorth Estate and for the next four years taught him everything he knew about life, money, politics, business and, of course, chemistry. Gregory was twelve when his grandfather died. For the next few years the company was run by one of Sir Elliot's senior executives, but according to the old man's wishes Gregory took over as CEO of the Galliard Group in 1989, fresh out of university. He might have been young but he was as tough-minded as his grandfather before him, and his talent for business was every bit as sharp as his scientific genius. The ruthless bastard has been top dog there ever since.'

'Your former boss,' Ben said.

'Correct. Billionaire, philanthropist, supplier of chemical weapons to terrorist regimes and murderer of anyone who gets in his way. You might say a chip off the old block, skipping a generation.'

'With one difference,' Ben said. 'Elliot Clarkson got away with it. Gregory isn't going to be so lucky.'

'I wish,' Miles said bitterly, picking up the picture of Suzie and gazing at it with a tortured look. 'He has it coming, and that's for sure.'

'I lost someone too,' Ben said. 'A long time ago. But it never goes away.'

'No. It never does. I loved her.'

'You want to talk about how it happened?'

Miles laid the picture down in his lap with a sigh. 'I've told you how Suzie and I found the documents in a safe in the basement of the Galliard building. Why Clarkson never had them destroyed, I'll never know.'

'The Clarksons have a careless way of leaving things lying around.'

'Like I said, there were the original lab reports written by Holloway, Watson and Liddell. Plus a load of technical data on the development of the Achlys-14 formula, and a heap of War Department correspondence that Elliot Clarkson had never disposed of. Maybe he enjoyed gloating over his handiwork too much to burn them, who knows? There was also an envelope containing what looked like period photographs of other incriminating notes that were all creased, as though they'd been folded up.'

The notes Wilfred had found inside the book, Ben thought. He said, 'So you stole them.'

'We were totally stunned, because we'd gone in there looking for evidence that Galliard were illegally shipping botulinum toxin, and instead found all this crazy stuff. We knew we had to stash it somewhere safe. Suzie had a friend,

Lynne, who owned a cottage in the Lake District. I couldn't get the time off work, and so it was Suzie who volunteered to make the drive up there in her Mini Cooper with the bundle of documents. But we'd been rumbled somehow. To this day I don't know how the bastards found us out. All I know is that . . .'

Miles's voice faltered, on the brink of cracking. Tears came into his eyes and he picked up the picture again, clenching it with shaking hands. '. . . that she never got there. The accident happened on a quiet stretch of road, far from anywhere. There were no witnesses. The police said she must have lost control of the car. It . . . it was . . .' He couldn't say any more.

'The documents vanished,' Ben said.

Miles looked up at him with pain-streaked eyes. 'Of course. Everything was gone. The evidence I'd have needed to take those fuckers down. And there was no way I could prove that Suzie had been murdered. Just like there was no way anyone could prove what they were doing with the botox, either. These bastards will just squash anyone who's a threat to them. Snuff them out, just like that.' He snapped his fingers, then was silent for a long moment, staring down at his feet. He shook his head. 'It felt like the end. I spent a lot of time wanting to die, too. I loved her so much. I should have been the one in that car.'

'Tell me how Carter Duggan comes into this.'

Miles wiped his eyes and sniffed. 'Duggan employed a computer geek in Canada,' he replied wearily. 'He was the one who tracked me down on the dark web, although I keep my real identity carefully hidden there. When Duggan approached me he said that he was an investigator working for the family of someone called Wilfred Grey. That name meant nothing to me.'

'Wilfred Grey died in 1924,' Ben said. 'Elliot Clarkson shot and killed him, claiming self-defence after Grey broke into his manor house. It was a minor incident at the time. Emily Bowman was his granddaughter, who hired Duggan to find out more about the reasons behind his death.'

Miles nodded. 'Duggan had spent a lot of time exploring old archives. Obscure newspaper reports from ninety-odd years ago aren't always available online, but the bigger libraries have everything catalogued on microfiche for researchers willing to put in the hours sifting through it all. Duggan was obviously a pretty canny investigator. He'd worked out the connection between his client's ancestor, Clarkson and Galliard, and picked up a scent, but he still lacked the knowledge about Galliard's dodgy history. That was what he was hoping to learn from me, because I'd been so critical of Galliard in my anonymous blog posts.'

'Did you write about botox and Achlys-14?'

'Never explicitly. I was too afraid to, even from behind a false identity. I danced around the subject, making plenty of insinuations and hinting at insider knowledge of their dirty dealings, past and present. Mostly I've always stuck to my general theme, which is how grasping and corrupt the whole pharmaceutical industry is, and has always been. It was enough to draw Duggan's interest, but I sensed it was just one of various leads he was following. I don't think he realised how potentially big this was until he met with Joe.'

'Brewster didn't tell him much.'

'Because he didn't know much. I was just using him as a buffer, to sound the man out. But what little information Joe did pass along was enough to get Duggan excited. He said he was as keyed up as a bloodhound following a blood trail.'

'He also said he thought Duggan was too interested in money. What did he mean by that?'

'We both agreed that Duggan was almost certainly a gold-digger. The hint of some kind of major scandal involving a big pharma company was clearly much more engrossing to him than his work for his client. That's why I decided there was nothing to be gained from meeting the guy, and to let it drop. People like that can't be trusted.'

Ben asked, 'Do you think Duggan tried to find out more about Achlys-14 on his own?'

'Maybe,' Miles replied. 'Though I don't see where he could have got the information from. The Galliard documents were the only source I know of. But we'll never know, will we? Duggan's dead.'

'Joe Brewster seemed pretty sure that he was killed by agents working for Galliard. Do you think that too?'

Miles made a sound that was halfway between a snort and a bitter laugh. 'They kill everyone else. What's one more?'

'Which means Duggan put himself on their radar somehow. Made himself a threat to them. How, if he didn't know the truth?'

'I have no answer to that.'

'Then I'll have to find the answer myself,' Ben said.

'What are you going to do?'

279

'Whatever I need to do to finish this,' Ben said.

Miles shook his head. 'How far do you think you can keep pushing before you end up just like everyone else who stands in their way? How long before they send their killers after you, too?'

'It's been tried before,' Ben said. 'And I'm still here.'

Miles said nothing. Ben looked at him and saw someone consumed with loathing and anger, but too paralysed by fear and his own sense of powerlessness to climb up out of the ditch and do something about it. He was a man trapped in his own private hell, and he always would be.

They had talked late into the night. It was raining harder than ever outside. Ben stood up. 'Thanks for the tea. Good luck, Miles. Get some rest. And stay out of trouble.'

Ben left the dingy flat without another word and walked outside into the downpour. He barely felt the cold rain as he headed back to the Land Rover. Because now he had all the pieces to determine who really had killed Carter Duggan – all bar one. It was time to pay a visit to Mr Gregory Clarkson, CEO of the Galliard Group.

Back in the damp, leaking Land Rover, Ben turned on his phone and found the number and address of the Galliard corporate HQ across the other side of the city. That was where his hunt would begin.

He was setting his sat nav when the phone rang.

'You thieving bastard,' said Tom McAllister. 'That's how you repay me for trusting you? By stealing my frigging warrant card? What the hell are you up to? I've been calling and calling.'

Ben replied, 'I did what I had to do, Tom. When this is

over you can arrest me for theft, for impersonating an officer, for whatever you like. But first I'm going to get the proof to set Jude free.'

'Yeah, well, you're a bit behind the curve, pal. Jude's already free. He escaped from Bullingdon Prison three hours ago.'

Chapter 37

Three hours earlier

It was after ten when the prison erupted.

With the facility locked down for the night, nobody would ever know how an inmate somehow managed to get past the guards, slip inside Mickey Lowman's single cell and garrotte him so brutally with a home-made cheesewire that he was almost beheaded. But once the deed was done, the cell floor awash with blood and the killer vanished like a ghost, the alarm was raised and sirens were soon sounding all through Bullingdon. As guards rushed here and there, two of them were expertly snatched and dragged into a storeroom where their throats were slit from ear to ear. The killers grabbed their keys and quickly, efficiently, set about opening cell doors.

Within minutes, Bullingdon was in the grip of total chaos as guards resorted to violence to subdue the torrent of raging inmates who overran the hallways and corridors, wreaking destruction all across the facility. A number of fires broke out and more alarms joined the cacophony. Several more guards were locked in cells, cornered and savagely beaten while others drew back and hid. Before anyone could do anything to get things in hand, disturbance had escalated into a full-scale riot such as Bullingdon had never seen.

Jude and his cellmate Big Dave had been relaxing in their bunks when it began. 'What the hell is going on out there?' Dave said, jumping up and going over to press his ear to the cell door. At first they thought it was an emergency like a fire, and Dave thumped against the door and demanded to know what was happening. But when they heard the urgent rattle of a key in the lock and the door swung open, it wasn't a prison guard standing there but one of Luan Copja's men. 'You come,' he said, stepping inside the cell and grabbing Jude's arm. There was blood on his clothes, but not his own.

Big Dave bristled and got between them, defensive. 'Hey, hey, leave him. What the hell are you doing?'

'Is okay, he is one of us,' Copja's man said, placing a palm against Big Dave's chest. 'He come with us.' Big Dave didn't like being touched and considered snapping the man's hand off at the wrist, but given who these people were he quickly thought twice. Copja's guy turned to Jude. 'You come with us, yes?'

'What are you talking about, come with us?' Jude asked, fazed. 'Come where?'

Copja's man grinned. 'You will see. Now come.'

'You okay with this?' Big Dave asked.

'I don't know,' Jude replied. Which was a true enough statement. But it was dawning on him that he was being offered a way out of his locked cell. And that didn't seem

283

like a bad thing. Something his father often said came into his mind. *Fuck it.*

'Must move quickly. There is no time.'

And before Jude really had time to think about what he was doing, he was being whisked out of the cell and found himself in the middle of the violent chaos. He and the Albanian quickly joined up with the rest of the gang, seven men in all, Copja among them. There was a glint of merriment in the crime boss's eye as the gang hurried through the prison, evidently heading somewhere in particular.

'I thought maybe you want to leave here, little man,' Copja rumbled, clamping Jude's shoulder in a massive, vice-like grip. 'You never think it happen so soon, eh? Your uncle Luan is full of surprises. You not worry, I look after you now.'

Jude hadn't asked for this, but they were giving him little choice. He was so confused that he barely understood what was going on, until he realised with a shock that Copja had been planning this jailbreak for some time. Past the inert and bleeding shapes of two guards; through a crowd of wild, baying inmates ransacking an office; finding one corridor blocked by fire and smoke and diverting along another, up a flight of stairs and then a second: they were heading for the roof. Through the tumult Jude thought he could hear the thump of a helicopter somewhere up above.

'Come! Hurry!' Copja's henchmen were hustling their boss along like presidential bodyguards, with Jude in his wake. Getting closer now. The roaring thud of the chopper was loud. They crashed through a door and pounded up a metal stair that led to the roof – a rush of fresh air – and Jude was blinded by lights and deafened by the noise and wind blast. The helicopter was touching down on the prison roof, its pilot skilfully avoiding the various antenna masts that jutted up into the night sky. The aircraft's skids flexing as it settled briefly; a hatch opening; the hurricane blast tearing at their hair and clothes as the gang rushed to meet it and clamber aboard. The chopper was small for the number of passengers cramming themselves in. Jude found himself squashed up between Copja's bulk and the man who'd freed him from his cell. The rotors clattered and howled. The hatch slammed shut. Then they were off, and it was only then that Jude felt the exhilarating thrill that this really was happening. He was escaping from this place!

Down below, the lights of the prison shrank away and then were shrouded behind a bank of low-drifting cloud and Jude saw no more. The Albanians were all high-fiving one another, whooping and laughing raucously. Copja patted Jude's shoulder and yelled in his ear, 'Easy as a pie. What you say to that, my friend?'

'Why me?' Jude asked over the roar of the chopper.

'It is like I tell you. You do something for me, I do something for you.'

The noisy, cramped flight lasted only ten minutes or so before the chopper came down to land and everyone hustled out. Jude had no idea where he was. They'd come down in a field, with not a single house or road in sight. Wasting no time, the chopper pilot gunned his throttle and took off again, disappearing into the night and leaving Jude and the gang alone in the middle of the dark field. Jude was uncertain what was coming next or what was expected of him, but it seemed to him that to say, 'Well, thanks for the lift, fellas. I'll be on my way now. See you around' wasn't quite what the Albanians had in mind. The gang were all talking in their own language, voices full of anticipation. One of the men pointed, and Jude looked around and blinked at the approaching headlights of four vehicles that had emerged from behind a thicket of trees and were bouncing across the field in their direction. Copja smiled in the lights and strode confidently towards them. There was a van, two SUVs and a saloon car. They pulled up four abreast and killed their engines, leaving their lights on as more men piled out.

Jude hung self-consciously around in the background until Copja turned and pointed him out to his associates, saying in English, 'Meet our new friend. He decided to join us.'

There was laughter. Jude thought, 'Hold on a minute. Join us in what?' He felt a slight chill as it occurred to him that there might be an unexpected price to pay for his ticket out of Bullingdon.

Two of the newcomers busied themselves unloading some large holdalls from the van, set them on the ground and unzipped them as Copja and his men gathered around to look. The blaze of headlights revealed spare clothing, stacks of cash and a small arsenal of automatic weapons. Copja nodded and muttered his approval. It was clear that the plan was to divide up the money and weapons and split into different vehicles.

That was Copja's plan, at any rate. It might not have been everyone's.

Jude perhaps didn't possess as well-honed a sixth sense as his father, but was anything but unperceptive and now, even as he stood there wondering what the hell he'd got himself into, he could see something was wrong. Something about the way that several of the newcomers were stepping back as Copja and his henchmen's attention was taken up with inspecting the contents of the bags. Something about the looks passing between them. The hands slipping furtively inside jackets.

Jude felt a sudden tingle of alarm as he understood that the bags were a decoy. Luan Copja was being double-crossed. Jude drew back out of the blaze of the lights, into the shadows.

A voice said, 'Hey, Luan, Armir Bajrak says hello.'

The blast of gunfire shattered the night. Luan Copja bellowed like a bull as bullets slammed into his chest and shoulder. Two of his men were cut down next to him, left and right. Another one dived to the ground and rolled under the van.

If his rivals couldn't get him inside prison, out here was the perfect opportunity to assassinate Copja. Jude could only guess that this Armir Bajrak had managed to infiltrate the enemy gang. But his hired thugs had done a clumsy job of it. Very clumsy, because a smart man would have ensured that the guns in the bag were loaded with dummy rounds. Copja staggered two steps, went down on one knee and snatched a small machine carbine from the holdall. White flame sputtered from its muzzle as he hosed a spray of bullets at his attackers. There was a scream. Car headlights shattered and went dark. More gunfire punched into Copja's body but he kept on firing until his gun was empty. Two of his loyal men who were still on their feet hurled themselves at Bajrak's guys. The one who'd freed Jude from his cell managed to twist a weapon free and turn it against them. Shots rattled out; then he was shot, too, and fell.

Jude dropped to the ground and flattened himself into the long grass as the firefight exploded wildly and bullets flew in all directions.

When he dared to look up again, there was dead silence. He clambered to his feet and peered cautiously through the gunsmoke swirling in the car headlights. Bodies were lying all over the ground. Nobody was moving. Stunned, Jude stepped through the scene of the massacre. The cars were riddled with bullet holes. He could smell burning and something fizzled under the bonnet of the van, as though it were about to burst into flames.

The body of Luan Copja lay sprawled face-down next to the holdalls. Jude went over to them. He ignored the guns, wanting no part of that. But the wads of banknotes crammed into bricks in the money bag were another story. If he was to go on the run, he was going to need all the cash he could carry. He rummaged in the bag of spare clothing until he found a few items that looked as though they'd fit him, crammed them in with the money and zipped the holdall shut. His legs were as shaky as jelly and his heart was pounding.

He was probably in much deeper trouble than before. But he was too excited to care. He was free.

Jude hoisted the heavy bag over his shoulder and ran like hell.

Chapter 38

Despite himself, on hearing of Jude's escape Ben's reaction after his initial shock was a tingle of pride that his son had managed to beat the system that had unfairly imprisoned him. It was the same grudging admiration he'd felt after Jude's performance at the bail hearing. But something told Ben this was far more serious.

'How the hell did this happen?'

Tom McAllister described the riot at Bullingdon, now under control. Jude's cellmate had reported to the authorities that Jude was removed from their cell and taken away by an inmate called Luan Copja and his gang of Albanian organised crime thugs, who had incredibly pulled off a daring helicopter escape during the disturbance.

'Last time anything like that happened was when the IRA boys got out of Mountjoy Prison using a hijacked chopper in 1973,' McAllister said. 'What Jude was doing mixed up with that bunch is anyone's guess. But he's not with them now, that's for sure. Copja and his boys were found shot to death an hour ago in a field near Chedworth, forty miles east of the prison. A local farmer heard gunfire and called the police. Looks like some kind of inter-gang warfare deal gone tits-up. They found a pile of dead Albanians, some shot-up vehicles, and a couple of holdalls. One full of clothes and the other full of guns. The thinking is that there might've been a third bag, that one full of walking-around cash for the escapees. But no sign of your boy. He's vanished into thin air.'

Ben listened grimly. His feeling of pride had been short-lived. Jude had done himself real harm by running like this, and getting mixed up in ugly business with criminals made it even worse. He was no longer the innocent citizen wrong-fully accused: that trump card had just been thrown away, by making himself a fugitive and a criminal.

The plan to pay a visit to Gregory Clarkson was now shoved aside. Ben looked at his watch and said to McAllister, 'I'm on my way. Don't do anything until I get there.'

McAllister gave a sour laugh. 'Chance would be a fine thing, in these exciting times we live in. On top of everything else someone's left Boars Hill looking like the Battle of Chalgrove frigging Field and guess whose job it is to pick up the pieces?'

Ben said nothing.

'I know that was you,' McAllister said. 'These things don't happen on my watch except when you're in town. You were the last person Emily Bowman called on that burner phone of yours before she died. That puts you in the frame. If Forbsie had the first notion of anything, he'd have launched a nationwide manhunt. Lucky for you, I'm the only person who's put two and two together. But my patience is wearing thin, Ben.'

'You're my kind of cop, Tom. I wish they were all like you.'

McAllister grunted. Not happy. 'If I didn't know better I'd think you flew your kid out of jail and shot up Copja's boys yourself. Where are you now? Let me guess. Norfolk?'

McAllister would have heard the reports of the happenings, there, too. 'London,' Ben replied, managing to be truthful and evasive at the same time. 'I can be with you in a couple of hours and we'll figure this out. We have to find him before the police do.'

'What are you talking about, *we* have to find him? I am the police.'

'I know what he's like, Tom. Now that he's free he'll go to ground and he'll do anything to prevent them from retaking him. He'll end up getting himself shot.'

'So what am I supposed to do, hold off the troops while you and I go hunting the length and breadth of the country for the wee skitter? Every hour that goes by, he's getting further and further away. By daybreak he could be on the Isle of frigging Skye.'

Ben sighed. The timing couldn't have been worse. 'I'm so close, Tom. Another day and I could have put an end to this whole mess. I think I know who really killed Carter Duggan.'

'Aye, well, I'd like to see you prove it,' McAllister said. 'Especially with your boy on the lam. He's just hung a great big guilty sign around his own neck.'

Ben drove hard out of London, or as hard as the ancient wreck of a Land Rover would let him. As he hacked across the city it started making ominous sounds from under the bonnet and the power response was feeling more and more sluggish. By the time he was on the motorway the damn thing wouldn't go more than fifty and the temperature gauge had pushed deep into the red.

The old banger's final voyage ground to a halt altogether on a stretch of quiet country road, somewhere in Oxfordshire at four in the morning. Ben tried and failed to rouse a taxi driver from his bed at that hour. Giving up, he hunkered down in the back of the dead Landy, tried to grab some sleep for himself and failed there too. He rolled the vehicle down an incline into some thick bushes, abandoned it and started walking.

Jude, where the hell are you?

It was dawn by the time Ben finally got to McAllister's cottage. The cop was already up and dressed in the dark suit he wore for work. He greeted Ben with a mug of hot black coffee and the surly words 'Give it back.'

Ben took the warrant card from his wallet and returned it.

He'd been expecting McAllister to be in a foul mood with him, but the cop seemed particularly irascible this morning. 'You ever do that again and I *will* arrest you,' he warned as they carried their coffees into the cottage's sitting room. 'If I haven't already it's only because you're in deep enough shit already.'

'That doesn't concern me right now. I'm more worried about Jude.'

'Then you'd best crack on looking for him, hadn't you?'

'Have you had your people check the vicarage?'

McAllister scowled. 'Do I look like Forbsie? I'm not stupid, you know. Of course we have. Every inch of the house and grounds. But beyond that, frankly I don't have a clue where the silly bastard could have gone. Does he have a girlfriend he might have gone to lie low with?'

'In America. She's history anyway.'

They spent a while throwing ideas back and forth, but to no avail. McAllister's dirty mood only seemed to grow worse as they talked. Now and then he turned a shade paler, and twice he pressed his palm to his right cheek and let out a low groan. At first Ben thought he was just stressed out, but it dawned on him that there was more to it.

'Something wrong?'

'It's this frigging toothache,' McAllister admitted. 'Started yesterday and it's got worse through the night. Frig it, I don't want to have to go to the dentist.'

'Get me a pair of pincers and I'll yank it out for you.'

McAllister looked at him as if he'd happily shoot him. 'You come anywhere near me with a pair of pincers, pal, and you'll wish you hadn't.'

Ben left him to his sufferings and wandered down the riverbank with a lit Gauloise and Radar trotting along at his heels. The morning mist was still clearing, drifting like smoke on the water. He was dazed. Everything he'd learned over the last couple of days seemed to have become irrelevant. The whole world had been turned upside down with Jude's escape from jail.

What was he thinking? And yet, how must it have felt for him, sitting locked up in a cell knowing that the real killer was still out there? Could Ben put his hand on his heart and say he wouldn't have done the same? The crazy Hope gene, striking again.

Ben had been sitting gazing at the misty water for a while

when McAllister came bursting out of the cottage to say that there'd been a major development. Ben jumped to his feet and raced up the riverbank to meet him. He looked animated, his toothache forgotten.

'Billie called,' McAllister said.

'Who's he?'

'Not Billy,' McAllister snapped impatiently. 'Billie, Billie Flowers. She's my Detective Sergeant.'

'Okay, so what's up?'

'We got him.'

Ben stared.

'Well, not quite,' McAllister corrected himself. 'But we're a big step closer. We've a pretty good idea where he went.'

The news of the sensational jailbreak had been splashed all over television that morning. The police had just had a call from a haulage trucker called Steve Kinnear who'd picked up a hitcher in the Cotswolds late last night, while en route to Penzance in Cornwall to deliver a load of engineering parts. On arrival at his destination he'd seen Jude's face on TV and reckoned the wanted man was the same person he'd given a lift to.

Ben asked, 'Reckons, or knows for sure?'

'A hundred per cent sure. He gave a pretty clear description, down to the clothes he was wearing. Said he was carrying a heavy holdall, which sounds like one of the ones found with the dead Albanians. Bet your arse it's the missing money bag.'

'Where'd Kinnear drop him off?' Ben asked.

'Out in the middle of the sticks, a few miles from Bodmin. Makes sense to me that a person on the run might pick that area. Pretty wild terrain, sparsely populated, easy to disappear.'

For Ben, it made even more sense. Because he suddenly knew exactly where Jude had gone.

Chapter 39

After a long and exhausting hike across the moor with the heavy holdall on his shoulder, as the early morning sun emerged from behind the hills Jude had finally found the lane that wound up towards Black Rock Farm. He followed its twisting, potholed course for half a mile further before he arrived at the familiar wooden gate, now a little more dilapidated than when he'd last seen it some years ago, but still bearing the hand-painted greeting that Robbie had put there to welcome visitors: PRIVATE PROPERTY – PISS OFF.

Safe at last. Smiling to himself in the certainty that nobody would think of looking for him here, Jude creaked open the gate and trudged the last couple of hundred yards along the rutted track to the house.

He and Robbie Brocklebank had been friends a long time, since they were both seven years old, though they hadn't been in touch for a while. Robbie had always been something of a tearaway, perpetually rebelling against his hippy parents – hippies of the bourgeois bohemian, open-toed-sandalled, pot-smoking liberal moneyed variety (Robbie's uncle, Sir Crispin Brocklebank, was a wealthy stockbroker) who'd brought their kids up to address them as Bertie and Meadow – yes, Meadow. When Robbie was eight they'd wanted to rename him River, but Robbie wasn't having it and had been at war with them more or less ever since. Which hadn't stopped him from making free use of the rundown Cornish farm that Bertie and Meadow had purchased as a holiday home many years ago but hardly ever visited.

Throughout his later teens Jude had attended more than a few wild parties in the big barn that Robbie had refashioned as a private rave venue and a concert hall for his thrash metal band, the Nazi Rocket Monkeys, while the house itself had seen its fair share of drunken debauchery, indulgence in mild narcotic substances and other teenage indiscretions. It had been during one of those wild parties that Jude had first met the man he would later learn was his real father. Ben had travelled here to break the news to him that Michaela and Simeon Arundel had been killed in a car smash. The encounter had marked the beginning of Jude's sometimes turbulent relationship with his biological dad.

He knew that Ben would go crazy when he heard the news of the prison escape. But what would he have done, in Jude's position? There probably wouldn't have been a stone of HMP Bullingdon left standing, so no lectures, please.

Reaching the house, Jude found that the front door was unlocked as usual. That didn't mean anyone was currently staying here – neither Robbie nor his parents cared much about home security, not that there was anything much inside worth stealing. Sure enough, a check of the rambling farmhouse's three floors, calling out 'Hello? Anybody home?' revealed that the place was empty. That suited Jude perfectly.

He picked out a small attic bedroom with peeling Led Zeppelin posters, a mattress on the floor and a view over the hills, found a sleeping bag that wasn't too fusty-smelling, then padded back down the creaky stairs to coax the old oil boiler into life and get some warmth into the place. There was a decent stock of tinned provisions in the kitchen, not all of it the tasteless organic vegetarian stuff Bertie and Meadow were into, and good old Robbie had left some pizzas in the freezer: triple cheese pepperoni! Best of all, Jude found a stack of lager six-packs in the fridge and more stashed under the kitchen sink.

Ravenous after his journey and the long, weary trek across the moor, Jude made himself a giant breakfast of baked beans and sausages and guzzled it down with something approaching ecstasy, slurping on a mug of fair-trade instant coffee. What a welcome relief it was, after his diet of prison food. Afterwards, full and belching and feeling extremely contented, he hefted his new holdall onto the rustic kitchen table, unzipped it and set about counting the piles of wadded banknotes inside. By the time he'd finished, he was sitting staring open-mouthed at a mountain of cash that entirely covered the table and amounted to over forty thousand pounds in used tens and twenties. He could only guess that this must have been intended as expenses money for Luan Copja and his cronies while they were on the run, before the gang was somehow infiltrated and the tables were turned. What did it matter any more?

Jude counted his blessings. He had supplies to last him a good two weeks, and enough cash to live on for much longer than that. Christ, he could survive for years up here in his remote bohemian hideaway if he had to. He also happened to know that Robbie's old Triumph Bonneville lived in one of the sheds, providing him with wheels for when he needed to scoot down to the nearest village, Warleggan, for more supplies. Venturing out into the public would be the risky part – but if he coloured his blond hair red with some of the hippy henna dye that Meadow kept in the bathroom and grew himself a bit of a beard, he reckoned he could avoid getting recognised.

He wasn't worried about Robbie turning up. Robbie would think it was the supercoolest thing in the universe to harbour a real-life fugitive from justice, and could be utterly trusted not to breathe a word to anyone. Meanwhile if Bertie and Meadow happened to make one of their rare appearances, Jude would just decamp to one of the barns and keep out of sight. The elder Brocklebanks were usually too stoned out of their heads to pay much attention to what went on around them, anyhow.

Boy oh boy, did this ever beat living behind bars! Jude neatly packed his money away, carried the bulging bag upstairs and threw himself down on his bed, laughing. In five minutes, he was drifting away into a beautiful, tranquil sleep.

Chapter 40

'You said the police know where he went,' Ben told McAllister. 'Maybe so, in the most general sense, but no more than that. You know what direction he went in. What county he's in. That's it. Whereas I've got him pinned down to the nearest square metre.'

'Are you sure?' McAllister asked.

'Pretty sure,' Ben said. 'There's no other reason why he'd have chosen to head to that region. It's a rough old farmhouse that belongs to the family of a school friend of his. They hardly use the place, by all accounts, and nobody else ever goes there. A perfect location to hide out in.'

McAllister looked thoughtful. 'So where exactly is this place?'

'That depends,' Ben said.

'Depends on what?'

'Depends on who I'm talking to here. Am I talking to the police? Or am I talking to someone who can think outside the box and be prepared to do this my way?'

'Try me,' McAllister said cagily.

'Here's how I see it. First of all, Jude might act stupid

sometimes, but he's not stupid enough to have asked Kinnear to drop him off anywhere too close to where he was going. He's a fit guy. Not SAS fit, but not too shabby. He could carry a heavy holdall for miles over rough country without breaking a sweat.'

'So?'

'So, now there's been a reported sighting, Devon and Cornwall police will have boots all over the Bodmin area hunting for him, right?'

'Right.'

'But we're talking about a big area,' Ben said. 'Remember your basic geometry?'

'Geometry. Give me a break, Hope.'

Ben said, 'If Jude hiked anything up to, say, seven or eight miles from the drop-off point in any given direction, that would equal the radius of the circle you need to cover in order to find him somewhere inside. The area of a circle is pi times the radius squared, which gives you a search zone of around two hundred square miles. If he walked just a couple of miles further, say forty minutes extra at a good pace, that area widens out to over three hundred square miles.'

'All right, all right. I get it.'

'Meaning the police will have to check every town, village, farmhouse, outhouse and henhouse in something like a hundred and ninety thousand acres of land. Even if they roll the air operations unit out of Exeter airport, a single helicopter will still have a hell of a job covering that much ground, plus they've only got a two-and-a-half-hour flight window before they have to return to base to refuel. It's needles and haystacks.'

McAllister had to grudgingly agree.

'On top of which,' Ben added, 'the place I think he's gone is pretty damn remote. The one time I went there, I had a hard time finding it.'

'But you'll remember?'

'Once I've been to a place I never forget how to find it.'

'What are you, a homing pigeon?'

'It buys us a lot of time. But only if we move fast.'

McAllister frowned. 'Us?'

'You, me and that clown car of yours, because I don't have one any longer.'

'Watch what you say about my car.'

'You can bring the dog along too. He might come in handy.'

Radar licked Ben's hand. He seemed to like the idea.

McAllister went on frowning, still not convinced. 'Why should I work with you on this?'

'Because it's the only way that leads to a happy outcome.'

'What outcome is that?'

'The one where we get Jude safely into custody, where some trigger-happy police sniper isn't going to drill a hole in him. At the same time, we nail the real killer and put an end to this thing once and for all.'

'Sounds like you have a plan,' McAllister said.

'Just half of one,' Ben replied. 'I'm still working on the other half. But what I have in mind, I can't do alone. I'll need your backup, Tom.'

McAllister was silent, thinking.

'I also need your answer now,' Ben said. 'The clock's ticking. Are you in, or out?'

McAllister said, 'You're forgetting one thing, pal. Forbsie might've pulled me off the case, but that was before the shit hit the fan at Emily Bowman's place. Now I'm back in charge of this unholy mess, which means that twenty minutes from now I'll be on my way to Cornwall where I'll be liaising with the local officers on the ground to supervise the search operation. Tell me how I'm supposed to do all that and still take part in this half-baked plan of yours.'

Ben leaned closer and peered frowning at the right side of McAllister's face. He winced. 'That's a hell of a swelling you've got there. All puffed up and bright red. Looks like a baboon's arse.'

McAllister scowled and defensively put his hand to his right cheek, which wasn't visibly swollen at all. 'What are you talking about, baboon's arse?'

Ben told him, 'You must be in agony. If I had a face like that, I'd get myself booked into the dentist's for an emergency extraction, PDQ, because there's no way you can supervise a major manhunt operation with a tooth that's about to explode. And I'd have to get someone to cover for me in my absence. Like Detective Sergeant Billie Flowers, for example. Who I'm sure is an extremely capable officer. I'm certain that your superior, Forbsie, will be full of sympathy and happy to cut you some slack. That's what having a chain of command is all about. One phone call, and you'll be good to go.'

'I can't—' McAllister began to bluster.

'Yes, you can,' Ben said. 'And it's what I'm asking you to do, because if you don't help me and Jude gets shot by some cowboy in a SWAT vest, that's on you.'

'What do I say to them when they see I've still got the tooth?'

'That the world's best dentist worked a miracle and saved it. Or if it's realism you want, get me those pliers and I'll be happy to oblige.'

'Damn you, Hope.'

'Damn me all you like. Just make a decision. And get out of that suit and those nice shiny shoes. Where we're going it might get a little rough.'

McAllister thought about it a little longer. But not too long. Then he heaved a huge sigh, slumped his shoulders in defeat and walked back into the cottage to get straight on the phone to Billie Flowers. Five minutes later he re-emerged, wearing jeans and hiking boots and a faded denim jacket.

'This had better be worth it,' he growled at Ben. 'Let's go.'

Chapter 41

McAllister opened up the driver's door of the massive Barracuda, left-hand drive like Ben's Alpina had been before it became a cube of metal. He angled the seat forward to let Radar hop excitedly into the back. Ben asked, 'You want me to drive?'

McAllister shot him a savage look. 'Don't push your luck, Hope.'

Ben walked around to the right side and settled into the high-back bucket passenger seat as McAllister wedged himself in behind the three-spoke wheel. The car was as wide as a boat, with enough leg and elbow room to spread out comfortably. They had a drive of over two hundred miles ahead of them, carving west through the Cotswolds and then plunging southwards by Bristol; down into Somerset: Bridgwater, Taunton, then into Devon, cutting through the heart of Dartmoor and onwards towards the south-western tip of England to Cornwall.

McAllister thundered through the lanes of rural west Oxfordshire, the clattering rumble of the big Hemi V8 reverberating in the verdant, sun-dappled tree tunnels. On straights the acceleration was stunning for a car that was pushing fifty years old; on tighter bends the thing wallowed like a water buffalo in a swamp. When they hit the open road the engine note smoothed out into a mellow roar and it seemed to find its long-legged stride, like it was home again on the NASCAR racetrack.

'I still think this is a bad idea,' McAllister said as the 'Cuda hummed down the motorway with eighty-five on the clock. Breaking speed limits was okay if you were a cop, even one who lied to his superiors and was technically signed off duty for a medical emergency.

'Then turn this bastard barge around, take me back, arrest me,' Ben said. 'Or try to, and see what happens.'

'Is that how it works: ask me for my help and then threaten me? A right charmer you are, Hope.'

'I've come this far,' Ben said. 'Nobody's going to get in my way until Jude's safe and the bad guys are in the bag.'

'Are you planning on shooting them, too?'

Ben looked at him. 'What makes you think I shot anyone? You want to frisk me for a concealed firearm?'

'Yeah, right. Listen, pal, doesn't bother me. If you can take out the trash and get away with it, that's no skin off my nose. Just try to do it a little more discreetly when you're on my turf, okay?'

'Tell me exactly how you managed to qualify as a police officer?'

McAllister ignored the question. He asked, 'So who are these bad guys anyway?'

'You'll find out soon enough,' Ben replied. 'If things go to plan.'

'You have the whole plan worked out now, do you?'

'I'm working on it.'

'A shitey auld deal this is,' McAllister grumbled, shaking his head. 'You drag me into a heap of trouble and you won't even tell me what's going on.'

'Are you going to bicker all the way to Cornwall?'

A silence; then McAllister muttered glumly, 'My tooth hurts.'

'Don't be such a wimp, McAllister. A big tough guy like you, making such a fuss for one measly little tooth out of thirty-two. I once knew a young trooper who hiked the best part of a forty-mile endurance march with half of them knocked out. He's still alive.'

'One of your fellow SAS nutters, I suppose.'

That would be the redoubtable Jaden Wolf, now living in Spain and, with any luck, doing a better job at staying away from trouble than his former commanding officer. Ben felt a pang of self-pity of his own, and wondered whether he'd ever be able to settle down to a peaceful life. Probably asking for too much, he decided.

As the morning wore on and they got steadily closer to their destination, the sky turned to a leaden grey and the landscape grew more barren and rugged. The Plymouth drank like a Sherman tank, a four-wheeled environmental disaster, and they had to stop twice for fuel. At the second stop, McAllister let the dog out to relieve himself and reluctantly let Ben take over the wheel for the last leg of the journey.

With the motorway behind them, the roads became increasingly empty and twisty and narrow, climbing up and down through the hilly moorland of Cornwall. A blanket of mist had descended from the grey sky, along with a thin sheeting rain that slicked the road surface and made the Barracuda's Goodrich tyres and wallowy suspension scrabble for grip on fast bends.

'Take it easy,' McAllister said, gripping the door handle as the rear end fishtailed out of line.

'Don't worry. If I wreck it, I'll buy you a new one.'

It was coming on for midday as Ben blitzed past the sign for Warleggan, the nearest village to Black Rock Farm. Driving through the greystone streets he passed the pub where he'd stopped to ask directions, the one time he'd been here before. 'It's all hippies up there,' the barman had said, eyeing Ben like he was a drug dealer.

'Well, your boy certainly picked the arsehole of nowhere to hide out in,' McAllister commented as they headed beyond Warleggan and climbed yet further into the remote hills. On a clear day you could see for many miles across the rolling moorland, but the mist had thickened to a yellowish fog and the visibility had dropped to less than thirty yards. Not a day for deploying Devon and Cornwall's police helicopter for a widespread manhunt. The roads were almost completely empty. If the cops were out in force looking for Jude, they must be combing some other sector of their wide search zone. Ben could tell that McAllister was itching to get on his police radio for an update on the operation. Twice he tried calling Billie Flowers on his mobile, but what little phone signal there was out here was made even weaker by the moisture-laden fog.

'Sounds like you get on well with this DS Flowers,' Ben said.

'Aye, she's a good officer. Sings jazz, too.'

'This is it,' Ben said as he saw the entrance to the rutted track, and he swung the car into it, the tyres pattering and slithering over the rocks and banging through deep ruts. 'It's a classic muscle car, not a frigging Land Rover,' McAllister complained. Further up the track, they reached the gate with the hand-painted welcome sign, and Ben knew that he'd found the place for sure.

'Private property: piss off,' McAllister muttered, reading the sign. 'Friendly folks the kid hangs out with.'

'They're an unusual kind of family. But I doubt we'll be meeting any of them.'

Ben let the Barracuda roll to a halt and cut the engine. The house was still a distance away, but if Jude was here he wanted to catch him unawares. 'We should walk from here,' Ben said.

They got out of the car. McAllister let Radar out of the back, and clipped him up on a short leash. 'Quiet now, boy.' The dog didn't actually nod, but the look in his keen amber eyes showed that he understood.

They walked. The place was utterly quiet. The only sounds were the soft crunch of their boots on the track and the panting of the German shepherd as he led the way, straining at his leash, ears pricked, primed and ready for duty. Ben's neck and shoulders felt tight with tension as the inevitable last-minute doubts began to creep into his mind. If he was wrong, he'd have wasted an enormous amount of time and would have no idea where else to start looking for Jude. For the first time since he could remember, he murmured a silent prayer.

'What a shithole,' McAllister said in a low voice as the dark shapes of the house and barns loomed up out of the fog. 'Makes Wuthering Heights look like Buck Palace, so it does.'

'Shhh.'

Ben could do nothing to stop the doubts rising as they walked closer to the house. The old farm was every bit as lugubrious and neglected as he remembered it. The house walls were streaked with green, nobody had cleaned the windows in years and a jungle of weeds sprouted everywhere. The large domed sheet-metal barn across the yard had been partially adorned with a clumsy attempt at psychedelic flower-child graphics, but the rust was showing through the paint. The first-glance impression was of a property that had lain abandoned and uninhabited for a long, long time.

Except it wasn't.

Ben was already noticing details. Like the asthmatic roar of a boiler flue venting gases and water vapour from the back of the house. And an old, scabby Triumph Bonneville motorcycle parked under a lean-to adjoining the side wall, with its side panel removed and a battery charger hooked up to an extension cable that snaked across the weedy ground into the big barn. There were no other vehicles in sight. Ben pressed two fingers to the charger. It was warm to the touch as the current flowed into the motorcycle battery.

Someone was here. Someone who'd arrived at the place on foot and was making attempts at getting some wheeled transportation up and running, while getting some warmth into the cold, damp house. And Ben would have bet his right arm that he knew who that someone was. His doubts drained away and he felt a tingle of excitement.

He motioned to McAllister to stay put while he quickly, silently checked the outbuildings. They were empty. Whoever was here, he was pretty sure he'd find them in the house.

The door wasn't locked, which seemed to suggest that the house's occupant was confident that nobody would come looking for them here. Careless. Ben eased the door open very slowly and cautiously stepped into the entrance hall. He caught the smell of damp, mixed with lingering traces of incense and the more recent aroma of cooking that wafted from the kitchen to the right of the hall. He nudged the kitchen door and saw that the room was empty. On a plain wooden table with one chair pulled up to it were the remains of a meal – pizza crusts, smears of baked bean sauce – and two empty lager cans.

McAllister had entered the house behind him and was standing in the hall with Radar, who so far was behaving himself. Ben quickly checked the tatty living room, the table-less dining room and the water-stained downstairs bathroom: all empty too. With McAllister right behind him and the dog padding in their wake, he climbed the stairs. They creaked badly and every step was a torture – but nothing stirred above. Reaching the first floor landing Ben saw three doors: another bathroom and two bedrooms. Nobody there. He continued upwards to the second floor. The smell of damp was stronger up here, and the boards were warped underfoot. Murky light filtered through a small, mossy roof window. Two more doors, pitted and peeling: one at the head of the stairs, the other at the end of a passage under the sloping angle of the roof.

Ben checked the first door and found an attic room someone had been using as an artist's studio. There was an easel, an antique dresser covered in candlewax dribbles and old dried-up watercolour paints and brushes, and about a thousand canvases displaying images of pink, green and rainbow-coloured unicorns that looked like mutant Labradors with narwhal tusks sprouting from their heads. Ben closed the door. The room at the end of the passage was the last one in the house left for him to check. If that was empty too . . .

Ben stepped quietly up to the door, paused outside and pressed his ear to it. What he heard inside the room made his heart jump. It was the soft, rhythmic sound of someone sleeping. He nodded at McAllister, who signalled back with a thumbs-up. Then he grasped the doorknob and oh-so-carefully eased it open.

The attic bedroom was shadowed by drapes drawn over its single window. Ben stood motionless in the doorway, letting his eyes adjust to the darkness. The only furnishings in the attic room were an astronomical telescope mounted on a tripod by the window, a wooden chair and a bare double mattress laid on the floor.

Curled up on the mattress, cocooned inside a sleeping bag, was the source of the soft, steady breathing Ben had been able to hear through the door. The sleeper was lying on their side with their back to the doorway. Ben couldn't see their face, but in the semi-darkness he was able to make out the mop of instantly-recognisable blond hair draped over the pillow.

And there he was, the desperate fugitive from justice with the law hot on his heels, sleeping like a princess without a care in the world.

Chapter 42

Ben stalked quietly into the room, not wanting to wake Jude up. Not just yet. At the foot of the bed was a bulky and bulging black holdall. He eased open the zipper, peered inside and saw the stacked wads of the Albanian gangsters' walking-around money that told him McAllister's guess had been right. He shook his head. *You bloody idiot.*

McAllister was still lingering in the passage, holding the dog. Ben stepped away from the bag of money, picked up the wooden chair and set it down at the bedside. He sat down and looked down at the still-fast-asleep Jude. Reached down and gently nudged his shoulder and said, very softly, 'Psst. Room service. How about a nice cup of coffee?'

Jude stirred, rolled, stretched out sleepily and gave a contented half-smile that turned into a cavernous yawn. He murmured, 'Hmm? Yes please, that'd be great.'

Then he suddenly woke up fully with a jolt as though ice water had been sloshed over him. He jerked rigidly upright in the sleeping bag, eyes widening in horrified panic, looking around him wildly. Then he saw Ben sitting there next to him and his alarmed expression collapsed into total confusion. 'What the hell are you doing here?' he gasped.

'I might ask you the same question,' Ben said. 'Decide to take a little holiday from jail, did we?'

'How did you find me?'

'A blind man could have found you, you silly sod,' Ben replied. 'Did you really think you could hide out here for ever?'

Jude stared at him. Still too shocked to move from the crumpled sleeping bag. 'I . . . who's that?' Catching sight of McAllister, who had walked into the attic bedroom and was closing the door behind him.

'That's the gentleman who's come to arrest you,' Ben said. 'His name is Detective Inspector McAllister.'

Jude's face twisted in horror. 'Arrest me? And you're going to let him?'

'Let him? I brought him here.'

'You can't do this to me! Are you crazy? I'm innocent!'

'You were,' Ben said. 'Now, not so much. I'm sorry. You've got to go back to jail.'

Jude struggled up out of the sleeping bag and jumped to his feet. Ben stood up, seized him by the arms and thrust him bodily into the chair.

'Why is it, Jude, that every time I come to this house looking for you, I have to grab you by the scruff of the neck like the stupid little twit that you are? Don't you dare move from that chair, do you hear me? Or I will tie you up in it.'

But Jude wasn't inclined to obey his father's stern command. He twisted free, writhed up out of the chair and ran for the door, shoving McAllister out of the way.

'Good luck with that,' McAllister said drily as Jude burst out of the room and into the passage, slamming the door so hard behind him that it brought a rain of plaster from the ceiling. 'Let's see how far you get.'

From outside the door came a low, deep growl, followed by the sound of rushing paws and scuffling footsteps in the passage, a squawk and then a soft thud. Ben and McAllister exchanged glances and rushed for the door. They hurried out of the attic bedroom to see Jude pinned against the wall by ninety-five pounds of muscle, fur and teeth. Left on sentry duty outside the door, Radar took his job seriously. He was up on his hind legs with his forepaws planted above Jude's shoulders and his snarling jaws an inch from his face.

'For Christ's sake call this bloody werewolf off of me!' Jude said in a strangled voice.

'He's a police dog,' McAllister replied. 'He knows a dangerous fugitive when he sees one.'

'Please!'

'Here's the deal, son,' McAllister told him. 'You need to decide if you're dealing with me, or with the dog. The choice is, you either come quietly or you risk getting your bollocks ripped off.'

'You can't do this to me, you bastard!' Jude yelled at Ben. He was about to say more, but another rumbling growl from deep inside the German shepherd's chest silenced him.

'You did it to yourself,' Ben said. 'While you've been sitting in jail, I've been running around gathering evidence that you were put there unjustly. I know who's responsible for killing Duggan. I was so close to proving it. All you had to do was trust me. All you had to do was wait it out a little longer. One more day, maybe two. But you couldn't do that, could you? Instead you had to go and screw it all up.'

Jude's face fell. He seemed to have forgotten all about the dog. 'You *know*?'

'And so will you, soon enough,' Ben said. 'I'm hoping you might even get to meet him. The same man who ordered the murders of Emily Bowman, Joe Brewster, a young woman called Suzie Morton and who knows how many others. Killing people seems to run in his family.'

'Wait till I get my hands on him,' Jude growled, looking as fierce as the German shepherd.

'That's not your job,' Ben replied. 'Your job will be to stay with my friend here while I finish what I started.'

'But if you can prove who killed Duggan, why do I have to go back to jail?' Jude pleaded miserably.

'Because it's better than getting yourself plugged by the tactical firearms squad,' Ben told him. 'And because you'll still have to answer for running.'

McAllister asked Jude, 'So what's it to be, son? Will you come quietly?'

Jude's shoulders sagged in defeat. 'Don't have much choice, do I? Okay. Okay. I will.'

'That's what I like to hear,' McAllister said. 'Radar, off.'

The dog instantly released Jude, dropped back down on all fours and sat on his haunches, tail thumping happily, suddenly as docile as a family pet.

'I hate to do this, son,' McAllister said. 'But I have to.' Taking out his police warrant card – the real one this time, in its proper leather holder with a silver detective's badge – he held it up for Jude to see and said in a solemn voice, like a judge handing out a sentence, 'Jude Arundel, you are hereby under arrest on suspicion of escaping the custody of prison and being unlawfully at large. You do not have to say anything but it may harm your defence if you do not mention when questioned something which you later rely on in court . . .'

'Such as the fact that it wasn't my idea to escape?' Jude said. 'The Albanians planned the whole thing.'

'Why would they bring you along for the ride?' Ben asked.

'Because I helped them. Luan Copja thought he owed me something.'

'Helped him how?'

'Some guy tried to shank him, okay? I happened to be there.'

Ben stared at him. 'In prison less than a week, and you get into a knife fight?'

'It wasn't exactly what you'd call a fight,' Jude protested. 'All I did was take the knife off him, like the way Jeff showed me. Copja's guys were the ones who did all the stabbing.'

McAllister rolled his eyes and cleared his throat loudly. 'Aye, well, be sure to tell the judge all about it. That'll really stand you in good stead with your defence. Now, am I allowed to finish giving this caution, or what? You're making me lose my thread. Where was I?'

'"It may harm your defence if you do not mention when questioned something which you later rely on in court",' Ben reminded him.

'I can't believe you're helping him to do this,' Jude muttered bitterly.

'Anything you do say may be given in evidence,' McAllister

finished, in the same solemn tone. In his normal voice he added, 'I should cuff you now, but I didn't bring them. Can I trust you not to run again, son?'

'Stop calling me son,' Jude muttered.

'He's not going anywhere,' Ben said. 'If he tries, you have my permission to sick the dog on him.'

'Oh, thanks so much, Dad.'

McAllister turned to Ben. 'That takes care of that. Now let's get out of here. Once we're on the road we can rendezvous with Billie and the troops and he'll be carted safely back into custody.'

'Hold on, Tom,' Ben said. 'I'm not finished here yet.' He asked Jude, 'Does this house have a landline telephone?'

Jude nodded glumly. 'There's an old dial phone downstairs. Why do you want to know?'

Ben replied, 'Because you can't get a mobile signal up here in the armpit of nowhere.'

'That's not what I meant. Who are you going to call?'

'Have to say I'm curious about that myself,' McAllister said.

Ben said, 'I'm going to call the guy who started all this. And I'm going to invite him to come over and join us. It's time he and I had a talk.'

Chapter 43

The phone was a GPO antique trimphone from the seventies, hard-wired into a socket in the living room and half-hidden under stacks of magazines. Judging by the thick coating of dust it hadn't been used for a long time, but when Ben lifted the handset he found to his relief that it was still working. He sat in the broken-down armchair next to it, pulled up the number of the Galliard HQ that he'd found the night before, and dialled. Jude and McAllister had followed him downstairs and stood watching and listening.

A cheery recorded female voice informed him, 'Hello, you've reached the main offices of the Galliard Group Pharmaceuticals Division' and directed him to various extensions, or to hold for general enquiries. He held, and another female voice came on the line with a bright 'Good afternoon; how may I help you?' A friendly bunch, the Galliard Group. But the welcome mat wasn't going to remain rolled out for very long.

'I want to speak to Mr Clarkson,' Ben said, and the receptionist sounded as stunned as though he'd demanded an audience with the Queen.

'*Mr Clarkson*?'

'Gregory Clarkson, the CEO of the company you work for,' Ben said. 'The man who runs the Galliard Group. That's when he isn't having people killed and peddling shipments of biotoxins to terrorists and dictators. Put him on right now.'

Not too subtle. Last night in London, Ben's strategy had been to mount a surprise attack on the enemy. That tactic was now out of the window. Now he wanted, needed, Clarkson to know exactly what was coming. And he was purposely being as aggressive and confrontational as he could with this poor innocent employee at her desk, because it was the only way to prevent her from simply giving him the brush-off. Ben had just declared open war on the Galliard Group.

After a dumbstruck silence she responded hesitantly, 'Ah, uh, Mr Clarkson isn't in the office today.'

'Then put me through to wherever he is, or find someone else who can,' Ben said. 'And make it quick, because I don't have a lot of patience. If I don't get to speak with him very, very soon, the information I have will be delivered to the national media. I hope I'm making myself clear. This is not a prank call.'

'Ah, who shall I say is calling?'

'The ghost of Carter Duggan,' Ben said. 'Your boss will understand.'

Flustered, she asked him to hold and disappeared off the line for a few moments while she conferred with someone higher up the ladder. When she returned, sounding extremely nervous, she said she was going to have to get someone to call him back. Ben hadn't really expected to be put straight through to the top man, just like that. There would be several layers of hierarchy to penetrate before his message got through. The mention of the name Carter Duggan would be sure to get Clarkson's attention, if nothing else. Ben repeated his warning to the receptionist that it had better be quick, and hung up. 'Bombs away,' he said with a smile.

Jude was looking doubtful. 'No way they're going to call back.'

'They might not,' Ben replied. 'But he will.'

'Who the hell *is* this Clarkson character?'

Before Ben could answer, McAllister fired off his own salvo of questions. 'Terrorists? Biotoxins? The Galliard Group? What the frig have you been digging into, Hope?'

And so Ben explained the whole thing to them. He laid out every detail of what he'd discovered. The assignment Emily Bowman had given to Carter Duggan, spelling doom for both of them. Her grandmother's long-forgotten memoir, rediscovered in Glencora Bowman's attic after her death. The crazy tale of the Forty Elephants, Kitty Kelly and Diamond Annie in 1920s London. The sad story of Violet and Wilfred, and the discovery that had led to the tragic deaths of their young son and of Wilfred himself. The deadly secret of Achlys-14. The conspiracy between Sir Elliot Clarkson and the British government during World War One that had brought about the worst, and most deeply covered-up, accidental genocide in history. The Galliard Group's suspected present-day illegal activities and the silencing of any company employee who got wise or tried to blow the whistle. The murders of Suzie Morton and, more recently, of Joe Brewster.

Jude and McAllister listened in silence, transfixed, by turns shocked, disbelieving and angry. It was a long story, but they had time – that was, as long as the cops didn't find Black Rock Farm too soon. Ben was betting that they wouldn't. His whole plan hinged on being left alone here in this remote spot for just a few more hours. After that, the entire British police could land on them en masse if they wanted to, and let the chips fall where they may.

As his long account finally wound to an end, Ben said, 'There's only one conclusion to be drawn from all of this. I believe that as his investigation went deeper, Carter Duggan pretty much lost interest in the job he was doing for Emily Bowman. Everything changed when he talked to Joe Brewster. That's when he realised that something much bigger, and much more lucrative, was behind all this. He didn't have all the facts, because he never got as far as talking to Miles Redfield. He didn't know the full truth about Achlys-14. He might not even have had the full story of what lengths the Galliard Group had gone to to suppress what Miles and Suzie had found. But that didn't stop him, because he'd learned enough from Brewster, plus whatever he'd figured out for himself, to bluff his way and come across as a real, serious threat to them, if what he knew fell into the wrong hands.'

'You're saying that Duggan blackmailed them?' Jude asked.

Ben nodded. 'Or he tried to, at any rate. It was a gamble, but he was a sharp character. Ex-cop, private eye; those guys aren't entirely weak in the head. I'm thinking he must have done a fair job of convincing them that he really had the evidence to take them down. But by doing that, he sealed his own fate.'

'How much do you suppose he asked for?'

Ben said, 'Your guess is as good as mine. A lot. But he should have known there was no way that Clarkson and whichever of his chief associates are in on this were going to let some upstart private dick from Ottawa bend their billion-pound corporation over a barrel and walk away with a single penny. To pay would be to admit guilt, and once they'd crossed that line there was nothing to stop him coming back and back for more handouts, because that's what blackmailers do. And if they believed he really did have the dirty on them, they weren't about to let him live. They've got so much blood on their hands already. What was one more? Duggan was either too naive or too greedy to see it. Then the rest fell like dominoes. Collateral damage.'

'And the bastards thought they could get away with it,' McAllister grumbled.

'Why not? Galliard have been getting away with it for a hundred years. They always cover their tracks. Or in Jude's case, some innocent person who just happened to blunder into the picture by chance becomes a convenient scapegoat. But this time their plans didn't work out quite as neatly as they might have hoped.'

'You can say that twice,' McAllister chuckled. 'Someone messed things up for them. And we won't ask who *that* was.'

'But is it true?' Jude asked, dumbfounded. 'The poison gas? All those millions of victims? It's so big I can't get my head around it. And then the botox thing, on top of all that. Can human beings really be this evil?' This, from someone who'd personally witnessed enough atrocities during his time in Africa to sicken the most jaded cynic.

'I can't say how much of it is true,' Ben said. 'But if none of it were, then Clarkson and his thugs wouldn't have so much of a deadly secret to protect, and people wouldn't be getting killed. It's not rocket science.'

'It's just unbelievable.'

'We can't change the past,' Ben said. 'But we can stop them from hurting anyone else.'

'How do we do that?' Jude asked.

'It's pretty simple,' Ben told him. 'And we couldn't have picked a better spot for it. Far away from anyone or anything. Clarkson will think the same way. That's what I want him to think.'

'You reckon you can draw him out here, do you?' McAllister said. 'Is that your plan?'

'I know I can draw him here,' Ben said. 'He won't refuse, when he's heard the proposition I have for him.'

Jude asked, 'What proposition?'

'The same proposition that Duggan made him,' Ben said. 'Clarkson sat up and took notice that time around. He'll do the same again.'

McAllister said, 'So you're a blackmailer now, are you?'

'I'm not interested in his money,' Ben replied. 'Just the pleasure of his company.'

McAllister shook his head, sceptical. 'All right, say he takes the bait. What then? Are you looking to turn this place into another frigging battlefield? I agreed to come out here and help you out. But I won't be party to any killing.'

'Who said anything about killing?'

'You didn't need to. I get the impression that's how you resolve most conflicts.'

'I don't know where you get these notions about me,' Ben said with a smile.

'So you just want to have a gentle conversation with the guy, I suppose?'

'Not a single person more is going to die,' Ben assured him. 'Not if I can help it. Though I doubt Clarkson has the same idea. Like I said, we couldn't have picked a better ground zero for what he'll have in mind.'

'You're crazy,' McAllister said.

'Maybe I am,' Ben replied. 'But whether I am or not, this ends here. Today.'

Jude chewed his lip anxiously and glanced at the phone. 'I still don't think he'll call,' he said, as though he was hoping he was right.

'And if he doesn't?' McAllister asked Ben. 'What's the plan then, Sherlock?'

'He'll call,' Ben said.

They waited. Ben lit another cigarette and relaxed in the armchair, breathing slowly, barely moving. Jude sat fretting and silent. McAllister paced the living room until he got bored and hungry, and went to the kitchen to see what he could rustle up to eat, complaining loudly at the lack of ingredients. Outside, the fog began to lift. Which was both a good thing, and a bad thing. Good, because it cleared the way for Clarkson to respond to Ben's challenge and get here fast. Bad, because Clarkson wasn't the only person out there looking to land on Black Rock Farm. The police manhunt could be hours away, or it could be minutes away, or they might never find this place at all. Ben's plan was a house of cards that depended uncomfortably on timing and chance.

But he'd bet everything on timing and chance before now, and won.

After half an hour, Ben was wondering if Clarkson was going to ignore his call. After forty-five minutes he was beginning to worry that his underlings might not have passed the message on at all.

And then, fifty-three minutes after Ben had made the call, the old GPO trimphone started to ring.

Chapter 44

Ben picked up the phone and said nothing, waiting for the caller to speak first.

'I'm willing to take an educated guess that I'm speaking with Mr Hope,' the caller said. 'Or should I say, Major Hope.' His voice was smooth and steady, soft and calm, but strong and full of authority. Sounding like a man in complete control of himself. Someone used to being in charge of everything and everyone around him. Accustomed to command, and to winning. Projecting an aura of utter confidence that he would inevitably come out as the victor this time too, once again.

Or that, at least, was the impression Clarkson wanted to give. He was doing a damn good job of it, too. Except Ben understood the psychology of his enemy and was perfectly aware that Clarkson was far, far less confident than he was trying so hard to appear. The very fact that he'd committed himself to calling a potentially unsecure landline phone, risking so much in order to find out what Ben wanted, was proof enough that behind the cool exterior Clarkson was as nervous as hell. And very frightened.

'You can call me Ben,' Ben said. 'And I'll call you Gregory.'

'Sounds as though you're interested in building a cordial relationship.'

'If it makes doing business that bit easier,' Ben said.

The calm, steady voice gave a chuckle. 'I was wondering to what I owed the pleasure of this conversation. Very well. Let's talk business. Your message, as cryptic as it was, seemed to indicate that you're looking to sell me something?'

'I am,' Ben said. 'Your freedom, along with the evidence I have in my possession that would deprive you of it for a very long time, if I were to pass it to certain people.'

Clarkson sounded unruffled, outwardly. 'I can't say I'm entirely surprised, judging by the tone of your initial approach. As I suspected, this sounds rather less like a business proposition and rather more like a cheap and nasty attempt at extortion. You should know that I don't truck with blackmailers.'

'No, you have them rubbed out instead,' Ben said. 'Which is what you did to Carter Duggan.'

'I'm afraid I have no idea what you're talking about.'

'You don't have time for bluff and bravado, Gregory,' Ben said. 'Duggan thought he had enough bare facts to scare you into paying him off. It didn't work out so well for him. But here's your problem. You knew full well that Duggan only had half the facts. Enough to make him dangerous, but the rest was smoke and mirrors. Unluckily for you, I'm not a big bullshitter like Duggan was. I'm also not as easy to take off the table. As you might have noticed.'

Clarkson's voice remained perfectly calm, but he was stepping out on a limb, committing himself entirely. This was a dangerous moment for him. 'Easy enough to say. You're going to have to convince me that you have something more substantial to bargain with.'

Ben replied, 'Try this on for size, Gregory. How about the fact that the secret weapon your dear grandfather developed for British Intelligence wasn't named after the Greek warrior Achilles, as Duggan thought? For a hotshot investigator he dropped the ball on that one. Close, but no cigar. Duggan picked his information up secondhand from Joe Brewster, another person whose name I'm sure is familiar to you. Whereas I have it from a much more knowledgeable source, one you haven't been able to get at because he's covered his tracks. It so happens that I have the original Achlys-14 lab reports sitting right here in front of me. It's all here, Gregory. Dates, signatures, technical notes. Right down to the last detail as recorded by Ivor Holloway, Alf Liddell and Cecil Watson. Liddell's account is the hardest to read, the poor guy knowing he was going to die the way both his colleagues had. Do you want me to go on?'

Now Ben was the one going out on a limb. He anxiously half-expected Clarkson to call his bluff. But all he heard was a terse, discomfited silence on the other end of the line.

Ben smiled and said, 'I know what must be going through your mind right now, Gregory. Of course, you can't say it, because you'd be incriminating yourself even worse than you have already. But you're thinking it can't be possible that I have those documents, since they were taken from the wreckage of Suzie Morton's Mini Cooper after you had your thugs run her off the road. I'm sure you probably had them destroyed, too. What you're missing is that Miss Morton and

330

her fiancé Miles Redfield had made copies of those documents, which they hid elsewhere. Did you really think they wouldn't have covered their backs, knowing the kind of people they were dealing with?'

More silence on the other end of the line. Ben sensed that Clarkson was badly rattled. He pressed on, moving in for the kill now.

'And that's not all I have here,' he said. 'Because Miles and Suzie weren't the only former Galliard employees to have caught the company with its pants down. Joe Brewster, the man you thought you'd zippered with your million-pound golden handshake, passed me enough documentary evidence on your illegal sales of botulinum toxin to destroy your corporation for ever. It fits nicely with the thick file of cooked accounts that Suzie Morton also had in her possession when she was murdered, the copies of which I now have. Put it all together and it really doesn't make the Galliard Group look so great, does it? Genocide, war crimes, commerce with terrorists and warlords. I have it all, Mr Clarkson. And I strongly advise you not to encourage me to use it. Mess with me and I will sink you to the bottom of the ocean.'

Clarkson said nothing.

'Hello?' Ben said. 'Are you still there? Do you believe me now?'

After a long further pause the voice at the other end of the line said, 'All right. Enough of the threats. You want to talk business, let's talk business. Suppose, purely for the sake of hypothesis, that the information you're referring to actually existed, relating to events that may or may not be purely imaginary and the figment of a deranged mind, but which could nonetheless cause a great deal of inconvenience were the knowledge of them to be made public. Naturally, in such a case one would prefer such information to be kept private.'

'I was sure you'd see it that way,' Ben said.

'What – again, speaking hypothetically – would be the cost of such a mutually beneficial arrangement?'

'The cost would be five million pounds in cash,' Ben said. 'That's pocket change, to a man like you. It's also a sum of money you could reasonably be expected to get together quickly. Luckily for you, I'm a reasonable person. A realist, and not too greedy. Or else I'd have asked for ten.'

'That would be an acceptable price, hypothetically.'

'Of course it would, you dirty bastard,' Ben said inwardly. Out loud he replied, 'I'm so pleased to hear you say so. I have two more conditions.'

'I'm listening.'

'First, I'd like to get this concluded nice and quickly, so I want the money today.' Ben looked at his watch. 'It's quarter to two. My location is approximately two hundred and sixty miles from London, very remote, very private. Not much over an hour's helicopter flight. Plus, say, another hour to get the cash together. To be generous, I'll give you until four o'clock this afternoon to deliver me the money.'

A pause. 'I can't promise, but that doesn't sound unfeasible.'

'You know what happens if you fail, Gregory. I'm not in the business of offering second chances. Now, my final condition.'

'There's more? You drive a hard bargain, Major Hope.'

'My final condition is that you bring the money to me personally. I want it from your own hand. In a nice leather case, which I get to keep, of course. Once I'm satisfied the cash is all there, we make the exchange, and I can guarantee that you'll never hear from me again.'

'You've obviously never seen five million pounds in cash before. It will take more than one case.'

'You do whatever you need to do, arsehole,' Ben said harshly, sounding exactly like the nastiest, cheapest, lowest scumbag extortionist he'd ever come across in all his years of dealing with ransom-hungry kidnappers. 'Just make sure you get me that money. You try to double-deal me, you'll wish you hadn't. Understand?'

It was a deal only an idiot would have offered, full of holes, no less of an open invitation to disaster than whatever Carter Duggan might have presented them with. Clarkson would be very much aware of that. Ben wanted the lure to be as irresistible as he could make it.

Clarkson was quiet for another long moment. Ben heard a muted exchange of voices in the background, as he conferred with someone standing nearby. Then Clarkson came back on the line and said, 'Very well, we have a deal. Give me your GPS location.'

Chapter 45

'He won't come,' McAllister said the instant Ben put the phone down.

'He will, because he has to,' Ben said. 'Because we're sitting ducks out here and this is too good a thing to pass up. And because we're so deep under his skin now that he's going to want to see us dead with his own eyes.'

'See *us* dead? I'm not sure I like the sound of that.'

'Don't be such a wimp, McAllister. What do you think I brought you here for? I said I needed the backup, remember?'

'Yeah, right. Two eedjits are better than one.'

'Three,' Jude said. 'I'm here too. I want to help.'

Ben shook his head. 'I know you do. But it's not what I want.'

'How many do you think he'll bring with him?' McAllister asked.

'As many as he can get on board a fast helicopter,' Ben said.

'And I suppose they'll be armed to the teeth.'

'I wouldn't have it any other way,' Ben said.

McAllister looked at him. 'What I said before, about you

being crazy? I take it back. I was wrong. Crazy's not the word for what you are. You're a bona fide raving frigging mental case. How the hell does one man on his own tackle a bunch of gun-toting maniacs, without killing anyone?'

'What about broken arms and legs, are they allowed?'

'I'll already have enough explaining to do when this is over. Can we lay off the fractures?'

'What about concussion, bruising, loose teeth?'

'Please don't mention teeth to me. Can you spell "reason-able force"?'

'I promise to be as gentle as I can,' Ben said.

Now all they could do was go back to waiting. They had a guaranteed time window of at least two hours before anything would happen. Ben went into the kitchen, hunted through cupboards and found a bag of rice and a tin of beef stew. He set a pan of water to boil on the stove. Dumped the contents of the can into a smaller cast-iron pot and started gently heating it up. As he searched the drawers for cutlery he came across a pair of walkie-talkies. They were old and scuffed, but the batteries still had juice in them. Interesting. Ben set them aside.

As he was preparing his meal, Jude joined him in the kitchen. Ben pointed at the walkie-talkies. 'What are those for?'

'Oh, those go back years. When Robbie and some of the gang used to have major parties where there were drugs going around, he used to get someone to keep watch on the driveway in case Meadow and Bertie turned up. They never did, though.'

Ben just nodded. Jude leaned on the counter, watching

him with a rueful expression. 'Listen, I don't know what to say. You did all this for me. If I hadn't run, you wouldn't be taking this risk.'

'Whichever way it went, it was always going to boil down to me and Clarkson,' Ben said. 'Maybe this is for the better.'

'What if the police get here first, looking for me?'

'We'll cross that bridge if we come to it,' Ben said. He stirred his warming stew. It reminded him of army rations.

Jude chewed his lip and frowned. 'I can't believe how calm you are.'

'If running around in a panic could help me,' Ben said, 'I'd do that instead.' He dipped a spoon into the rice, tasted a grain, added some salt to the water, tasted another. 'This is nearly done. There's too much for me. You want some?'

'I couldn't eat another bite,' Jude said, shaking his head. 'My stomach feels all knotted up and I can't sit down. How can you eat at a time like this?'

Ben smiled. 'It's like I always used to tell my troopers. There's nothing like a good warm meal before going into battle.' The rice was done. He strained it off, ladled a pile of it into a bowl and dumped the meat stew on top, then pulled up a chair at the table to eat.

'Sometimes I realise how different we are,' Jude said, watching him. 'I know I've got into a few scrapes, but I was always terrified. I'm terrified now. But you, you enjoy this kind of thing, don't you? You're actually looking forward to having a showdown with these people.'

'What I look forward to the most is going home afterwards,' Ben said. 'And you'll be going with me, when the time comes.'

'Home,' Jude reflected sadly. 'I was thinking about home. When this is all over one day, I don't think I can ever return to that house.'

'You grew up there. Your mother and Simeon loved it.'

Jude shook his head. 'There are nothing but bad memories there for me now. I'll always see Duggan lying there. I was thinking I should sell it, but I wanted to ask you first. I know how much you love the place, too.'

'It's your choice, Jude. You don't have to rush into anything.'

'Yeah, I'll have plenty of time to mull over it while I'm back in bloody prison again,' Jude said bitterly. 'Christ, I can't stand this waiting around. I'm going for a walk.'

Alone, Ben quietly finished his meal. He washed it down with the last of the beer, and then took out his cigarettes and lighter. He was down to his last Gauloise. As he lit up, he thought about what was coming in a couple of hours' time. This might really be his last Gauloise.

Ben spent a few minutes pondering what arrangements he needed to make, in the event of things turning out badly. In addition to various other assets there was a respectable sum of money in a secret personal account that he never touched, which would become Jude's and would – as long as he didn't go crazy with it – last him a good long while. Ben took out the small notebook that he carried, cleared aside his plate and wrote a short note to Jeff Dekker to instruct him to do the necessary, by whatever means were required. Even if Jude were still a criminal suspect on the run, Jeff would find a way to get the money to him.

He found McAllister in the living room, still pacing restlessly up and down and pressing his hand against his cheek with a soft groan of pain, a recumbent Radar watching him from a sofa. With Jude out of the way Ben said, 'Listen, Tom, when this kicks off things might get a little hot around here. I need you and Jude to be far from the action. If anything happens to me, take off and keep going.' He handed him the note. 'I'll also need you to send this. I've written the address on the back.'

McAllister took the note gravely. He asked, 'If I'm far from the action, how will I know what's happening?'

'With one of these,' Ben replied, giving him a walkie-talkie. 'I'll radio at five-minute intervals from when they arrive. If six minutes go by and you haven't heard from me, it means I'm dead.'

McAllister accepted the radio, but he didn't look happy. 'If anything happens to you, and if I'm not around to arrest them, the bad guys get away with it. And I suppose if I tried, they'd kill me too. Either way they're home free.'

'Unless the police could make the connection with Achlys-14, the botulinum and Duggan.'

'Without any real proof to go on. Good luck with that,' McAllister said. 'In which case it's bye-bye for the mitigating evidence that would exonerate Jude. He'd still have the murder charge hanging over him, on top of the escape. Come the trial, he could be looking at twenty years.'

Ben nodded. There was no avoiding that possibility.

'In which case,' McAllister said, 'I was never here, and I never laid eyes on him. I'll let him run, and he can take his chances out there. I won't let an innocent man spend his life in prison.'

Ben shook McAllister's hand. 'You're a decent guy, Tom. Even if you are a cop.'

'I'll take that as a compliment.'

They waited. Time seemed to have slowed to a crawl. Going out of his mind with frustration, Jude skulked off to nap on the threadbare living room sofa. As four p.m. dragged closer, Ben did a reconnoitre of Black Rock Farm and its various long-disused agricultural features, barns, pens and storerooms. Once upon a time, many years ago, Bertie and Meadow Brocklebank had made a half-hearted stab at quitting their townie existence and becoming proper smallholders. All that remained of their failed attempt was a mouldering store of organic fertiliser and a variety of shovels and picks and hoes, never used, now speckled with rust. In another corner was a weathered heap of building timber for some outbuilding renovation project that had never happened.

While Ben was doing his round of the property, McAllister headed off down the track to move the car away from its conspicuous position by the gate. He parked it in an agreed spot quarter of a mile the other side of a small hill, behind some trees where it was less likely to be noticed from the air. Nearby was the ruin of a stone barn, predating the farm by a century or more, where he and Jude would take cover when the showdown began. While McAllister was in position he and Ben tested their radios to make sure they would be in range of one another.

McAllister returned to the farm on foot. He and Ben shared a mug of coffee in silence. They waited. The police didn't come. The hour drew nearer. And nearer. Ben still felt calm. He climbed the stairs to the top floor attic room and positioned the astronomical telescope to scan the horizon to the north-east, the direction from which he expected the enemy to approach. Land-spotting optics showed their images the right way up, but their stargazing counterparts produced an upside-down view: the picture Ben could see in the eyepiece was of the inverted hills weirdly suspended above a sky now almost completely clear of cloud cover. A fine day for a high-speed helicopter journey halfway across England, to rid yourself of your enemy at the end of it.

Three-thirty p.m. came and went. Three-forty-five. Ben returned downstairs to send Jude and McAllister away.

'I don't want to leave you alone here,' Jude said, visibly emotional.

'Don't you worry about me,' Ben assured him.

McAllister wished him luck, and then they were gone, making the quarter-mile trek over rough ground to the ruined barn. Ben headed back up to the attic room and resumed watching the sky.

Four o'clock ticked by. Clarkson didn't come.

Ten past. Quarter past.

Clarkson still didn't come.

Then at last, Ben spotted the tiny dark speck over the hills. He watched intently as it grew into the shape of an approaching helicopter, heading out of the north-east straight for the farm. As it got closer, he could see in the upside-down image that it definitely wasn't a police aircraft. The pale sunshine glittered off its red fuselage. The distant thud of rotors became a roaring clatter.

They were coming.

The helicopter settled down to land on a patch of open

ground a hundred yards from the edge of the farm property, flattening a wide circle of long grass with its downdraught. The pilot shut down the turbine and its howling note dropped in pitch. The side hatches opened. Ben watched as the pilot and passengers all got out. The diminishing hurricane from the rotors tore at their hair and clothes as they hurried away from the aircraft, heads low.

There were seven men. Two of them were distinctive from the others: one a tall, slim, authoritative-looking middle-aged man in a long and elegant black coat. Gregory Clarkson had met the challenge to make a personal appearance at this showdown. Scurrying along at his side was a smaller, younger man who from his appearance was obviously another company executive, incongruous out here in his suit and shiny shoes.

Exactly as Ben had expected, there was no sign of a nice shiny leather attaché case filled with money, let alone the several cases it would take to accommodate five million pounds. Clarkson was never going to bring the cash. And exactly as Ben had also expected, what Clarkson had brought instead were the five large, powerfully built and heavily armed companions who fell into formation like bodyguards around their boss as the group hurried away from the chopper and started walking purposefully towards the farm.

The five looked much more in their element than Clarkson and his corporate colleague. They were dressed for combat in boots, fatigues and tactical vests, and they clutched their automatic weapons in gloved fists. Serious, gruff, grim-faced professionals, none under thirty-five. One of them, the pilot, had the walk, the attitude, the buzz-cut look of an ex-military operative and he held his weapon like a trained man. Ben had no doubt that the other four could handle themselves pretty well, too, whether Clarkson had picked his team from the private security industry or from other, less kosher, sources of manpower.

Ben stepped away from the telescope and headed for the door. He knew what he had to do next. He was ready for them.

Game on.

Chapter 46

Jasper Hogan, Gregory Clarkson's right-hand man, partner in crime and highly-paid company vice-director, was extremely nervous. He felt queasy from the chopper ride and his mouth was dry as he hurried in his boss's wake through the long grass. His handmade John Lobb Oxford brogues weren't made for this kind of terrain. There wasn't a molecule of his being that belonged for a single second in this godforsaken wilderness. He deeply resented having been pressured into leaving his comfortable office for this reckless, in his opinion wildly misguided, cod-military expedition to sodding Cornwall and a confrontation with the man who'd already laid waste to a good number of their hired hands. Hogan was afraid of the surly heavies with guns, who towered over him and barely spoke, acting like they were mercenaries in some foreign war zone. He was afraid of Gregory Clarkson. But most of all he was afraid of Ben Hope.

Hogan's boss was striding over the rough ground with a look of steely purpose, grimmer and more determined than the vice-director had ever seen him. Hogan had to jog to keep up. Speaking just loudly enough to be heard over the noise of the helicopter he pointed towards Black Rock Farm and asked Clarkson for the twentieth time, 'How can we be so sure Hope is even here? This could be a trick.'

'Oh, it's a trick all right,' Clarkson snapped back at him, eyes fixed on the distant farmhouse. 'He might be a better bluffer than Duggan was, but he's still a bluffer. He doesn't have a thing on us.'

'Then what are we even doing here?' Hogan asked, again for the twentieth time. 'Why take such a risk? With all respect, sir, I still think this is a bad strategy.'

Clarkson turned towards him with a flash of venomous anger that made Hogan almost flinch. 'Get this through your head, Hogan,' Clarkson seethed at him. 'When you have a rat in your house, you don't just ignore it and hope it goes away. You make damn well sure the thing is as dead as dead can be. Then you pick it up by the tail and you fling its filthy little body into the fire. That's what we're doing here. I want that man out of my life for good, and I won't settle for being told about it by some moronic underling who's getting paid to tell me what I want to hear. Understand? Good. Now keep your fucking mouth shut.'

Turning towards his men he said more loudly, 'Spread out. I doubt you'll find him in the house. He'll use that as a decoy and be hiding in one of those outbuildings instead, so concentrate on those. Surround the property and shoot anything that moves. This man is dangerous and he can't be allowed to get away. Remember the bonus for the one who takes him down. All right? Now get moving.'

The fact was that, for all his outward confidence and commanding authority, Gregory Clarkson was every bit as nervous as Hogan. He'd never had too many scruples about following in the footsteps of his grandfather; ordering the elimination of troublesome individuals and being indirectly responsible for the deaths of many, many more, whose names and nationalities he'd never even know and didn't much care about, gave him no moral qualms. Likewise, the actions he'd been forced to take over the Duggan affair hadn't kept him awake at night for any reasons of conscience – no, what racked him with worry was the thought of the damage that could be done to him and his company by anyone getting too close to the secret of his clandestine operations. First it had been that blasted Canadian. Now it was Ben Hope, a more dangerous threat by far.

These last few months had been a fraught time for Clarkson's precious company. It had never aspired to become the biggest of its kind in Europe, far from it – the Galliard Group was dwarfed in size by many of its competitors, the Pfizers and GSKs of this world – but it had always punched well above its weight and share prices were up and up. Even so, it wasn't so rich and powerful as to be impervious to ruin. Last October the company had been hit by a class-action lawsuit over the claimed side effects of one of his most profitable above-board pharmaceutical products, a diet pill that caused kidney damage to a small percentage of users. He'd been getting away with it for years, but after a particularly determined lawyer had produced enough clients and medical evidence to torpedo his business he'd eventually caved in and settled out of court for a crippling seven-figure sum that still made his eyes water when he thought about it.

Clarkson had only narrowly dodged further injury by

resorting to his usual means of bribery and intimidation to keep the fiasco from becoming public knowledge. The last thing his weakened company needed right now was another scandal. And the horrible truths that stood to be revealed by his enemies went way beyond the realms of the merely scandalous. If it came out that he had been raking in illicit fortunes from well-organised terror groups and UN-subsidised tin-pot regimes who were secretly stockpiling Galliard-produced botulinum for use in biological warfare, it would do more than sink him financially. He and his co-conspirator Jasper Hogan would probably spend the rest of their lives behind bars.

For that reason, Ben Hope must die. He must die today. Right here, right now. And, Clarkson reflected with a smile, he couldn't have picked a better location for his own demise. This was perfect.

The track leading to Black Rock Farm lay to the east side of the property, and the smaller outbuildings and abandoned animal pens were clustered at the far end, to the west side, with most of the fields and paddocks extending northwards beyond the back of the old farmhouse, which was partly hidden from view by a hulking domed metal shed that was the largest of the barns. There was no sign of movement within the farm, except for a rusty bit of corrugated iron that hung loose from the side wall of the big barn and flapped in the wind.

As they got closer, Clarkson and Hogan slowed their pace and hung back, letting the armed men move ahead. Obeying their orders the five spread out so that they could approach the house from multiple angles. Two of the men, Reynolds and Webster, worked their way around the west side of the farm while two more, Nelson and Shaw, curved around towards the east side, forming a pincer movement. The fifth man, the ex-military pilot whose name was Pearce, took the middle line straight towards the house. Their eyes were sharp and their weapons were cocked and ready.

Everyone was certain that Hope would be expecting an assault. He might start shooting at any moment, a prospect that made Hogan cringe and hold his breath. Even Clarkson seemed to have lost some of his steely composure, the nervousness beginning to show. But no rattle of gunfire sounded from the farm as the five men reached the fence and clambered over its hanging barbed wire strands into the property. Nothing. Just the clank-clank of the flapping loose iron sheet, the dwindling whip-whip of the helicopter rotors behind them and the moan of the rising wind. A weather front was racing in from the west; the sky that had been so clear and blue just minutes earlier was now darkening as a solid mass of pendulous, gravid storm clouds gathered overhead.

Pearce, the ex-military pilot, was the first over the fence. Check the barns, the boss had said, and Pearce was inclined to agree that was where Hope was most likely to be lurking in wait for them. The big metal barn was closest. Pearce stalked towards it, and got there just as the clouds opened. The raindrops began slowly but in moments had intensified into a deluge, water streaming down the curve of the barn's roof. Pearce moved quickly, cautiously around the side of the building to a sheet metal doorway that hung open a few inches, swaying in the wind.

He paused, then stepped inside with his weapon raised,

swinging the muzzle from side to side. Safety off, ready to rock'n'roll. It was just like the old days for him. Pearce had served for seven inglorious years with the British Army before getting kicked out for dealing in stolen weapons. He was very sure of his capabilities and certainly wasn't intimidated by going up against some pumped-up ex-Special Forces prick. Those guys weren't all they were hyped up to be.

Pearce didn't have a very high opinion of his teammates, either. He was the only real soldier of the five – in his own estimation by far the most proficient and skilled killer, with some highly accomplished jobs under his belt – and he was itching to get at the arsehole who'd taken out several of his associates, two in particular who were his old pals from back in the day and had never returned from the Emily Bowman hit. Pearce was going to take particular pleasure in dragging Hope's dead body out to present like a trophy to the boss. Not to mention the £10,000 extra bounty on offer to the man who nailed the bastard. For Pearce, there was no doubt about who would get the prize.

It was dark and murky inside the big barn. The hammering rain sounded like machine-gun fire against the tall domed metal roof. Pearce trod carefully to avoid the bits of junk and old bottles that littered the compacted-earth floor. At the far end was a kind of makeshift wooden stage, covered in a mess of big black boxes that he identified as music amplifiers and PA speakers. Looked like a bunch of wannabe rock stars hung out in this place. Losers.

He moved deeper into the building, listening and watching for the slightest movement. His high-velocity bullets would punch through the thin metal walls like hot needles through butter, and he needed to be sure of his target lest he accidentally shoot one of his team – or, much worse, shoot the man who was paying him. Pearce's finger rested lightly on the trigger and his right eye was pressed to the ACOG optical sight on his weapon. Moments like this were what he lived for. He was pumping with excitement at the prospect of flushing Ben Hope from his hiding place. *Come out, come out, wherever you are.*

In fact Pearce was so excited that while he was on full alert to detect and destroy any enemy that might suddenly appear in front of him, he'd forgotten his training and neglected to look up at the thick, strong rafters overhead.

The massive blow hit him from above. Something very heavy but quite soft came crashing down on his head and flattened him to the floor with a muffled thud that was all but lost over the sound of the hammering rain. The big hessian bag of organic fertiliser that had been dropped on him from a height of twenty feet split open with the impact, and Pearce was covered in mouldy, powdery pellets as he lay there groaning and dazed. He was barely conscious of the second light thud of someone jumping down from the rafters to land next to him. Or of the knee that pressed against his carotid artery, cutting off the oxygen to his brain. Once fully unconscious, he couldn't possibly have been aware of being dragged away across the barn floor, rolled into the shadows and quickly, expertly tethered up with a length of electric guitar cable and gagged with a piece of sacking material. He'd be out of action for several minutes before he came to, writhing and struggling against his bonds. By then, it would all be over.

Across to the west side of Black Rock Farm, Reynolds and Webster were much less concerned about their team colleagues than with their own personal safety as they crept towards a rickety, ancient milking shed that looked like the kind of place a crafty and dangerous opponent might hide. The pounding rain soaked through their hair and ran into their eyes. The dirt of the yard was rapidly getting churned up into slippery mud by the deluge. They flanked the doorway of the milking shed, nodded to one another and then slipped quickly through, Reynolds first, Webster following right behind. They covered each other well as they burst into the shadowy interior. The windows were streaked with green filth and very little light penetrated inside. The shed stank of damp straw and there was moss growing on the concrete stall dividers where now long-dead cattle would once upon a time have been set in rows to be hooked up to the milking machinery. Disused farm equipment and old windows and stacks of crates and pallets, broken tools and bits of timber were piled up here and there, offering lots of hiding places where their enemy could be lurking in wait, ready to attack. They trained their weapons left and right, covering every inch, willing him to come out. If Hope was hiding in here, he was a dead man for sure.

Reynolds froze, thinking that he'd heard something. A tiny rustle among the straw, barely audible over the steady roar of the rain pounding the shed roof. He couldn't be certain, but it seemed to have come from the shadows behind a heap of mouldy old timber. He signalled to Webster, who paused mid-step and followed the line of Reynolds' pointing finger in the direction of the sound. The two of them stood very still, barely breathing, listening hard with their guns clasped tight against their shoulders and aiming blind into the darkness. Reynolds could hear nothing but the storm outside and the flutter of his own heart. What he'd heard was probably just a rodent, he thought. The place must be crawling with them. He signalled again to Webster and shook his head. *False alarm.* They moved on a few steps, trying to make as little noise as possible.

Now it was Webster's turn to stop and motion to his colleague, thinking he'd seen something. He was pointing at some corrugated sheets that had been propped at an angle against a wall to form a triangular nook, into which a man could have wedged himself. Reynolds nodded. He trained his sights on the dark triangle, ready to start blasting, as Webster tiptoed through the shadows up to the sheets, reached tentatively out to grasp the edge of the nearest, and quickly yanked it away from the wall to reveal . . . nothing but a patch of cobwebbed brickwork and some startled woodlice that scuttled away in panic.

Reynolds heaved a sigh. *Bollocks.* They'd obviously drawn a blank with the milking shed. He turned to Webster and was just about to say, 'Let's go, he ain't in here' when Webster suddenly toppled forward and crashed down onto his face.

For the first brief fraction of a second Reynolds thought his companion had tripped over some object hidden in the matted straw. Before he could react, a dark shape appeared at his side and something hit him extremely hard across the side of the head, and his lights went out.

Chapter 47

Ben stepped out of the shadows and stood over the limp bodies. They weren't moving, but all the same he gave each of them another hefty whack of the axe handle to make sure they were definitely out for the count. Reasonable force; nothing like it in the world.

He quickly trussed their wrists and ankles with some lengths of baling twine he'd found in the milking shed. The thin nylon cord might have been bright pink and not very macho stuff, but it was immensely strong and no man alive could break it with his hands. The knots were almost impossible to pick, too. When his work was done, he dragged them between a couple of stall dividers where they'd be reasonably protected from what was about to happen next.

The rainstorm seemed to be hammering down even harder. Anything that cut noise and visibility were fine by Ben. He checked his watch, the diver's illuminated face glowing green in the gloom, and counted down the last seconds before another five-minute interval was up. Right on cue he thumbed the talk key on his radio and reported to McAllister, in a whisper, 'Still here. Stand by for some fireworks. Over.'

McAllister came back an instant later, 'Copy that. Watch your back, pal.'

Ben picked up one of the fallen weapons. It was a nice enough piece of kit, identical to the one his first victim had been carrying, now stripped and scattered into pieces: an IWI Galil Ace, the latest Israeli variant on the time-tested Kalashnikov assault rifle design, straight out of the box, fully loaded up with a thirty-round magazine. Clarkson must have some pretty hot contacts within the UK to get hold of these toys. Ben set the fire selector to full-auto, flipped off the safety, pointed the muzzle towards the floor away from his feet and squeezed off a short blast. Bits of shredded straw flew up and a stream of spent brass flew from the ejector port. The rattle of gunfire was massively loud inside the shed and would be plenty audible outside it. Which, at this point in the execution of his plan, was just what Ben wanted.

The expected commotion from outside came moments later: Ben heard the running footsteps and raised voices as the fourth and fifth of Clarkson's men came dashing across the yard from wherever they'd been hunting for him, suddenly alerted to the sound of the rifle shots. Ben let off another deafening burst for good measure to leave them in no doubt where he was. If they'd known that their comrades were down and trussed like turkeys on the floor, they'd have opened fire on the milking shed and he'd have been caught inside like a rat in a trap. But they didn't know that – in the confusion it was just as possible that at least one of their guys was standing and it was Ben on the ground, full of holes.

As the two came charging inside the milking shed to find

out what the hell was happening, Ben stepped quickly across to the piece of sturdy four-by-three wooden post that was the only thing holding up the cowshed roof. He'd sawn through enough of its original supports earlier to have made the entire structure dangerously weak. He lashed a hard kick at the base of the wooden post and dived under cover between the concrete stall dividers as the roof buckled and then collapsed inwards with a groan and a rending crash.

Through the falling wreckage Ben caught a brief glimpse of Clarkson's men: one of them staring upwards in paralysed horror as a ton of cobwebbed dry-rotted timbers and asbestos sheeting came down on top of him, the other trying to bolt back towards the doorway but not making it before he, too, was buried and pinned to the floor.

Ben was blinded for a few seconds by the swirling dust. Deliberately collapsing a building onto his own head was something he'd never done before. *Maybe I am mad*, said a fleeting voice in his head. But he didn't have a lot of time to dwell on it. As the clouds of dust began to subside he saw the gaping hole where a collapsing beam had taken down part of the wall. Coughing, eyes stinging, he pulled himself out from under his sheltering place still clutching the Galil rifle, shouldered aside a broken asbestos roof sheet that blocked his exit, and crawled out over the debris into the pounding rain.

He looked back at the flattened ruin of the milking shed and doubted whether any of Clarkson's four men trapped inside had been crushed to death. One thing was for sure, they wouldn't be going anywhere in a hurry.

Five men down, no permanent casualties. It was time to

354

move on. Clarkson and his company associate were Ben's main concern now.

He glanced all around him, blinking as the rainwater washed the dust out of his eyes. The farmyard was a deserted sea of mud. Past the side of the big barn and beyond the fence he could see the Galliard helicopter sitting empty on the wet ground, its rotor blades static and drooping.

He shouldered the Galil, took aim through its optical battle sight, centred the dot reticle on the area of the chopper's fuel tank hatch, and fired. The ripping report wasn't as loud as inside the shed, but still damn loud. Bullet holes appeared in the side of the aircraft's fuselage, drawn in a ragged vertical line by the climb of the recoil. It was no target rifle. Ben adjusted his aim and fired another sustained blast, and this time the chopper did what he wanted it to do, and exploded in a great mushrooming fireball that sent a tower of black smoke rising up to be dispersed by the wind. The boom of the explosion rolled across the barren landscape.

Ben lowered the rifle and gazed with satisfaction at the blazing shell of the helicopter. Just in case Clarkson and his man decided to try their luck at escaping by air. If they wanted to get away, they'd have to hoof it. Ben had no intention of letting that happen. He scanned the surrounding moors for two little running figures, but could see nothing. He ran back to the big barn in case they might have slipped in there. The only living soul inside was the bound and gagged gunman he'd left there earlier, now awake and struggling in vain to get free.

Ben hunted through more of the various smaller sheds

and outbuildings. They weren't hiding under the lean-to where Jude had moved the motorbike, with its spark plugs removed in case anyone got ideas about riding off on it. They weren't lurking inside the disused henhouse or the woodshed, either.

Ben could think of just two remaining options. Clarkson and his companion must have either totally dematerialised and vanished into the aether, or else they'd skulked inside the farmhouse.

Minutes had ticked by. As he raced for the house Ben radioed McAllister again. 'Still here.'

'Pleased to hear it, pal.'

Ben reached the house and pushed through the door with the Galil rifle to his shoulder. His plan had been to start checking each ground floor room in turn and work his way upwards, but he didn't get that far. Because standing there in the hallway at the foot of the stairs, boggling at him in terror and holding up his hands, was Clarkson's corporate associate. His shoes were caked in mud, his suit was rumpled and the rain had plastered his hair over his pasty brow. He looked as though he'd been about to bolt upstairs when Ben burst in.

'Stay right where you are,' Ben told him. He aimed the rifle at his chest. Point-blank range. Unmissable. If Ben had pulled the trigger he'd have splattered the guy's heart and lungs all over the stairway.

'P-please d-don't shoot me,' he quavered, almost fainting at the sight of the gun.

'Where's Clarkson?'

The man's mouth opened and closed like a landed fish's.

He looked as though he was on the verge of fainting from fear. 'I . . . I . . .'

'I said, where is he?' Ben demanded.

'Right behind you,' said a voice.

Then Gregory Clarkson stepped out of the kitchen doorway. He was smiling. He was holding a big black semi-automatic pistol. And he was pointing it straight at Ben's head.

Chapter 48

There was no way that Ben could get turned around fast enough with the rifle to avoid being shot. He'd have had to swivel its barrel through a whole hundred and sixty degrees from where it was pointing at the guy by the stairs and fix his new target in less time than it would take Clarkson's trigger finger to give a tiny twitch and his bullet to cross the six feet of air between the pistol's muzzle and Ben's skull.

Certain death. Zero chance of survival.

'Whoops,' Clarkson said. 'The great SAS warrior, caught napping. Looks as though the shoe's on the other foot now, doesn't it? Now, let's be a good fellow and turn that weapon over to my associate, Mr Hogan. Then maybe I won't put a bullet in your head. At least, not right away. I want to savour this moment.'

Clarkson was standing just too far away for Ben to attempt any kind of disarming move. A lot of amateurs would have thrust the pistol out at arm's length, which was almost the same thing as letting Ben have it. But Clarkson was holding it low, tight against his side. And that gave Ben no choice but to do what he was told.

Ben put the rifle on safe, flipped it over and handed it to the man called Hogan. Hogan took it as though he was almost as afraid of the gun as he'd been of its business end moments ago. His hands were shaking and sweat was pouring down his cheeks.

Clarkson grinned. Triumph was flashing in his eyes. 'Excellent. You see, Hogan? I was right as usual. It was worth making this journey after all. Now, Major Hope, put your hands up. Lace your fingers over the top of your head, so I can be sure you won't get up to any more of your tricks.'

Ben slowly raised his hands. Laced them together over his head. On the way up, he was able to get a glance at his watch. Exactly four and a half minutes had gone by since he'd checked in with McAllister.

'You see how compliant he can be, Hogan?' Clarkson said. 'You pull his teeth, he's as compliant as a lamb. Now, Major, let's see you get down on your knees.'

Ben was counting the seconds in his head. Very slowly, with his hands still laced together on his head, he sank down until he was kneeling on the floor like a man awaiting execution. He was still counting the seconds. Five minutes since he'd checked in with McAllister. His radio deadline was up.

Ben said, 'You're enjoying this, aren't you, Clarkson?'

'Oh, very much so. It's even better than I imagined. But don't expect it to last, Major Hope. I have a fairly low boredom threshold. Soon enough I'll lose interest in humiliating you, and I'll just blow your brains out, like the worthless piece of scum you are.'

'Where's the money?' Ben said. 'I thought we had a deal.'

'Games, games to the last,' Clarkson chuckled. 'Let me tell you something, Major. You should never bluff a bluffer. I suppose you brought along your cast-iron proof of my guilt, did you? As though you actually thought I'd fall for that one.'

'It's somewhere safe,' Ben said. 'You shoot me, there's no telling where it might end up. And then the whole world will know what you've been up to.'

'What I've been up to,' Clarkson sneered. 'What gives you the right to judge me? I'm a businessman, nothing more. I sell legitimate, tested and approved beauty products to the highest bidder and it's no concern of mine what my customers choose to do with them afterwards.'

'It seems that your illustrious ancestor wasn't too concerned about the consequences of his actions, either,' Ben said. 'Your drug addict daddy never hurt anyone but himself, so I'm guessing the psycho gene must have skipped a generation.'

Clarkson's sneer melted into a look of anger and his cheeks flushed at the mention of his disgraced parent. 'Don't give me that moralistic crap. Yes, and so what if my grandfather's patent killed millions of people? Who even remembers them now? They'd be dead anyway.'

'They might not have died in agony with blood pouring out of their ears and eyes and their lungs turning to mush,' Ben said.

'We've all got to die of something, old chap. Some idiot gets a deadly virus; whether it was manufactured in a lab or created by nature, what difference does it make? Some other idiot, such as is imminently about to happen in your case, gets a bullet from my gun.'

'One more here, one more there,' Ben said. 'What does it matter in the great scheme of things? I think I'm beginning to understand how your mind works, Clarkson.'

'You're absolutely right. As far as I'm concerned, the human race is nothing more than vermin and its members only matter worth a damn if they can make me richer. Otherwise, to hell with them. And as for the ones who stand to make me poorer—'

'Like Carter Duggan?' Ben cut in.

Clarkson snorted contemptuously. 'There's another idiot. Thought he could carve himself out a nice fat slice of my fortune. Didn't work out too well for him, did it? But the biggest idiot of them all was that imbecile of a son of yours. Though, in actual fact, he did me a real favour. If he hadn't blundered in and gone and incriminated himself the way he did, I'd have had far more work to do covering my tracks. Now I gather he's managed to escape from jail, which suits me well as it only makes him look even more guilty. Good luck to him. He's going to need it.'

'Looks like you beat us all,' Ben said.

'Yes, I did,' Clarkson replied. 'I always win. It's what I do. And to the victor belong the spoils. Now, Major, I have to say I'm getting somewhat tired of this conversation. I did warn you that I get bored easily. So I think we'll end it on that note, and I'll shoot you. Goodbye.'

Ben had been counting in his head the whole time. Nearly eight minutes since his last radio check-in with McAllister. At the same time, he was coming up with his plan for just how exactly he was going to get that pistol out of Clarkson's hands and prevent himself from getting shot, with a rifle to his back. It wasn't a bad plan. It might even have a ten per cent chance of working.

But Ben wasn't going to need it.

Chapter 49

Before Clarkson could pull the trigger, the farmhouse door crashed open and the hallway was suddenly filled with a wild snarling flurry as Radar came streaking in from outside. The German shepherd didn't need long to evaluate the tactical situation. Like a canine guided missile he launched himself at Clarkson, who was standing nearest the entrance.

Clarkson jerked the gun away from Ben and fired at the pouncing dog, but missed in his panic. Then he screamed as the dog's long, sharp fangs sank into the forearm of his gun hand and he was dragged to the floor. Radar shook his head violently from side to side as though he was killing a rat, with Clarkson's arm clamped tightly in his jaws. The pistol spun out of Clarkson's grasp.

By then, Ben was already on his feet. Hogan was yelling like a lunatic as he pointed the rifle this way and that, unsure of who to shoot first, the ninja SAS assassin or the wild wolf that was savaging his boss. But Hogan was unable to fire it at all, because the safety catch was still on and he didn't know how to work the gun. Ben ripped it out of his hands and smacked him down hard to the floor with the butt end.

Clarkson was still screaming, pinned on his back and desperately kicking as the dog remained latched onto his arm. Ben used the command McAllister had used, 'Radar, off!' and the dog instantly let go and backed away a step, eyeing Clarkson as if he'd like nothing more than to have a gnash at the rest of him.

That was when Radar's master appeared in the doorway, dripping with rain and out of breath from the quarter-mile run to the house. 'Missed your call, buddy. Thought you could use a little help.'

'Welcome to the party,' Ben replied. There were times when the police turning up at your door was actually a good thing. McAllister clipped Radar up to his leash.

Clarkson was still on his back, gibbering in pain and fear and nursing his ripped arm. Ben scooped up the fallen pistol, made it safe and tossed it to McAllister. Not to use, but as evidence. He asked, 'Where's Jude?'

'Here,' Jude said, stepping into the house. He scraped back his wet hair, eyed the two men on the floor and asked, 'So, which one of you bastards do I have to thank for ending up in the clink?'

'Both of them,' Ben said. 'But this one here is the main man.' Ben stepped up to Clarkson, reached down and jerked him roughly to his feet.

'Can I clobber him?' Jude asked, clenching a fist.

'You'd have to ask the cops,' Ben said, pointing at McAllister. 'You're in his custody now, remember?'

'As if I could forget. Just let me hit him once. Please?'

McAllister shrugged. 'Jeez. If it makes you happy, go for it.'

'Are you the police?' Clarkson yelled at him. 'You can't let him do that to me. It's illegal!'

'Shut your hole or I'll clobber you myself,' McAllister warned. Clarkson was about to yell something more when Jude's fist cracked into the side of his jaw and decked him back down to the floor. Hogan still hadn't got up.

'That's enough of that, now,' McAllister said to Jude.

'Confession time,' Ben said to Clarkson. 'You're going to repeat everything you just admitted to me.'

'I'm not saying a word!'

'Suit yourself. Then we'll let this dog eat you alive.'

'Oh, please don't say a word,' Jude told Clarkson with a nasty glint in his eye. 'I want to see you get gobbled up.'

Clarkson gaped in horror at Radar, who was straining so hard on the leash to get at him that McAllister had to hold on with both hands. 'This is extracting a confession!'

'Works for me,' McAllister replied. 'Now I'd do what the man says, if I were you. Make this easy on yourself and start talking.'

The prospect of being devoured alive worked wonders on Gregory Clarkson's loquacity. Every word was recorded on McAllister's phone as the details came babbling out: the illegal drug deals with terror contacts and corrupt regimes in several countries. The murder of Carter Duggan, perpetrated by one of his hired killers, a man called Todd Pearce.

McAllister paused the recording and said, 'If you think you're going to make this easier on yourself by squealing on your pals, you're wrong. But thanks anyway for the tip-off. He won't be at large for very long.'

'You can arrest that man there for Pearce's murder,' Clarkson yelled, pointing at Ben. 'He killed him. You'll find the body somewhere on this farm!'

'Wrong,' Ben said. 'If Pearce was one of the men you brought here today, he's alive and well, just like the other four.'

'You're lying! You killed them like you did the others! Arrest him!'

'I know this man,' McAllister declared solemnly, flashing a sideways glance at Ben. 'He's a law-abiding citizen and never killed anyone in his life. You're another story.' He pocketed the phone. 'I think we've got enough here to be getting on with. Gregory Clarkson, I hereby place you under arrest for the murder of Carter Duggan.'

'Don't forget all the others,' Ben reminded him. 'Suzie Morton, Joe Brewster, Emily Bowman, her housekeeper and her manager, and whoever else it will turn out he's hurt. Not to mention all the poor bastards who've been poisoned by his company's illegal toxins.'

'Sounds like we have a lot to talk about, Mr Clarkson,' McAllister said. 'We'll figure that out as we go along. And I'm sure that the boys from the National Crime Agency will want to get in on the fun, too.'

Next, Ben hauled the half-dazed, snivelling and miserable Hogan to his feet and McAllister arrested him too. 'Shite, I forgot,' he said. 'I'm not carrying any cuffs.'

'Try this,' Ben said, taking more of the baling twine out of his pocket.

Jude stepped forward eagerly. 'Allow me?' With McAllister's permission he tied Clarkson's wrists behind his back, then Hogan's. His knots were pretty good.

'We'd better gather up the others,' Ben said. Jude and Radar stood guard over the prisoners while McAllister joined Ben in the task of hauling the debris of the collapsed milking shed roof off the bruised, battered but still perfectly alive bodies of four of Clarkson's men. The fifth, who would later turn out to be Todd Pearce, the hired assassin responsible for murdering Carter Duggan, was duly dragged out of the big barn and dumped with his trussed-up associates.

With that job completed, it was time to bring in the troops. McAllister called Billie Flowers.

Chapter 50

Within an hour Black Rock Farm was swarming with scores of officers and the track and yard were jammed solid with police vehicles and ambulances. The Devon and Cornwall force's helicopter thudded overhead while the remains of the Galliard one went on quietly burning. Ben watched from a distance as McAllister spoke with the local commander and his detective sergeant from Thames Valley, who was a petite and very attractive Afro-Caribbean woman in her early or mid thirties. She seemed somewhat perplexed by McAllister's presence here in the middle of the Cornish countryside, when he was officially supposed to be laid up at home with a dental emergency. He was going to have some explaining to do.

Ben anticipated that the cops would have an awful lot of questions for him, too, but for the moment he was left alone to watch from the sidelines. As the uniforms milled around the house and outbuildings and a forensic unit combed through the scene gathering evidence, the Galliard Group's CEO and vice-director and their five henchmen received on-site treatment from paramedics for their minor injuries before they were restrained with proper handcuffs, loaded into separate vehicles and taken away. So was Jude – but this time, as the apprehended fugitive set off on his journey back to jail he was grinning from ear to ear. Before they closed him into the back of the van he gave Ben a last wave and a thumbs-up.

Ben had been right about the ton of questions he'd have to face. He and McAllister travelled separately to the Bodmin police hub, thirteen miles away, where a sour-faced local plainclothes inspector called Parfitt accompanied Ben and a pair of uniforms into a windowless interview room, sat him down at a table, and the interminable grilling began. Ben was ready for their interrogation. He was polite, calm and cooperative. The account that he gave them was plausible enough, being mostly accurate with just a few omissions and embellishments. He consistently stuck to his version of events down to the last detail, secure in the knowledge that Tom McAllister would be doing the same in another room within the station.

He and McAllister had had plenty of time before the cops' arrival to get their stories straight. McAllister's report would state that, as a result of Mr Hope's lawful personal investigations into what he believed was the false imprisonment of his son, Gregory Clarkson and his associates had travelled to Cornwall with the intention of protecting their crooked business interests by killing him. This was fully backed up by the recorded confession of the Galliard Group CEO, which admitted culpability for a host of crimes and was clear evidence that Jude Arundel was innocent of the murder of Carter Duggan.

As for that shining example of a law-abiding citizen Mr Hope, McAllister would bear witness to the fact that he had used no more than the minimum of reasonable force to protect his own life, as well as Jude's and that of a police officer, namely McAllister himself, who had also come under fire from Clarkson's armed thugs. Naturally, anything that the suspects tried to assert to the contrary would be just a pack of lies.

With regard to the perplexing matter of the destroyed helicopter, on which the cops focused with particular suspicion and were obviously gunning to try to pin on Ben considering his known background and degree of expertise, McAllister would attest to the fact that one of Clarkson's men had accidentally blown it up himself during the incident, with a stray bullet that had been intended for Mr Hope. At no time had Mr Hope fired a shot or used a firearm in a threatening manner. The forensic evidence would show that none of Mr Hope's fingerprints were to be found on any of the weapons recovered from the scene.

The grilling dragged on until ten o'clock that evening, by which time Ben's interviewers had run out of steam and reluctantly had to admit there was nothing they could hold him for. 'All right,' muttered Detective Inspector Parfitt. 'Then it would seem that you're free to go. Thank you for your cooperation, and have a safe journey home.'

As Ben emerged from the police station wishing he had a Gauloise, he found McAllister sitting waiting for him on the wing of the Plymouth Barracuda parked outside. Radar's tail thump, thump thumped on the ground as Ben walked over to them.

McAllister said, 'There you are at last. Thought they'd keep you in all night. How'd it go?'

'Fine,' Ben replied. 'What did you expect? I'm a model citizen.'

'That Parfitt's a bit of a gobshite, isn't he?'

Ben shrugged. 'What about you? Are you in the shit with your superiors at Thames Valley?'

'Bah,' McAllister said with a dismissive wave of his hand. 'No more than usual. Forbsie will likely want to tear a strip or two off my arse when I get back, but there's not a lot he can do to an officer who's just taken down a corrupt corporate executive who was consorting with terrorists and warlords and having folks bumped off left, right and centre. I'll be the hero of the hour, so I will.'

'Congratulations.'

'Aye, all in all, not a bad day's work,' McAllister replied, looking pleased. 'And you even managed not to shoot anyone for a change. Maybe you're learning, Hope. Who'd have thought it?'

'I resent that accusation.'

'Which one?'

McAllister's phone started burring in his pocket and he fished it out. 'Just got a text message from Billie.'

'Is she back in Oxford?'

'No, she's at a pub just down the road and wants to meet us for a drink.' McAllister smacked his lips. 'Just the thing I needed. Jesus, what I wouldn't do for a jar or two of real Cornish ale on tap.'

Ben's mouth felt parched after hours of talking to the cops. 'I reckon I might try one of those myself.'

'My treat.' McAllister slid down from the wing of the car and yanked open the driver's door, jerking his chin at Ben to get in the other side. 'Come on, let's go. Billie's a great gal. You'll like her.'

'You say she sings jazz?' Ben asked.

Chapter 51

Following several sessions of much more intensive questioning than Ben had had to undergo and involving the joint forces of Thames Valley Police, Metropolitan CID, the National Crime Agency and counter-terrorism elements of British Intelligence, Gregory Clarkson, Jasper Hogan, the five men employed in the assault on Black Rock Farm and eight more senior executives made full confessions of their parts in the company's many illegal activities and were charged with a variety of criminal offences including, in Clarkson and Hogan's cases, attempted murder, conspiracy to murder, bribery, firearms offences, corruption, and aiding and abetting terrorism and war crimes. Meanwhile, dawn raids on addresses across London and the south-east led to the arrest of a further seventeen less senior Galliard Group staffers who were implicated in the company's botulinum racket and faced only slightly lesser charges.

More than a hundred company employees in total were questioned. Those accused faced the prospect of years of trials and a couple of centuries behind bars between them. Miles Redfield was looking forward to being there in court the day the judge's gavel fell and watching Suzie's murderer get what he deserved. Then, and only then, would Miles be able to start putting his life back together.

Meanwhile, Galliard's stocks plummeted so sharply within forty-eight hours of the news breaking that financial analysts forecast the early bankruptcy and almost inevitable closure of the company. After more than 110 years in business, Sir Elliot Clarkson's proud firm would soon be no more.

Three days after being temporarily returned to prison, Jude received a visit from his lawyer, Dorian Simms, bringing the not entirely unexpected news that Jude had been cleared of the murder charge. Also not unexpectedly, though, he wasn't off the hook quite yet – he'd still have to face justice for escaping. It was a mixed celebration for Jude that night, with freedom hanging in the balance. His hearing was due to take place in two more days, at the same courtroom in Oxford where he'd been sent away.

Ben had checked into a local hotel for those few days rather than travel back to Le Val. Unable to find a single rental company willing to risk letting him have a hire car – his past record with those being a catalogue of wanton destruction and wreckage – he was privileged to get the loan of Tom McAllister's precious Barracuda ('you be fucking careful with her, mind') while its owner made do with an unmarked cruiser from the police pool.

Ben spent the daytime mooching restlessly around in his hotel room or driving by old haunts, and his evenings at the riverside cottage in the company of McAllister and Radar. Fine meals were shared, a great deal of wine and the detective's favourite Langtree Hundred ale consumed. Ben was beginning to appreciate how well McAllister lived. He'd also come to realise that the cop was probably one of the most unusual people he'd ever known. As well as a true friend. Ben had been blessed with a few of those in his life; now he'd added another to that list.

But through those days Ben felt ill at ease and unable to relax. He dreaded the coming hearing and the pronouncement of the judge that might, just might, result in Jude's imprisonment for a good while longer.

The day finally came. The morning of the hearing was grey and overcast, and if Ben had been a superstitious man he might have taken that as a bad omen. He was up early after a restless night and couldn't face breakfast. He walked from his hotel and met Dorian Simms outside the courthouse in Speedwell Street. McAllister was tied up at work and couldn't make it. Simms was very noncommittal about Jude's situation. 'It could go either way, depending on the judge's mood. Jude could walk out a free man today, or he could be made to serve another twelve months, maybe longer.'

Soon afterwards, Ben and Simms took their seats in the courtroom where District Judge Crapper would once again preside over Jude's fate.

The proceedings started out like a replay of the first hearing, which seemed as though it had taken place months ago. Ben had an unsettling sensation of déjà vu as Jude was brought in, was requested to identify himself before the court and the judge asked him if he understood the very serious charge brought against him. Escaping from the custody of one of Her Majesty's prisons was no small matter, Crapper explained gravely. Even if you were innocent of the original crime, you were not to take the law into your own hands, but instead to trust the time-honoured judicial system to take its course. What had the accused to say for himself?

In Ben's nightmares during the wee small hours, Jude had answered that question by leaping wildly over the railing, thrusting an obscene gesture in Judge Crapper's face and screaming out, 'Yes, you ugly old fart, damn right I broke out of that shitty horrible place. And I'd do the same again tomorrow!'

But dreams can be worse than reality, and Jude behaved himself perfectly. He hung his head and looked suitably penitent as he replied that yes, he understood the charges; yes, he admitted what he'd done was wrong; and he accepted he must pay the price. The judge seemed sympathetic, almost benevolent, towards Jude – or was it just wishful thinking on Ben's part?

The lawyer for the Crown Prosecution Service, a man called Barclay with a sardonic leer permanently imprinted on his face, took a very different view. 'Now, Mr Arundel, I'm sure I needn't remind you that the last time you appeared in this very same courtroom, you openly stated that it was your intention to escape from prison. Is it not the case that you simply acted on your threat?'

'I was angry and upset when I said that,' Jude replied. 'I didn't really mean it at the time. How could I have known the riot was going to happen?'

As the morning rolled on, various witnesses were brought out to testify to their part in the drama of the now infamous Bullingdon Prison jailbreak. The court heard from a guard who had been injured in the riot, his arm still in a sling, who described the violence of that night as nothing like he'd ever seen before. An officer of the Gloucestershire Constabulary, who'd headed up the police unit that had found the bodies of crime boss Luan Copja and his Albanian gangsters in the field near Chedworth, gave a detailed depiction of the abortive escape, as best as the police had been able to figure out exactly what happened. Much of it was still a mystery.

After a short recess, the next witness to appear was Jude's former cellmate at Bullingdon, a large but softly-spoken inmate called David Flynn. He was wearing the regulation sweatshirt and jogging pants of a convicted prisoner and seemed happy to have been let out for a few hours to testify. A pair of prison guards hovered nearby, ready to collar him if he decided to copy Jude's example and make a break for it. They needn't have worried.

Dorian Simms, as the lawyer for the defence, was the first to question the witness. Judge Crapper listened intently to Flynn's account of the moment when Jude had been plucked from their cell by one of Luan Copja's men.

'Did it seem to you as though Mr Arundel had been expecting these men to take them with him?' Simms asked.

'No, sir,' the big guy replied respectfully. 'Jude looked pretty confused when the guy turned up, like he had no idea what was happening. Neither of us did. It was a weird moment.'

'Had you any reason to believe that Mr Arundel might have been involved in any way with the gang, prior to his stay at Bullingdon?'

'No, sir,' Big Dave repeated. 'He'd never had anything to do with them before. I know that for a fact.'

'And how do you know this?'

'Because it was me who pointed them out to him, in the mess hall, just a couple of days before the riot happened. He'd never heard of Luan Copja until that moment. I believed him. He's not a liar.'

Again, predictably, come his turn to question the witness, Barclay the prosecutor went straight into offensive mode, claiming that Jude had intentionally hooked up with Luan Copja's gang in the knowledge that they were planning to escape. Big Dave deflected all his lines of attack with polite, simple replies, until Barclay's most damaging question stopped him in his tracks: 'If Mr Arundel was unknown to Luan Copja, then please explain to the court why the gang chose to single him out to take along for the ride, when they could presumably have chosen anyone in the prison, or nobody at all?'

Big Dave couldn't answer that, but Jude was given the opportunity some time later when he was recalled to the stand. 'I don't know,' he replied innocently as Barclay fired the same question at him. 'I got the impression that Copja wanted me to join his gang for some reason. I couldn't say why. Maybe he'd run out of real hard guys to recruit.'

There was a small ripple of amusement in the court. Judge Crapper, Ben and the two lawyers were the only ones not smiling.

Once all the witnesses had testified, all arguments been heard and the defence and prosecution rested, the moment had come for Crapper to make his judgement. He reflected

378

for a long moment, apparently undecided, then sighed and called another short recess. Simms whispered in Ben's ear, 'Keep your fingers crossed.'

Fifteen minutes later, Crapper re-emerged from his chambers, resumed his position at the bench, cleared his throat and addressed the court.

'In light of the evidence, the particular circumstances of this case and his proven innocence of the charge of murder, I see no legal basis for returning the defendant to prison. Foolish he may have been in some of his actions, but he is no criminal. Mr Arundel, on behalf of this court I hereby sentence you to six months, suspended.'

And with that, it was over. An hour later, Jude walked out of the courthouse more or less a free man. The conditions he'd have to meet for the next six months required him to do a few hours' community work a week, and he was forbidden to leave the country. He couldn't stop grinning.

'It's no big deal. The only downside is that I won't be able to come with you to Le Val,' he said to Ben as the two of them headed on foot towards the bustle and noise of Oxford's city centre. It was after midday and the rain had given way to a clear blue sky. Sunshine gleamed off the towers and cathedral spires of Ben's old college. He was smiling, too. It was good to be alive.

'Le Val's not going anywhere,' Ben told him. 'When you've served out the six months you can come and stay as long as you like. What are your plans now?'

'I've decided to sell the vicarage, Dad. I'm going to put it on the market right away, and live in the annexe until it's sold. After that, I don't know what I'm going to do. I feel like I've been stuck in a rut, not really *doing* anything with my life. Maybe I'll finish my marine biology degree.'

'You've always loved the ocean. I can see you doing something in that line.'

'But right this moment all I can really think about is a big pile of bacon, sausages and chips, and a thousand pints of beer to wash it down with. Let's celebrate!'

'I think we can manage that.'

The Turf Tavern was one of Ben's favourite Oxford pubs from the past. They sat outside in the leafy, sunny beer garden to eat. Jude had his mountain of food, but as he dug into it his cheeriness seemed to have left him.

Ben said, 'You look very pensive all of a sudden, for a bloke who just got his freedom back.'

Jude shrugged. 'Sorry. It's just that the last couple of days I've been doing a lot of thinking about Achlys-14, all those millions of people those bastards killed or made sick with their poison. It haunts me. I still can't bring myself to believe it's true.'

'There are lots of things men do to one another in warfare that you wouldn't believe,' Ben said. 'Speaking from experience. That's why I never wanted you to belong to that world.'

'I never will,' Jude replied resolutely. 'That's for sure.' He paused while he munched reflectively on a chip, then asked, 'Do you think it could ever happen again? If they had the biotechnology to create something like that a hundred years ago, think what even more awful shit they could cook up now.'

Ben thought about all the awful shit that was already cooked up and lurking in thousands of labs around the world, ready for use. Most people had no idea of the extent of it. He said, 'In a war, you mean?'

'In a war, sure. But I was thinking generally, too. Think of the power something like that would give to an evil maniac secret ruler of the world, over nations, over economies, over everything. Even if the virus wasn't half as lethal as Achlys-14. Even if it only killed one per cent as many people. Imagine the fear it would cause today, what with social media and all the ways information spreads around the world in the blink of an eye nowadays. I mean, total apeshit panic. Everyone afraid of each other, people terrified to go outside in case they get it and drop down dead. Whoever had that sort of power could shut the entire system down and make slaves out of the lot of us, force whole populations to do whatever they wanted. They could herd us all into containment camps, or keep everyone in isolation, locked down under house arrest wearing gas masks. The world we knew, suddenly turned into a hell on earth. One you *can't* escape from.'

Ben smiled. 'That's one hell of a vivid imagination you've got there.'

'Maybe I'm thinking that way because I've just come out of prison,' Jude said. 'But it's true, isn't it? It's possible. Then you'd have a hundred pharmaceutical companies just like Clarkson's lining up to make a trillion quid out of some untested vaccine that'd probably hurt more people than it cured.' He shook his head and took a glug of his beer. 'I don't know. The idea scares the shit out of me. I was lying there in my cell the last two nights and I couldn't sleep a wink thinking about it.'

Ben clapped him on the back. 'You worry too much, Jude. I'm sure it'll never happen.'

'Yeah, maybe you're right. Let's hope it doesn't, anyway.' Jude went back to eating, and the tasty feast on his plate soon restored his spirits. 'So what now?' he asked as he polished off the last chip with a satisfied flourish and settled back in his seat, patting his full belly. 'Off home to France?'

Ben nodded. 'I'll be heading back soon. Maybe late tonight, or maybe early tomorrow. There's just one last thing I need to take care of before I go.'

EPILOGUE

Ben stepped out of the London taxicab and lingered for a moment on the pavement to look at the building. The tea room was still open for business, serving its last few afternoon customers before closing for the day. It was an old-world kind of establishment, unrestored all these years but lovingly maintained, a throwback to bygone times in the midst of all this sleek, plastic modernity. The fancy gingerbread wood-work facade was painted glossy emerald green and the signs etched into the two large front windows either side of the entrance displayed its name in florid, cursive script: KITTY RYAN'S, with a shamrock underneath.

The Irish theme was even more pronounced inside. Anything that wasn't painted emerald green was decorated with more shamrocks and Celtic knots. Ceilidh music was playing on the scratchy sound system. The Chieftains, Ben thought. Behind the green counter were display shelves and cabinets filled with home-baked Irish soda bread, cakes and scones whose aroma mingled with the scent of fresh-brewed tea and ground coffee. A handful of clientele, mostly older ladies, were finishing up their slices of cake before closing time. A teenage girl in a Bee Happy T-shirt was going round clearing up the empty tables.

Ben walked up to the counter where a young red-haired woman in an apron, a green off-the-shoulder top and black leggings was tidying away dishes. He watched her for a moment. She was the classic Irish redhead, with curling Pre-Raphaelite locks halfway down her back, very fair skin with freckles on her shoulder and vivid green eyes that hinted at a fiery temperament. She looked exactly, uncannily, the way Ben had imagined Kitty Kelly from Violet Bowman's memoir, except she couldn't be more than about twenty-three. Which made her about a hundred years younger. Much too young to be her granddaughter. A great-granddaughter, maybe, he wondered.

She saw him and smiled, wiping her hands on her apron. Slender hands with long fingers and trim nails, no rings. She said brightly, 'Hey there, stranger. What can I get you?' No trace of Irish accent. The heritage was clear enough, but it was generations down the line.

Ben said, 'Nothing.'

Her eyebrows rose. 'Nothing?'

'It all looks good,' he said, pointing at the displays. 'In fact it looks great. But I'm not here for that.'

'Then why are you here?' she asked him quizzically, cocking her head to one side, eyeing him with a widening smile. Flirtatious, but also genuinely curious.

'To deliver something,' Ben replied. He took the memoir from his bag and placed it carefully on the counter, wrapped in plastic.

'I'm intrigued,' she said, looking at it. 'May I?'

'Be my guest.'

She peeled away the plastic wrapping with her long, slender fingers. 'It's a book.'

'It's a little bit more than that,' he told her. 'More like a little slice of history.'

'Is it for me?'

'That depends,' he said. 'I came here to pass it to the descendant of Kitty Kelly, the founder of this place. Is that you?'

The green eyes narrowed a touch. She pointed at the window. 'Sign says Kitty Ryan's. How did you know about Kitty Kelly?'

'You should read the book,' he said. 'It's all in there.'

'Kitty Kelly was my great-grandmother.'

'Then I guess it belongs to you now,' he said. 'It was written by a very old friend of hers, a long, long time ago.'

'So, how come you had it? Are you a relative?'

He shook his head. 'That's a long story.'

'They always are, aren't they?' She picked up the memoir and leafed delicately through some of the pages. Then shook her head, making the curly red locks swirl around her shoulders. She laid the book back down on the counter. 'No, this wouldn't be for me. It's my nan you should be giving it to.'

'Your nan?'

'Orla. Orla O'Casey. She used to be Orla Flanagan. That was her mother's married name.' The green-eyed redhead let her gaze linger on him for another long moment, as though she was considering whether to trust him. 'My name's Shannon. What's yours?'

'It's Ben. Ben Hope.'

'That's a nice name. Are you a nice man, Mr Ben Hope?'

'I try to be. It's not for me to judge.'

'Because if I thought you were a nice man, instead of just passing it on to her I'd invite you back here to meet my nan and give it to her in person. She's old. She doesn't get a lot of visitors these days.'

'I would like that very much,' Ben said. 'And I wouldn't take up much of her time.'

A moment's hesitation. Then Shannon flipped up a hatch in the counter and beckoned him through. She called to the girl who was clearing the tables, 'Lizzy, watch the front for me, will you?'

Lizzy called back, 'Okay.'

Shannon led Ben through a door and along a passage to a back room. She tapped softly at a door before going in.

'Nan, you have a visitor. Someone called Ben. He's come to bring you something.'

Sitting at a table in the small storeroom that doubled as a laundry room was an old, old woman. An ironing board lay across the tabletop in front of her as she worked her way through a laundry basket of real cloth napkins embroidered with little shamrocks. A stack of them sat on the table at her elbow, immaculately pressed and folded. The room smelled of hot steam and clean, fresh linen.

'I don't know anybody called Ben,' she said, laying down her iron and reaching for her glasses. Her voice was still strong for her age.

We think history is in the past, but it's closer to us than we realise. Ben was looking at the daughter of Kitty Kelly. By the look of her she must have been born around 1930, when Kitty was young, not too many years after Violet had quit the Forty Elephants and fled London. Orla O'Casey was in pretty good shape and had obviously been a spectacular beauty, back in her day. Now Ben could see where the grand-daughter had got it from.

'Mrs O'Casey, my name's Ben Hope. You're right, you don't know me. But I have something here for you.'

He handed her the slim book. She took it, removed her glasses and held it close to examine it. 'What is this?'

'It's a story,' Ben said. 'The story of your mother's best friend. Her name was Violet.'

The name triggered the old woman's memory, still sharp as a knife. 'Violet Littleton,' she said. 'My mam used to talk about her all the time. They were like sisters once. Then Violet left without a word and never got in touch again. It broke her heart.'

'It broke Violet's, too,' Ben said. 'She'd have wanted Kitty to know why she had to go away. This would have helped your mother to understand. Now it's yours. It's only right that it should end up in your family. It has no other home to go to. Not any more.'

'It was nice meeting you, Ben Hope,' Shannon said at the tea room door as he was leaving. 'You sure you don't want a coffee or something?'

'Nice to meet you too, Shannon,' he replied, and started walking.

He looked back after twenty paces and saw her still leaning there in the doorway, watching him.

After thirty paces he looked back once more, but this time she was gone.

He kept going. Empty taxis came by, but he felt like walking.

No other home to go to. Ben's own words lingered in his ears as he thought of Le Val. The place he most wanted to be. The place he would soon be returning to. And from now on, nothing, no more intrigues, no more crazy adventures, were going to persuade him to leave there ever again.

As though that were true.

Ben Hope returns in a thrilling new book

The Crusader's Cross

Coming November 2021
Available to pre-order now

EVIL NEVER RESTS.

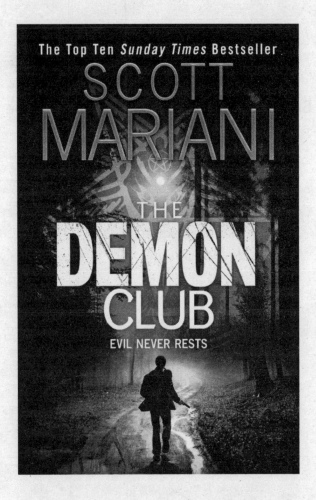

The only way for Ben to save himself and his
loved ones is to declare war on the forces of evil.
But who will win?